W9-AAW-534

THE LOST TEMPLE

ALSO BY TOM HARPER

The Mosaic of Shadows
Knights of the Cross
Siege of Heaven

As Edwin Thomas

The Blighted Cliffs
The Chains of Albion
Treason's River

THE LOST TEMPLE

TOM HARPER

THOMAS DUNNE BOOKS
ST. MARTIN'S PRESS ☙ NEW YORK

This is a work of fiction. All of the characters, organizations, and events portrayed in this novel are either products of the author's imagination or are used fictitiously.

THOMAS DUNNE BOOKS.
An imprint of St. Martin's Press.

www.thomasdunnebooks.com
www.stmartins.com

Library of Congress Cataloging-in-Publication Data

Harper, Tom.
The lost temple / Tom Harper.—1st U.S. ed.
p. cm.
ISBN-13: 978-0-312-38060-1
ISBN-10: 0-312-38060-7
1. Adventure and adventurers—Fiction. 2. Archaeologists—Fiction. 3. Caves—Greece—Crete—Fiction. 4. Tablets (Paleography)—Fiction. 5. Treasure troves—Fiction. 6. Mediterranean Region—Fiction. I. Title.

PR6120.H644L67 2008
823'.92—dc22

2008024943

First published in United Kingdom by Century an imprint of Random House Group Limited

First U.S. Edition: November 2008

10 9 8 7 6 5 4 3 2 1

For Oliver Johnson
the Special One

When, by chance, this story had fallen into my hands, I—eager to tell the truth of history—felt compelled to spread it more widely: not out of vanity, but rather so that I might provide entertainment for an idle mind.

Preface to *A Journal of the Trojan War,* Dictys of Crete

Eastern Mediterranean 1947

PROLOGUE

Crete, 20 May 1941

LEGEND SAID this was the first place men flew. Like artificial birds, they had dressed themselves with beeswax and feathers, launched themselves from the lofty palace and soared over the jewelled sea. They had climbed high, ever nearer the sun—until one, a boy, flew too close, melted his wings and fell. By the time the last feather settled on the water, the boy had slipped beneath the waves, into myth. Now there were men in the sky again. Instead of feathers they flew on wings of silk, and the webbed harnesses which held them would not melt in the sun. *Fallschirmjäger*, they called themselves: hunters from the sky. They did not fall, but swooped down to the earth like hungry eagles.

Pemberton saw them from his office window. He had known he was in trouble when the bombing stopped. For the past week it had been a regular terror: the drone of the engines, then the howl of the diving Stukas and the ground shaking under their explosions. Sometimes the bombs had come so near the villa that the artifacts shivered in their display cases, rattling like loose teacups on saucers, until the staff moved them down to the basement. Now the bombs had stopped. The illustrious refugees who had made his life a misery had departed and the staff were all gone—Pemberton had sent them home to their villages and families that morning. He was the only one left. And it was time for him to go.

He grabbed his knapsack from the hatstand in the corner and turned it out over the desk. A week-old sandwich fell limply on to his desk, followed by a half-empty thermos, his camera, torch and penknife, and a few crumpled chocolate wrappers. He kept the torch and the penknife and discarded the rest, though he made sure to pop the film out of the camera. Then, trembling with haste, he unlocked the desk drawer and pulled out the notebook. Dust had spidered the creases in the soft brown leather, and the gold monogram in the corner had almost worn away. It had been a gift from his wife, almost her last, and he treasured it—but that was not what made it most valuable. The invaders could have everything in the villa—the artifacts and museum pieces, the clothes and the furnishings imported from England, even his beloved library—but not that.

There was nothing else he could do. He buckled the knapsack and walked to the door. He stepped out into the sun, while above him a multicolored canopy of silk clouds—white, red, green, and yellow—drifted earthwards from the sky.

Pemberton had waited until he was certain, until he saw the first parachutes blossoming in the afternoon sky. Now it was too late. The whole valley throbbed with the echo of the Junkers-52 transport planes roaring overhead, and he could already hear the staccato thump of gunfire from round the bend that led north to the harbor at Heraklion. The Germans must have landed south of the town, cutting him off, and with every passing moment more reinforcements were jumping in from the Junkers. He wouldn't get through that way. So he went south, up into the hills and toward the mountains.

He walked quickly. He had been on Crete since before the war, two years now, and his long hikes into the island's interior had become legendary among his colleagues. The flab that had begun to creep over his belt after too many college dinners had retreated, and if the sun had bleached the last traces of black out of his hair, it had compensated by breathing new health and color into his cheeks. He was fifty-six, but felt younger now than he had ten years earlier.

When he had gone about a quarter of a mile, he looked back. In the dip below, the excavated walls of the palace of Knossos were just visible in the ring of pine trees. The palace had been his life's obsession and even in his hurry he felt a stab of loss at abandoning it to the invaders. As a student before the Great War he had helped the legendary Sir Arthur Evans dig it out of its three-thousand-year sleep—a golden age, when it felt as if they tunnelled into myth itself and every day brought new finds that turned legends into history. Thirty years later, widowed, he had returned as the site's curator. Archaeology's age of heroes had passed: the swift charge of discovery had given way to the meticulous crawl of scholarly analysis, but he had been happy enough. He had even managed a few discoveries of his own—and one that would have astounded even Evans. He reached behind his back and squeezed the knapsack, making sure yet again that the notebook was still there.

Another plane swept in low from the north. In the clear air he could see it plainly: the squat nose, the black cross on its side, even the white ribbon of the static line trailing behind. It must have reached the end of its drop run; in a moment it would swing round, wheeling back to the mainland for another cargo. Except that it didn't turn. It carried on over the palace and up the valley, straight for him.

Pemberton was no coward. He had stood in the trenches in Flanders and forced himself over the top with the others, but the sight of the oncoming plane froze him still. He tipped back his head and spun round as it lumbered overhead, the beat of its engines so slow he thought it must drop out of the sky. The square hatch in the fuselage gaped like a wound.

Pemberton jumped: a figure had appeared in the hatchway and was peering out. He must have seen Pemberton, and for a second Pemberton felt a strange communion as their gazes met. Then the man fell. Arms outstretched like wings, he dropped from the plane, hung there a moment, then was whipped away by the slipstream. A long tail unravelled behind him, pulled taut and blossomed into the white dome of a parachute, jerking him upright like a marionette. Even then, he still seemed to be falling with terrifying speed.

It had taken seconds, but already there were more men in the air behind him. The plane hadn't finished its drop run at all. Pemberton looked down. The wind would carry the paratroopers past him, but not so far that he could escape them. He was trapped. With no alternative, he turned back toward the palace in the trees.

He scrambled up the four-thousand-year-old steps and collapsed behind a wall, breathing hard. Evans's ambition had not been satisfied simply by excavating the palace: in places he had actually tried to rebuild it and the result was a clutch of half-built rooms emerging from the ruins like ghosts. Some visitors found them evocative, others an insult to archaeology; Pemberton, though professionally expected to disapprove, had always been secretly fond of them. He had never thought he would find himself hiding for his life there. He twisted round and lifted himself to peer out of the window in the resurrected wall.

For a moment he dared to hope that perhaps the paratroopers had headed inland. Then he saw them. They were even closer than he'd feared: in the few minutes it had taken him to run back to the palace, they had extricated themselves from their parachutes, formed up and begun maneuvering down the valley. He could see them spread out in a thin line, moving through the dappled olive groves that sloped down to the palace. He counted six of them, in tight-fitting rimless helmets and baggy green smocks that seemed strangely impractical for fighting. If they had taken the road to the west, they would have gone well past the ruined palace. As it was, they would walk straight into it.

From away behind him something hard and metallic grated on stone. He spun about in terror—then, belatedly, remembered the men in the valley. Had they seen him? No. They had vanished under the shadow of the south wall and were temporarily out of sight. He looked back, more careful this time. In the great courtyard, where the ancients had once danced on the backs of bulls, a huge crimson parachute lay spread out like a bloodstain. The fabric writhed and shivered in the breeze, while behind it a tangled mane of black ropes trailed out to a steel canister about the size of a coffin. Pemberton could see the crack of the impact in the gypsum slabs and he felt a flash of anger at such casual vandalism.

The first of the German soldiers, a sergeant, hauled himself over the parapet and ran across the courtyard to the canister. The others followed, crowding round him as he knelt and opened the lid. Some of the men were stepping out of the baggy overalls they had worn for the drop, revealing the gray battledress and bandoliers beneath, while others took the weapons the sergeant was handing out.

But away from the soldiers, something was moving. From the corner of his eye, Pemberton saw a figure creeping across the roof of the shrine that stood a little way to his left. He wore a white smock, with a black scarf tied over his head, every inch the traditional Cretan farmer. In his hand, held carefully to avoid scraping it on the stone, was a rifle. It looked even more ancient than the man himself—it could hardly have seen use in the half-century since the Turks were chased off the island—but there was no doubting what he meant to do with it.

Pemberton edged out from behind the column that sheltered him and flapped his hand, trying to attract the Greek's attention without alerting the Germans. They seemed oblivious to the danger: three of them had lit cigarettes and stood there smoking, while the others packed their equipment into rucksacks. One of them made a joke, and nervous laughter rippled around the courtyard.

"Psst," Pemberton hissed through clenched teeth, pushing caution to its limits in his desperation to stop the Greek. What was the man thinking? The Germans had almost finished unloading the canister and were ready to go. In a few more seconds they would be on the move—and Pemberton would be safe.

The Greek must have heard Pemberton. He turned sharply, angling the gun; then smiled broadly as he recognized the English archaeologist, a familiar presence in the valley. A broken row of teeth gleamed very white against his wizened brown skin. He lifted the rifle to his shoulder, squinted down its rusted sights and fired.

Blood exploded from the German sergeant's throat as the shot reverberated around the courtyard. On the roof of the shrine, the Greek was frantically trying to reload, tugging on the heavy bolt of his rifle. But the Germans had seen him. Jagged lightning flared from the muzzles of their machine pistols and a torrent of bullets tore into him. The force of their impact rolled him backward, leaving a sticky smear of blood across the flat roof.

The guns went quiet. In the far distance, Pemberton could hear the battle for Heraklion still raging, but the sounds were flat and unreal after the savagery of the *Schmeissers*. One of the soldiers ran forward, up a shallow flight of stairs to the roof of the shrine where the dead Greek lay. He kicked the body, then fired a single redundant bullet into the corpse's skull. Pemberton shuddered and edged further round the column that shielded him. Evans's reconstructed rooms were little more than showpieces, with no more depth than the Wild West façades of a Hollywood studio. With men in the courtyard and now to his left as well, there was precious little space for Pemberton to hide. He pressed his back against the pillar, not daring to move.

Opposite, by the back wall, a shadow moved in the doorway. Pemberton froze, then breathed again. A tiny kitten had sauntered through the door and was standing in the sunlight, staring at him with wide eyes.

"Go away," Pemberton mouthed, craning over his shoulder to make sure the German on the roof couldn't see him. What if the cat's movement attracted his gaze?

The kitten sat down on its hind legs, lifted a paw and began licking itself.

"Shoo." Glancing around, Pemberton could see the soldier was still on the roof across from him, using it as a lookout to scan the area for more partisans. If he looked over now he would surely see Pemberton.

The men in the courtyard shouted impatiently. Their sergeant was dying and they were keen to get him help. With a last look down the valley the soldier on the roof turned back. Pemberton's shoulders slumped forward and he hugged his knapsack with relief.

But the cat had stopped washing itself and was standing very still, wobbling a little on its stubby legs. A crow had flown down and perched on the bullet-riddled corpse, oblivious to the German standing a few feet away—or to the young predator crouched in the shadows. The kitten's tail quivered and its open jaw made a strange clicking sound. Then it pounced.

After that, everything happened too fast for Pemberton to see. The man on the roof spun round, spraying an indiscriminate stream of bullets into the open room. His comrades in the courtyard could see even less, but they were in no mood for caution. They opened up with everything they had, and suddenly the air was filled with a storm of lead, concrete, stone and plaster. Something sliced open Pemberton's cheek, just missing his eye, but he barely felt it. He leaped to his feet and, still clutching the bag, hurled himself through the opposite doorway. He never saw what happened to the cat.

The palace of Knossos was no longer the labyrinth it had been in legend, but there were still ways to lose yourself in it and Pemberton knew the layout better than any man alive. He burst through the door, almost oblivious to the shouts that followed, and dropped over the edge of the balcony into the open ruins below. A slit opening led into an underground chamber, beneath the room he had come from, then out into the sunlight again. Here a succession of long corridors stretched out to his left but he ignored them and turned right. They had not excavated much here, afraid of disturbing the foundations of the ruins above, but they had driven a couple of test tunnels under the great courtyard. One of them went all the way to the far side. If he could get there he might be able to work his way down to the east gate and slip out among the trees at the bottom of the valley. Footsteps pounded on the terraces above him and he pressed himself flat against the buttress wall. If anyone looked over the edge now he would be in plain sight. But no one came. There was the opening, a black hole in the embankment a few yards away. He ran to it and squeezed in. It was not much wider than Pemberton himself: several times, he banged his shoulders on the old timber joists that shored up the ceiling. Fine streams of loose dirt sifted through the cracks, settling in the creases of his shirt and trickling down his collar. Worst of all, there was no room to look back to see if anyone had followed him. He could only struggle grimly on, pushing his bag in front of him, toward the small square of light that winked at the end of the tunnel.

At last he reached it. With a final heave, he pushed the bag out so that it dropped on to the floor, then slithered after it. He was now in the shaft of the grand staircase, the best-preserved part of the palace. That had not satisfied Evans, who had embellished it still further with replica frescoes and painted columns, so that it looked almost as it must have done those thirty-three centuries earlier. To his right, a flight of stairs led up toward the courtyard, while another flight disappeared down on his left to the lower levels. If Pemberton could only get down there . . .

Flat footsteps rang out on the stairs above. Before Pemberton could move, they rounded the corner and stopped short on the landing. A German paratrooper stared down on him. He was limping slightly, perhaps from the parachute drop, but the gun in his hand didn't waver.

"*Was haben wir hier?*" His young eyes widened as he took in the strange sight. He had expected another farmer, or maybe a lost soldier, not this bedraggled, bespectacled English archaeologist. "*Was bist du denn für einer? Engländer? Soldat?*" He jabbed the *Schmeisser* at Pemberton. "*Spion?*"

Pemberton wrapped his arms round the bag and closed his eyes. Everything had been for nothing and now he would die here: one last skeleton in the minotaur's labyrinth. Irrelevantly, he thought of all the tombs he had broken open during his career and wondered if their angry denizens would be waiting to abuse him in the afterlife. At least he might see Grace again.

A shot rang out, echoing around the gloomy shaft. To his surprise, Pemberton didn't feel a thing. Perhaps the soldier had missed—or perhaps he was already dead. He waited for what seemed an eternity for the man to finish the job. When nothing happened he opened his eyes.

On the landing, the German soldier lay flat on his back, his toes in the air and the soles of his boots pointing toward Pemberton. Blood dripped from the step. Before Pemberton could hoist in this sudden reversal, a dark figure had flitted past. He ran up the stairs three at a time, checked the German's pulse then turned back. He was not wearing a uniform, but there was a pistol in his hand and what looked suspiciously like a knife bulging from his boot. His tanned face was frowning, troubled by something.

He stared down at Pemberton. "Are you the King of Greece?"

Pemberton gazed up blankly at the man who had saved him. Sunlight from the shaft above cast a slanted shadow over his face, revealing a tough mouth, weather-beaten skin and stubble that suggested he had left his bed in a hurry that morning. Dark eyes glinted in the gloom.

There was nothing Pemberton could think to say except, "Do I look Greek?"

The man shrugged. "They told me he might be here."

"He was." Pemberton struggled to his feet, not quite sure how he had come to be having this conversation. "He stayed at my house." He still remembered the shock of returning to the villa and finding the Greek monarch there: the New Zealand guards patrolling the garden, the liaison officers shouting into the radio they had erected in his study, the redundant courtiers sitting on the terrace chain-smoking their way through endless hands of cards. "They moved him on—to Chania, I think."

"Well, he's not there now." The man snapped open the breech of his revolver and replaced the spent cartridge from the pouch on his belt. "He escaped this morning—no one knows where he went. They told me to look out for him here."

Pemberton squinted at him. "Who are you?"

"Grant." He didn't offer a hand.

"John Pemberton. I'm the curator here."

"Good for you." Grant holstered the revolver and knelt down to pick up the machine pistol. He rifled through the dead German's uniform, extracting three spare magazines and—to Pemberton's horror—two hand grenades.

"Surely you won't use those here?"

"Why not?" Grant tucked the grenades into his belt and slung the machine pistol over his shoulder. "If you're worried about chipping the paintwork I'd say you're a few thousand years too late." He turned back up the stairs. "Wait here."

Pemberton's mouth was very dry. "Where are you going?"

"To find the King of Greece."

Pemberton waited, huddled in the shadows in the crook of the stairwell. Grant's footsteps died away quickly and he was left in silence. Trying not to jingle the buckles, he opened the knapsack and reached in. The notebook was still there, thank God; he ran his fingers over the leather and wondered what on earth he was doing. Where had Grant come from? Would he come back? Even if he did get rid of the soldiers in the palace, how would they ever manage to evade the others that must be swarming all over the island? Pemberton was no stranger to warfare, but for twenty years he had only experienced it through the muffled blanket of archaeology: scorch marks on walls, bronze blades pitted and notched, very occasionally a skeleton to be photographed, tagged and displayed. Now he was in the middle of it, and the idea that he might become fodder for some future archaeologist was not a pleasant thought.

Shouts rang out, very nearby, followed by three quick shots. Pemberton flinched. This was a dangerous place to be—he needed somewhere darker, more out of the way. Treading softly on the broad stairs, he tiptoed further down, toward the Hall of the Colonnades.

Grant knelt beside the bodies of two German soldiers and slotted three new cartridges into his Webley. It was a habit he had learned early on, always to reload when you had the chance. He'd lost count of the number of times the extra bullets had saved his life.

He holstered the Webley and gripped the *Schmeisser. Two more*, he thought. He had been watching the valley from a hidden lookout all day, ever since a panicked adjutant had arrived at his billet gibbering that the King of Greece had gone missing. He had seen the planes streaming in, the blizzard of paratroops falling over the island and the smoke rising from the towns, and felt his rage mount. Why should he be sidelined because some idiot politician was worried about a king whose own subjects didn't even want him? He had seen Pemberton leave the villa, then watched the squad of paratroopers make their landing up the valley. That was when he had left his post and crawled down the slope to the palace. SOE hadn't sent him to Greece to gawp at royalty; they had sent him to kill Nazis. And that was what he intended to do.

Keeping low, he crept down the eastern slope of the palace. He had had plenty of time to study it from above, but now that he was down among the ruins it was almost impossible to reconcile his bird's-eye view with the sprawling chaos around him. It was a sniper's dream, so much cover spread across so many different levels that he didn't know where to look.

"Patience," he murmured to himself. It had never been his strong point. But there were still two Germans prowling this labyrinth, and if he blundered about he would make easy prey. Better to . . .

A fragment of stone on the wall beside him exploded under the impact of a bullet. He hadn't seen where the shot came from; instinctively, he grabbed the *Schmeisser* with both hands and swung round to lay down a suppressing fire. Two bullets spat out of the muzzle; then—nothing. *Jammed.* He tore it off his shoulder and threw it away, diving to his right as more shots whistled over his head. *The bastard was above him.* Staying on his stomach, he wriggled along the shallow trench that had once been a royal corridor. A dark chamber loomed at the end of it, a cellar built into the hillside. If he could make that, he would at least have a roof to protect him. Blood pounded in his ears; he could hear the German soldier scrambling down after him. Abandoning caution, he flung himself through the open doorway as another volley of bullets chased him in.

He had come into a long, thin room, with a succession of bays opening off on either side like cattle stalls. Low walls divided them, and each seemed to be occupied by massive clay urns, every one taller than Grant himself. For a moment he thought about trying to crawl inside one to hide—then dismissed the idea. He'd be trapped like a rat in a bag.

More shots flew through the doorway, kicking up plumes of dust from the dry floor. He ran to the end of the chamber, looking for a door, even a hole in the wall. There was nothing—the door he'd come in by was the only way out. *Just my luck*, he thought grimly, *the one solid room in this whole bloody ruin*. The last bay on his right was empty: he hurled himself into it as his pursuer came running through the door.

For a moment there was silence, while the German waited for his eyes to adjust to the darkness and Grant crouched behind the wall. He tried to peer out, but the fat-bellied jar in the next bay blocked his view completely.

"*Rudi*," he heard the soldier call. "*Komm. Ich habe ihn.*"

There was no reply. That was good, thought Grant. Better still, the voice had sounded uncertain. He didn't know where Grant was and he didn't want to find out on his own. That was very good.

Quiet as a cat, Grant eased himself over the low wall and dropped down into the bay on the other side, behind one of the massive jars. Thumbing back the hammer on the revolver, he leaned round, feeling the clay coarse and cold against his bare arm. Where was the German?

His gun came out from behind the jar and a beam of light from the door caught its barrel. Only for a second, but it was all the nervous paratrooper needed. A burst of gunfire raked the room and thick lumps of clay flew off the jar. One struck Grant's right hand; before he knew it his fingers had sprung open and dropped the revolver. It fell to the ground and another layer of sound joined the cacophony in the chamber as the shock of the impact triggered the firing mechanism.

Grant dived back behind the jar. Thank Christ the Minoans had built it to last: the bullets had cracked it but not broken it. Meanwhile, the shot from the Webley seemed to have given the German pause for thought. He had stopped shooting—perhaps he was waiting for his comrade to join him. Peering underneath the jar, Grant could just see a pair of polished black boots standing to the right of the door.

Now he knew where the German was, but he had no way of getting him. The Webley lay on the sandy floor, almost close enough for him to stretch out his arm to grab it, just far enough that he would certainly die if he tried. He had the knife in his boot, but he'd never get sufficiently near to use it. That left . . .

Grant looked down at the two stick grenades tucked into his belt. He thought of the poor archaeologist, the horror on his face when Grant had taken them from the dead German.

"Sorry, old man," he whispered. Then he unscrewed the cap in the grenade's handle, felt for the cord inside and gave it a sharp tug. *One . . . two . . .* He stood, bent his arm and lobbed the grenade toward the far end of the passage. *Three . . .* It spun through the air and vanished out of sight. *Four . . .* A knock as it struck the rim of the jar next to the soldier, then a hollow thud as it dropped inside. *Five . . .*

A cloud of clay shards enveloped the German as the jar disintegrated. Grant didn't hesitate. He threw himself into the passageway and grabbed the revolver, rolled into a crouch and squeezed off three quick shots almost before he stopped moving. The second two were unnecessary. The paratrooper slumped to the ground among the pulverized remains of the jar. His face had been mashed into a bloody mess and blood trickled from the small hole just below the eagle insignia on his left breast. He didn't move.

Grant looked down at the pile of clay and dust, unrecognizable as the great artifact it had been. *That'll give the archaeologists something to piece together*, he thought.

And that was when he heard the shot.

John Pemberton was terrified. Not since Passchendaele had he felt dread like this—and at least then, for all the horror, he had had his men around him. Now he was alone. From somewhere nearby, maybe just the other side of the wall, he heard a furious fusillade of gunfire, a pause, then a deep booming explosion that seemed to shake the palace to its foundations. Had the bombers come back? Echoes from the blast lapped around the stone shaft; he didn't hear the shots that followed—nor the footsteps creeping quietly down the stairs.

The first bullet caught Pemberton in the shoulder, spinning him round so viciously that the second missed completely. The third tore through his shoulder blades and erupted from his chest. He fell forward, then rolled over on to his back. A dark mist clouded his eyes. At the bottom of the steps he could dimly see a snarling monster advancing toward him. In the strange criss-cross shadows of the hall, it almost looked as if horns had sprouted from the rimless helmet he wore.

Even in his dying moments Pemberton only had one thought. *The book*. He reached for the knapsack—but it was not there. He'd dropped it when the first bullet struck. Squinting through the blood-soaked haze, he saw the bag lying beside the pillar. He turned on to his side and stretched toward it.

A heavy boot came down hard on his hand. He barely felt the pain, but the sickly sound of fingers cracking made him scream aloud. The monster laughed, enjoying his agony.

"*Wünschst du dieses*?" The voice was harsh and indistinct, the bovine mockery evident. Keeping his rifle trained on Pemberton, the monster reached down and picked up the knapsack, dangling it just out of Pemberton's grasp. Pemberton flailed, but could not touch it. His lungs were racked with pain now, each breath barely worth the effort, and a pool of blood was spreading around him. The monster had unlatched the bag and was rooting inside it: he pulled out the torch, the penknife, two bars of chocolate—and then the notebook.

Pemberton groaned with despair. The monster laughed—a horrid, snorting sound that turned to uncomprehending snuffles as he pawed through the pages.

"*Was ist das?*"

"Go to hell."

It took all of Pemberton's energy just to say it—but it enraged the monster. Rearing up, he threw the book aside and upended his rifle like a club. Pemberton didn't even have the strength to flinch. Over the monster's shoulder he saw a dim shadow moving behind the columns on the stairs like the flicker of a flame. But of course there had not been a fire in here for three thousand years.

Behind the column, Grant couldn't see the German, but he saw the black shadow looming across the dying archaeologist. Forgetting his pistol, he pulled the knife from his boot and vaulted down from the open stair. Two silent bounds took him across the chamber. The German began to turn, but too late: Grant crooked his left arm round the German's throat, pulled him back and plunged the knife hilt-deep into his neck. For a second the man's head tipped back and he bellowed with agony. Then, with a twist, Grant pulled the knife clear. Blood sprayed from the wound, soaking Grant's face, and the German went limp. Grant shoved him aside and looked down.

One glance told him that Pemberton would not leave that room alive. His cheeks and lips were white, his body drained. But there were still a few drops of life in him. He raised a trembling arm and pointed to something behind Grant. His mouth stretched and puckered in a succession of grimaces, trying to force out a few last words. Grant knelt beside him, putting his ear to Pemberton's lips while his eyes followed the outstretched arm. There, in the corner a small brown notebook lay splayed open on the floor.

"Arch . . ."

Pemberton broke off in a fit of choking. Grant cradled his head against his chest. He wanted to tell him not to speak, to save his strength, but he knew there was no point. Whatever the old man had to say, he might as well get it out.

White hands, suddenly strong again, clutched the collar of Grant's shirt. Dull eyes sparked into life and fixed on him. "Archanes," he whispered. "The house with the apricot trees. Take it to her."

Then the hands went limp, the eyes closed and Grant smelled the familiar, lavatorial stench of death.

He carried the archaeologist's body outside and laid it in the palace's open foundations, covering the corpse with rubble to protect it from scavengers. One of the stones had a strange mark cut into it, a three-pronged design like a pitchfork or a trident, and he used that as a headstone. He took what he could from the dead paratroopers and reloaded the Webley. Then, like the heroes of old, he went in search of battle.

I

Oxford, March 1947

RAGE. THE first word ever written in Western literature, it sets the theme for all that follows."

The undergraduate glanced up from his essay, obviously hoping for a reaction. Opposite, a pair of pale-blue eyes stared steadily over his shoulder and examined the smear of ice that clouded the window. A coal fire hissed and spluttered in the grate, but it stood little chance against the freeze, which had gripped all England since January. Least of all in the drafty medieval rooms of an Oxford college, whose stones stored five hundred years of accumulated damp and chill.

The undergraduate cleared his throat and continued. "All the characters in the *Iliad* are defined by rage. Some think they can manipulate it; others are overwhelmed by it. Mostly, they die because of it, which explains why the story has such resonance almost three thousand years after Homer wrote it. As recent history shows, rage and violence continue to be the dominant passions of the world. The *Iliad* is not a story about the past; it is the story of the present. We can only hope that we, like Achilles, will eventually allow humanity to master our rage and pride and build a better, more just future."

A pause. Across the book-lined room, Arthur Reed, Professor of Classical Philology, was frowning.

"Did I say something wrong?"

The blue eyes drifted down from the window and settled on the undergraduate. "A poem."

The student blinked. "Sorry?"

"It's a poem. Not a story."

The undergraduate scowled, but swallowed whatever he wanted to say and stared at his essay. "Shall I go on?"

Reed settled back in his chair and sighed. The war had changed everything. In the thirties the undergraduates had been a callow bunch, eager to please and easily awed. This new generation were different. What could he, who had spent the war behind a desk, teach them about heroes?

A soft tap at the door interrupted the tutorial. A porter appeared and bobbed his head, studiously ignoring the undergraduate. "Beg your pardon, Professor. A Mr. Muir in the lodge to see you."

Wrapped in his wing-back chair, with a blanket over his legs and a thickly wound scarf almost swallowing his head, Reed was all but invisible to the porter in the corridor. But the undergraduate opposite could see him well enough—and saw the strange look that crossed his face, as if he'd bitten into a sour apple.

"Tell him I'll come down when I've finished."

"He was awful insistent, sir."

"So am I, Mr. Gordon." Reed took off his glasses and began polishing them on the tail of his scarf—a sure sign, to those who knew him, that the discussion was over. With another bob of his head the porter disappeared.

Reed stared at the ash-white coals in the grate, so long that the undergraduate wondered if he'd been completely forgotten. Then, with a strained smile and obvious effort, Reed forced his gaze back to his student. "Where were we?"

An hour later, with the undergraduate slightly older but—Reed feared—little wiser, the porter returned. He had hardly opened the door before the visitor pushed past. He was a slim man, wiry and taut, who didn't so much move as bristle. His ginger hair was cropped close as a scouring brush. Without taking off his coat he strode across the small room and dropped into the threadbare sofa opposite Reed. The aging cushions sagged underneath him, doubling him up in an awkward, angular sort of crouch. Leaning forward, his legs spread apart, he gave the unsettling impression of a leopard poised to pounce. He rubbed his hands together.

"I'm sorry for keeping you waiting," said Reed mildly.

"You damn well should be. I'm a busy man."

"But you came all the way out to Oxford to see me. You could have phoned."

"I did. Five times—yesterday—and twice the day before that."

"Ah, well, I dare say the porter lost the messages. Anyway, you're here now. How can I oblige?"

Muir pulled a cigarette from an ivory case and struck a match. He didn't offer one to Reed. When the tip was glowing, he reached inside his pocket and extracted a stiff brown envelope which he tossed on to the coffee table between them. "What do you make of this?"

Reed took the envelope. Inside was a single photograph printed on heavy paper. He squinted at it, then unfolded himself from his chair and crossed to the desk against the wall. He took a thick magnifying glass from a drawer and held it above the image. "A clay tablet—or part of one. There's a black band across the bottom of the picture that makes it rather difficult to see. There seems to be some sort of inscription on the tablet, though the picture's too blurred to make it out clearly. Nothing else, except a wristwatch laid flat beside it." Reed put down the magnifying glass. "Did John Pemberton take this?"

Muir stiffened. "Why do you ask that?"

"Did he?"

"Maybe. Why?"

Reed tapped the photograph. "The watch. Pemberton always used it for scale when he was photographing artifacts. Rest his soul." He peered at the photograph again, then at Muir. "You've obviously heard of him? I hadn't imagined you as an enthusiast for archaeology."

"When he wasn't digging up lost civilizations, Pemberton worked for us." The cigarette had already all but vanished; Muir took the butt and flicked it into the fireplace. It raised a few forlorn sparks.

"*Us?*" Reed queried.

"Military Intelligence. We recruited him before the war—asked him to keep an eye on things in case Hitler set his sights on Crete." Another cigarette was already shrinking visibly in Muir's mouth—at least he was doing something to heat the room, Reed thought. "This is all confidential, of course."

"Of course."

"We used Pemberton to liaise with the locals, establish contacts, that sort of thing. As an archaeologist he could wander pretty much anywhere and no one took any notice. It was a damn shame when he died on the first day of the invasion—set us back six months."

"A terrible pity," agreed Reed, shooting Muir an oblique glance from under his snowy eyebrows. "And now you're looking through his snapshots?"

"We found the picture in a German archive after the war."

Reed scratched his neck where the scarf itched. "You're not seriously suggesting . . . ?"

"That Pemberton was a traitor?" Muir gave a short, humorless laugh. "No. When the Germans captured the island they made Pemberton's villa their headquarters, so they had plenty of opportunity to rifle through his belongings."

"Then why . . ."

"Never mind why." The second cigarette butt followed the first into the fire. Muir flipped open his case and instinctively reached for another, then checked himself and snapped the lid shut. He drummed his fingers on the ivory, a fast beat like a machine-gun. "All I want to know from you is what this picture shows."

Reed picked up the magnifying glass again and reexamined the photograph. "Probably late Minoan or early Mycenaean . . ."

"In English?" The cigarette case flew open as Muir's impatient fingers gave up on self-restraint.

"Very well. The clay tablet in the photograph probably dates from about the fourteenth century BC and comes from Crete or mainland

Greece. Not as old as the pyramids, but before the Trojan war." He smiled. "If, of course, you believe in that."

"So it's Greek and it's old as sin. What about the writing?"

Reed sighed and put down the picture. "Come with me."

He struggled into his overcoat and jammed a fur-lined hat over his head, then led Muir down the wooden stairs, across the quadrangle and out through the main gate of the college. Shovelled ramparts of dirty snow lined the road, almost waist high, and the few pedestrians who braved the icy pavements were hunched over by the wind that whistled down Turl Street. Roofs groaned under the burden of snow and icicles hung like knives from the gutters, while the college walls—so golden in summer—seemed gray as the sky.

"Were you here?" asked Reed as they shuffled across Broad Street and past the Gothic turrets of Balliol College. With their crusting of snow, they looked like something out of a fairy tale. "As an undergraduate, I mean?"

"Cambridge."

"Ah," said Reed, with what appeared to be genuine sympathy. "*Procul omen abesto*."

They walked on in silence, past a snowbound churchyard and across a street to the Ashmolean Museum. Its enormous neoclassical portico seemed out of place amid the medieval austerity of the colleges. A nod from Reed carried them past the guard, through the empty galleries, to a gloomy back room. It seemed to be some sort of cupboard for the clutter of forgotten civilizations. Tall statues stood shrouded in dust sheets, marble toes sticking out under the hems; gold-framed paintings leaned against the walls; and display cases with the glass taken out were pushed into corners like unused school desks. Most of their contents seemed to be missing, marked only by the dark shadows they had left in the bleached backing board, but one case still held a few exhibits. Reed crossed to it and pointed.

Muir leaned closer. The piece Reed had indicated was a clay tablet, blackened by age and split by three large cracks. Its edges were rough, but the face was smooth. Scratched into the surface, almost invisible in the dim room, were hundreds of tiny, spidery characters.

Reed turned on the lights and handed Muir the magnifying glass.

"What is it?" The bite had temporarily gone from his voice.

"It was discovered—the writing, that is—in about 1900. Sir Arthur Evans found it on Crete at Knossos and named it Linear B. As he was also curator of the Ashmolean at the time, a fair number of the pieces ended up here."

Muir put down the magnifying glass and held the photograph next to the tablet. "You mean there's more than one of these things?"

"A few score. Maybe a hundred and fifty all told—though some of them are only fragments." Reed shrugged. "It's not really my subject. I don't know why you fagged out to Oxford through this terrible weather to bother me with it. You could have taken a taxi to the British Museum and found out as much. They're very helpful there."

Muir ignored him. "Can you read it?"

Reed gave a short, shocked laugh. "Read it? Scholars have been trying to break this for almost fifty years. They've all failed. Solving it would be the most extraordinary breakthrough since Champollion cracked the Egyptian hieroglyphs. And he had the Rosetta Stone to work from, of course."

"Have you tried?"

Reed shook his head. "As I said—not really my thing. And I don't know why . . ."

"I needed an answer quickly and you're the only man with the clearance for this." Muir had put down the photograph and was striding around the room, chewing on an unlit cigarette.

"Clearance?" echoed Reed, baffled. "If this ever held a secret, it was more than three thousand years ago. I suspect it's declassified by now."

"That's where you're wrong." Muir spun round and advanced toward Reed. "I want you to have a run at this. After the work you did on Ultra it should be money for jam. This stuff's obsolete."

"It's not really . . ."

"And I may need you in Greece. If that was where Pemberton took this photograph, who knows what else he found there?"

Now Reed looked genuinely appalled. "To *Greece*? But there's a civil war going on there at the moment."

Muir gave a wolfish laugh and stubbed out his cigarette on an empty plinth. "At least it'll be warmer than this fucking morgue."

It was dark by the time Muir got back to London, to the gray building off Victoria Street. Most of the staff had already gone home, but the night clerk let him into the archives. It took four hours, but at the end of it he had a name and a file. He started reading from the back, flipping quickly through the dry pages. Like most of the files in this section, it began in late 1938, sporadically at first—medical records, training assessments—then more urgently. Between 1940 and 1944 the reports came thick and fast, a Cook's tour of the war's many fronts—Paris, Moscow, Athens, Heraklion, Alexandria, Cairo—headed with a mind-numbing variety of ever-changing code words. In 1945 they slowed abruptly, ending in a few paper dribbles as the bureaucracy discharged him. And, on the final page, a single telegram. After the yellowed sheaves of war records the paper was crisp and stark.

Muir whistled under his breath. "You silly bugger." He spent another five minutes checking back through the records, then picked up the phone.

"I need to get to the Holy Land." A pause. "No I don't care if it takes a fucking miracle."

2

Qaisariyeh, Mandate of Palestine

THE CASTLE stood on a promontory, a thumb of land sticking out into the calm Mediterranean. French knights had built it some eight hundred years earlier, to keep out invaders tempted by the flat coast and the tranquil sea. In the end they had failed, but the castle survived: a monument to the crusaders' extraordinary aptitude for war, gently crumbling through the centuries.

Now a new generation of colonizers had revived it, embellishing the medieval ramparts with innovations unimaginable to the men who built it. Barbed wire ran along the massive walls, and the crossbowmen in the towers had been superseded by Bren guns. But they were no longer there to keep enemies away. The castle had been turned in on itself, and the stout fortifications now protected the realm by keeping men in rather than out.

The car pulled up outside the gate just before midnight. Leaving the engine running, the driver jumped out and ran to open the rear door. If he had learned one thing on the long drive from Jerusalem, it was that his passenger was not a man to tolerate delay.

"Wait here," came the curt instruction. "I won't be long."

A wand of light cut through the darkness and in a moment a fair-haired man in an officer's uniform emerged from the arched gateway carrying a torch. "Lieutenant Cargill, sir."

"How do you do?" The visitor didn't introduce himself, nor take the hand that hovered in front of him as it wondered whether to shake or salute. "Don't you have electricity here?"

"The generator conked out this afternoon, I'm afraid." Cargill seemed eager to please; he hadn't yet discovered that this was a lost cause where Muir was concerned. "How was your journey, sir?"

"Fucking terrible." Muir followed Cargill through the arch, down a vaulted passage and out into a courtyard that had become home to a colony of Nissen huts. "Have you been to Jerusalem recently? Our esteemed government's turned the center of town into some sort of miniature Birkenau and locked themselves inside it. Wrapped themselves in barbed wire. Even then they can't protect themselves against these fucking Irgun guerrillas." He shook his head in disgust. "Anyway, our man's still here?"

Surprised by the change of tack, Cargill took a moment to answer. "I've had him moved to the interrogation room ready for your arrival. Actually, we weren't sure what time you would arrive—he's been there a few hours now."

"Good. Soften him up. He's a hard bastard, this one, according to his file. All sorts of heroics in the war. Picked up a DSO, and they didn't hand those out for digging latrines."

"Really?" Cargill sounded surprised. "Not a man you'd expect to find running guns to the Zionists."

Muir chuckled. "Three months after they pinned the medal on his tit he disappeared. Deserted. A complex fellow, our Mr. Grant."

They reached the far corner of the courtyard, an old stable that had been fitted with a corrugated iron roof and a steel door. Cargill unlocked it.

"Will you need help, sir? I could fetch a couple of sergeants . . ."

"No need. Wait here in case there's any trouble. You're armed?"

Cargill touched his holster.

"Keep it ready, then. If anyone walks out through that door without knocking twice on the inside, shoot him."

"Do you really think . . ." Cargill looked appalled.

"I told you: he's a complex fellow."

The door clanged shut behind him as Muir stepped into the cell. Like the rest of the fortress, it was a strange mix of old and new: medieval stone walls topped and tailed with an iron roof and a hastily poured concrete floor. As in the Middle Ages, it was lit by flame: in this case a Coleman lantern hung from a crossbeam. In the middle of the room, two wooden chairs faced each other across a steel table, and there, his right arm handcuffed to the table leg, sat Grant.

Muir studied him for a moment. The file photograph must be almost ten years old, but it was impossible to say whether the intervening decade had been good to Grant or not. He had aged, of course—but so had most men who survived the war. In Grant's case the changes were neither better nor worse. He had scars—one on his left forearm that snaked almost from the elbow to his wrist—and lines at the corners of his mouth and eyes, but they hadn't changed the underlying face. It was as if the years had taken the young man in the photograph and simply sharpened him up, clarified him somehow. Even cuffed to the table, he managed to slouch back and offer Muir an easy, sardonic smile.

Muir flipped open a notebook and began reading. "Grant, C. S. Born October 1917, County Durham. Educated . . . nowhere that matters. Left school 1934. Emigrated to South Africa, then Rhodesia. Travelled extensively in southern Africa as a prospector for the Kimberley Diamond Company. Rumored involvement with indigenous anti-Belgian elements in Congo. Returned England 1938, recruited to Military Intelligence, later transferred to Special Operations Executive. Active service in Greece, North Africa, Balkans and Soviet Union. July 1944, awarded Distinguished Service Order; October 1944 missing, presumed deserted, following an incident near Impros, Crete. Subsequently linked to black marketeering in London; later rumored to be working in the eastern Mediterranean, running guns to the so-called Democratic Army of Greece, the Irgun, the Haganah and other elements in the Zionist underground. Whereabouts currently unknown. Correction: whereabouts currently handcuffed to a table in a shitty little cell in the asshole of nowhere, looking at a long stretch at His Majesty's pleasure for supplying arms to the enemies of the Empire."

Muir snapped shut the notebook and dropped into the empty chair. Grant stared back, his eyes wide with mock awe. "Anything else?"

His voice was not what Muir had expected. Somewhere at the bottom of it he could detect the rough vowels of a boy from the north, but it had been layered with so many other accents and inflections that it was impossible to pin down: a true mongrel.

"Only that the arms you've been smuggling appear to have been looted from caches that were supposed to supply the Greek resistance in the war."

Grant shrugged. "No one was using them. The Jews spent most of the last ten years looking down the wrong end of a gun. I thought the least I could do was give them something to shoot back with."

"But they're our fucking guns. And they're shooting them at us."

Grant shrugged. "Us? I didn't think I belonged in the club any more."

"So you thought you'd get your revenge by selling our guns to our enemies?" Muir breathed a contemptuous stream of smoke through his nostrils.

"Just the money."

"I suppose that's the benefit of working for Jews."

Grant didn't answer, but held Muir's gaze across the table.

Muir tapped a fresh cigarette on his ivory case. "Anyway, I couldn't give a squirrel's shit what you're doing at the moment. I came here to talk about Crete and a Mr. John Pemberton." A spark of flame. "You knew him."

"Did I?"

Grant did well to keep his face impassive, but Muir had conducted enough interrogations to see past the façade.

"Crete—the day the Nazis arrived. We'd sent you to look for the King near Knossos. Instead you bumped into Pemberton. You were the last man to see him alive."

"And the first to see him dead. So?"

"According to your report, he handed over his notebook before he died."

"And?"

Muir leaned across the table. The glowing tip of his cigarette hovered a few inches from Grant's face, and smoke drifted into his eyes. "I want to know what you did with it."

"I gave it to his widow."

"Pemberton didn't leave a widow, you prick. She predeceased him."

"Maybe it was his sister." Grant's eyes were tearing from the smoke, but he never blinked. He held Muir's gaze for a long moment—then blew the cloud of smoke straight into Muir's face, so suddenly that Muir shrank back. "What do you think I did with it? I didn't have time to visit the library. I binned the book and tried to find some Nazis to kill. If you read my report, you'll know I managed that pretty well too."

Muir leaned back in his chair. "I don't believe you."

"I don't suppose you spent much time on the front line."

"I don't believe that a man spent his dying breath giving you this book and the first thing you did was throw it away. Weren't you curious why it was so important to him?"

"He could have given me his lucky matchbox and a locket with his lover's hair and I'd have done the same." Grant shook his head. "I flipped through the book, but it was all gibberish and mumbo-jumbo. I had a lot of ground to cover and I couldn't afford to be weighed down. So I lost it."

Muir stared at him a moment longer, then abruptly stood. "That's a pity. If you'd had it, or knew where it was, I might have been able to help you out of here. Might even have been some money in it. After all, I don't suppose the Yids will be paying you now." He looked down expectantly. "Well?"

"Go to hell," said Grant.

The car nosed into the copse of trees and rolled to a halt. Its headlights threw a pool of yellow light round the clearing, illuminating a battered

Humber truck with its canvas sides rolled down. A group of young men in mismatched combat uniforms lounged against it, smoking and checking their guns. They made a terrifying sight—but if the occupants of the car were worried they didn't show it. No one got out. In the back of the car a handle squeaked as the passenger wound down the rear window.

One of the men walked over and stooped to look inside. The night was warm, but nevertheless he wore an overcoat and a black beret jammed down over his close-shaved gray hair. He carried a machine pistol.

"Are you ready?" The tip of a cigarette glowed in the back seat, but the face behind it was invisible in the shadows. "You found what you needed?"

The man in the beret nodded. "It was in the truck—as you promised. We are ready."

"Then don't cock it up. And make sure he gets out alive."

They took Grant back to his cell, a vaulted cellar from the crusader castle crammed with three wooden bunks. In the utter darkness he had to feel his way to his bed. He flopped on to the mattress, not even bothering to take off his shoes.

A match flared, illuminating a young face with floppy dark hair and olive skin on the bunk beside him. He lit the two cigarettes pursed between his lips, passed one to Grant and blew out the match before it burned his fingers.

Grant took the gift gratefully. "Thanks, Ephraim."

"Did they beat you?" The boy couldn't have been more than fifteen or sixteen, but his voice was matter-of-fact. *And why not?* Grant thought. Ephraim had been in the prison far longer than he had, almost three months now, sentenced for throwing rocks at a British policeman in Haifa.

"They didn't beat me."

"Did they want to know where they can find Begin?"

"No." Grant lay back, arms behind his head, and blew smoke at the ceiling. "It wasn't the usual goons. Some spook from London. Wasn't interested in the Irgun—just wanted to dig up some ancient history."

"Did you tell him?"

"I . . ."

Even through the meter-thick walls they felt the explosion. The bunks rocked and dust rained down from the ceiling. Grant swung round and leaped to the floor, pulling the boy Ephraim with him. They crouched in the darkness. Shots rang out—first panicked and sporadic, then methodical and constant as the Bren guns started up.

"They're getting closer." Holding Ephraim's shoulder, Grant led him across the room until his hand felt the cold metal of the door—still locked. Flattening himself against the wall, he pushed Ephraim to the opposite side of the door frame.

"Get ready—someone's coming."

Lieutenant Cargill returned to his office and poured a long drink from the bottle he kept in his desk. He had met plenty of disagreeable men during the war, and afterward here in Palestine, but few who exuded the same calculated unpleasantness as his nameless visitor.

A knock sounded at the door. Whisky slopped over the rim of the glass. Had the visitor forgotten something?

"Engineer, sir. Come to repair the generator."

Cargill sighed with relief. "Come in."

The engineer was a small man, with wire-rimmed spectacles and an ill-fitting uniform that looked as though it had been cut down from a larger size.

"Rather late to be mending the generator, isn't it?" Cargill dabbed at the spilt whisky with his handkerchief. "Wouldn't it be easier to wait for daylight?"

The engineer shrugged. He seemed to be sweating profusely. "Orders, sir." He was still walking toward Cargill, a holdall clutched in his left hand. "Now, sir, if you'll just give me your keys."

"You don't need my keys to get to the generator. You'll find it . . ."

Cargill looked up, to see the muzzle of a Luger hovering six inches from his nose. "*What the hell?*"

"Your keys."

As the man stretched out his hand, the sleeve of his ill-fitting shirt rode up. Tattooed on his wrist, in a bruise-purple color that would never fade, ran a row of tiny numbers.

"You will not be the first man I have watched die. Give me the keys."

Followed every inch of the way by the Luger, Cargill unclipped the ring of keys from his belt and laid them on the table. Then the engineer—*the Jew*, Cargill corrected himself—took a length of electrical wire from his holdall and tied Cargill's wrists to the back of his chair and his ankles to the legs of the desk. Cargill bore the humiliations in stoic silence.

"Those keys might unlock the cells, but they won't get you through the front gates. You won't just walk out with all your Irgun gangster friends trailing behind you."

"We will find a way."

The words were hardly out of his mouth when a massive explosion shook the castle to its very foundations. It must have been close by. Cargill rocked on his chair, couldn't keep his balance and toppled over with a yelp of pain, his legs still tied to the desk. Through the dust and smoke that swirled around the room, he saw the Jew snatch the keys, then touch his cap in farewell.

"*Shalom*."

The footsteps were closer now. There was a definite rhythm to them: approach, pause, approach, pause. With each pause, Grant could hear shouts and the clink of metal. Another burst of machine-gun fire from outside drowned the sounds for a moment; when it stopped there were keys jangling right outside the door. Grant tensed in the darkness. There was no handle on the inside—all he could do was wait as the key slid into the lock, turned, clicked . . .

"*Rak kakh*."

The door swung in, but the squeak of the hinges was drowned out by the squeal of delight from Ephraim. "*Rak kakh!*" he shouted back, repeating the Irgun slogan. "*Rak kakh*. Praise God you came."

"Praise God when we get out of here," muttered Grant.

Their rescuer had already moved on to the next cell by the time they stepped out, but the corridor was teeming with freed prisoners. At the far end an Irgun commando was standing by the exit doling out small arms from a sack.

"Like a bloody Hebrew Father Christmas," said Grant.

Ephraim looked at him in confusion. "Who's Father Christmas?"

They pushed their way down the corridor, past the commando—who had run out of guns—and into the main castle courtyard. Eight hundred years had raised the ground almost a meter above the original foundations and a trench had been dug along the front of the building to allow access. Now it was filled with the ex-prisoners and their rescuers, engaged in a furious firefight with the English garrison by the gatehouse. On the far side of the courtyard a pile of smoking rubble and a massive hole showed where the Irgun had blown their way through the castle wall.

"Who's in charge?"

He had to bellow it in the ear of the nearest fighter, a lean young man blasting away with what looked like a First World War carbine. In the time it took him to jerk back the bolt, slot it home again and aim, he somehow managed to indicate a tall figure in a black beret and overcoat, halfway down the trench. Grant crawled across.

"Where's your escape route? Through the breach?"

The Irgun commander shook his head. "That's how we came in," he said in English. "We go out the back door." He nodded to his left, where the western wall pushed out into the sea. As Grant stared, he could see a file of men creeping along the shadows at its base, invisible to the British soldiers who were concentrating all their fire on the prison block.

"Do we swim?"

"Not if you hurry."

Grant glanced back to the gatehouse. From the top of the tower the lightning muzzle flash of a Bren gun burst through the ancient arrow loops. While they were in the trench they were safe, but the moment they abandoned their position they'd make easy pickings in open ground.

"You'll need to shut that up before we go."

The commander looked at him. "Are you volunteering?"

"Why not?"

Lieutenant Cargill's night had been going to hell ever since the mysterious visitor arrived. His ankle ached where it had twisted when he fell, but that was nothing against the agony of having to lie on the floor, tied to the office furniture, and listen impotently as the battle raged outside. He couldn't even tell who was winning. Nor was he under any illusion that things would improve when it was over.

The door burst open. Trapped behind his desk, Cargill saw a pair of worn brown boots pound across the room. He craned his neck up, just in time to see a motley, unshaven face peering over the desk in surprise. A plea for help died stillborn on Cargill's lips.

"You're the gun-runner." A horrible thought crossed his mind. "This isn't to do with your visitor, is it?"

Grant didn't answer: he was pulling the drawers from Cargill's desk and turning them out on the tabletop. He lifted a brown leather holster from the bottom drawer. The walnut handle of a Webley revolver jutted from under the flap. Grant pulled it out and checked the chamber.

Helpless and defenseless, Cargill nonetheless put on a brave face. "Are you going to shoot me in cold blood?"

Grant shook his head. "No point. I'll leave it to the army, when they find out what a balls-up you've made of this." He thought for a moment. "What's your hat size?"

Outside Cargill's office a worn flight of stairs climbed to the ramparts. Grant took them two at a time and ran along the wall toward the gatehouse tower. In the confusion no one had remembered to lock the door. Grant slipped inside. This part of the tower had been gutted, except for four steel pillars supporting the gun platform on the roof. They gleamed in the darkness, flickering with the reflections of light from the battle outside, while the drafty chamber echoed like a drum with the thump of the Bren gun above. Grant jammed Cargill's peaked cap over his tousled hair, touched the Webley that was now buckled securely round his waist, then shinned up the wooden ladder bolted to the wall.

The gunner on the roof could hardly have heard Grant, but he must have noticed the movement out of the corner of his eye. He eased off the trigger and glanced round.

"What the hell do you think you're doing?" Grant bellowed, in his best regimental English. "Keep those Yids pinned down."

The voice, and the familiar silhouette of the officer's cap, was all the reassurance the gunner needed. He couched the Bren gun against his shoulder and let off another furious volley. It gave Grant all the time he needed. He crossed the roof and with one well-aimed kick sent the gunner rolling across the wooden floor in agony. Two more deft punches and the hapless gunner lay sprawled out, unconscious.

Grant pulled off the man's belt and used it to tie his wrists behind his back. That done, he returned to the Bren gun, shifted it round and loosed a long stream of bullets in the vague direction of the British troops. He grinned as he saw confusion overwhelm them. Some of the more alert soldiers sent a few shots back toward him, cracking splinters off the stone battlements, but most of them seemed in complete disarray. Over by the prison block, meanwhile, the shooting was tailing off as the Irgun used the distraction to make good their escape.

Grant squeezed off a final burst, then picked up the Bren gun—taking care to avoid touching the scalding barrel—and staggered across to the far wall. He heaved it into the dry moat. By the time anyone found it there, Grant hoped he'd be long gone.

There were only half a dozen fighters left in the trench. A couple more lay dead on the ground, but most seemed to have escaped. Grant made his way to the black-bereted commander. "Just in time," he grunted. He broke off to slap another magazine into his machine pistol. "We need to get to the boat." He turned to his right and handed the gun to the fighter beside him. "Keep those English pinned down until we're over the wall."

The fighter's arms sagged as he took the weight, but the determination in his young face was unbending.

Grant's eyes widened. "Ephraim?"

The boy hoisted the gun on to the earthen parapet and squinted down the barrel with fierce concentration. Grant turned to the commander. "You can't leave him here."

"We need someone to hold off the British until we're away."

"I'll do it," Grant said, without even thinking.

The commander shrugged. "Do what you want, English. They hang you if you stay."

"They'll hang the boy if I go."

Ephraim shook his head and gave a white-toothed grin. "They cannot—I am too young. By the time I am old enough to hang, Israel will be free."

"You'd better hope so."

Grant looked down at the boy, his floppy hair and his bright eyes shining with a desire to strike at the hated colonizers. Maybe Grant had looked the same at that age, the day he stepped on to the quay at Port Elizabeth with nothing but a suitcase to his name. Part of him—the young man who had run away to South Africa—wanted to stay with the boy and live his heroic dreams. But another, colder part knew what he had to do.

Grant reached out and ruffled Ephraim's hair. "Keep moving around," he told him. "It'll make them think there's more of you."

Ephraim smiled, then leaned over the weapon and squeezed the trigger. The gun almost leaped out of his hands, before he slowly wrestled it under control.

The Irgun commander tugged Grant's sleeve. "We have to go."

They ran along the base of the wall. Grant felt horribly exposed, but Ephraim's ragged bursts of gunfire were still keeping the garrison distracted. At the bottom of the furthest tower he found a rope ladder.

With a quick scramble he was up it, standing on the rampart and looking out on a moonlit sea. Just off the rocks, where the wall met the waves, thirty men sat huddled in a motor launch.

"Down we go." A rope dangled from one of the ancient battlements. Grant took hold of it, swung himself out and slid down—so fast he burned his palms on the coarse rope. Two steps on the slippery rock and he was looking down into the boat. Another step and an almost headlong plunge, and he was sprawled in the bilge. He heard a thud from nearby as the Irgun commander jumped down. Then the big engine opened up and Grant was tipped back as the launch gathered speed over the calm sea. No one spoke. Every man was tensed, waiting for bullets to rip apart the open boat. But none came.

Grant pulled himself up and managed to squeeze on to the bench that ran along the side of the boat. After about quarter of an hour one of his companions lit a match, and a few moments later the boat was alive with glowing cigarettes and whispered jubilation. Grant picked his way aft and found the Irgun commander. "Where are we going?"

"We have a cargo ship waiting off shore. She'll take us up the coast to Tire." He opened his hands. "After that, wherever you want."

Grant thought for a moment. Muir's visit had planted an idea in his mind—though he had never expected to be able to act on it so quickly. He took a drag on his cigarette and blew smoke into the moonlight. "Can you get me to Crete?"

3

Archanes, Crete. Two weeks later

THE LOCALS called the mountain the Face of Zeus. It towered over the village and its surrounding vineyards, a high fist of rock clenched against the sky. In prehistoric times the bull-worshipping Minoans had built a shrine on its summit; thousands of years later a small, whitewashed church had replaced the shrine, but every August the villagers still made their pilgrimage up the slopes to take offerings to the sanctuary. Even the comings and goings of gods could not change the island's routine.

At about eleven o'clock on that April morning, any god looking down would have seen the old bus rattle into the town square and discharge a gaggle of passengers—mostly farmers returning from the market. Many drifted toward the *kaphenion* to continue their arguments and gossip over coffee, but one walked in the opposite direction and turned down the narrow lane that led up toward the foot of the mountain. No one paid him much attention, though everyone noticed him. They had grown used to strangers passing through their village, ever since the Germans came. Hard experience had taught it was always safest to ignore them.

Grant walked to the edge of the village where the lane became a track running between apple orchards. The ground rose to meet the mountain and there, just where cultivated fields gave way to rock and wild grass, a stone house stood. Hens pecked around a rusty grape press in the front garden and bundles of unplanted vines leaned against the wall, but the shutters were freshly painted and a thin trail of smoke rose from the chimney. At the side of the house the first leaves were beginning to appear on the small grove of apricot trees.

Grant stood there for a moment, watching, then let himself through the gate and walked softly up the stairs to the front door which—as usual with Greek village houses—was on the first floor. He didn't knock; instead, he whistled a few bars of a mournful Greek marching song.

The wind coming off the mountain snatched the notes from his lips and whisked them away. Wildflowers rustled in the breeze. A loose shutter banged against the wall. Afraid that his hat might blow away, Grant took it off and tucked it under his arm. He'd bought it in haste at the bazaar in Alexandria, three days earlier, and the band was a little loose.

He waited another minute, then decided to come back later. He turned round—and stopped.

Even with all his training, he hadn't heard her come up behind him. She wore a plain black dress, and a black scarf covered her head. If you had seen her from behind you would have taken her for one of the old women who inhabited every Greek village, as gnarled and wizened as the olive trees and just as much part of the landscape. But if you looked from the front, you would have seen that the dress was pulled in at the waist, tracing the curves beneath, and that below the hem of the skirt her ankles were smooth and slender. Her dark hair was pulled back under the scarf, except for one loose strand which hung over her cheek. It only seemed to accentuate the wild beauty in her face.

"Grant?" The face screwed up and her dark eyes blazed. "I didn't think you'd come back. I didn't think you'd dare."

Her voice was the same as he remembered it, with a quickness like a lick of flame in the way she pronounced the English words. He put his hat back on, just so he could lift it in mock courtesy. "Marina. I . . ."

"If I ever wanted to see you again, it would only be to kill you."

Grant shrugged. "Time for that later. I came to warn you."

"The same way you warned Alexei?"

"I didn't kill your brother." Grant spoke deliberately, coldly.

"No?" She had begun to move toward him, carried away by her anger, and Grant braced himself. He had never underestimated her. Most of the men who had had regretted it "Three days after the ambush he went to meet you in the gorge at Impros. Neither of you ever came back—but only one of you is alive now."

"I promise you, his death had nothing to do with me." That wasn't entirely true. He could almost taste the poison bile that had clogged his throat as he'd waited in the gorge with the Webley, the sweat stinging his eyes like tears. "Christ, he was almost like a brother to me."

There was a lot more he could have said, but that would only have made things worse. And he didn't have much time. He glanced over his shoulder, then back at Marina. "I came to warn you." He'd already said that, he knew. "You remember the book?"

She looked up, caught off guard. "What?"

"The book. The archaeologist's notebook I gave you to hide. You remember it?"

A gust of wind suddenly lifted her scarf and snatched it away. It sailed across the garden, catching in the branches of a tree by the wall. Marina's long hair billowed out behind her, savage and untamed.

"I don't remember it."

"Yes you do. Two days after the invasion. I brought it here—the archaeologist asked me to. You were upset because he'd been killed."

"Pemberton was a good man," said Marina softly. "A *good* Englishman." She stared at Grant a moment longer. A tear glistened in the corner of her eye. It wouldn't fall, but nor would she wipe it away. Grant just stood and waited.

She seemed to decide something.

"Come inside."

The house was exactly as he remembered it: a kitchen, a bedroom and a living room, all simple but impeccably tidy. A charred log smoldered in the stone hearth, and bunches of wildflowers and dried lavender were arranged in vases on the windowsills. Photographs hung on the walls: a man in a broad-brimmed hat sitting on a donkey, struggling to keep still for the camera; two young women laughing by a river bank; a young man in a conscript's uniform, his face grainy and drawn as he tried to look brave. Grant didn't look at that one.

Marina disappeared into the kitchen, returning a few minutes later with two tiny coffee cups and two glasses of water. She had also brushed her hair, Grant noticed. She put the drinks down on the lace tablecloth and seated herself across from him. Grant sipped his coffee cautiously and made a face. It was thick as tar.

"Have you lost your taste for Greek coffee?"

"Just checking it for strychnine."

Marina laughed, despite herself. "I promise you, when I kill you it will be with my own hands."

"That's all right, then." Grant tipped the cup back and drained it in one gulp. He watched as Marina drank hers. She must be twenty-seven now, he thought—thinner than she had been the day he limped into her house, but still with the same wild, unpredictable beauty. Even then, she and her brother had been making names for themselves with the *andartiko*, the Greek resistance. In the months that followed, helped and supplied by Grant, they had become one of the most formidable thorns in the Germans' side. And more than that, Grant and Marina had become lovers. It had been a clandestine affair, hiding from Germans and Greeks alike: brief moments snatched in shepherds' huts and behind broken stone walls, usually during the heat of the day before their nighttime missions. Grant could still remember the taste of the sweat on her neck; the rustle of the myrtle and oleander; her moans and the way he had tried to silence them with kisses. They had been brutal, savage times, but that had only made the sex more urgent, more vital. Until it all ended on that blisteringly clear April day, in a gorge in the White Mountains, with the smell of rosemary and cordite.

Grant realized she was watching him and quickly took a sip of water.

"So you came to warn me. About what—Pemberton's notebook?"

She had mastered her emotions now and was calmer, speaking with clipped politeness. Though there was still a flush in her cheeks.

"It's . . ." He hesitated. "It's a long story."

"Then tell it from the beginning." She leaned back and folded her arms across her breasts. "Tell me what happened after you left Crete."

"I went back to England." Even that simple statement hid a multitude of stories: an inflatable boat racing in to a beach near Dover under cover of darkness; a threadbare bedroom on Old Compton Street over a café, twitching the curtains each time a bobby walked down the street; midnight meetings in the shells of bombed-out houses. "Then one day I was walking down Baker Street and a man bumped into me. Literally—more like a rugby tackle. Terribly apologetic, frightfully sorry, insisted on buying me a cup of tea. He was so keen I said yes."

"He was a spy?"

"I think he worked at Marks & Spencer. A clothes shop," Grant added, seeing her blank look. "But he was a Jew. He told me about some friends of his who were trying to persuade our government to hand over Palestine to the Hebrews. God knows how they found me, but they had this idea I could help them lay hands on some weapons."

"And?"

"I could. We'd stashed guns all over the Mediterranean in the war and it was a fair bet some of them had been left behind. They handed over some cash, I bought a boat and we were in business. You know how it is. You get into something, word goes around, soon other people come knocking on your door wanting the same thing. We've finished one war but there's another one starting already. Only now the amateurs have got a taste for it, they all want to catch up with the professionals and they're willing to spend."

"So you give them the guns to kill each other."

Grant shrugged. "They'd kill each other anyway. I just help level the playing field. But it all went to hell three weeks ago. The army found out about it; they were waiting for me on the beach." He leaned forward. "And that's where it gets interesting. A man came to visit me in prison—an English spy. He didn't give a damn for Palestine and he didn't care much about my guns. He wanted me to tell him where Pemberton's notebook was."

Marina was leaning forward too, now, drawn in to the story. Grant tried not to notice how close their faces were. "But how did he know?"

"I must have mentioned it in my report—that Pemberton gave it to me when he died. The man who came to see me was just fishing. But he was hungry. He must have been—he'd come all the way from London just to ask me what I knew. Offered me money, a ticket out of jail. Probably a bloody knighthood if I'd pushed him."

"What did you tell him?"

"What do you think? I told him to go to hell."

"But he still let you out of the prison."

"I escaped."

"And came straight here—why? To take the book for yourself?"

Grant suddenly reached forward and took her hands in his. She gasped with surprise and pulled back, but she couldn't break his grip. "To warn you. This English spook came all the way to a dungeon in Palestine to find out if I had it, six years after the event. I don't think he's a nice man. He knows I had the book; he knows my connection to you and he knows your connection to Pemberton. It's not going to take him long to join the dots." He stared into her eyes. "Have you got the book?"

Marina squirmed against his grip, tossing her head with anger. "What will you do with it? Sell it to this man?"

Grant let go, pulling his hands apart so fast that Marina flew backward into her chair. Her chest heaved against her dress and the loose lock of hair tumbled forward again over her flushed cheek.

"That depends what we find. If this is about a few broken pots and some rocks in the ground, why not? But if there's something more worthwhile . . ." He paused. "You worked for Pemberton—you told me once that when you were a kid Knossos was practically your sandpit. If he found something valuable, something worth all this bother, don't you want to know what it was?"

4

MARINA LED him down to the ground floor, a barn-cum-storeroom under the main house. Well-oiled farm tools hung on the walls, while chaff and straw covered the floor. Kneeling down in the far corner, she brushed it away with her hands until she had exposed a square crack running round one of the flagstones. She took a crowbar from a peg on the wall and levered it in, slowly prising back the stone. Grant didn't offer to help; instead, he stood by the door and scanned the surrounding countryside. Something felt wrong, some intuition that he couldn't place. He could have dismissed the feeling—but he had learned from experience it rarely paid to ignore it.

Iron clattered on stone as Marina put down the pry bar. With one last look out through the door, Grant joined her and peered down into the hole she had opened. It sank about three feet into the ground, two feet square and lined with dusty planks. Inside he could see three bundles wrapped in goatskins leaning against the wall and a battered box of ammunition at the bottom. Marina lay down on her stomach, stretched in and pulled it out. The catches snapped; the lid squeaked and there it was. The cream pages had yellowed and gun oil stained the cover, but there was still enough gold on the monogram to read it: JMHP.

"Well hidden," said Grant. "How did you know it was so valuable?"

"There was a man here in forty-three, a Nazi named Belzig. You were on the mainland then. He was an archaeologist—but not like Pemberton. He was a pig. He forced people to work for him like slaves: many died. And he wanted the journal. I heard from my cousin that he ransacked the Villa Ariadne looking for Pemberton's journal. When he did not find it, he rounded up the staff who had worked there and did unspeakable things to them, trying to discover what happened to it."

"What did he want with it?"

"I never met him to find out—I'd have killed him if I had."

Grant stared at the book, his mind racing. What was in it that could be so important? He remembered seeing Pemberton die: an old man who had spent his life in the safety of the past, only to be overwhelmed by the violence of a new chapter in history writing itself. What had he discovered that could possibly have mattered in the last three thousand years?

"Did you ever read it?" he asked Marina.

"No."

"But you worked with Pemberton. Weren't you curious?"

She twitched her head dismissively. "The war came. I forgot that life. I forgot archaeology; I forgot Pemberton. If you hadn't come back, they'd probably have dug up the book in a thousand years and put it in a museum." She glared at him. "I wish you hadn't come back. Then I could have forgotten you also."

"I'll be off then." Grant stretched out his hand to take the book. Marina didn't move.

"What will you do with it?"

"Read it. See if . . ." He broke off as Marina burst into laughter. "What?"

"Nothing." Her voice was brisk, but the corner of her mouth twitched. "Take it. Read it." She tossed it to him across the barn. Grant caught it one-handed and flipped it open. He looked at the page, then turned through a few more with mounting frustration. "It's all in Greek."

"Ancient Greek. Even if you could read Greek as well as you read English, for you it would be like attempting to read Chaucer."

"I never tried."

She made a face that told him she wasn't surprised. "Lots of the words would look the same, but some would not mean what you thought and some you would not recognize at all."

"Christ. He didn't make it easy for us."

"He always kept his notes in ancient Greek. He said it made him feel closer to the past."

"Well, he's close to it now." Grant wondered if, down the valley, the corpse still lay where he had buried it in the foundations of Knossos. "How the hell am I supposed to read this?"

"Get a dictionary." Her face was alight now with the uninhibited passion he remembered so well. "A dictionary of archaeology, also. And a pile of history books. Even if you could read it, it would take you six months to understand what he was talking about."

Grant looked down at the book. The neat rows of indecipherable letters seemed to swim in front of his eyes. Marina was taunting him, but she was taunting him with the truth. Of course he could just sell it—track down the bastard from SIS and strike a deal. But how could he get the right price if he didn't know what he was selling? More than that: he couldn't let go of the simple, stubborn desire to find out what someone didn't want him to know.

"I don't suppose . . ." He shot her a sideways glance. She was standing beside the hole, dust and straw clinging to her dress, her face glistening with sweat from the effort of pushing back the stone. Her lips were slightly parted in a triumphant smile and her dark eyes flashed the challenge. Her mind was already made up—but she would make him ask for it.

He cleared his throat. "Will you help me work out what Pemberton was up to?"

They took the book inside the house and laid it on the table. Grant wanted to start at the end, reasoning that whatever Pemberton had discovered must have been not long before he died. But Marina insisted on opening the book at the first page and reading through, muttering the words under her breath. Grant lit a cigarette. A few goat bells clanked in the distance, and the leaves of the apricot trees rustled in the wind. In the village below, the locals would be closing their shutters for their afternoon siestas. Otherwise the only sound in the room was an occasional pop from the burning log and the crisp slice of pages being turned.

Grant stared out of the window. Away to his left, where the road to the coast snaked down the valley, a car was crawling up the hill. It disappeared behind a bend, reappeared and vanished again, flashing in and out of the sun like a mirror. Grant felt a familiar prickle in his gut.

"How much longer?" he asked, trying to be casual.

"Forever, if you keep interrupting." Marina's face was set in a scowl of concentration. "There's a lot of Linear B in here I can't understand. I think Pemberton was trying to decipher it."

Grant didn't know what Linear B was, but just at that moment he wasn't interested. The car had disappeared into the village's tightly packed streets. Maybe it was just a local bigwig showing off his wealth, or an official from Heraklion come to impress the populace, he told himself.

"Do you get many motor cars around here?"

"Yorgos up the valley has a Ford."

A few hundred yards away a black snout inched its way through the narrow lane, on to the track between the apple orchards.

Grant touched the Webley tucked into his waistband. "Were there any bullets in that ammo box?"

"Just the book. I used the bullets on the Germans." More curious than exasperated now, she looked up. "Why?"

The car halted outside the front gate. The engine throbbed for a moment, then abruptly died away. Two men in dark hats and overcoats got out; one went round to the boot and pulled out a long, snub-nosed package wrapped in brown paper.

"Because we've got visitors."

Grant squeezed through the small window at the back of the house and dropped to the ground. Round the corner he could hear the iron clop of hobnailed boots stamping up the path to the front door. Whoever they were, they weren't worried about being heard. Grant wasn't sure if that was good or not.

The footsteps stopped at the door and a fist thudded against it—the clumsy sound, Grant thought, of a heavy man trying to be casual. Another thud and the tap-tap of the boots shifting impatiently.

"Maybe it's just the man from the Pru," Grant whispered.

A sharp crack ripped through the garden, followed by the tearing of wood and a bang as the door flew in—probably under the impact of a hobnailed boot, Grant guessed. A few moments later came the rumble of furniture being overturned and the clatter of drawers being tipped out over the floor. Next to Grant, Marina's face was drawn in fury and he grabbed her arm, digging his nails into her wrist.

"Is there a window at the other end of the house?"

She shook her head.

"Good. Let's go."

Shielded by the house, they ran across the broken ground, vaulted a tumbledown stone wall and slid into a shallow gully in the hillside. Loose stones and gravel crunched underfoot, but the men in the house were making a thorough business of tearing it apart, and their noise drowned out anything Grant and Marina did. He could hear angry shouts from inside, though muffled by the walls he couldn't make out the language. Was it English?

Lying on their bellies, they wriggled up the gully. When Grant judged they'd gone far enough he waved Marina to stop. The noon sun blazed down and his shirt was damp from the effort of crawling up the slope. Gripping the Webley, Grant inched himself up and peered over the lip of the gully.

The house had fallen silent. From where Grant lay, the front door and the car parked beyond were hidden, but through the living-room window, framed in the curtains, he could see a dark figure standing in the middle of the room. From the way he moved and gesticulated, Grant guessed some sort of discussion was under way. He turned to Marina. "Still got the book?"

She half lifted it to show him. A few more grazes had scuffed the worn leather binding, but otherwise it was unharmed. "Is that why they came?"

"I don't think it was for the pleasure of your conversation."

"Who are they?"

Grant had a fair guess, but he hid it behind a bland shrug. "No one we want to meet."

He looked back down the hill. The dark figure had vanished. On the far side of the house an engine coughed into life and a few moments later he saw the car pull away down the road toward the village. It squeezed down the narrow lane between the houses and disappeared. Marina started to rise, but in an instant Grant's hand was on her wrist and dragging her back down, so quick she almost fell on top of him. She rolled away with a growl of fury—as she came back up, Grant saw that a small knife had appeared from nowhere in her hand.

"What are you doing?"

Her tumble had disarranged her dress, dragging down the neckline. She seemed not to notice.

"You can't go back there," he said. Very deliberately, he let his gaze drift from the hovering knife to the exposed skin below her collarbone. A bud of white lace peeked out from under the black dress.

She tugged it back into position with a snort of disgust. "Why not? First you come, when I never wanted to see you again, and an hour later there are two *malakies* tearing apart my house like animals. Am I supposed to think that's a coincidence?"

"Almost certainly not."

"Then how in hell can you tell me what to do?"

"Because if you walk through that door, it'll be the last thing you ever do." Grant pointed. Through the window they could see a mess of splintered wood, smashed china, broken photographs and scattered ornaments littering the floor. The barrel of the gun was almost invisible against the chaotic background. Even if you'd seen it, you might have mistaken it for just another piece of debris lying on the floor. Only when it twitched did some incongruity of light and shadow alert the eye.

Marina, who had spent long hours of reconnaissance looking for exactly those tell-tale signs, saw it at once. "One of them stayed behind." She lowered herself back into the gully. "Do you think he saw us?"

"If he had, we'd know about it."

"Then we can surprise him." Her eyes gleamed with savage delight—the look he knew so well from the war. As the Germans had found to their cost, there was nothing the Cretans loved so much as a blood feud. "You've got your gun. I'll distract him by the door and you can get him through the window." Doubt flickered into her eyes as she saw Grant shaking his head. "Why not?"

"Because every hour he sits there waiting is an hour we've got to get away."

They walked for most of the day, toward the great massif of mountains that rose across the eastern horizon. Just before dusk they found an empty shepherd's hut in a high meadow, whose previous occupant had left wood, blankets and two tins of field rations, probably relics of the war. Grant built a fire and they huddled round it in their blankets. Down in the valleys it might be spring, but up on the mountain winter lingered. Patches of snow filled the hollows in the north-facing hillside and the summit still wore its white winter coat. A chill wind whistled around them and Grant pulled his blanket closer. It would have been the most natural thing in the world to wrap it round both of them, as they'd done so often on cold nights during the war, but he didn't try.

After they'd eaten, Marina took out the book. She held it up to the fire, letting the flames play over the pages. Grant fought back the fear that a stray ember could end their quest before it even began.

"Two months before the invasion, Pemberton went to Athens. I thought it was strange he went then—everybody knew the Germans were coming and he almost couldn't find space on the ferryboat with all the soldiers going to the front. But he said he had to go. When he came back, something was different. He didn't say, but I could see he had some new obsession. It was always the same, if he found a new site, or some artifact he couldn't place. The lights in the villa burned late, and he became distant and tense. Of course, everyone was tense in those last days, so we didn't notice so much. In April he disappeared for a week on his own. Afterward I found out he had been on the east of the island, toward Siteia. He was looking for something."

"Which is why you've brought us east?"

"Yes." She stared at the book, her smooth face wrinkled in concentration. "If he found something, he would have written it in here." She combed her fingers through her loose hair. "But I can't find it."

Grant edged round to peer over her shoulder. Row upon row of neatly printed symbols swam in the firelight, as distant and unknowable as the men who had first devised them. The Greek letters he recognized—he could even make out some of the simpler words—but a large portion of the page seemed given over to characters he had never seen in his life. He reached forward, brushing Marina's shoulder, and pointed. "What are they?"

"Linear B."

He remembered she had mentioned it earlier, in her house, before the thugs showed up. "What's that?"

"An alphabet. An ancient system of writing. It was discovered about fifty years ago at Knossos."

"So it's Greek?"

She shook her head. "Long before Greek. It comes . . ." She thought for a moment, playing with a strand of hair. "You've heard of Theseus and the Minotaur?"

"The myth?"

She laughed. "Where Pemberton worked—where I worked—is the place where history and myth meet each other like a river and a sea." She dug her fingers into the earth and pried out a small rock. "This stone is nothing. But if I do this . . ." She laid it on the ring of stones that made the fireplace. "Suddenly it has meaning. Somebody will find this in the future, maybe two thousand years from now, and even if they have never seen a fireplace or even imagined one, they will know that a human being made this thing for a reason. And they will try to guess what that reason was. Maybe they will find traces of ash in the middle of the circle and scorch marks on the stones; perhaps a rusted tin can and your cigarette butts. And they will deduce . . ."

"That we ate our supper here?"

"That this was the site of a primitive pillar cult, no doubt with phallic implications. That the stone circle was the foundation of a wooden column which we, in our primitive ignorance, worshipped. That we brought food offerings in metal containers and smoked this mildly psychotomimetic substance to induce a state of divine ecstasy. They will think that the ashes and the scorch marks come from a fire, possibly linked to invasion or war, when the sacred pillar was burned down. They will publish this in their learned journals and then they will argue as to whether the similar sites they find all across the island constituted an official religion, or simply parallel local traditions. And they will be completely wrong."

She picked up the rock and tossed it away into the darkness. Grant waited, watching the firelight dance over her face. "What's that got to do with the Minotaur?"

"Only to say that the myths survive when everything else has been forgotten. And that sometimes the myths, for all their slippery deceptions, tell us more about the past than ruined walls and broken pots. For three thousand years no one believed that there had ever been a great prehistoric civilization on Crete—but in all that time they never forgot the story of Theseus and the Minotaur. Even children knew it. Then, fifty years ago, Evans came here and went to the place the legends said. He found everything. A palace like a labyrinth. Drinking vessels shaped like bulls, figurines of bulls, stone horns—even paintings of young men performing acrobatics on bulls."

"Not a human skeleton with a pair of bulls' horns sticking out of the skull and a ball of string next to it?"

"No." She pulled her knees close to her chest. "Of course, myth distorts the past. But here on Crete you had the very first civilization in Europe—more than a thousand years before the golden age of Greece and fifteen hundred years before the Caesars—and for three millennia afterward the only place it was recorded was in the myths. Without them the palace at Knossos would just be piles of stones. And when Evans finally brought it to light, he named its civilization 'Minoans' after the legendary King Minos."

Her face shone in the golden firelight as if—like some ancient sibyl—she could see back through thirty centuries of history. She didn't even seem to notice Grant's frank gaze fixed on her until, with a discreet cough, he asked, "What's this got to do with the writing in the journal?"

"The Minoans left more than just ruins and artifacts. They left us their writing. There were two forms—a primitive one, which Evans named Linear A, and a later development he named Linear B. Most of the examples were found scratched into clay tablets, which baked when the palace burned down."

"And what do they say?"

"No one knows—no one's ever been able to decipher them. It's one of the greatest mysteries of archaeology."

Grant looked back at the book. "Did Pemberton ever try to crack it?"

"You couldn't work in this field and not try. To the archaeologists it was like a crossword or a riddle, something to puzzle over on winter evenings by the fire. As far as I know, Pemberton never made any breakthrough."

"What about in the book?"

"No." She turned through a few pages. "It's too neat. He's copied some inscriptions, but there's no attempt to translate them."

"What about that?" Grant stabbed a finger into the book and held down the page. Above a few lines of the angular Linear B script, the page was filled by a simple line drawing. It looked almost like something a child might have drawn: two triangles flanked a small spiked box, with two rows of jagged lines running below. At the top, in the center of the page, some sort of stylized animal seemed to float above a rounded dome, with birds on either side.

"It must be Minoan," murmured Marina. "But I've never seen it before. It wasn't in the collection at Knossos." She turned to the next page. It was empty, except for four lines of Greek. After that, the book was blank.

"What does the Greek say?" asked Grant.

Now here, now there, the carcasses they tore:
Fate stalk'd amidst them, grim with human gore.
And the whole war came out, and met the eye;
And each bold figure seem'd to live or die.

Perhaps it was the smoke blowing from the fire, but Marina's voice was hoarse and tears rimmed her eyes. "It's Homer. The *Iliad*. Pemberton must have been reading it when the Nazis came. It was the last thing he ever wrote. Nothing to do with the picture." She turned back to the previous page and stared hard at the sketch, as if by the effort she could burn away her tears. "The iconography . . ." She took a deep breath. "The iconography seems to date it as middle to late Minoan. The zigzag lines are probably purely decorative, though some might see them as denoting water. The animal at the top . . ." She squinted, holding the book out to the fire. "Maybe a lion or a sphinx—either way, it would symbolize a protector or guardian. Possible royal connections as well. The birds are doves, which usually signifies place sanctity. In this case the identification is supported by the shrine in the center of the image."

"How do you know it's a shrine?"

"The bull horns on top. It's a standard depiction of a Minoan shrine. Like how a cross on top of a building tells you it's a church."

Marina stared into the flames. Whether she was puzzling over the image or thinking of Pemberton, Grant didn't know, but he pulled the book away before she dropped it in the fire. He looked at the picture—then rested the book on his knee and forced the pages flat. The spine cracked in protest and Marina looked up.

"Be careful."

"What does . . ." Grant licked his lips as he picked out the unfamiliar letters. "*Pha . . . raggi . . . ton . . . nekron* mean?"

"*Pharangi ton nekron*? Where do you see that?"

Grant held it up to show her. On the inside of the page, almost buried in the crease of the binding, three Greek words were written vertically down the side of the picture. Marina snatched the book from him and stared.

"Of course," she murmured. "*Pharangi ton Nekron.*"

"Who's he?"

"It's a place—a valley. On the east coast, near a village called Zakros. It means . . ." She thought for a second. "It means the Valley of the Dead."

"Sounds promising."

5

Valley of the Dead, Crete

RED ROCK walls rose stark above them, glowing in the sun, but in the cleft of the gorge a tangle of plane trees and oleanders shaded the valley floor. Grant peered up through the leaves, shading his eyes against the brightness. They were in a vast canyon, curving gradually toward the sea. High above, a series of dark holes riddled the cliffs.

"Those are tombs." Marina's black dress was gone, traded in a village they'd passed for a pair of surplus green military trousers and a short-sleeved blouse, unbuttoned just far enough to draw Grant's eyes when he thought she wasn't looking. Her dark hair was tied back in a loose ponytail and, though she wore no make-up, three days walking across the mountains had burnished her skin to a lustrous brown. A coil of rope was looped over her shoulder.

"People have been buried in those caves since Minoan times," she continued. "So, the Valley of the Dead."

"Doesn't look too frightening to me. Sun's shining, wildflowers are out, birds are singing."

"Actually, to the Greeks, birds were often seen as harbingers of death, messengers to and from the underworld."

"Oh." A sinister note suddenly crept into the trill chirruping around them. "Has anyone ever explored the caves?"

"Always." She wrinkled her nose. "It doesn't take long for the sacred relics of one generation to become pickings for another. Archaeologists have found a few ancient burials, but most of them disappeared a long time ago."

"Then why . . ."

"We're not here for the tombs." She pulled a piece of paper out of her pocket, a copy she had sketched of Pemberton's drawing. "You see the horns? We're looking for a shrine."

"Not the same thing?"

"The Minoans didn't bury their dead in their temples. No one did until the Christians came along. The ancients would have been shocked by the idea of bringing the dead into the places of the living. They put them in the cities of the dead—necropolises. Like those caves."

"So where do we look for the temple?"

Marina considered it for a moment. "Hogarth—another archaeologist—excavated at the mouth of the gorge in 1901. He found a few Minoan houses, but no shrine."

"Maybe Pemberton found something he missed." Grant took the drawing from Marina and squinted at it. "You said these zigzag lines might represent water?"

"Or they might be purely decorative. There's no way . . ."

"Look." Grant held the paper upright, looking straight down the valley. "These two triangles on each side—those are the sides of the gorge. You've got the sea in front of them. And here"—he jabbed a finger in the center of the picture—"the temple."

Marina looked doubtful. "I don't think you can assume that the Minoans used spatial relationships in their art like that."

"Bollocks. They drew it as they saw it."

"Really?" Her tone hardened. "And how do you know how they saw the world, so many thousand years ago? For that matter, how do you explain the lion floating in mid air? Did they draw that as they saw it?"

"Perhaps it's a cloud."

"And the dome underneath it? A rainbow, perhaps?"

"Well, have you got a better idea?"

She sighed. "No."

But Grant's victory was short-lived. The canyon ended almost half a mile from the coast, spilling out into a few dusty farm fields.

"The ruins Hogarth found must be somewhere here," said Marina, exasperated. She looked at the sketch again. "What did Pemberton see here that made him think of the Valley of the Dead?"

In one of the fields a gaunt ox was dragging a plow through the dry earth. A farmer in a tweed jacket stood beside it, swatting its flank with a cane, while a stout woman in a headscarf looked on. They watched silently as Grant and Marina approached.

"*Kalimera sas*," Marina called.

"*Kalimera*." The farmer leaned on his stick and stared at her. Beside him, his wife looked at Marina as if she'd stepped off the stage of a Paris revue.

Stammering slightly, Marina launched into her question. Grant's Greek was probably good enough for him to have followed it if he'd paid attention, but he didn't bother. Something was troubling him. Pemberton had written "Valley of the Dead" in the margin of his notebook, but this wasn't the valley. He turned and looked back up into the gorge. It curved away to the left, so that from where Grant stood it looked as though the valley ended abruptly in a sheer rock face where the wall swept round. And there, seeming to rise straight over the middle of the gorge, stood a domed hill.

"He says they never saw anyone."

"What?"

Snatched out of his thoughts, Grant turned back. Across the field the farmer still stood impassively and watched them. His wife had turned away and was ostentatiously driving the ox forward.

"The farmer. He says they never saw a British archaeologist. He might be lying—the British aren't so popular here since you started propping up the puppet government in Athens."

"Nothing to do with me," demurred Grant. "But look behind you."

Marina looked round. "What?"

"That's the view." The paper flapped in the breeze as Grant held it up, transposing it over the landscape. “The cliffs on either side, the sea at this end and the hill in the middle of the valley.” High above the domed summit a hawk hovered lazily in the sky. “You’ve even got the birds.”

“And the flying lion?”

“Sleeping.” Grant grinned. “Let’s see if we can wake him up.”

They threaded their way through the trees and fallen boulders that littered the dry stream bed. Inside the gorge, with the cliffs looming over them, they quickly lost sight of the summit, but they pushed on, trying to keep as straight a path as possible.

“The Minoans often put their shrines on hilltops,” said Marina, breathing hard. It was almost noon and her shirt clung to her skin. “Perhaps we should try the top of the cliffs.”

“It wouldn’t look the same from up there,” said Grant stubbornly. “And in the picture, the temple’s under the summit.”

“I told you, you can’t . . .” Marina broke off with a cry of surprise. She pushed past Grant toward a boulder at the edge of the path. On top of it, almost hidden by the fronds of an oleander, four rocks were arranged in a small cairn. She pulled them apart. A smoothed-out square of thinly beaten silver glittered underneath.

“Minoan treasure?” asked Grant.

“Fry’s Turkish Delight.” She turned over the foil to show him the wrapper. “Pemberton loved it. Every time he went to England he came back with some.”

“Full of eastern promise,” Grant muttered, astonished. “I wonder what other surprises he left for us.”

Marina scrambled over the rock and vanished into the undergrowth. With a rueful shake of his head, Grant followed her through the trees until they gave way to a bare hillside. A few yards away Marina was kneeling beside a rocky overhang.

“Is that the temple?” The rock looked too low for anyone to be able to crawl under it.

“See for yourself.”

Grant crouched down. Laid out on a piece of sacking under the rock were a pickaxe, a spade and a paraffin lantern. All were coated in rust, but he could still read the letters stencilled on the wooden handles: B.S.A.

"The British School at Athens," Marina explained. "They ran the excavations at Knossos. They were Pemberton's employer."

Grant pulled out the spade and banged it against the rock. A few flakes of rust fluttered to the ground and a mournful clang echoed through the valley. Grant looked around guiltily.

"I thought we were trying to be secret," said Marina, cocking an eyebrow at him.

"We haven't found anything worth keeping secret yet."

Marina slipped the coil of rope from her shoulder, lashed one end to the pickaxe's handle and began clambering up over the fallen boulders. Grant waited long enough to be sure that the stones she loosened wouldn't come tumbling down on his head, then followed.

At first it was easy enough, scrambling from one boulder to the next. But soon the large rocks gave way to small pebbles, which slid away underfoot the moment Grant trod on them. Climbing the slope became a race, a frantic effort to keep lunging forward faster than the clattering pebbles could drag him back. Then that too ended, in a sheer red cliff face, and Grant had to grab on to an exposed tree root to stop himself sliding all the way back down the hill. Just to his right the rope end dangled down. Grant snatched it and hauled himself up hand over hand until, in a torrent of sweat and curses, he heaved himself over the cliff.

"Is this what you used to do with Pemberton?" he asked, breathing hard.

"No. But he obviously did it himself."

Grant pushed himself to his feet, raised an arm to brush the dust off his shirt—and stopped in astonishment. They had climbed higher than he thought and arrived on a rock shelf almost halfway up the thousand-foot cliffs. They loomed above, so dizzyingly steep that Grant didn't dare look up for fear of losing his balance. Below, the green ribbon at the bottom of the gorge wound its way toward the sea sparkling in the distance. But in front of him, where the cliffs met the shelf, a dark crack split open the rock, just wide enough for a man to squeeze through. Above it, almost invisible in the shade of an overhang, a stone plaque sat in a recess cut into the rock.

Grant edged toward it. Three thousand years had ground down the carving; what remained was only a faint impression of the original proud design. The claws and teeth had lost their sharpness, the mane wilted, the crouched muscles wasted away. Even so, Grant recognized it at once. He pulled the crumpled sheet of paper from his pocket and held it up. "There's your flying lion."

Marina shook her head, though Grant couldn't tell if it was wonder or exasperation. She picked up Pemberton's lantern and shook it. A few drops of ancient paraffin sloshed inside.

"There's no wick."

Marina took a knife from her hip pocket, unclasped it and sliced a thin band of cloth from the sleeve of her blouse. She twisted it between her fingers and threaded it into the lamp.

Grant held out his lighter. "Allow me."

Flame licked along the cotton wick, almost invisible in the harsh sunlight. Marina moved toward the crack in the cliff, but Grant was faster. He twisted the lantern out of her hands and stepped in front of her, then pulled the Webley from its holster. "I'll go first."

Grant pushed through the crack. After about ten yards the passage widened. He paused, holding up the lamp to guard against nasty surprises—and barely had time to adjust his eyes when a sharp elbow dug into his back, pitching him forward. He stumbled into the room, flailing the lamp so as not to dash it to pieces on the floor. When he had managed to stop himself he turned round.

Marina stood in the doorway, a half-guilty expression spreading across her face. "Sorry. I didn't see you stop."

"Lucky there wasn't a bottomless pit waiting to swallow me."

But Grant had no time to nurse his anger. The cleft had opened into a chamber, whose walls were still pocked with the millennia-old scars of the copper chisels that had carved it out of the rock. A stone bench ran across the far end, above which an upturned vase sat in a deep niche. A wood-framed sieve leaned against the bench, together with a trowel, a plumb line, a brush and another chocolate wrapper. On top, laid out almost as if in a museum, sat a row of figurines and artifacts. Grant and Marina crouched in front of them—perhaps in the same way as worshippers had knelt there all those thousands of years ago.

"This must be some kind of lustral bowl," said Marina, picking up a shallow dish carved from purple stone. Her voice was low with awe. She put the piece down reverently and picked up another. This was a painted figurine, wasp-waisted, with ruffled skirts and its arms held aloft like wings. It looked almost like an angel. Except, Grant noticed, that the cropped jacket it wore had been pulled apart to reveal a pair of breasts thrusting out, squeezed almost perpendicular to the body.

"Nice tits."

Marina scowled. "It's a Minoan goddess figure. She was their principal deity—the source of all fertility and power. These sorts of idols are quite common."

Grant leaned closer, affecting to examine it. "What are those wavy lines on her arms?"

"Snakes." Marina held it up to the lamp. Close to, Grant could see it clearly: a writhing serpent running up one arm, across her bare shoulders and down to the other wrist. The lines on her chest that he had taken to be the hem of the jacket turned out to be two more snakes, one coiled round her breasts, the other hanging down over her hips and between her skirts.

"A dangerous woman," said Marina tartly. "You wouldn't stand a chance."

"Goddesses aren't my type."

Marina put down the figurine and surveyed the rest of the hoard. Most of it was in fragments, which Pemberton had sorted according to type: pieces of ivory, half a dozen seal stones with miniature engravings; two doubleheaded axes and lots of pottery shards arranged in different piles.

"This is interesting." Marina took two of the pieces from the furthermost pile and held them together. "Most of the finds are mid-period Minoan—say three and a half thousand years ago—but these are much more recent. It's almost as though the shrine was abandoned, then rediscovered later."

"How much later?"

"Say three thousand years ago."

Grant yawned. "It's all old news to me, sweetheart." He cast his eye over the assorted artifacts laid out on the bench. "How much is this lot worth, anyway?"

"From an archaeological point of view, this could be quite significant. The goddess statue is hardly unique, but it's a very fine example. The pottery's probably most valuable—if we can get a good chronology it will tell us a lot about settlement patterns in this part of the island." She frowned. "It would be useful to know its stratification. I'm surprised Pemberton didn't . . ." She trailed off as she noticed the bored scowl on Grant's face. "What?"

"I don't give a damn how fascinating it is to archaeologists. I want to know how much it's *worth*."

"Is that all you care about?" Her voice was bitter. "Half the world is lying in ruins and the other half can't even afford to feed itself. You won't get rich peddling the crumbs of a civilization most people have never heard of. If you want to make your fortune, go back to your guns. Men always find money for killing."

She turned away, but Grant reached out and spun her round. "Do you really think I'm interested in carting this junk down to some pawnshop to get my sixpence for it? *Think*. That nice man from Secret Intelligence came all the way to Palestine to see if I had Pemberton's book and I don't think it was because he's collecting for the British Museum. They think there's something valuable in the book—valuable to the sort of men who deal in steel and oil and guns and lives. So I'm asking you: is this valuable? Because if it isn't, either they've got the wrong end of the stick, or we've come to the wrong place."

He stepped back. Despite the stifling air in the cave, Marina was shivering.

"There are a few things here that would be interesting to scholars," she said flatly. "Otherwise . . . I don't see anything."

"How about that?"

Grant turned the lantern toward the alcove in the back wall. At first he had taken the object inside for an upturned vase, but looking closer he could see it was a piece of stone, about two feet high and vaguely bullet-shaped, with a web of criss-crossed lines carved in relief out of its sides. A shallow impression dented its top.

"This . . ." Marina stared. "This is very unusual. Not valuable, of course," she added acidly, "but very rare. I think it must be a baetyl."

"A beetle?" asked Grant, confused.

"A *baetyl*. A sacred stone. Possibly a meteorite originally, though this is obviously a copy. Perhaps that indentation in the top held a fragment of the original rock—or maybe some sort of cult idol." She ran her hands over the cold stone, almost caressing it. "Have you been to the oracle at Delphi?"

"I blew up a train near there once. Didn't have time to see the sights."

"There's something similar there. The *omphalos*, they call it—the navel of the world. As far as Crete goes, there are frescoes that show equivalent objects, but no one's ever found anything like this."

"But I still don't see why . . . What was that?"

Grant swung around. The Webley gleamed in his hand—until, with a deft movement, he reached inside the lantern and pinched out the wick. Instantly the room was plunged in darkness.

"Stay back." Grant swept out an arm and pushed Marina into the corner of the chamber, taking two silent steps to his left so as to be out of the line of the door.

"What is it?"

Grant didn't need to answer. From outside, drifting down the passage, came the clatter of falling rocks—then the unmistakable sound of a voice cursing in English. Grant trained the Webley on the door. He heard scrapes and muffled curses as someone tried to squeeze through the narrow aperture, then soft footsteps. His finger curled round the trigger.

The wan beam of a flashlight pierced the darkness in the room, flitted like a moth from floor to wall to ceiling and came to rest on the barrel of Grant's revolver.

"I hope you're not fucking thinking of shooting me."

6

GRANT'S GUN never wavered. Undeterred, the new arrival ducked into the small chamber and stood in the door, little more than a silhouette against the dim daylight that filtered through behind.

"Who is this?" asked Marina.

"I don't think I introduced myself last time." The man shone the torch on his own face, revealing tightly cropped red hair, a spare moustache and a narrow, pointed face. "Muir." He didn't offer his hand. "Grant and I have met. And you must be Marina Papagiannopoulou. Better known to us—and to the Germans, when they were in business here—as Athena."

"You seem very well informed."

"I've followed your exploits with interest. And for the last three days I've followed you with even more interest." He chuckled. "You didn't make it easy for us. We almost lost you when you snuck away from Archanes."

"Maybe you shouldn't have sent in your goons."

Muir held up his hands in innocence. "Nothing to do with me."

"Who were they, then?"

"Competitors. They . . ."

An almighty sneeze exploded down the passage behind Muir. He threw himself to the side of the room—just in time, as the thunderous roar of the Webley filled the chamber.

"Jesus and fucking Mary," said Muir. "You'll have someone's eye out.

With the gun still ringing in his ears, Grant heard a quavering voice calling in terror from down the passage, "Don't shoot."

Grant swung the gun back toward Muir. "Take one step closer and we'll have Mr. Muir's brains all over these walls," he called down the corridor. Then, to Muir: "Who did you bring with you?"

Muir's torch had fallen to the floor, but in the tiny room it still cast enough light to see the paleness of his face. "No one you need to worry about."

Grant hesitated for a moment, then made up his mind. "Drop your gun and walk slowly toward me."

"I don't have a gun," protested the panicked voice. "Shall I . . ."

"Just get in here."

Marina picked up the torch and shone it down the passage. There was a cough, the shuffle of leather on stone. Blinking hard, his arms raised as high as the low ceiling would allow, he stepped into the light. A thatch of snowy white hair framed a round face, lined but still oddly youthful, its cheeks and nose crimson with sunburn. A pair of pale-blue eyes peered out beneath the eminences of two magnificent white eyebrows—anxious, but turning to wonder as he slowly took in the surroundings. "Remarkable," he breathed.

A change had come over the room—a calm. Grant felt his control slipping away from him. "Who's this?" he asked, jabbing the Webley at Muir.

"His name's Arthur Reed. Professor of Classical Philology at Oxford."

"May I?" Reed reached toward Marina. Utterly disarmed, she let him take the torch from her hand.

"Remarkable," he said again, gazing at the artifacts ranged along the back wall. "This, I presume, must be some sort of baetyl."

"That's what we thought," said Grant. Suddenly, he didn't know why, he felt as if he had to be on his best behavior—like a boy dragged out of his tree house and forced to have tea with a distant aunt.

Muir reached for his pocket, froze as he saw Grant's hand tighten round the Webley, then laughed. "Don't worry." He fished out the ivory cigarette case. "Want one?"

Grant would almost have killed for a cigarette, but he wasn't ready to accept Muir's generosity yet. "How about you tell me what in hell's going on here?"

Muir struck a match, adding the warmth of flame to the torch's electric glow. "I suppose you think I owe you an explanation?"

Stone grated at the back of the chamber and all three of them spun round. Reed was kneeling on the bench by the niche in the wall. He seemed to have lifted the stone baetyl off its perch, or at least managed to tip it back, revealing a shadowy hollow within.

"Could somebody help me, please?"

Grant and Muir stared at each other across the barrel of the Webley. With an exasperated huff, Marina stepped toward Reed.

"There's something underneath," he explained. "Can you reach it?"

Marina leaned in. After a couple of seconds her hand emerged clutching something small and flat and hard. She examined it, turned it over and almost gasped with surprise. Wordlessly, she handed it to Reed.

"Remarkable," he whispered.

Grant flipped up the safety catch on the Webley. "Now," he said, "would someone please tell me what this is about?"

They sat on the ledge outside the cave, blinking and squinting to be out in the sunlight again. Reed had put on a broad-brimmed sunhat; he sat on a rock and peeled an orange. Marina held the Webley, still trained on Muir, while Grant turned over the object in his hands. It was a clay tablet, a quarter of an inch thick and about the size of his palm, with rounded corners and smooth surfaces—except at the bottom, where a jagged edge suggested part had been broken off. Age, earth and fire had mottled the clay, but the designs wrought in it were clear enough. One side was covered with strange, miniature symbols—row after row, carved into the clay when it was wet, then baked into eternity.

"Is this Linear B?"

"Yes." Reed and Marina answered in unison, then looked at each other with the delighted surprise of shared understanding.

Grant ran a finger over the symbols, tracing the rough edges and deep whorls, as if by touching he could somehow feel the pulse of its ancient secrets. *What did they say?* He turned the tablet over. There was no writing on the underside: the clay was flat and smooth, still showing the impression of the hands that had kneaded it out. But it was not empty. Grant balanced Pemberton's notebook on his knee, using the tablet to weigh down the page, and looked between the two. One was drawn in Pemberton's strong ink strokes, the other in paint that was badly chipped and faded, but there was no mistaking the similarity. They were the same. Two mountains, the sides of the valley; a domed hill, a horned shrine and a pair of doves. And hovering above them all a lion, the same animal that still watched them from its perch above the crack in the rock.

"Pemberton must have hidden it in the cave when he left," said Reed. He took the diary and the tablet from Grant and examined them again, turning through some of the pages until he came to the final Homeric quotation. He grimaced. "*Each bold figure seemed to live or die*. That was John Pemberton. A bold man."

"A good man," added Marina.

"A dead man." Grant turned to Muir. "But what I want to know is: what did he find that's so damn valuable? And why are you so desperate for it?"

"That's classified." Muir bared his teeth. "Secret."

"A secret worth taking to your grave?" Grant glanced over the cliff edge. "The fall's probably enough to kill you—but you'll be dead before you land."

To Grant's right, Marina kept the Webley pointed straight at Muir. If her slender arms struggled with the weight, they didn't show it. Muir looked between the two of them. Nothing in their faces gave him the least hope.

Moving very slowly, Muir lit another cigarette. Each sound seemed unnaturally loud in the hot afternoon air—the click of the case, the flare of phosphorus, the crack as Muir snapped the spent matchstick in two. A shadow passed across his face: a hawk hovering in the sky.

"All right." He took a deep drag and his mouth curled in something like pleasure. "I'll tell you what I can."

"You'd better hope it's enough."

Muir took a bundle of photographs from his shirt pocket and passed one to Grant.

"It looks like our tablet."

"It was found by the Americans in the dying days of the war, at a scientific facility they'd captured in Oranienburg, Germany."

Grant raised an eyebrow. "Wasn't that in the Soviet sector?"

"They managed to drop in before the Russians got there. Liberated umpteen crates of Nazi papers and paraphernalia—mostly reports, technical documents, tedious crap. Anyway, someone had to have a look at it, so they shipped it back to the States for some sub-committee of nobodies to dig through and tell them there was nothing to worry about. Forgot the whole thing. There was so much coming out of Germany and nobody wanted to spend their time looking back to the dark old days. But these beaks kept plodding away and a couple of months ago they turned up something interesting."

"This photograph?"

"In a cardboard box with some files, which wasn't unusual—and a steel flask, which was. Inside was a piece of metal, about the size of a golf ball. They didn't know what it was, so they sent it off to the labs for analysis. And what they found was something no one had ever seen before."

"What's that?"

"Well, no one had ever seen it, so it didn't have a name. They called it Element 61."

"Element 61?" repeated Grant. "Like a chemical element?"

"Exactly. You've seen the periodic table? Well, apparently there are some holes in it. It's like an incomplete deck of cards—you know how many you should have and where the missing cards would go, but you haven't got them all. Same with these missing elements. The scientists know they have to exist and they know where they'd fit, but they've never managed to get their hands on the stuff. This Element 61 is one of those missing cards. So, naturally, the boffins got excited and wanted to know where this rock had come from."

"Is it valuable?"

"Valuable?" Muir ground the remnant of the cigarette under his heel and lit another. "It's fucking priceless. It's unique. So far as anyone's ever known, it doesn't exist on earth."

There was silence as they digested this information.

"It's from a meteorite," Reed said. Looking at him, Grant could see this story was as new to him as to anyone.

"Correct." Muir looked pleased. "But that's not the whole story. Take a look at these." He tossed over three more photographs. "This is the sample they found. Front, top and bottom. Notice anything?"

Grant looked at the pictures—a shiny lump of rock illuminated against a black cloth. From above and in profile it appeared smooth, almost fluid, pocked with miniature craters like hammered gold. But the third picture was different: here the surface was almost flat, scored by a series of vertical lines into successive ridges.

"It looks like something's cut through it."

"Those lines you can see are the strokes of a saw blade. The piece they found in Germany is just the tip of the iceberg—or, in this case, the meteorite."

"The baetyl," murmured Reed.

Muir's head whipped round. "What?"

"Nothing."

"Anyway, the Yanks read through the files, but all they got was that this had been found on Crete by the Germans. The Krauts didn't have any more idea than the rest of us where it came from—but they did find the photograph of the tablet with it. Nothing else to go on. Greece is our playground—or was, until Attlee picked up his toys—so the Americans handed it over to us to sort out. And now we're here."

"Why do you want it?" Marina's voice was hard. "Why is this Element 61 so important?"

Muir took a long drag on his cigarette. "You think they tell me? I'm just the bag man. Half of what I've told you even I don't know officially. But what I do know is that the Yanks are desperate for this thing and they're lining up to piss money on whoever finds it. So you can shoot me off this cliff like a fucking fairground duck if you like—but if you've any sense, you'll join my jolly crew and start digging."

"Join you?" Grant threw the photographs back at him. "What's to say you won't stick a bullet in my back the moment I put this gun down?"

"Because you're useful. You're so far off the map no one will suspect you're working for us, and you know how to operate incognito in this part of the world." He jerked his thumb at Marina. "Her too. Plus she knew Pemberton better than any of us."

"And when we stop being useful to you?"

"You'll stop being useful when we find that lump of metal. Then you can fuck off with your share of the loot and never see me again." He tried to contort his sharp features into something like a pleasant smile. "What I said in Palestine still stands. You're a wanted man; I can make that all go away. And as for you . . ." He turned to Marina. "I know all about you and your brother. Quite a double act, weren't you. Shame the way he died. Single bullet at close range—must have been someone he knew. Did you ever wonder who pulled the trigger?"

Marina was staring at him, her gaze as black and lethal as the barrel of the gun. "What do you mean?"

"We've got a file on your brother in London. Do right by me and I can let you see it when this is over. You'd be amazed what's in there."

He cocked an eyebrow toward Grant, who tried to look unconcerned.

"You're full of shit."

"Actually, I'm dying for a piss. So make up your minds. Are you with me or not?"

"Does it make any difference? The meteorite's not here."

Muir scowled and flicked his cigarette butt over the cliff edge. "I didn't say it would be easy. Maybe we've got the wrong place."

"No." Reed had sat out the negotiations unnoticed, perched on a rock and staring vacantly at the lion over the doorway. Now the quiet certainty in his voice surprised them all. "This is where the meteorite was. Come and have a look."

One by one, they squeezed through the crack into the rock-cut shrine. Muir lit the paraffin lamp and together they stared at the snub-nosed shape of the carved stone in its niche.

Once again, Grant was struck by how much it looked like a bullet. "What are those ridges round it?" he asked.

"The original meteorite was probably covered in some sort of sacred mesh or web," Reed explained. "When they carved this copy, they also copied the ropes."

"They?" Muir sounded tense enough to snap. "Who the fuck are *they*?"

"The people who took the original meteorite away." Serenely oblivious to Muir's simmering anger, Reed stared at the baetyl. "You see the small hollow in the top? I expect that held the fragment that Pemberton found. They'll have sawn it off and left it here, to give the effigy the power of the original. A propitiation to the gods, if you like." He gave a small smile—lost on Muir.

"They . . . *they* . . . Who are we talking about here? Pemberton? The Nazis? Some Cretan shepherd who wandered into the wrong cave?"

"Oh no." Reed knelt down and started examining the piles of pottery laid out on the stone bench. "The meteorite was gone long before that—probably at around the time the Bible was being written."

Muir paled. "You're saying we're two thousand years too late?"

"Not the New Testament." Reed seemed to lose his train of thought completely as he peered closely at a piece of painted pottery. He held it up to the lamp, turning it this way and that. Then, just as suddenly, he continued, "They took the meteorite around the same time that Moses was leading the Jews out of Egypt. Three thousand years ago—give or take the odd hundred."

"Jesus Christ." Muir slumped against the wall and pushed an unlit cigarette into his mouth. Grant and Marina looked at each other uncertainly, while at the far end of the chamber Reed busied himself with the potsherds.

"What do we do now?" Muir asked no one in particular.

Reed stood and brushed the dust from his knees. Lamplight smoldered in the lenses of his glasses and a stray tuft of hair cast a hornlike shadow on the wall behind him. "Actually, I think I know where they took it."

7

SS Kalisti, North Aegean. Four days later

"SO EXPLAIN this to me again."

They were sitting out on deck as the ferry steamed across the Aegean. The sea lane had always been a busy one: in its time it had seen heroes, gods and a thousand vengeful ships on their way to sack a city, all sailing by. Some were still there, watching from above: the Gemini, the twins Castor and Polydeuces who sailed with Jason on the *Argo*; Pegasus, who had carried Perseus and Andromeda over the sea to Greece; Hercules, who had travelled this way to perform his labors. They glimmered in the night sky, while below the moon laid out a silver path on the water.

"I think Pemberton guessed. Those lines from the *Iliad* he wrote down—he wasn't only thinking of the Germans. He must have been reading them because he'd made the connection." Reed shifted slightly on the hard wooden bench and pulled his scarf closer round his neck. Around him, Muir, Grant and Marina all waited like students in a tutorial. On the table between them lay two fragments of pottery, the clay tablet and Pemberton's journal.

"To understand this story you have to begin with the Minoans. Or rather, begin with their ending. Around 1500 BC they were at the height of their powers. What they achieved then in architecture, painting, sculpture and writing was the high point of all European civilization for a thousand years afterward. Then . . ."

"Bang."

Reed gave Grant a severe look over the rim of his spectacles. "Are you familiar with this story, Mr. Grant?"

"Lucky guess. In my experience, when everything's going so swimmingly, that's when it's time to load your gun."

"In this case, *bang* is the literal truth. A vast volcanic eruption on the island of Thera—or what used to be Thera. Now it's a ring of islets round a very large hole in the sea. It blew its top—must have shaken the earth to its core. You can imagine what followed: earthquakes; tidal waves sloshing around the Mediterranean like a bathtub; ash covering the islands like snow. All the Minoan cities were destroyed. Civilization collapsed."

"But that wasn't the end of the Minoans," Marina objected. "They were devastated, but they weren't wiped off the map."

"Indeed not." Reed paused as a steward put four cups of steaming coffee on to the table. "Once the dust had settled, so to speak, they picked themselves up and tried to carry on. But now there's a new complication. Suddenly, Minoan culture starts popping up all over mainland Greece."

"Maybe it got washed up by the tidal waves," Grant suggested. Reed ignored him.

"At the great centers in Greece—Mycenae, Tiryns, Argos—Minoan art and pottery become increasingly influential. Meanwhile, on Crete we start to find all sorts of exotic foreign objects. New types of swords and spears, chariots—weapons the peaceful old Minoans never had any use for."

Muir sipped his coffee. "Sounds to me as if the Greeks took advantage of the disaster to get one over on the Minoans."

"Or perhaps it was the other way round," Marina countered. "Perhaps the Minoans started making colonies in Greece."

"Un-bloody-likely." Muir rolled his eyes. "The tanks come one way and lorries carrying the loot go back the other. Never changes."

"Scholars debate this," said Reed smoothly. "The evidence is inconclusive. Personally, I find myself agreeing with Mr. Muir. Crete was ravaged by the volcano just as the mainland Greeks were hitting their stride. It would be reasonable to expect that the Minoan survivors naturally fell into the Mycenaean orbit."

"Just like us and the fucking Yanks. One country's misfortune . . ."

Grant cleared his throat. "Who are the Mycenaeans?"

"Greeks," said Marina. "From the great age of heroes."

"Pre-Greeks," Reed corrected her. "The era that the Greek myths hark back to and that Homer describes. The civilization of Agamemnon, Odysseus, Menelaus and Achilles. If you believe the legends. Historically speaking, they were probably a culture of warriors and pirates, a loose federation of semi-independent city states who paid allegiance to a high king whose capital was Mycenae. They flourished in the later stages of the second millennium BC—then, suddenly, around 1200 . . ." Reed gave Grant a pointed stare. "*Bang*. Everything was lost and Greece lapsed into a dark age that lasted five hundred years. Invaders moved in—the true ancestors of the modern Greeks, most likely. They looked at the remains the Mycenaeans left behind—the vast walls, the finely worked treasures, the intricate arms and armor . . . In the darkness of their own existence, they couldn't conceive of men ever creating such things, so they invented myths to explain them. The massive stone foundations could only have been laid by Cyclops and giants; magical craftsmen must have wrought the jewellery; only heroes descended from gods could have wielded those swords. Like all barbarians, rather than rise to the challenge of civilization, they explained away its achievements in order to excuse the poverty of their own."

"Though afterward those people laid the foundation for all your Western civilization," said Marina tartly. She seemed to have taken Reed's sermon as a personal affront. "Philosophy, democracy, mathematics, literature. And as for the myths, there's another theory about those."

Muir groaned. "There's always another fucking theory with you people."

"The time we stop proposing theories is the time the barbarians take over," said Reed firmly.

It earned him a more sympathetic look from Marina. "What if the myths weren't written by the invaders?" she said. "What if they were the stories the Mycenaeans wrote themselves, remembered down the generations?"

"It seems unlikely," said Reed. "The myths are so convoluted and contradictory—even the Greeks struggled to make sense of them when they tried to write them down."

"What about Homer?"

"Homer was a poet." Reed's tone, normally mild, suddenly took on unexpected strength. "Myth was the yarn he used to weave his creation, but the result is pure . . . poetry."

Muir yawned. "Is this relevant?"

Reed muttered something under his breath about barbarians, while Marina drank her coffee and made a sour face.

"From a crudely teleological perspective, all that need concern you is that the Mycenaeans—probably—came to Crete in the latter half of the second millennium BC. If they followed the usual practices of invading armies, we can perhaps assume that they carried off a number of treasures. Including, possibly, the baetyl—the meteorite. Certainly, some of the pottery we found in the cave shrine seems to be Mycenaean in origin."

"That explains the picture on the tablet," said Grant, glad to have something useful to say amid all the academic argument. "The waves," he added, answering the quizzical looks he drew. "They're in the foreground. It's drawn as you'd see it from the deck of a ship. In fact . . ." He picked up the tablet and stared at it. The picture of the valley filled most of the space, but in the bottom right-hand corner—just by the jagged fracture where the tablet had been broken—he could make out a dark brown blob. He might have mistaken it for a stain or a smudge of earth, but the edges were too distinct. He showed it to the others. "This could be the prow of a ship."

"Or the tip of another pair of sacred horns," said Marina doubtfully. "Or—anything. I told you, you can't assume that ancient artists saw the world the same way you do."

"We seem to have done all right so far."

"Let's hope your luck continues." Muir tossed a cigarette butt over the ship's side. "Anyway—the Mycenaeans came to Crete and did what invading armies usually do: knocked down the palaces, helped themselves to the women and looted the treasure. Then they took away our sacred meteorite—where? Why not Mycenae?"

"They could have—but I think not." Reed glanced around. That late, most of the passengers had found space inside, but with Easter only three days away the ship was overladen with islanders travelling home. Dark lumps broke the line of the deck where men and women curled up to sleep, while further forward a group of conscripts knelt round a bollard playing cards for cigarettes. A graybearded Orthodox priest sat on a bench under a bare light bulb and spun a string of silver worry beads in his hand. Slap—against his knuckles; slap—against his palm. It was a timeless sound, as natural as the creak of the ship or the lapping of waves.

Reed leaned forward. "The Mycenaeans had nothing against the Minoan religion. The whole idea of a war of religion—fighting someone because he worships a different god, then giving him a choice of conversion or death when he loses—is a much more modern invention. Another innovation for which we have Christianity to thank. The ancients were far more broad-minded and acquisitive in their dealings with the gods. If you defeated an enemy, the only logical thing to do was to take away his relics and his holy objects and use them for yourself. No point letting divine power go to waste."

Three long blasts from the ship's horn underscored his words, as if the gods themselves bellowed out agreement. Grant looked over the rail. Across the water a red beacon winked against the sea; ahead, a straggle of lights rose in the darkness. The flat deck began to come to life: men rubbing their eyes; women wrapping their shawls round them and stroking their children. Conscripts stuffed cigarettes and cards into their pockets. Only the priest sat still, forever whirling his beads.

"Here we are." Muir drained the last of his coffee. "Lemnos."

·

"According to Homer, when Zeus got tired of his wife's meddling, he strung her up from Mount Olympus with a pair of anvils tied to her feet. Her son, Hephaestus, the smithing god, came to rescue her—so Zeus threw him out of heaven. He fell all day and landed, I imagine with something of a crunch, here on Lemnos."

Reed waved his arm to embrace the island. They were sitting at a *kaphenion* on the waterfront, a shallow bay lined by the houses of the island's capital, Myrina. Once it must have been bright and picturesque, but like everywhere else, the war had drained its color. Faded paint peeled off crumbling plaster; newspapers flapped over broken windows and gulls nested among the shattered roof tiles. Even the island seemed to have turned against its inhabitants: round the sweep of the bay, the line of houses was frequently broken by huge upthrusts of exposed rock, as if a giant hand had reached out of the earth to crush the town in its fingers.

Grant sipped his coffee—mercifully they had Nescafé here, so he was spared the usual Greek mud—and kept silent. Like generations of students before him, he was quickly learning that the professor conducted his lectures on his own terms.

"Hephaestus was nursed back to life and set up his forge here with his two sons. Now—*they* are very interesting . . ."

Muir stifled a yawn.

"They were called the Kabyri. Demigods, or *daemons* as the Greeks called them: strange creatures who live in that murky space where folk tales, myths, religion and magic blur. In some way they're not unlike the English ideas of faeries—magical creatures with powers that fall short of full divinity."

Muir covered his eyes. "Please tell me we haven't come to chase fucking pixies."

As a man who had spent most of his life in the international flotsam of diamond prospectors, special operations agents and bandits, Grant usually didn't notice swearing any more than comments about the weather. But somehow, in Reed's presence, he found himself embarrassed by it—like a schoolboy ambushed on the playground by his mother. It didn't seem to bother Reed, who simply rolled his eyes as if he were dealing with a particularly stupid pupil.

"In this case your unimaginative language is unusually apt. The Kabyri were the center of a mystery cult that lasted for centuries."

"What was the mystery?"

Reed gave a weary sigh. "Obviously it's a mystery. Only members of the cult knew their secrets and they had to undergo all sorts of initiatory rites before they found out. In all probability it began as a sort of guild, a way of passing on the skills of the smithing fraternity. Much like the Freemasons, I shouldn't wonder. Over time, though, it became a broader cult with all the usual mystery preoccupations: death and the underworld; life and fertility—which no doubt led to certain sexualized rituals. In art the Kabyri are often depicted with implausibly outsized genitalia. Hence your, erm, fornicating pixies."

"It seems a bit of leap," said Grant. "From a Working Men's Club for blacksmiths to the local cathouse."

"Not at all." Reed leaned forward, his coffee forgotten. "Smithing was one of the most esoteric skills of the ancient world, much more magic than science. The furnace wasn't just a fireplace where you controlled a chemical reaction. It was a portal, the host of a sacred process whereby simple rock ore was transmuted into the essential tools of life. Using it without adequate preparation would be like walking into a church and just gobbling down the communion bread and wine before it's been consecrated. There would be rituals to prepare the tools, to purify the smith, to summon up the alchemical powers from the gods. And in their eyes one of the closest parallels was with procreation."

"Going at it hammer and tongs?"

"The sacred union of the elements of life, wrapped in the mysteries of the womb, mirrored the fusion of copper and tin in the crucible. Remember, this was the Bronze Age—they hadn't yet discovered ironworking. Heat, sweat, blood—and of course, an ever-present risk of death. In legend, Hephaestus married Aphrodite, the goddess of love, to symbolize the union. Even today a lot of primitive cultures use worked metal as a fertility charm."

For once, Grant looked interested. "They have the same idea in Africa. In Rhodesia we found furnaces decorated with pictures of a woman giving birth."

"Life-giving creation," Reed agreed. "Metal tools were the foundation of all agriculture and civilization. The man who knew the magic of metalworking wasn't just a technician or a craftsman—he was a priest, a shaman who could commune with the gods. No wonder he kept himself wrapped in ritual and mystery." With his eyes wide, his thatch of white hair blown awry in the harbor breeze, Reed's demure donnishness had all but vanished. Instead, it seemed he might himself be a shaman, his blue eyes staring into an ancient, magical past to commune with its ghosts.

"Fascinating," said Muir. He lit a cigarette. "But what about the bloody meteorite?"

For a moment Reed seemed not to have heard him. Then, abruptly, he shook himself, looked around in mild surprise and smoothed down his hair. "Well, obviously they'd have brought it here."

"Obviously."

"The meteorite would have been almost pure metal. Where else to bring it but the sanctuary of the Kabyri?"

Muir's eyes narrowed. "Please tell me there's more to go on than that."

Reed pulled out his handkerchief, then unwrapped it to reveal a triangular fragment of pottery inside. Its yellow glaze was chipped and cracked, but the decoration was clear enough. Framed by burning tapers against a background of stars two figures stood out in red. One was tall and bearded, the other short and clean-shaven, but each carried a hammer in one hand and a cup in the other. As Reed had warned them, each had an enormous penis dangling between his legs. "Meet the brothers Kabyri," said Reed. "Pleasant little chaps."

"Why are they holding cups?" asked Grant.

"Probably pouring sacred offerings—though in Greek literature the Kabyri are notorious drunks." Reed handed the fragment to Marina. "This came from the cave shrine in the Valley of the Dead—but it isn't Minoan. This is a Mycenaean piece and I'd wager enough claret to sozzle the Kabyri that it was brought there by the men who took the baetyl away."

"But the cult of the Kabyri spread all over the Aegean," objected

Marina, who had eaten her breakfast in silence until then. "Further—to the shores of the Bosphorus, even the Black Sea. Lemnos was the origin of the cult, but not the only center. Why not Samothraki, or Thessaloniki, or Thebes?"

Reed waved away her suggestions. "The cult only spread much later. We're still deep in prehistory here—1200 BC or thereabouts. Lemnos was one of the earliest inhabited islands in the Aegean. Even the Greeks couldn't trace their ancestry back far enough: they recorded that it was settled by Pelasgians, a quasi-mythic race of people who were there before the Greeks. Probably Mycenaeans. Besides, Pemberton thought so too." Reed opened the journal to the last page and pointed at the Homeric quotation Pemberton had scrawled. "This isn't a description of one of the Trojan battles. It comes from book eighteen, when Hephaestus forges new armor for Achilles in his workshop on Lemnos." He looked around, beaming triumphantly. "The workshop we can safely equate to the sanctuary of the Kabyri."

Muir stubbed out his cigarette in the remains of his coffee and waved at the waiter to bring them the bill. "Is it signposted?"

"It shouldn't be too hard to find. According to Eustathius of Thessalonica, a commentator on Homer, the sanctuary of the Kabyri is right next to the volcano." He caught sight of Marina's surprised stare. "What?"

"I'm sorry to tell you this, Professor." Grant thought he detected the edges of a smirk on Marina's lips. "There is no volcano on Lemnos."

Reed blinked twice, while Muir's match hovered unstruck against the matchbox. It was left to Grant to ask, reasonably, "What about all these?" He nodded at the plugs of rock rising up around the town—and the huge outcrop topped by a castle at the mouth of the bay. "Those are volcanic."

"Lemnos is certainly a volcanic island," Marina allowed.

"Of course it is," said Reed peevishly. "Eustathius, Heraclitus, all the ancient commentators agree that the temple of the Kabyri is next to the volcano."

"Then perhaps they should have visited the place before they wrote about it. There hasn't been a volcano on Lemnos for millions of years. That's before the Minoans," she added for Grant's benefit.

"Christ. Is there anything left? A crater or something?" Muir threw a few coins on to the table.

"We can do better than that. The sanctuary of the Kabyri—the *Kabyrion*—was discovered and excavated ten years ago by Italian archaeologists." Marina smiled at Reed. "Nowhere near the volcano."

"Wonderful. How the hell do we get there?"

Muir's manners might be crude, but his talent for taking hold of a problem and battering it into submission was undeniable. Although it was Good Friday, when most of the townspeople had retreated to their homes to prepare for the weekend's celebrations—Muir was relentless, banging on doors and shouting through windows. Eventually, slumped over a backgammon board in a taverna they had all assumed was shut, they found what they wanted. At first the fisherman looked frightened at the strange quartet of foreigners asking about his boat, then profoundly suspicious, but the wad of banknotes Muir pressed into his hand seemed to dispel his fears. He grinned, and led them down to a broad-beamed caïque moored against the jetty. The wooden hull was scratched and scarred, and there seemed to be almost as much water inside the boat as outside it.

Reed looked around nervously, trying to find a place to sit that wasn't stained with oil or fish blood. "Is there really no alternative?"

"During the war the Germans didn't trust the fishermen. Thought they might use their boats to carry intelligence and spies." Grant gave a slightly shamefaced grin. "They weren't wrong about that. But it destroyed the islands. Without fish they couldn't work and they couldn't eat. Lots of the fishermen were forced to sell their boats, or had them smashed by the Nazis."

"What's that?" Muir, bored, was staring at the high end post that rose almost vertically from the bow, a cutlass ready to slice through any headwind. Wide blue eyes were painted on either side, and nailed below them was a small copper amulet in the shape of a bulbous, apelike man.

Marina laughed. She had untied her hair, letting it whip loose round her shoulders, and as the boat gathered speed the wind pressed her blouse close against her skin. "Do you believe in omens, Mr. Muir? That's one of the Kabyri. They were often associated with sailors: they appeared in storms to guide ships to safety. The islanders still use them as charms today."

Grant looked up at the sky, wondering if the ship that had sailed from Crete three thousand years ago had been protected by a similar charm—and if it had worked. On that Good Friday there was not a cloud in sight: the air was so clear they could see the white cone of Mount Athos, the holy mountain, rising out of the horizon. They rounded the headland under the castle and the fisherman opened the throttle, leaving a wake of diesel smoke billowing behind him. Even so, Grant made his way to the bow when the others weren't looking and touched the amulet. *Just for luck*, he told himself.

8

IT WAS mid afternoon before they nosed into the sandy cove—too late to return to Myrina that day. They unloaded blankets and tinned food from the caïque, then arranged for the fisherman to come back the next morning. He disappeared round the point in a cloud of smoke and they were left alone on the beach.

"In classical times there was an annual festival where all flames on the island were extinguished for eight days. On the ninth, a ship came to the sanctuary of the Kabyri bringing new fire—sacred fire—from the temple of Apollo on Delos. It must have put ashore here." Reed looked around and again Grant felt that unsettling feeling that the professor saw things he didn't.

"So where's the sanctuary now?"

They followed a goat track up the slope that rose out of the cove. A riot of wildflowers blanketed the hillside—poppies, buttercups, mayflowers and more—but thornbushes lurked among the flowers and their trousers were soon scratched to threads. Straight ahead an artificial terrace had been cut into the hillside, hanging out over the foaming sea below. It was about the size of a tennis court, and flat except where a few column pedestals and foundation stones broke the surface. A forlorn skeleton of wooden poles, with a few strands of thatch blowing in the breeze, was the only relic of the archaeologists who had discovered it.

"Lovely spot," said Muir. "But as excavations go, I've seen latrines that were more spectacular."

"There's more over there." At the far corner of the terrace a crumbling path led round the shoulder of the hill to a second terrace above the next cove. Exposed foundations showed the clear outlines of a rectangular building, a columned hall and a screened-off sanctuary at one end. Even so, none of the walls survived much more than a foot high.

"This is more promising," said Marina optimistically. "The first courtyard held a Classical temple. This is Archaic."

"It all looks fucking archaic to me."

Marina gave Muir a withering stare. "Historically speaking, the Archaic period began in about 750 BC. The Classical period follows around three hundred years later with the rise of the great Greek city states."

"That's still too late." Grant's brain was slowly getting used to the deep depths of the past that these academics inhabited—a period that until recently he would have dismissed as all *once upon a time*. "You said the Mycenaeans died out in 1200 BC."

Reed looked at him with the benevolent approval of a schoolmaster. "Quite right. But we are getting closer."

Grant looked out to sea, wondering if it was too late to signal the fisherman to come back. But there was no sign of him: only a smudge of smoke further out where a trawler was lying off the coast. It didn't seem to be moving.

All afternoon they picked their way through the ruins, examining every last scratch in hope of finding writing or carvings. There was nothing. When they'd exhausted the site, Grant clambered down to examine the shoreline. A rock shelf ran along the bottom of the cliffs, slanting into the water, and he followed it back toward the bay where they had landed. Out at sea the trawler still wasn't moving. From Grant's height it was little more than a blur on the horizon.

"Hello." In front of him the shelf split open and a square-cut channel of water lapped deep into the rock. He lay down on his stomach and leaned over the edge, wincing at the touch of the hot stone through his shirt. If he hung his head almost upside down, he could see the channel continuing back under the overhang, into what looked like a shallow cave. The ripple of waves breaking over the beach inside drifted out, soft and haunting.

The water didn't look too deep. Grant untied his boots, slipped off the Webley and removed his wallet from his trousers. Then he braced himself against the sides of the narrow inlet and lowered himself into the water. The current was stronger than he'd expected—the waves almost lapped his chest as they swelled into the channel—but by pressing his arms against the rock walls he managed to keep his footing and work his way forward. He ducked under the overhang, pushed off and half stumbled, half swam on to the beach inside. He wiped the water from his eyes and looked around.

The cave was almost tall enough for Grant to stand, a rough dome about twenty feet round, divided almost evenly between a shallow pool of water and a pebble beach rising gently to the rear wall. The opening to the sea allowed in plenty of light: it played off the water, reflecting soft silver tangles on the ceiling, but all it revealed were a few pieces of driftwood washed up at the back of the cave.

Shit. Grant gave a rueful smile. In the near corner, almost parallel to the sea channel, a narrow passage led through the rock into a thin cleft of sunlight. He looked down at his sodden clothes. *Waste of bloody effort.* With a final look around he squeezed through the passage, almost on his hands and knees, then twisted round so that his head emerged blinking in the open air. From above, it just looked like a fissure in the rock. He must have stepped right over it.

"Ah. Pratolaos emerges."

Trapped in the fissure, Grant squinted up. A floppy white sunhat was peering over the cliff above. "It's only me."

"Pratolaos," Reed repeated. "One of the central rites of the Kabyri cult was a rebirth ritual—the first man, Pratolaos, reborn in a cave and emerging whole from the earth. The sources say his emergence was accompanied by 'unspeakable rites.'" He sounded as though he relished the prospect.

"There's nothing unspeakable down here. Just a pile of driftwood."

"Well, we may need that too." Reed pointed to the west. The sun had disappeared behind the headland and a red haze colored the sky. "Muir says we should make camp for the night."

"I'll come up."

They laid out their blankets on the terrace and built a fire. It was all a far cry from the unspeakable rituals and sacred knowledge that had once happened there, Grant thought, as he sat on a foundation stone and ate stew from the can.

Reed licked his spoon. "I've been thinking about your cave. I wonder if it's the one in the story of Philoctetes."

"Who?"

"Philoctetes was a Greek archer during the Trojan war. Only he didn't make it to Troy with the fleet. He upset one of the gods—always a hazard in those days—and the offended deity arranged for him to be bitten by a snake. The wound swelled up and festered: it smelled so awful that the Greeks refused to take him any further. They marooned him here on Lemnos. Poor chap lived in a cave for ten years—until the Greeks found out from an oracle that they'd never take Troy without Philoctetes' bow and arrows. It was actually the bow of Heracles, you see, that he'd inherited. So Odysseus came back, no doubt pinching his nose, picked him up . . . and the rest is history."

"Is it?" Grant threw another branch into the fire, watching the sparks spit up in the darkness. "I thought the Trojan war was just a legend."

Reed chuckled. "Of course it is. The Mycenaeans were pirates, raiders—probably not much different from Vikings. All their stories would have involved sailing around plundering cities, the bloodier the better. Afterward, as later generations reworked the stories, they decided to tidy them up a bit: introduced the beautiful princess kidnapped by the wicked eastern lothario; made the hero a wronged husband trying to rescue his wife, rather than a warlord who no doubt raped his way the length and breadth of the Aegean. Magic armor, fantastical contraptions, sea nymphs—they turned it into a fairy tale."

Grant picked up his empty stew can and tossed it into the darkness.

It rolled over the cliff edge and tumbled down to the sea, clanging like a bell as it bounced on the rocks. "Let's hope we're not left here as long as Philoctetes."

Grant woke with a start. The night was cold and his shoulders were stiff from the hard earth under his blanket. He lay there for a moment, letting his ears get used to the background noise: the scratching of insects, the surge of waves at the foot of the cliff, Reed's gentle snoring. But none of those were what had woken him. He listened again, straining his ears. It was a low sound, further away but unmistakable: the idle throb of an engine. Then, suddenly, it cut out.

Grant pushed back the blanket, patting the ground until he felt the Webley. He got up and crept quietly to the edge of the cliff. The white surf shone with an almost phosphorescent glow in the moonlight, but there was no sign of any boat.

Probably just a fisherman putting out his nets, he told himself. He craned his neck round to his right, looking for the beach where they had landed that afternoon, but it was hidden behind the headland. He thought about waking Muir, but he could imagine his scorn. Marina? He glanced back to the fire. Her blankets, like his, were thrown back into a flat heap. *Where was she?*

He made his way slowly away from the terraces, over the hill and down the goat track toward the cove. He heard the men coming up the path before he saw them. First the crunch of loose stones under hard boots; then a snatched curse, perhaps as someone blundered into one of the spiky bushes. Grant glanced around desperately. Away to his left, a few yards off the path, he could see the silhouette of a humped boulder. With two strides he was behind it, biting his lip against the thorns that ripped into his calf.

"*Shto eta?*"

Suddenly Grant was back in the war, crouched in the darkness with only the Webley for company, listening to an enemy patrol and praying they hadn't heard him. But that war was over: now the enemies spoke Russian.

Another voice muttered something in reply. The footsteps paused; Grant crouched lower behind the rock, feeling the spines dig into the seat of his trousers.

"*Shto eta bila?*" A third voice. Now Grant was beginning to worry. The three men held a brief discussion, while Grant squeezed the Webley's trigger guard so hard he thought he might snap it.

The footsteps started up the path again. Grant saw them a moment later, wending their way up the hill knee deep in scrub. His heart sank as he counted them off—*five*—all with guns in their hands. He didn't dare move—if they looked back now they would surely see him.

They didn't. Grant waited until they had crested the ridge, then tiptoed to the path and followed. He knew he should be thinking of a plan, but he needed all his wits just to keep quiet on the loose path. Beyond that, all he could think of was a simple equation: five men, six bullets. He was pretty sure Muir must be armed, but whether he could warn him in time . . . Even then, they weren't good odds.

Grant came to the top of the ridge. In front of him the ground leveled out a little, then dipped down to the sanctuary terrace. In the far corner he could just make out the faint glow of embers and the dark outlines of the blankets spread around the fire. Muir and Reed would be fast asleep, completely oblivious to their danger. Two of the Russians were already on the terrace, creeping slowly toward them. Grant's gaze swept across the scene. *Where were the other Russians?* A shadow moved on the rock wall above the terrace, just visible against the broken ground behind. *Three*. Something coughed at the foot of the slope and Grant saw the glint of moonlight on steel. *Four*. That still left one unaccounted for.

But there was no time. The two men on the terrace had almost reached the blankets. One hung back, while the other moved purposefully toward Reed. *They know what they're looking for*, he thought. He craned around again. *Where was the fifth man?*

Never start a fight if you don't know where your enemy is. It was a lesson he'd learned long before they taught it at SOE. But they'd also taught him: *never hesitate*. The Russian was almost beside Reed. There was only one way to warn him. Keeping one eye shut to protect his night vision,

Grant trained the Webley on the nearer of the two Russians and pulled the trigger.

After two thousand years, smoke and fire and hot metal filled the sanctuary of the Kabyri again. Grant saw his target drop, caught square between the shoulder blades. Surprise gave him time for another shot, he reckoned, so he turned left, sighted on the man on the hillside and fired again. Then he dived to his right, rolling down the hillside as a bullet dug up the ground where he'd just been standing. They were fast—faster than he'd expected. He twisted round. The first man he'd shot was still down, possibly permanently; the second, on the hill above, he couldn't see. Meanwhile, at the far end of the sanctuary, he could see three figures struggling with each other. The shots must have woken Reed and Muir. *That's good*, he thought. It would be hard for the Russians to shoot with one of their men tangled in with their targets. Though that meant they could only aim at . . .

A volley of bullets punctuated the thought before he finished it—closer, this time. But in the dark they couldn't shoot without revealing themselves. Grant registered the muzzle flares—one from the hill, one from the edge of the courtyard. He aimed at the nearer one and fired. A howl of pain told him he'd aimed well—though not well enough if the man was able to shout about it. And now it was their move. Grant didn't wait; he flung himself headlong down the hill, rolled the last few yards and came to rest behind a large block of masonry. Had they lost him? More shots and a shower of stone splinters from above said no, but at least he was behind cover now. *Three bullets left*. Would they try to outflank him?

He scrabbled in the earth until he found a loose rock, small enough to throw, big enough to make a noise. He lobbed it to his right. It made a gratifyingly loud rattle as it landed—but then, nothing.

Either they've lost interest, or they've wised up. At the far end of the terrace, not so far away now, he could still hear the frantic sounds of struggle. He edged round the chiselled block, trying to keep in its cover. In the dark, with only the moon for light, the wrestling shadows blended together to make a three-headed monster that writhed and roared on the ancient terrace. Then one figure split off, sprawling off-balance.

That seemed to change things. The remaining two began to move—still struggling, but less viciously. One seemed to have the other locked in a grip and was dragging him across the courtyard. Grant lifted the Webley—but whom was he supposed to shoot?

The man who had been left behind got to his feet and began to run after the others. Grant swung the gun toward him, then checked himself. Even as a blur in the dark, there was something unmistakable about him. *Muir*.

Two flashes—and for two instants Grant saw everything in the courtyard captured like photographs. In the first, two men were stumbling across the terrace, one dragging the other by his hair, while Muir pursued them. In the second flash Muir was down. Grant didn't see who had fired, but he saw where the shots had come from. He fired back—twice—then, when nothing happened, once more. A heavy object toppled through the bushes and dropped on to the sanctuary floor. Grant leaped out from behind the rock, forgetting caution, and sprinted to Muir's side. The pool of blood was black in the moonlight.

"Don't waste your time," Muir groaned. "They've got Reed."

Grant looked around. The Russian and Reed had already vanished off the terrace, presumably somewhere in the scrub making for the cove. How many of them had he got now? Three, maybe four? For a moment he considered going back to reload the Webley—but that would take time he didn't have. Hoping there wasn't a Russian with his sights set on him, Grant ran across the terrace, up the far slope and down the other side. The hill dipped, rose again and spread out down to the cove. There was the boat, bobbing in the water just off the beach—and there were the men, dark shadows against the silver sand. The Russian was struggling to get Reed into the boat: standing knee deep in water, he had to cover the professor with a pistol in one hand while trying to pull the engine's choke cord with the other.

The engine coughed into life—there was his chance. He jumped down the sandy embankment on to the beach and sprinted toward the Russian. His footsteps were soft in the yielding sand, silenced by the noise of the engine. And the Russian was still distracted with Reed. He jabbed his gun furiously, but the professor refused to move. In fact, he was slowly edging backward out of the water. The Russian fired; Grant's heart almost stopped, but it was only a warning. The bullet burrowed harmlessly into the sand. It had the desired effect, though. Reed halted, trembling.

The Russian strode out of the sea toward Reed—just as Grant covered the last few yards. Even in the darkness the Russian must have noticed something. He half turned, but too late. Grant crashed into him. The gun flew from his hand, skidded down the beach and spun into the surf. The two men grappled at the water's edge. Grant swung a punch that didn't quite connect; he tried to get a hand to the Russian's throat, but the man held him too close. Salt water splashed in his face as they rolled in the water: he was underneath now, choking as the Russian held him down.

But the tide had turned; now time was against the Russian. With a last jab to Grant's kidneys, he let go and began wading out toward the boat. Grant got up and spat out a mouthful of seawater. Behind him, Reed was shouting something almost unintelligible.

"Stop him! *He's got the tablet.*"

The Russian had reached the boat and was trying to haul himself inboard. Bruised and winded, Grant summoned the strength for one more effort. A few feet away, wet metal gleamed in the moonlight where the surf rippled over the Russian's gun. Grant picked it up and aimed.

"*Stop,*" he shouted.

The Russian turned, still gripping the boat for balance. His other hand was sliding inside his jacket.

"*Stop!*"

Three shots rang out. The Russian screamed once, then let go the boat and slid silently into the waves. Grant spun round. Marina was standing on the beach behind him, her bare legs slightly apart, both hands holding a pistol. Though she must have run to get there, her breathing was calm and controlled.

"Why the hell did you do that?"

"He was reaching for a gun."

"I had him covered." Grant splashed out to where the dead Russian floated in the water and dragged him back to shore. He hauled him out of the water and laid him on the sand. A startled crab scuttled away.

"Anyway, where did you go? And what brought you here just in the nick of time?"

She looked down at the sand. "I couldn't sleep; I went for a walk. When I heard the shots I came back and found Muir."

"It would have been nice if you'd come earlier. They almost killed us up there."

"I know. I'm sorry."

"And the gun?"

"I took it from Muir. He wasn't going to use it."

Grant shook his head and looked down at the dead man. He was squat and solid, with wide cheekbones and a now permanently downturned mouth. Grant rifled quickly through his sodden pockets. There was no wallet or identification, just a penknife, a few drachma coins, and a sodden wad of brown cardboard that had once been a pack of cigarettes.

"What could they want with us?"

"Maybe this." Grant reached into the last pocket and felt his fingers close round the hard clay slab. It was lucky Marina hadn't shattered it when she shot the man. He pulled it out, brushed it off and handed it to Reed. "Whatever they wanted, they knew exactly where to find it."

9

Myrina, Lemnos. Next evening

GRANT STOOD on the hotel balcony and breathed the night air. The harbor lights twinkled before him, crisp as stars, each one twinned with a flat reflected smear on the water. At that moment Grant felt like a man trying to navigate by the reflections alone.

"What do we do now?"

Grant turned round. The shutters were pulled back and the room behind him, bathed in a nicotine-yellow light, was framed like a painting. Reed sat on a chair by the dresser, apparently hypnotized by the ceiling fan, while Marina perched on the end of the bed and darned the sleeve of a blouse. Muir lay propped up against the pillows behind her, a cigarette jammed into his scowl. One trouser leg was rolled up to the knee to fit the fat bandage that wrapped his calf and shin—though the doctor who had seen him claimed the bullet had missed anything that mattered.

The question hung unanswered in the smoky air. They hadn't spoken much that day. No one had slept after the gun battle: they had sat up through the night, twitching at every rustling branch and breaking wave. At first light they had gathered the Russians' corpses and sunk them in their boat in the bay, weighed down with stones. Then they had sat down to wait for the fisherman. Much to Grant's surprise, he had come.

Muir flicked ash into the ashtray beside his bed. "I want to know why the fucking Russians were there in the first place."

"They wanted the tablet. They almost got it." Grant pointed to the dresser, where the tablet lay on a lace mat bathed in lamplight. "Whatever it is, your Element 61, they're after it too. Which makes me wonder: what's so special that both the Yanks and the Soviets are so eager to have it?"

Muir stared him down. "I told you: I'm just the bag man. The real question you should be asking is, how did they find us."

Grant poured more wine from the half-empty bottle on the balcony and threw it down his throat. "There's a civil war going on in this country. Soviet military advisers crawling all over the place. Half the population supports the EAM."

"Those bodies we sank weren't a bunch of military attachés who got lost in the dark. They knew what they wanted—as you said—and they knew where we were. Even we didn't know where we'd be two days ago. Someone told them. And you don't have to look too hard for the bloody fifth column in this room."

The hard silence that followed was broken by a flash and a flat bang echoing off the harbor. Grant spun round, his hand instinctively going to his hip. But it was only a firework, a prelude to the bombardment that would be let off when midnight struck on Easter Sunday.

"It's funny how these traditions rub on with Christianity," said Reed. "It's such an ancient idea, trying to drive away evil spirits with loud noises."

He had spoken to nobody in particular and nobody paid him any attention. Marina was staring at Muir, with much the same look on her face as when she shot the Russian on the beach. Though this time Muir had wisely kept his gun close to him. "What are you saying?" she hissed through bared teeth.

"I'm saying it's a queer business how you went for a walk just as the Soviets turned up on our doorstep. Queerer still how you finished off that last chap before he could tell us anything. And let's not forget the small matter of your dear departed brother."

"He wasn't a Communist," spat Marina. "He was a hero."

"He was thick as thieves with the Communist Party of Greece."

"Because they were the only people willing to organize the resistance against the Germans when all the politicians just wanted to crawl into their pockets. Alexei didn't care about Stalin or the dictatorship of the proletariat—he just wanted to fight the Nazis."

"And when they were gone? Who was going to take over?"

"Did it matter?" Marina's face burned with hatred. "Stalin or Truman or General Scobie—what's the difference? You all just wanted to take Greece for yourselves." She made a half-turn round the room, fixing Grant, Muir and Reed with a smoldering glare. "You know, there's a legend that once upon a time the women of Lemnos got together and killed all the men on the island in one swoop. Maybe they had the right idea." She stormed out of the door and slammed it behind her. For a moment the echo drowned out the fireworks in the harbor.

Muir rasped a match against the box. "Good fucking riddance."

Grant looked at him in disgust. "You know her brother wasn't a Communist."

"As far as she's concerned he was. And she's hiding something."

"She's angry as hell because of what happened to her brother."

"Then why don't you tell her the truth about it? Is there any more wine in that bottle?"

Grant picked up the bottle of Moschato. It was unlabelled and covered in dust from the hotel owner's cellar. He jammed in the cork and lobbed it across the room to Muir. Muir winced as he stretched to catch it.

"Marina knew Pemberton, she knows the archaeology and she can handle herself in a fight. She probably saved our skins on the beach last night."

"Grow up. She killed that Russian because she had no choice. If we'd captured him he'd have spilled the beans on her."

Grant shook his head. "I don't buy it. She could have shot me instead. You were down, Reed was unarmed, the Russian had the tablet.

They could have jumped in the boat and been halfway to Moscow by now."

A chair scraped on the floor. Reed had stood—and flinched, as two angry stares pinned him back. "I, er, thought I'd get a little air."

"No you fucking won't. We've almost lost you once already this weekend. Don't know what nasties are lurking out there." Muir gestured out of the window. The street below was filled with noise and light as the townsfolk hurried to church for the midnight Easter service.

"I'll go with him." Like Reed, Grant was desperate to get away from the stale anger in the room.

"Keep your eyes open. Especially with Marina on the loose."

Grant buckled the Webley's holster round his waist, then pulled on a jacket to cover it. "We'll be careful."

The fresh air was a relief. They stood on the hotel's porch and breathed it in for a few moments, not speaking. They didn't have a destination in mind, but the moment they stepped into the street they found themselves carried on the current of the crowd. They were all dressed in their Sunday best: fathers in three-piece suits, however threadbare; mothers in high heels dragging along children with scrubbed faces and pigtails. All of them, even the smallest child, carried long white candles.

"I hope Marina's all right," said Reed. "She seemed rather upset about her brother."

"She should be. We killed him."

"Oh." Reed grimaced and didn't ask any more. After a pause: "I suppose you're not troubled by this sort of thing. Midnight raids. Russian spies trying to kidnap you. Guns being waved all over the place. People dying."

"Troubled?" Grant laughed. "Maybe. You get used to it."

"It's funny. I suppose, in a way, I've spent all my life with war. Homer," Reed added, seeing Grant's surprise.

"I thought you said that was a fairy tale."

"Some of the stories are. But Homer . . ." Reed paused, his eyes half shut, as if savoring a fine wine on his tongue. "He puts the truth back into them. Not the literal truth—though actually, his poems are far less fantastical than most versions. The poetic truth."

"Don't believe everything you read in the papers, Professor. There's not much poetry in war."

"'My subject is War, and the pity of War. The Poetry is in the pity.'"

"Wilfred Owen was a hopeless romantic. There's not much pity in war either. I learned that much from my dad."

Reed, far too steeped in the ways of an Oxford don to enquire further, fell silent. They walked on with the crowd, out of the town and toward the church on the headland at the mouth of the bay. The flash of fireworks lit up the sky like a distant storm.

"It was the smell, you know."

"Pardon?" Surprised from his thoughts by Reed's unexpected remark, Grant looked up.

"The story Miss Papagiannopoulou . . ."

"Call her Marina," Grant interrupted. "It'll save you years of your life."

"The story she referred to. The women of Lemnos didn't just spontaneously murder their menfolk. They did it because they'd been shunned. They'd been afflicted by a curse that gave them terribly bad breath—they'd offended Aphrodite—so, naturally, their husbands refused to kiss them. Or offer other, erm, marital favors. So they killed the men."

"Doesn't exactly solve the problem."

"That's what they discovered. A few months later Jason and the Argonauts popped by on their way to find the golden fleece. The women practically held them at spear-point until the Argonauts obliged them."

"Must have been a hard life, being an Argonaut."

"Hm?" Reed wasn't really listening. "It's funny how all these old stories about Lemnos revolve around odor. Philoctetes' stinking wound, the women's foul breath. Almost as if Lemnians had a reputation."

He trailed off, lost in his own thoughts as they reached the end of the promontory. A square, whitewashed church rose above them—but they couldn't get any nearer, for the crowds had completely surrounded it. From inside, Grant could just make out the drone of the priests chanting the Easter liturgy, though no one seemed to be paying much attention. Children chased each other through the forest of legs, while adults greeted each other and gossiped quietly.

"Not quite C of E, is it?" Reed grinned.

A hawker, with pairs of candles hanging from his arms like onions, moved up toward them. Grant would have sent him packing, but Reed beckoned him over and, after some brief haggling, came away with two candles. He handed one to Grant. "The Greeks say if you burn it down it burns away your sins."

Grant squinted down the length of the slender taper. "Do they come any bigger?"

A hush fell over the crowd. Up on the hilltop a spark appeared in the door of the church. It hovered for a second, divided in two, then again and again, multiplying from candle to candle as it passed through the crowd.

"The original light comes from Jerusalem," Reed whispered. "Every year the patriarch of Jerusalem crawls into the Holy Sepulcher—Christ's tomb—and a holy fire spontaneously kindles itself out of the air. The patriarch lights a candle from it and passes the flame on to his congregation."

"Sounds like hocus-pocus to me. He's probably got a lighter stuffed down his pants."

"Maybe." Again, Reed seemed to filter out everything but the sound of his own thoughts. "Extraordinary to think, though, that in ancient times the islanders waited for the boat to bring the sacred fire. And here we are, three thousand years later, doing exactly the same thing."

Grant trawled through his memory. He felt as if he'd learned more history in the past week than all the previous thirty years of his life combined. "You mean the fire ritual? The one where they turned out all the lights for nine days?"

"Indeed. Interestingly, according to one of the sources, the ritual was meant to purify the island after the episode I told you about earlier. The darkness was a time of penance, symbolic death to atone for the historic murder of the menfolk. Then the light arrived, symbolizing new life and rebirth."

"Pratolaos." The name jumped into Grant's mind. "The first man, reborn in a cave."

"Not so different from another man who was buried in a cave and came back to life." Reed stopped talking as the man in front of him, a burly farmer in an ill-fitting suit, turned round. Grant braced himself for a complaint, but the man only smiled and reached out his candle, tilting toward Reed's. The wicks touched; Reed's took the flame and flared into life. A bubble of wax trickled down toward his fingers.

"*Christos anesthi*," said the farmer. *Christ is risen*.

"*Alithos anesthi*." Reed replied. *He is risen indeed.* All around them the greeting and counter-greeting whispered through the crowd, like moths on a summer night. He turned to Grant and offered him the flame. "*Christos anesthi*."

"If you say so." Grant lit his candle and held it awkwardly, trying not to drip wax on his shoes.

"Are you uncomfortable?"

Grant gave a bashful grin. "Confused. I'm not sure if I'm burning away my sins, apologizing for those husband-slaughtering women, worshipping Jesus or conjuring up Pratolaos."

Reed smiled. "Now you're getting the idea. But you mustn't hog the fire. You're supposed to pass it on."

Grant turned round. The fire had already spread beyond him: most of the candles behind were lit. But one seemed to have missed out. He reached forward. The two candles collided, knocked against each other a few times in a clumsy courtship, then finally settled long enough for the flame to leap between them.

"*Christi anesthu*," Grant mumbled.

She retracted her candle and held it up in front of her. Orange light shone on her face and the reflected flame burned in her eyes.

"Marina?" Grant almost dropped his candle. "Jesus Christ!"

". . . Is risen indeed." She turned away; Grant half lifted a hand, but she was only passing the fire on to the man behind her. When she had finished she turned back. She had been crying, and even among the crowd she looked strangely vulnerable, as if she couldn't decide whether to spit in his face or run away.

"I'm sorry about Muir," said Grant. "He's . . . He's an asshole."

"I didn't sell you out to the Russians." Her voice was brittle.

"I never said you did. But you can see why Muir's jumpy. Someone must have told the Reds where we were. And it's a shame you shot the Russian. It would have been useful to find out what he knew."

He gave her a sideways glance, which she answered with an uncompromising glare. "There was a bulge under his coat and he was reaching for it. What would you have done?"

"That was the tablet."

"Then it's lucky I didn't hit it."

He reached out a tentative hand and brushed back a strand of hair that had fallen over her cheek. She didn't stop him.

"Anyway, Muir doesn't matter any more." A breeze stirred through the crowd and Grant cupped his hand round the candle to protect it. "There's nothing at that sanctuary. This trail was three thousand years old before we started. It's not just cold: it's bloody frozen in the depths of time. Might as well give up now and go back to Crete."

There was a discreet cough from behind. Grant and Marina turned, to see Reed watching apologetically. With the candle clutched in his hand, he looked like a choirboy on Christmas eve. "Actually, I think the trail's warming up nicely."

Grant and Marina stared at him in disbelief. "How?"

Reed tapped the side of his nose. "The clue was in the ancient stories." He smiled. "You just have to follow your nose."

10

Therma, Lemnos. Next morning

ARE YOU sure you've got this right?"

They were standing in a shallow valley at the end of a dirt road. It was a pleasant spot: poplars and cypress trees shaded the stream that bubbled down the valley, while in front of them stood a neat, four-square, neoclassical building. It felt vaguely Swiss to Grant: its red-tiled roof and vigorous white walls; the fresh paint on the doors and the starched curtains in the windows. Everything seemed healthy and efficient. Everything except the smell, which festered in the valley: the eggy, noxious stink of sulfur.

"Perhaps not," said Reed. He sounded unaccountably cheerful. "But this is where the hot springs are. I don't know why I didn't think of it earlier. They've been in use since at least Roman times."

"I hate to be the one to tell you, but a hot spring isn't the same as a volcano. Even the ancients probably knew the difference."

Reed shrugged. "All the legends about the foul-smelling Lemnians will have been rooted in some sort of collective memory. If this was the place where they had their shrine, they must have smelled rather unpleasant after nine days of rituals."

They had walked the few miles from Myrina that morning. There wasn't much to be found in the town on Easter Sunday, but between them Grant and Marina had managed to scrounge a few tools, an oil lamp, a length of rope and a donkey to carry it all to the spa at Therma. Now they were there, breathing in air that seemed anything but healthy to Grant.

"So what do we do? Ask the attendant if he's found a three-thousand-year-old meteorite in the bath?" He pointed to the locked door and the dark rooms behind the lace curtains. "It looks shut."

"Bank Holiday." Reed peered around. "But the thermal springs don't rise inside the spa. The water gets piped in from somewhere. Let's have a look."

A brief reconnaissance of the buildings didn't reveal much. They left Muir with the donkey and spread out, gradually working their way further up the valley behind the spa. The sulfurous smell faded away, drowned out by the sticky scent of wildflowers, and their pace slowed as they waded through the long grass. At the top of the valley the stream disappeared. Grant spent a fruitless quarter of an hour looking for its source but found nothing. He sat down on a rock in the sun, watching the lizards dart among the stones. The withered husk of a snakeskin lay coiled at his feet.

"What's over there?" Reed had come up behind him, his face flushed under the sunhat. He was pointing up the hill, where a mounded hilltop swelled out of the rolling landscape. The valley had hidden it, but from the ridge they could see it quite clearly. Reed took the field glasses that hung round his neck and pressed them against his spectacles, then handed them to Grant. Unsure what he was looking for, he twisted the dial until the blurred image came into focus.

"There's a cross on top of it." It was a steel cross about six feet tall, held in place by four guy ropes. A hawk was sitting on one of the transepts, preening itself.

Grant lowered the field glasses. "I know I'm not a historian, but aren't churches a bit later than what we're looking for?"

"Have you ever been to the Roman forum? When Christians took over the empire, they just bricked up the pagan temples and turned them into churches. You can still see the classical columns built into the walls. The Parthenon in Athens was used as a church—and a mosque when the Ottomans captured it. Buildings come and go, but sacred places have a way of persevering."

"I suppose we can try."

Picking their way over the loose stones, they worked their way toward the summit. From the ridge it had looked like a normal hilltop, but as they edged round its shape changed. The far side seemed to drop precipitously—then, as they came a little further, they saw that there was no far side at all. The whole face had been hollowed out under the summit, so that the hill swept over like a wave poised to break. The cavern underneath must have been at least a hundred feet high. Nestled inside, almost hidden in its shadow, was a tiny whitewashed courtyard with a church against its far wall.

"Sacred places," murmured Reed.

Marina nodded. "It's almost as if nature made it for this. A giant rock womb—or a furnace."

"Even looks a bit like a volcano, if you squint," Grant conceded.

"And look." Marina pointed to the gatepost. On a mosaic in the wall, blue tiled letters spelled out ΑΓΙΑ ΠΑΝΑΓΙΑ on a golden background.

"*Ayia Panayia*," Reed elaborated. "A title of the Virgin Mary. It means 'All Holy.' It emphasizes her aspect as God's partner in the conception of Jesus. If you're inclined to think heretically, you can derive it back from the ancient cults of an all-powerful, all-fertile goddess who herself gives birth to gods." Reed saw Marina's appalled look. "From an anthropological point of view, of course."

They passed through the open gate into the small compound. The air went suddenly cold as they came under the shadow of the hill, and the noise around them deadened. The only sound was the splash of water, pouring from a spout in the wall shaped like a serpent's head into a marble basin. Grant sniffed it and smelled the familiar odor of rotten eggs. "Sulfur."

But Reed and Marina didn't hear—they were already at the church door. They tried the handle and the door swung open. Grant followed them in.

It was a simple church: a low, oblong room with plain walls, slit windows and a barrelled roof. Skeletal bundles of dried flowers quietly disintegrated in the corners, and a few red glass jars clustered on the step by the altar, though the candles they held had long since burned out. At the back of the church a single icon of the Virgin Mary stood facing toward them, her legs apart and her hands held up as if in blessing. The infant Jesus peered out at them from a golden circle in her stomach.

"If you think there's something familiar about that pose, you're entirely correct." Reed pulled out Pemberton's battered journal and turned to an early page. An ink sketch leaped out: a wasp-waisted woman with long skirts, bared breasts and a snake writhing along her outstretched arms. "The Minoan mother-goddess."

"She's got better tits than the Virgin Mary," said Grant. He didn't look at Marina, though in the corner of his eye he saw her cross herself.

"And look at the Christ figure. He seems to be inside her—in her womb." Reed made a half-turn, taking in the whole church. "Are you familiar with the Hindu concept of the *avataram*? Aspects of the gods' incarnations change, but the underlying truths are eternal."

Marina frowned. "If you're going to dismiss two thousand years of Christian teaching, could you at least do it outside?"

"New religions are terrible magpies—they love to build on the foundations of the faiths they've barged out of the way. Both theologically and physically."

"Are you proposing we demolish this church?"

"No. But we do need to do what the archaeologists do."

"What's that?" asked Grant.

"Get to the bottom of things."

Reed paced the length of the room, staring at the heavy stones paving the floor. Three yards back from the altar, he suddenly went down on one knee and started scrabbling at something. Marina and Grant crouched beside him. An iron ring was set flush into the floor. Reed pried it up and tugged. Nothing moved.

He turned and looked apologetically at Grant. "Would you mind?"

Grant planted one foot on either side of the stone, crouched and heaved. The cracks around it were thick with dirt—it must have lain shut for years—but it slowly yielded to his pressure. A crack opened and Marina slid the blade of the shovel inside. Together they heaved and levered the stone away until they had opened a hole wide enough to climb through. A dark chasm loomed below.

"I wonder what's down there?"

Grant took one of the glass candle holders and dropped it through. It thudded against something hard, but didn't break. Reassured, Grant swung his legs through the hole and lowered himself down. He had only reached shoulder height when his feet touched solid ground: his head was still sticking up through the church floor and he had to wriggle down to see underneath. He struck a match.

He was standing on a beaten earth floor, in a low chamber whose dimensions seemed to be the same as the church's. All around him stone pillars sprouted out of the ground to support the church floor. Some were intact, still crowned with ornate capitals, but others had obviously snapped at some point in the past and been cemented back together, or repaired with crude fieldstones. Strands of straw scattered the ground and a few tools lay resting against the far wall. Grant could make out a masonry trowel, a bucket, a rake and a scythe. Otherwise, it was empty.

"Is there anything down there?" Reed peered in, his face almost completely blocking the light from above. At the same time Grant felt the heat of the flame burning toward his fingers. He dropped the match and was suddenly in darkness.

"Nothing except some gardening tools. There's a scythe—does that symbolize something? Death?" Grant thought of the weathervane on top of the pavilion at Lord's. "Time?"

"The caretaker probably uses it for cutting the grass." Reed disappeared and the blue-tinged daylight filtered back in.

"We'll have to start digging."

They fetched the donkey. Muir came too. Grant hung the lanterns between the supporting pillars, while Marina drove a row of stakes into the ground about a yard back from the innermost wall. In the flickering lamplight they crouched on the earth floor under the altar and stared at the walls.

"The church is Byzantine," Marina explained. "But these foundations are Hellenistic—about 200 BC, when a lot of the mystery cults flourished." She pointed at the crudely cut stones mortared together. A few of them seemed to be missing and layers of flat bricks filled the gaps. "You can see where they were repaired when the church was built. But it's possible that the site goes back considerably further than that."

She indicated the line she had staked out. "This is the north wall of the church. But I think there's evidence that the sanctuary was reorientated during the Christian period so that its altar would face east." She swept her arm round, pointing out each of the walls in turn. "Do you notice anything about the south wall?"

Grant stared, trying to probe the shadowy recesses where pillars blocked the lamplight. "The stones look smaller—and they're not as well put together."

"Exactly." Marina looked pleased. "This was probably added later to partition the existing foundations into something small enough to support the church. It's likely the courtyard gives a more accurate outline of the original temple's dimensions. In which case the sanctuary would have been somewhere near here."

"Then let's get started."

It was slow, aching labor. Unable to stand upright, they had to stoop low and attack the packed earth with short, ungainly jabs. After a while, once the ground was broken, they evolved a system whereby Marina, Reed and Muir filled the bucket with soil, which Grant then hauled away and tipped out on the hillside. The air in the cellar, stuffy to begin with, grew stifling. Marina knotted the tails of her blouse together round her midriff, while Grant stripped off his shirt and worked barechested. Even Reed removed his tie and rolled up his shirtsleeves.

Grant was just taking out another bucket of earth when something caught his eye at the foot of the hill across the valley.

"What's that?"

"What?" Reed was lying in the grass, resting while Muir spelled him. He was staring right at it, though he didn't seem to have noticed. Grant could never quite be sure what he was seeing.

"There." It came again—a series of sparkling flashes, winking at them from the edge of a ridge, near a blackened pine tree. Grant tried to count them, wondering if it could be some sort of message. But to whom?

"It might be a scrap of cigarette foil, or a piece of broken glass," Reed suggested.

"Or someone watching us." Grant pulled on his shirt and buckled the Webley round his waist. He made his way down the slope, picking a cautious path through the tangled scrub and loose stones. He had to watch his footing carefully; when he looked up he couldn't see the flashes any more.

He crossed a small stream at the foot of the hill and began climbing up the far side. As he got closer to the ridge he slowed. He could see the black branches of the burned pine tree poking over the escarpment above. A breeze stirred—and among the wildflowers and grasses he smelled a wisp of tobacco smoke. Someone must be there. But he heard nothing.

He crept to his left, edging his way round the ridge to try to get round the back. A butterfly flitted across his path; the bushes around him buzzed with the sounds of bees and flies. Anywhere else, it would have been a perfect day to lie back in the grass with a cold beer and a girl. He gripped the Webley tighter.

With a sudden roar a motor kicked into life on the ridge above. Forgetting caution, Grant ran the last few yards up the bank and looked down. A cloud of dust was slowly settling on the dirt track that wound away behind the next hill. Grant ran down it and round the corner—just in time to see the blur of a motorbike disappearing out of sight. He stared after it for a moment—but there was nothing he could do.

With a curse, he walked back to the hillside. A little hollow indented the slope, just behind the ridge that looked across to the hooded mountain top. A section of grass had been flattened there and half a dozen white tubes littered the ground. Grant picked one up and sniffed it, then squinted down the cardboard barrel. They were cigarette butts—but a good inch of the cigarette was hollow, as if the manufacturer had only been able to afford to fill half the tube with tobacco. Cheap tobacco at that, Grant thought, smelling it.

There was only one place Grant knew where they made such awful cigarettes. He'd smoked a few himself during his brief stint on the Eastern Front, as much for warmth as for the nicotine. The five men they'd sunk in the bay obviously hadn't been the only Russians on the island.

"They've been watching us."

"Damn." Muir threw his cigarette butt into the marble basin. It hissed and fizzled out. "How long were they there for?"

Reed blinked. "I'm afraid I never noticed them."

"Well, pay more fucking attention from now on." He turned to Grant. "Do you think they'll come back?"

"Maybe. After the other night, they'll be careful about getting too close."

"Let's hope so."

The day grew darker. Clouds rolled in from the west, brooding over the hooded hilltop. On one of his trips to empty the bucket, Grant saw the sun low between the clouds and the sea, a furious crimson mess. The next time he emerged it was gone. Night fell, but the cellar remained in perpetual lamplit twilight. The trench against the wall was almost two feet deep now: when Grant came down the others looked like dwarves toiling in the bowels of the earth.

Work slowed. They had exposed the upper foundations and come down to a lower level, broad slabs laid without mortar. Now the ground was harder, filled with as much rubble as earth. They had to remove it piece by piece. Soon their hands were chafed raw, their nails split and their muscles in agony.

At nine o'clock they paused for supper. They sat in the courtyard, shivering slightly in the cool air, and ate the bread and cheese the hotel owner had given them that morning. There were no stars.

"How far down have we got?" asked Grant.

"Those ashlars—the big stones—are very old." Marina had Reed's jacket wrapped round her shoulders and her eyes were glazed. "We must be close."

"If there's anything to find," Reed cautioned. His earlier exuberance had vanished, broken by the sheer effort of their labor. "It might be in another part of the temple—or this might be the wrong place altogether."

"Only one way to be sure." Grant took a last swig of water and picked up a spade. "I'll dig."

But his effort was short-lived. He had only been working for a quarter of an hour when he felt a jarring impact. He knelt in the trench, scraping away the soil with his fingers to try to find the edges of the rock he had hit. All he felt was stone. Soon, working with hands and spade, he had uncovered an unbroken rock surface that ran from one side of the trench to the other.

Marina unhooked one of the lanterns and lowered it into the hole. "Bedrock." She swore under her breath. "This must have been the floor of the original temple. You can see the marks where they used chisels to level it."

"At least we don't have to dig any deeper." Grant let the spade drop to the ground and rubbed his blistered hands together. "It's too late to get off the hill now. We'll have to go back in the morning."

Grant collected the equipment and passed it out to Reed. Marina ignored them. She stood waist deep in the trench and examined the ashlar wall, occasionally sweeping away the crust of earth with a small brush. When Grant had handed up the last of the tools, he turned. Marina was crouched beside the wall, her face inches from the stone as she traced something with her finger. But it was her face that really stopped him. It shone with a fierce concentration, and her dark eyes were wide with awe.

Grant's weariness fell away in an instant. He scrambled across the low room and joined her in the trench. She didn't say anything, but grabbed his hand and pressed it against the wall. Her skin was warm against his, the stone beneath it cold. She moved his hand down the wall in a slow, sinuous arc. "Do you feel it?"

He did—a curve of tiny ridges carved into the rock. He took his hand away and stared closely. Three thousand years had worn it down to almost nothing, little more than a shadow, but his hand had told him what to look for. He traced it again, a crescent moon turned on its side. A pair of bull's horns.

"We need to pull it out." Marina took her pocket knife and tried to work her blade into the hairline crack along the edge of the slab.

"It must weigh a ton," said Grant doubtfully. The stone was about a yard wide, a foot high and looked to be almost as deep. "You'd need dynamite to get that out."

"The Mycenaeans didn't have dynamite." Marina kept prying away with the knife. Worried that the blade might snap, Grant stepped back out of the trench.

Muir popped his head through the hole in the church floor. "Are you going to spend all night down there?"

"Marina thinks . . ."

Grant whipped round as a huge bang echoed round the cellar. Marina was in the trench holding her knife and even in the lamplight he could see her face was white as dust. A stone slab lay at her feet, shattered into three pieces by the impact on the bedrock. Above it, a dark chasm had opened in the wall.

"It was a panel." She was trembling—she must barely have avoided being crushed by the falling slab. "A door."

"Someone forgot to oil the hinges." Grant jumped down into the trench. The aperture was about the same size as the slab that had disguised it, barely high enough for a man to squeeze through. He stuck in his arm and felt around.

"It opens out a bit once you get through the wall. Not a lot, but perhaps enough to give you some wriggle room."

He took the lantern from the edge of the trench and pushed it through the hole. The fire shone on smooth-cut stone walls, but beyond it all was darkness.

"Let's see what's inside."

II

It was like posting himself through a mail slot. Grant had been in some tight spaces before—chasing diamonds in Rhodesia in the thirties—but never anything like this. He twisted his head flush with his body and sucked in his stomach; he wriggled and squirmed into the stone mouth, while Reed and Marina pushed from behind. Then he was through. He lay flat on his belly, breathing hard.

Something touched his ankle, still sticking out into the cellar, and he kicked instinctively.

"I've tied a rope to your foot." Marina's voice was already frighteningly distant. "If you find something, jerk it twice. If you get stuck, jerk it three times and we'll pull you out."

Grant didn't bother to reply. He was in a tunnel, taller than the hole he had squeezed through but no wider. If he got on to his hands and knees, his back scraped the roof. There were no stones or mortar to be seen: it must be cut into the rock itself.

"At least there's no danger of it collapsing," he consoled himself.

He crawled forward. The tunnel wasn't high enough to hold the lamp; he had to push it along the ground in front of him, then crawl after it. The air was thick—surely no one had breathed it for three thousand years. More worrying was the sour tinge of gas he smelled. *Where's a canary when you want one?* he thought.

He crawled on. The only sounds now were the scrape of the lantern as he slid it forward and the dead rustle of his clothes against the rock walls. Whoever had cut the tunnel had done a remarkable job: it never deviated, but thrust straight into the heart of the hill. He tried to imagine the men who had made it. How long had it taken them, with their stone hammers and copper chisels?

"And what were you trying to get to?" he wondered aloud. Had it been worth it?

He shook his head. Ahead, something was gleaming in the lamplight. He hauled himself closer, pushed the lantern forward again, then snatched it back just in time to keep it from toppling over. A shiny-faced pool of water stretched out in front of him, cut into the floor of the tunnel. Grant extended an arm and held the lantern above the surface. The water was clear; ripples of lamplight touched the rocky bottom, about three feet down. It would have been easy enough to splash through, Grant thought. Except that on the far side, rising sheer and impossible out of the water, the tunnel and the pool ended together in a rock face.

Grant stared at it for a moment, then drew his right leg up and twitched it twice. It was an awkward maneuver in the tight space—for a moment, he wondered if they'd felt it. Then he heard a noise behind him—far away, it seemed. The grunts and groans of someone trying to squeeze into the tunnel.

While he waited, he turned his attention back to the pool. It must be fed from an underground spring: it couldn't have stayed like this for so many centuries otherwise. Was it the same source that fed the fountain in the church compound? He leaned out over the water as far as he dared. It certainly had the same sulfurous smell. And if there was a way for the water to come in . . .

He lowered the lamp so that its bowl almost touched the water. It was hard to see at that angle, but it looked as though the far wall didn't reach all the way to the bottom. Instead, there seemed to be the dark shadow of an opening at its base.

The shuffling noise that had been growing louder in the tunnel behind him stopped. A hand squeezed his foot and he craned his head round. Dark eyes watched him from the black midnight behind.

"Here we are. Theseus and Ariadne in the labyrinth."

"Let's hope there's no Minotaur."

Grant rolled on to his side, pressing himself against the wall so that Marina could see past him. Her eyes widened.

"What do we do now?"

"I don't think they cut their way down here just because they were thirsty. Untie my boots." Grant pointed to the yawning shadow at the foot of the rock face, though it was invisible to Marina. "There's an opening. I'm going to see where it goes."

Marina unlaced his boots and tugged them off, leaving the rope still fastened round his ankle. He didn't take off his clothes: there was no room.

"Be careful." Her voice was small and hollow in the gloom.

Grant pulled himself forward and slid face first into the water. It was surprisingly warm—almost like a hot bath. He immersed himself in it, enjoying the rare feeling of space. He could even spin himself round to look at Marina. She had crawled forward to the water's edge and for a second their faces almost touched.

"Give me two minutes," he said. "Then pull like hell."

The water closed over his head like a coffin. He duck-dived to the bottom, pawing out with his hands until he felt the opening in the far wall. It seemed to be about the same size as the tunnel above—wide enough to move forward, too narrow to turn round. He kicked himself through, banging his knee on the rocky floor. The minerals in the water stung his eyes, so he closed them—there was nothing to see anyway. All he could do was press his palms against the sides of the tunnel, washed smooth by the ages, and kick on.

Two minutes. How long was that? In a place without light, without sound, without up or down, how could you measure time? Grant didn't know how long he had been there—nor how far he had come. Did it matter if you didn't know how far you had to go? At first he tried to keep count of his kicks, but he soon lost track. A slow ache crept into his lungs and his thrusts weakened. He would have to turn back soon. *Two minutes.*

The tunnel widened. The walls pulled away from Grant's reach and his last contact with the solid world disappeared. He was suspended in space—weightless, senseless, timeless. He forgot everything and became nothing. He was alone with the gods, a little fish wriggling forward, driven on by a destiny it could not understand.

A flash of pain cracked through his skull. He must have floated up and banged his head on the rock ceiling. His lungs were burning now, but when he parted his lips it was only to get a mouthful of water. There were no air pockets here. Did he even have enough in his lungs to get back?

He opened his eyes—and stared despite the stinging pain. Ahead of him the water seemed to shimmer with a golden light: the warmest, kindest light he had ever seen. He wanted to be near it; he knew that if he could only reach it everything would be all right. The pain disappeared; his body relaxed. He kicked out again, almost in a dream. The golden light was nearer now, all around him, and he was rising, rising . . .

His head broke the surface with a splash and a gasp of relief. Pain flooded back, but this time when he opened his mouth he tasted air. He gulped it down, screwing his eyes shut against the water cascading off his face. Only when his lungs were satisfied, when they no longer felt as if they were about to split apart inside him, did he wipe his eyes and open them.

The light almost burned through his eyeballs, and a hot breath singed his face. He splashed back in terror as the flames licked up in front of him and water droplets sizzled into steam. He shut his burning eyes, then cracked them open a fraction. He had come up in a pool in another small chamber, but instead of a rock face, this one was barred by a wall of fire. He gaped, amazed. The flames seemed to lick out of the rock itself, and the walls round it were black with soot, softly moulded like melted wax.

Treading water, Grant extended a toe until he found the bottom. It wasn't too deep. Still marvelling at the fire, he let himself stand—and almost immediately collapsed as a tug on his leg pulled his feet out from under him. *Marina.* He splashed wildly, scrabbling against the walls for a grip. Marina was strong—she was pulling hard, almost desperately. It was all he could do to hold on, fighting to keep himself from being dragged back into the tunnel. It felt as though his leg would be ripped off. He tried to kick off the noose but it was too tight, and there was no way he could reach it with his hands without losing his grip. All he could do was hold on and pray.

The rope went still. Grant gave it two deliberate tugs with his leg, waited a few seconds, then gave two more. A moment later he felt two tugs in reply. The rope went taut again, then started to twitch like a plucked guitar string as Marina hauled herself along it, hand over hand. Grant braced himself against the chamber to anchor her. Ever closer—then a hand wrapped itself round his calf, let go and she broached the surface like a dolphin. He put out an arm to hold her back from the flame at the far end.

She shook the water from her head and pushed back the hair that was slicked to her face.

"Careful," Grant warned. "Open your eyes slowly."

She gasped. The sound sighed round the chamber. "What is it?"

"A gas vent." Now that he'd had time to think, Grant could remember an evening by a campfire near the Zambezi, yarning and bragging with the diamond company geologists. "Methane gas escapes through holes in the rock and spontaneously ignites. No one quite knows how it works. Apparently . . ." He unbuttoned his shirt and peeled it off, rolling it into a loose bundle. With a quick movement, he breasted his way through the water and pressed the shirt into the flames. With a hiss of steam, the cave was plunged in darkness.

Grant whipped the shirt away and stepped back—straight into Marina. She cried out and grabbed him, wrapping her arms round his bare chest for balance. Her nipples pressed against his back, her sodden blouse leaving little barrier between their skins. Just at that moment he had no time to appreciate it. The flames had leaped up again, as steady and constant as a gas fire in a suburban sitting room.

Just as they had said. "It always relights itself," he marvelled.

"Is it dangerous?"

"You don't want to cover it too long in case the gas builds up." That prompted another thought. "But if it burns, it's getting air from somewhere. The water seals the way we came. There must be something behind it."

With a hint of reluctance, he pulled away from Marina's embrace, stepped forward and smothered the flame again. There was a splashing in the darkness behind him, then a spark. A new light filled the cave as Marina held her lighter aloft. By its glow, they could see a dark tunnel continuing on the far side of the gas vent.

Grant slipped the rope off his ankle and handed the end to Marina. "Wait here."

She shook her head. "You're not going down there alone."

There was no time. The smell of gas was already beginning to seep into the cave and if it caught the lighter flame they would—literally—be toast. "You have to. We can't leave the vent shut, and I'll need someone to put it out again if I come back. When I come back," he corrected himself.

Grant hauled himself out of the water, taking great care not to dislodge the shirt, and pushed forward. A second later he felt the heat on the soles of his feet as Marina whipped the shirt away. He could see the passage now. It was still as low and tight as before, but this time the air was fresher. There was the unmistakable billow of a breeze on his face. He carried on, faster, crawling over the shadow cast by the fire behind him.

The tunnel ended in another rock wall—and this time there was no pool of water at its base. He twisted his head round. The light from the gas vent barely penetrated this far down the passage, but there was still a faint glow in the air. As his eyes balanced with the gloom, he thought he could make out a dim circle of light, a halo hovering over him in the tunnel roof. He reached up a hand and felt nothing except the cool rush of air.

He felt around the rim of the hole above his head. The black basalt had been ground smooth, polished to a sheen that had not faded in thirty centuries of darkness. It was almost perfectly round, but it seemed terribly narrow. Narrower even than the slot he had squeezed through to enter the tunnel.

"Nowhere else to go," he told himself. He unbuckled his belt and slid off his trousers—if he was going to get through, there wouldn't be a fraction of an inch to spare. He sucked in his stomach and pulled himself up so that he was squatting directly under the hole. He raised his arms over his head and pressed them together, like a diver preparing to take the plunge. Then he stood.

The stone was tight as a noose. He writhed and squirmed against it, squeezing himself through inch by agonizing inch. The rock was not quite as perfectly smooth as he'd thought: against his body, each tiny ridge became a razor, scraping his bare skin raw. He gritted his teeth against the pain—at least the blood lubricated the edge of the hole a little. His shoulders were through; then his ribs, though it felt as if the breath had been squashed out of them. Now he could use his hands as well as his feet—and just as well: he needed all his strength to lever his hips through. If they could actually make it. Perhaps he would end up trapped, unable to move up or down, until the flesh rotted from his bones and the noose finally released his skeleton.

Something gave—not within him, thank God, but around him. He was through. With a final heave, he hauled himself out and emerged—naked, bloodied and wet—into the most extraordinary room he had ever seen.

12

After being squeezed in the tunnel so long, the space was vast and dizzying. He was lying on the floor of what looked like an enormous beehive: a round stone chamber whose sides slowly curved in until they met in a point high above him. Directly below it, a few yards away from where he lay, a round hole was sunk in the floor like a well. But there was no water in the bottom: this was a well of fire. Flames licked round the edges, a giant gas ring that illuminated the whole chamber with a murky orange glow. On one side, just in front of the opening Grant had crawled through, a pair of stone horns stood atop a monolithic stone altar.

Grant moved round the walls. The decoration was almost unimaginably intricate, bands of concentric friezes bordered with a menagerie of birds and animals all carved into the stone. They were caked with soot, but the underlying images were still clear enough. On one level Grant could make out the gnomic figures of the Kabyri, bulbous and ludicrously well-hung as they danced and revelled in the firelight. On the level above, armies marched to war and peasants gathered crops in the fields, a lost civilization immaculately preserved in stone.

"Grant?"

The voice echoed round the domed chamber, quickly overtaken by a gasp of amazement. Marina's head had popped through the hole in the floor and she was staring at her surroundings with wide eyes—that widened still further as her gaze fell on Grant. She gave a short, embarrassed laugh and looked away, blushing in the firelight. Grant realized that he was still stark naked.

"Nothing I haven't seen before," she said, trying to sound matter-of-fact and not really succeeding.

"I was waiting for the unspeakable rites to start."

"I think you're too late." She reached his bundled trousers out of the hole and tossed them across the room. "*Ela*. Cover yourself before the Kabyri get jealous."

Grant pulled them on. "I thought I told you to wait by the gas vent."

"I didn't want you disturbing the site before a proper archaeological investigation."

"It's quite a sight." He reached down to pull her through the hole, then hesitated. "Can you get back down the tunnel?"

"I hope so."

"Then you'd better fetch the others. They won't want to miss this."

To Grant's disappointment, Marina was able to squeeze through the entrance hole without having to undress. As for Reed, he almost leaped through it like a jack-in-the-box. Far from traumatising him, the ordeal of getting through the tunnel seemed to have filled him with energy. He bounded around the chamber like a boy in a toyshop, examining everything and murmuring awed exclamations under his breath. In one corner he found a pair of three-legged iron pots, their legs bent over like stalks.

There lame Hephaestus the goddess found,
Obscure in smoke, his forges flaming round,
While bathed in sweat from fire to fire he flew;
And puffing loud, the roaring billows blew.
That day no common task his labor claim'd:
Full twenty tripods for his hall he framed.

"Just as Homer described it. This must have been the first cult center, before it moved to the coast." He shook his head in wonder. "We've just been inducted into a club that hasn't had a new member in two thousand years."

"Lucky there was no one here to blackball us." Muir's head poked through the hole. Grant and Marina hauled him up.

"Obviously there were certain ritual elements missing . . ." Reed drifted away to peer at a frieze. "The tunnel we took would certainly have been the path of initiation into the cult. First of all the symbolic death in water . . ."

"It almost wasn't symbolic at all," said Grant, remembering the total emptiness in the black pool. "But I thought water was just supposed to purify you."

"To the ancients, death and purification were intimately linked. The water that cleanses your body or your soul can also wipe clean your memory. Lethe, the river of forgetfulness, was what you crossed to get into Hades. As far as the Greeks were concerned, if you forgot who you were you might as well be dead. Even today, if you think of Christian baptism, the water doesn't just cleanse you. When you're dipped in it you die to sin. Then the fire kindles new life, you squeeze through the birth canal and pop out here, naked as a baby. Pratolaos, reborn into the sacred mysteries of Hephaestus and his sons, the Kabyri."

"Fascinating," said Muir. "Now see if you can solve the mystery of that fucking meteorite."

They spread out to search the sanctuary. Grant and Marina moved around the edges, poking into every niche and shadow; Muir went the other way. Reed seemed curiously detached from the work. He had managed to bring a flashlight through the tunnel and contented himself with staring at the friezes, picking out the frozen stone figures in the beam.

"Over here."

Grant joined Muir on the far side of the room, behind the horned altar. What he had taken to be another niche was in fact a door which led on to a small side chamber. This was square and much plainer than the main dome, with only a single band of relief carved round the wall.

A flat-topped boulder—a hard, blue-tinted stone—rose knee high in the middle of the room; at the back a bowl-shaped impression about a foot wide had been bored out of the floor. Curved fragments of pottery lay all around it.

"What's this?" asked Grant. "Another shrine?"

"I think it's a primitive furnace." Marina squeezed past them and knelt beside the impression in the ground and reached in. Her hand came out black.

"I think I can guess where the meteorite went."

"Where?" Muir spun round, his eyes raking the room. But there had been no triumph in Marina's voice—only weary resignation. Grant's gaze followed hers down, to the dark jaws of the furnace that opened at her feet.

"You said that apart from the Element 61, the tests showed the meteorite was mostly iron."

A horrible thought began to grow in Grant's mind. "You said this was the Bronze Age," he objected. "I thought the Iron Age came later."

"It did." Reed had entered the room and was standing in the doorway. A distracted thought creased his brow. "It's interesting—the idea of an Iron Age originally comes from the poet Hesiod. A near-contemporary of Homer. For him it had nothing to do with technology, but with the lustre of a civilization. He thought it went the other way: from the gilded accomplishments of a golden age, down through silver and bronze, to the lumpen ugliness of iron. It's only in our scientifically minded times that we've come to see iron as progress. Harder, sharper, cheaper—much better for hammering into guns and engines and barbed wire."

"I'm sure that's fascinating, Professor." Impatience strained Muir's voice. "But could the Mycenaeans work iron?"

Reed looked surprised by the question. "Of course."

"But you said it was the Bronze Age."

"A new age doesn't begin at the stroke of midnight. Iron Age, Bronze Age, Stone Age—they're labels of convenience. The transitions between them would have been gradual and sporadic: a process of decades, perhaps centuries. And then there are the practicalities. It's my understanding that *working* iron isn't terribly difficult, just a matter of bringing it to the right temperature. *Extracting* iron from ore, that seems to have been the dicey part."

"The earliest pieces of ironworking are all meteoritic," Marina confirmed. "Axe blades, arrowheads, knives . . . In fact, the ancient Egyptian word for iron literally translates as 'metal of heaven.' They didn't know any other source."

Exhaustion overtook Grant. Outside, in the world where time had not stood still for three millennia, it must be almost midnight. He flopped down on the flat-topped boulder and stared at the ground. "So the Mycenaeans found this juicy lump of iron—mixed with Element 61—at the shrine on Crete and brought it here . . ."

". . . to melt it down." Marina's words rang in the stone chamber.

"Well of course. They'd have had to. You're probably sitting on the anvil where they hammered it out."

They all stared at Reed, thrown into confusion by his cheerful, almost excited manner.

He in turn looked utterly baffled by their gloom. "Didn't I tell you? Come and have a look."

Back in the main chamber, Reed's torch played over the stone frieze that ringed the room at about head height. The yellow beam only deepened the shadows round the carved figures, so that they seemed to leap out from their stone frames and come alive in the air.

"*Each bold figure seemed to live or die*. Do you remember the lines from the *Iliad* in Pemberton's notebook?"

"You said it came from a bit describing Hephaestus's workshop."

"Did I?" Reed sounded surprised. "Well, yes. After a fashion. It would have been more accurate to say it describes a piece of metalwork Hephaestus makes in his forge. Are you familiar with the *ecphrasis*?"

"No."

"An *ecphrasis* is where the poet breaks his narrative to give a long, minutely detailed description of some precious artifact, usually weapons or armor."

"Going off on a tangent, in other words," said Muir.

"Tangential to the story, perhaps, but integral to the poetry. Some of the most dramatic passages in all Homer are these *ecphrases*. And the longest, most magnificent of them all takes place here on Lemnos, in the workshop of Hephaestus. He forges a shield, inlaid with the most intricate decoration imaginable. A microcosm of the world—scenes of daily life and scenes of war. A cross between a Brueghel painting and the Bayeux tapestry. In the cities, men and women dance and revel, while lawyers and politicians argue in the forum. In the fields, the seasons turn: crops are sown and harvested, grapes pressed to wine. Shepherds drive their sheep to pasture. Armies invade, wars are fought. All depicted on the shield."

As Reed spoke, Grant had the extraordinary feeling of floating free of reality. The torch beam darted around the room, flashing across the frieze from panel to panel, so that for a split second each one was illuminated. The pictures ran together in his mind like the frames of a film, a panorama of the world. There they were: youths and supple maidens dancing, so lifelike they seemed to sway in the trembling torchlight. Oxen pulled plows over fields and the furrows sprouted wheat that the drovers, now armed with sickles, harvested and tied in bundles. A ribbon of men wound its way over distant hills to a great city, where two armies vied beneath the walls. Under a leafy oak tree a placid bull sat hobbled on the ground, while women plaited ribbons through his horns and men sharpened their knives.

The torch beam stopped its whirling dance and came to rest as Reed finished his description. The film was over, the cave was still again.

"I thought it was a fairy tale," Grant said at last.

"So did I. But this . . ." Reed spoke tentatively, testing each word as if he couldn't believe it would hold the weight of its implications. "This is what Homer describes. This is where he describes it."

"On a shield?"

"The shield of Achilles." He spoke the name in wonder. "I suppose it makes sense. In the Bronze Age, iron was the rarest metal there was—forty times more valuable than silver. Finding a piece as big as that meteorite would have been like finding the Koh-i-Noor diamond. They wouldn't have melted it down for pocket knives and axe heads. They would have turned it into something extraordinary—something legendary. Something the poets would sing about for generations, that even three thousand years couldn't obliterate."

Reed leaned against the altar. The stone horns that decorated it curved round him like wings.

"So where do we find it?" asked Grant.

13

"To understand this story, there are certain things you need to be aware of." Reed turned his torch back to the frieze, to the stone army under the city walls. "The Greeks who went to Troy were the cream of their age. Menelaus, king of Sparta, whose wife was Helen of Troy. Agamemnon, his brother, the high king of Mycenae. Odysseus, the strategic genius, and Ajax, as strong as an ox. But greater than any of them, the one man the Greeks couldn't do without, was Achilles.

"Now there's a common belief that the *Iliad* tells the whole story of the Trojan war: the thousand ships, the ten-year siege, the death of Achilles and the final sack of the city.' Reed pursed his lips, the weary look of a man who had spent his life in a war of attrition with ignorance. "In fact, the *Iliad* only deals with about a fortnight's worth of the war, in the last year of the siege. Agamemnon and Achilles fall out over a division of the spoils—in this case a slave woman—and Achilles goes off in a huff to let the Greek army see how well they can cope without him. Not very well, it turns out: led by Prince Hector, the Trojans take advantage of Achilles' sulk to almost wipe out the Greeks. Achilles refuses to budge, but his companion Patroclus dresses up in Achilles' armor and goes out to battle. Everyone thinks it's Achilles; the tide turns and it's all going splendidly for the Greeks, until Hector turns up and rather spoils the illusion by killing Patroclus and taking the armor for himself."

The torch beam darted on, moving round the cavern to the next panel. Now the armies opposed each other across a great river, hurling spears across it, while chariots rushed up reinforcements behind.

"This leaves Achilles in a bit of a bind. He's desperate to get revenge on Hector, but he hasn't got any armor. So his mother—the sea nymph Thetis—goes to the forge of Hephaestus on Lemnos and commissions him to produce a new set of arms and armor. The shield is undoubtedly the pièce de résistance, but there are also greaves, a breastplate and a helmet to go with it. Suitably attired, Achilles finds Hector on the field of battle, fights him in single combat and kills him. Then he lashes the corpse to his chariot and drags it around the city until the Trojan king Priam, Hector's father, comes to Achilles' tent and begs for his son's body. Achilles is so moved by the old man's grief that he at last lets go of his anger and hands over the body. End of story, and they all live happily ever after. Except, of course, that most of them don't."

"I thought Achilles was killed by a poison arrow in his heel."

"Actually," said Reed, "that's a common misconception. Achilles' heel is something of a myth."

"It's all fucking myth," said Muir disparagingly.

Reed looked irritated. "I'm coming to that. What I was trying to explain is that Achilles' heel isn't part of the original legend. There's nothing in any of the earliest sources to say he was struck in the heel, or even that he was especially vulnerable there. It doesn't appear in any written source until the first century AD—seven or eight hundred years after Homer. Homer never tells the story of Achilles' death. The *Iliad* ends before he dies and the *Odyssey* picks up the story some time afterward."

"Well, if Homer doesn't talk about it, who does?"

Reed leaned forward. "By the end of the Classical period Homer had become the absolute bedrock of Greek civilization. His poems were like the Bible, Shakespeare and King Arthur all rolled into one. But Homer didn't invent the stories—he adapted them for his poetry. The tales of Troy already existed, in overlapping and sometimes contradictory versions, oral poems and folk tales, myths and legends. At first, his interpretation would have just been one version of many. Gradually it became the preferred version, then the authoritative one. That was the power of his poetry.

"But the rest of the tradition survived too: Homer's poems wouldn't make sense if it didn't. There's a vast literature from other poets, authors and playwrights who took the Trojan war as their theme: Sophocles, Aeschylus, Virgil—to say nothing of Shakespeare, Tennyson, Chaucer . . . The list is literally endless because it's still being written, more than two and a half thousand years after Homer first put pen to paper."

"So what did happen to Achilles?"

"The tradition records that he was killed by Paris—possibly shot in the leg by an arrow—while fighting at the gates of Troy. According to a précis in the *Odyssey*, the Greeks then cremated him and buried his ashes in a golden urn, near the mouth of the Dardanelles."

> *Now all the sons of warlike Greece surround*
> *Thy destined tomb and cast a mighty mound;*
> *High on the shore the growing hill we raise,*
> *That wide the extended Hellespont surveys;*
> *Where all, from age to age, who pass the coast,*
> *May point Achilles' tomb, and hail the mighty ghost.*

Grant looked up. "Is that true? Is the tomb still there?"

"There are tumuli on the shores of the Bosphorus," Marina answered. "Archaeologists have excavated them, but never found anything significant. Certainly not a shield."

"Besides," Reed added, "cremation was an Iron Age practice. The Mycenaeans at Troy would have buried their dead in tombs. It's an anachronism in the poem."

Muir stood. "An anachronism? It's all fucking anachronistic. We're trying to find something of vital national urgency, and all you can give me is hocus-pocus and a three-thousand-year-old ghost trail. It doesn't matter a damn if Achilles was shot in the heel or the head, if he was cremated or buried. *He didn't fucking exist*."

"Someone existed." Reed's voice was unyielding. "He may not have been called Achilles, his heel probably wasn't any more vulnerable than the rest of him and I rather doubt his mother was a sea nymph—but *someone* existed. If the smiths on Lemnos forged that shield, someone took it. Someone extraordinary, worthy of such a priceless and holy piece of armor. Someone who would inspire stories and legends, however corrupted and confused they became. Someone whose life left an indelible mark on history."

"*History*? I thought we were talking about literature. Myth."

"A hundred years ago everyone thought the Trojan war was pure myth, total invention. Then Schliemann started digging. No trial and error, no years of searching. He went straight to Troy and stuck his spade in. Then he went to Mycenae, Agamemnon's capital, and did exactly the same thing."

Grant stirred. "How did he know where to go?"

"Everybody knew." Reed had wandered into the center of the chamber. Light from the gas flame seemed to wrap itself round him. "That's what's so extraordinary. The knowledge was never lost. We still have guidebooks from two thousand years ago describing these places for classical tourists. What we lost was the belief—the faith that there was any truth in the stories. All Schliemann had to do was believe."

Muir ground out his cigarette on the altar and tossed it into the fire pit. "All right." His voice was hard with mocking disbelief. "So what do you want me to do? Go to Turkey and dig up every mound of earth to see if there's a shield inside?"

"There's no need for that." Reed's voice was milder now. "If the stories are true, the shield won't be there."

"You said Achilles was buried at Troy."

"He was. But his armor wasn't buried with him. It was too valuable. The Greeks held a contest to see who should inherit it and Odysseus won."

"Jesus Christ—doesn't this end? What did he do with it?"

"No one knows. That's where the shield of Achilles drops out of legend completely. Odysseus doesn't, of course—his ten-year journey home to Ithaca is the subject of the *Odyssey*. But as far as I know, there's never any mention of Achilles' armor in the *Odyssey* except a brief allusion to Odysseus having won it. Now Odysseus was shipwrecked so many times on his voyage that it's inconceivable it made it home with him."

Muir opened his ivory cigarette case; his fingers scrabbled inside, but it was empty. He looked up and his eyes met Reed's. "Let's cut through all this crap and mumbo-jumbo. Do you have any idea where we can find this shield, or should I cable London and tell them the hunt's over?"

For a moment, Reed and Muir stared at each other.

"I don't know where the shield is."

The case snapped shut. Muir turned to leave.

"But I know where I'd start looking."

14

Paleo Faliro, Athens. Two days later

IT WAS a clear, bright spring morning. The lower slopes of the mountains that circled the city were green from the winter rains, and snow still glistened on their heights like marble. Grant and the others sat out on the hotel terrace by the waterfront—between the mountains and the sparkling sea, between winter and summer, between the past and . . . who knew what? Just at that moment Grant didn't care. He felt as if he'd spent the last week in darkness—midnight ferries, sea caves, claustrophobic tunnels and caverns. For now, sitting in the sunshine with a cold beer in his hand was enough.

This was a Greece he hadn't seen before—a Greece of money and middle classes, far away from the poor hamlets and fishing villages he was used to. Elegant turn-of-the-century villas lined the foreshore, while fat-trunked palms shaded the tramlines on the esplanade and slim yachts filled the moorings at the marina below the hotel. Here, you could almost forget the civil war that still ravaged the country.

Across the table, Reed sipped his cup of tea.

"We need to go back to the beginning." He unwrapped the clay tablet and laid it in the middle of the table. After all their adventures, Grant was amazed it was still in one piece. "It all seems to have started when Pemberton found this. I think the first question has to be: where did it come from?"

Marina put down her drink and picked up the tablet, running her finger over the angular characters like braille. "He might have found it in Crete, but I think it was here. It was when he returned from his last trip to Athens that he seemed to get excited."

"Quite so." There was just a hint of impatience in Reed's voice. "But where did it come from in the first place? It must have been dug up somewhere. These Linear B tablets have been found all over Crete and at Mycenaean sites on the mainland, but so far as I'm aware they've never turned up in Athens. I think we can discount the possibility that Pemberton stole it from a museum. Either someone must have given it to him, or he stumbled across it in one of the antiquities shops here. Now—"

He broke off with a vexed frown. The roar of propellers drowned out his words as a small floatplane swooped overhead. It dropped toward the sea, bounced once and skidded across the waves in a fountain of spray. Probably some shipowning heir trying to impress a girl, Grant thought.

"Does this really matter?" Muir blew smoke through his nostrils. "We've got the tablet, that's what counts. If you could read the fucking writing, maybe it would be worth something."

"If you'd left me alone in Oxford I might have made some progress. Rather than dragging me here to be shot at, almost kidnapped and dragged from one end of the Aegean to the other." Reed stared over the rim of the teacup. Down in the bay, the floatplane was taxiing toward the dock. "But the point I was trying to put to you is that even if I had deciphered the Linear B—and even if it does point the way to the shield—it would only take us so far." He held up the tablet and stroked a finger along the ragged edge where it had been snapped. "Halfway, give or take."

"You mean there's more of it?" Muir slammed his cup down on the table. Tea slopped into the saucer. "How the hell are we going to find that?"

"By finding out where this one came from." Reed put down the tablet and hid it under his napkin to avoid the stares of the other guests. "A piece this significant hasn't been lost in someone's attic for a hundred years. My guess is it must have been excavated shortly before Pemberton found it, just before the war. With all the upheaval then, it would hardly be surprising if it had escaped notice—or made its way on to the black market."

Grant frowned. "It could still have been found by accident. A farmer plowing his field or something. Grave robbers, maybe."

"Unlikely. Of all the Linear B tablets that have come to light, I don't think any were turned up by accident. Whatever the tablets say, they were pretty exclusive playthings. They've only ever been found in palace complexes—and those take some effort to excavate." Reed turned to Marina. "I'd be grateful if you would go to the Ministry of Culture. Find out who was issued archaeological permits in 1940 and 1941. Half the world was at war at the time, so there can't have been many."

He stood, picking up the tablet still wrapped in the napkin.

"Where are you going with that?" Muir asked suspiciously.

"To my room, and then to the library."

"I'll go with you." Marina jumped up, and she and Reed disappeared into the hotel. Grant swilled the last of his beer round the glass and drained it. Across the table, Muir was peering over his shoulder, watching the floatplane moor at the dock. A tall man in white trousers and a white open-necked shirt jumped down from the cabin and started talking animatedly with the marina attendants.

"You'd better go with Reed." Muir turned back. "Athens must be crawling with Reds. Don't want our professor falling into the wrong hands. And buy yourself a suit. You look like bloody Gunga Din at the moment."

Grant ignored the insult. "Do you really think he's up to it? Breaking the Linear B?"

Muir shot Grant a crooked look, weighing his words carefully. "He did some work on codes for us during the war. That's where I came across him. That's confidential, by the way. He may seem as though he's wandered out of Gilbert and Sullivan, but he's absolutely fucking brilliant. He broke the Hungarian foreign office cipher in three days flat."

"Was that a difficult code?"

Muir gave a sardonic laugh. "I've no idea. The point is he doesn't speak Hungarian."

Grant caught up with Reed and Marina outside the hotel, and together they took the tram into the center of Athens. Marina had swapped her army fatigues for a simple blue dress, drawn in at the waist. She sat primly with her knees pressed together, her hair pinned back and her bag in her lap: just another young woman on her way to the shops or the pictures. Reed stared out of the window at the passing city. An open lorry full of armed soldiers pulled past them; grim-faced women pulled their children back from the road. In the rest of Europe the war might be over, but in Greece the quiet savagery of a civil war smoldered on.

"Who was Schliemann?" Grant asked, remembering something Reed had said in the cave.

Reed looked up, surprised. "Schliemann? An archaeologist. *The* archaeologist, really. He practically invented the discipline—made it up as he went along."

Marina pursed her lips. "That's not all he made up."

"I think what Marina is referring to is his, um, enthusiasm. Schliemann, as I said, was a great believer in the truth of Homer. A romantic. He was also a compulsive showman. It's possible that he occasionally let his preconceptions and his sense of theater dictate the presentation of what he discovered."

"There were rumors that half the treasures he found he'd planted himself," Marina sniffed.

Reed waved a hand airily. "Details. He didn't plant the Cyclopean walls of Troy, or the Lion Gate at Mycenae. You can disapprove of his methods and dispute his interpretation, but you can't deny his achievement. He rescued the Trojan war from the realm of myth and planted it firmly in the real world."

Grant stared at him. "But if Schliemann proved the stories were true, why did you keep insisting they were fairy tales?"

Reed gave an embarrassed smile. "My faith wasn't as strong as

Schliemann's. Or rather, I was an apostate." A faraway look came into his eyes. "I saw him once. I was ten years old. He gave a public lecture at the Royal Geographic Society; my father took me. We went up on the train and he bought me a lemon ice at Paddington. Funny what you remember. Anyway, Schliemann made an extraordinary impression. Bounded in wearing his frock coat and German accent like some combination of Allan Quatermain and Captain Nemo. The hour passed like a dream, like a summer afternoon leafing through your favorite books and reading all the most exciting bits. Except this time, it was *all true*. That night, I decided I wanted to be like Schliemann."

"What happened?"

"I grew up." A wistful sigh. "I went to Oxford—and stayed there. It seemed the best place for a young man with a passion for the Classics. Instead, it slowly leeched the passion out of me. You can't spend a lifetime just basking in the magnificent glow you get from Homer. You have to study, analyze, explain. And the closer you look, the further away you get. That first emotional burst gets broken down into eminently rational components, which get broken down again and again. It's like dissecting the family dog to find out why you love him so much. By the time you're finished, it's gone." Reed wiped his face with his handkerchief. The crowded tram was warm and sweat beaded on his forehead. "Besides, even with everything Schliemann found, it's still an enormous leap from a couple of ruined hill forts, however evocative, to saying that Homer got it all right. Respectable academics don't stand for that sort of thing. We're professional skeptics. If you do believe, you keep it a rather guilty secret. In time, it becomes an embarrassment, then a joke. Eventually you can't remember what it was you ever saw in it."

"But you changed your mind."

"In the cave. Seeing all those carvings, exactly as Homer described them . . ." Reed shook his head in wonder. "I remembered what inspired me that night in Kensington. It wasn't the poetry—that came later. It wasn't even the stories, exciting though they were. It was the possibility, the hope, that buried under all that scholarship and legend there might be something real. Something true." He gave a bashful smile. "I started to believe again. Just like Schliemann—or Evans. Speaking of whom . . ."

He jumped up and pulled the bell cord. The tram lumbered to a standstill. Grant rose, but Marina stayed seated.

"Not my stop. I'll see you back at the hotel."

"Keep your eyes open."

She lifted her handbag a little. It looked surprisingly heavy—more than the usual lipstick and powder. "I can take care of myself."

Grant and Reed stepped off and found themselves at the gates of a large white neoclassical building, set back from the street in spacious grounds and surrounded by a high stone wall. A brass plate on the gatepost announced THE BRITISH SCHOOL AT ATHENS.

"The place looks half asleep. They might as well have hung out a *Do Not Disturb* sign."

"Most of the staff are probably away for the Easter holidays. But with any luck . . ." Reed pumped the doorbell enthusiastically, until a young woman in a gray jersey dress emerged from the house. She eyed them with suspicion—Reed in his outmoded suit and floppy sunhat, Grant in his boots and shirtsleeves—but Reed's name seemed to have some talismanic power. The mere sound of it turned her hostility into something more like starstruck awe. She led them through the gate and up a hill, through a garden of olive trees, pines, cypresses and oleanders, into the cool of a high-ceilinged hallway.

"I'm afraid the Director is away today, or he would have come to meet you himself. He'd be so honored by your visit, Professor Reed. If you could just sign in the visitors' book." She slid the book across the table and held out a pen. Reed signed with a flourish and passed the pen to Grant.

"Do all visitors have to sign in here?" Grant scribbled something meaningless and illegible under Reed's name, a small piece of subterfuge that had become habit.

"Of course. Even our most esteemed guests." She flashed Reed an apologetic smile.

"Do you mind if I have a look?"

Grant leafed back through the book. It looked like an artifact in its own right, a relic of the past that had been dusted off and propped back on its shelf. Page after page, row after row of names and dates whose regular spacing gave no hint of the erratic passages of time they represented. Sometimes there were a dozen or more on the same date; more often days or even whole weeks passed without the book being disturbed. Then, just once, something different: two neat ruled lines like a scar across the page, dividing April 1941 from January 1945. *Four years*, Grant thought. Four years when the world had done its best to tear itself apart. All in the white space between two parallel lines.

On the page before the divide, Grant found what he was looking for. He turned the book to show Reed. "Pemberton was here: 21 March 1941."

"You knew John Pemberton?"

"We met once. Were you here then?"

She shook her head. "Most of us have only been here since the war."

Grant thought for a moment. "You said this place funded Pemberton's digs on Crete. Would you have records of his expenses?"

The girl looked taken aback at the request. She glanced uncertainly at Reed, who gave a reassuring nod. "I can look for you. It may take a little time. If the records are anywhere, they're probably in the cellar."

"We'll be in the library."

Grant had never been much of a man for libraries; Reed was in his element. While Grant sat by the window and skimmed through a three-week-old copy of *The Times*, Reed flitted among the shelves, gathering books and piling them on the table like a bird making its nest. Grant glanced at the gold lettering on the spines: *Through Basque to Minoan*; *A Clue to the Cretan Scripts*; *The Palace of Minos* by A. E. Evans, in four table-bending volumes. Grant's heart sank. There were more books there than you could get through in a year.

"Are you really going to read all of them?"

Reed's head popped up from behind a particularly forbidding volume. "Maybe. People have been trying for fifty years to crack this particular riddle. In some respects, it makes Ultra look like a Bank Holiday crossword."

"Ultra?"

Reed blushed to the roots of his snowy hair. Mumbling something about Muir, he sank back behind the safe rampart of books. Grant reopened his newspaper.

A knock at the door provided a welcome interruption. It was the girl, clutching two dog-eared cardboard folders tied together with string. She put them on the table in front of Grant. The delicate scent of rose-water and lilies wafted down as she reached over him.

"These are the Knossos accounts for the first months of 1941, before the staff evacuated. Are you interested in anything in particular?"

"I want to know if Pemberton bought anything on his last visit to Athens."

She sat down beside him and turned through the ledger. Across the table, Reed hummed and sucked the end of his pencil.

"There isn't much for that period. The digging season hadn't started." She gave him a sideways glance, obviously uncertain how much he knew about archaeology. "To be honest, I don't quite know why he stayed on in Crete."

You'd be amazed, Grant thought. He limited himself to a noncommittal grunt.

"Here's something." The sleeve of her dress brushed his arm as she held down the page. "Fifty pounds on 21 March. All it says is 'Museum Acquisition.' Signed off by the Director."

"Does it say where he got it?"

She untied the second file and turned out a jumble of ticket stubs, coupons, requisition forms and receipts. "It's a bit of a mess. They can't have had time to file it before the Germans came." She shuffled the papers in her hands and started dealing them out like a croupier. Despite her schoolmarmish appearance, her nails were painted a vivid red. "No—no—no . . . What's this?"

She laid a crisp sheet of cream notepaper on top of the pile. The receipt had been written out in thick blue ink, copied in both English and Greek. *Late Minoan clay tablet (partial), uncertain provenance. 50*

British Pounds. At the top of the page, the letterhead was engraved in flamboyant curlicues: *Elias Molho, Dealer in Rare Antiquities*. There was an address below.

"He didn't get that from a flea market." Grant felt the ridged paper between his finger and thumb. "Do you know where this address is?"

Grant left Reed behind his barricade of books and took a bus downtown. He didn't have a map, but he had spent enough time in Greece to have picked up the local custom of just asking at every news-stand and kiosk. Gradually the answers that came back changed from occasional nods to a steady pulse of recognition, a sort of human sonar. Soon enough, it guided him to a quiet, gently dilapidated street lined with shops that had seen better days. Many of the buildings were still pocked with bullet holes, though whether Fascist or Communist, domestic or foreign, Grant couldn't tell. Even the locals had probably lost track. A few children kicked a football against a plane tree at the far end of the street and a scrawny ginger kitten chased its tail on the steps of a defunct bakery. Otherwise it was deserted.

Grant found the address on the paper—number twenty-three. Elias Molho, Dealer in Rare Antiquities was still there, but only in the memory of faded letters above the doorway that no one had bothered to paint out. The shop itself had become a tailor's. Grant groaned.

He heard the slap of running footsteps behind him. He turned, and saw a man sprinting down the empty street toward him. Two things about him caught Grant's eye: first that he had no shoes on and second that he was carrying what looked like a bottle of vodka with a rag trailing out of its neck. Grant went for the Webley, but the man barely noticed Grant. He ran straight past him and kept going.

The children, who only a moment earlier had been happily kicking their football, had suddenly vanished. The only men in the street were the fugitive and Grant. Grant didn't know who he was or why he was running, but he had seen enough similar scenes in the war to know that trouble wouldn't be far behind. He ran up the steps and stepped smartly into the tailor's shop, just as an American jeep driven by Greek soldiers veered round the corner.

A stooped old man looked up from his newspaper as Grant walked in. Racks of suit jackets and flannel trousers gathered dust against the walls. The jeep roared past. "I'm looking for Mr. Molho," he said in Greek.

The old man gave him a long, penetrating stare.

"Mr. Molho is not here." He spoke slowly, pronouncing every word. It might just have been his age, but there was a light in his walnut-brown eyes that made Grant suspect there was plenty of life left in him. In the distance he heard the screech of tires, then shouts and a fusillade of shots.

"Do you know where he went?"

"Away." The old man picked up a measuring tape and a chalk disc, and advanced from behind his counter. "Perhaps you want a suit?" His look said Grant could use one.

"Where did he go?" He edged behind a display table that held a tray full of ties. "I need to find him."

"He went away," the tailor insisted. "In the war. Away."

He flapped the tape measure at Grant, who knew when he was beaten.

"If he does come back, give him this." There was a pad on the counter. Grant took a pencil and quickly wrote out his name and the address of the hotel in Greek capitals. He thrust it at the tailor, who recoiled and stared at the floor. His nervous hands had twisted the measuring tape into a knotted tangle.

"You are not understanding. He will not come back. He was *Evraios*. A Jew. He does not come back."

"A fucking dead end. Literally." Muir speared a piece of lamb with his fork. Blood and fat dribbled out of the meat. The hotel restaurant was virtually empty. Grant, Reed, Marina and Muir sat in majesty in the center of the grand dining room, heavily outnumbered by the sullen staff who loitered by the kitchen doors, gossiping and smoking.

"She had more luck." Muir jabbed his knife across the table at Marina. "Flashed her tits at the Minister and found out all sorts of things."

Marina shot him a look of barely controlled disgust and played with the clasp of her handbag. "There were only four archaeologists issued permits for Minoan or Mycenaean sites in the winter of 1941. One was Pemberton . . ."

"We know that," Muir interrupted through a mouthful of lamb.

"Two others were Swiss carrying out secondary excavations at Orchomenos. The fourth was a German, Dr. Klaus Belzig, looking at a new site in Cephalonia."

"Belzig?" Grant shared a look with Marina.

"You know him?" said Muir.

"He was on Crete in the war, looking for Pemberton's journal. Some of the things he did . . ."

"Sounds like our man. But what the hell was a Kraut doing in Greece before the war?"

"The government was doing everything it could to avoid invasion, right up to the last minute. They didn't want to give the Germans any excuse."

"And he was digging in Cephalonia, you said?" Reed looked up from the soggy mass of wild spinach on his plate. "Cephalonia," he repeated, as if the name held some secret meaning. "Remarkable."

Muir swung round to Reed. "What's so bloody marvellous about Cephalonia?"

"Cephalonia is the main island in the group that includes Ithaca. The home of Odysseus. If he took the armor . . ."

"Can we stop chasing fairy tales? If this armor exists, we're not going to find it guarded by a one-eyed giant and a pair of singing mermaids. How did you get on with the writing on the tablet?"

Reed stared at his plate and toyed with the tendrils of spinach. When he looked up, his eyes were clear as the sky. "I made some progress."

"How long until you crack it?"

Reed gave a short laugh, so condescending it verged on outright pity. "Some of the best minds in the business have been trying for half a century. It's going to take me more than an afternoon. I haven't even got the symbols yet."

"What do you mean?" asked Grant.

Reed pushed away his plate and leaned back in his chair. "If you think about it, all writing is a form of code. The writer takes language and converts it into visual symbols, which the trained eye then converts back into the words they spell out. Modern cryptography is all about transforming it—usually mathematically—to such an extent that only someone with a pre-arranged key can transform it back. Now, normal written languages have a great many recurring patterns. Common letters, common combinations of letters, common sequences of words. Given enough text to work from, a straight substitution cipher—one where each letter is always encoded by the same other letter or symbol—can always be broken if you know the patterns of the original language. So modern cryptographers spend a great deal of effort, time and ingenuity turning sequences of letters—i.e. sentences—into strings of numbers so convoluted as to seem almost completely random."

"You seem to know a lot about it," said Marina.

"I've dabbled." A dangerous glance from Muir discouraged Reed from being any more forthcoming. "The problems that confront us with the tablet are very different. We can assume that the men who wrote the tablets weren't trying to disguise what they wrote. On the contrary, they probably wanted it to be as plain as possible. But three thousand years later, we've lost not only the key to the code, but also any knowledge of the language that's been encoded. There are two ways of approaching it. You could start by looking at the symbols—or you could attempt to guess the underlying language, and then work out how the symbols represent it."

"But these tablets are over three thousand years old," Grant objected. "How would we know what they spoke?"

"We wouldn't. But that hasn't stopped scholars trying to fit other languages—or their hypothetical antecedents—to the pattern of Linear B. They've proposed everything: Hittite, Basque, archaic Greek, proto-Indian, eteo-Cypriot, Etruscan—which is particularly fanciful, as no one's managed to translate *that* yet. Most of it's a load of nonsense, a rather hopeless blend of tenuous coincidence and willful optimism."

"Sounds like another dead end."

"I agree. So rather than go straight for the language, we attack the symbols. We try to discover their patterns, their internal logic and the rules that govern them, to see what we can learn about the underlying language. The problem is, we don't even know how many symbols we're dealing with."

"Presumably they're all written out on the tablet," Muir said acidly.

Reed raised an eyebrow, a mild gesture that had driven many an undergraduate to despair. "Are they?" He pulled a fountain pen from his jacket pocket and drew a cursive letter on the tablecloth, oblivious to the waiters' horrified stares. "Which letter is that?"

"A '*g*,'" said Grant.

"A '*y*,'" said Muir.

"A '*P*,'" said Marina, who was sitting across the table from Reed and reading it upside-down.

Reed settled back with a mysterious air of contentment. "Is it? Or is it a '*j*' or an '*f*'? Or '*if*'? Or '*of*'? Or maybe Miss Papagiannopoulou is reading it the right way up and it's '*Pn*' or '*Pr.*' Or perhaps it's just a slip of the pen. The Minoans and Mycenaeans didn't set their alphabet in typefaces. They scratched it into wet clay with reeds and sticks—possibly in a hurry, or balancing the tablet on their knees. Even in their perfect forms, lots of the symbols seem to be extremely similar. Judging how much of the difference is genuine and how much is just variation in handwriting requires the wisdom of Solomon. And that's just to get to the starting gate."

A glum silence fell over the table. Grant picked at his food, while Muir watched a long finger of ash droop from his cigarette.

"Did I miss anything?"

The dining room's double doors burst open as if blown in by a gale. A tall, broad-shouldered man was pushing through the field of empty tables toward them. There was something drearily wholesome about him: the tennis shoes; the adolescent haircut; the white trousers and white open-necked shirt, as crisply pressed as his smile. Even if you hadn't heard the accent, there would still only be one word to describe him: American. If he noticed the four astonished pairs of eyes staring at him, his beaming face showed no awareness.

"Jackson," he introduced himself. "Marty Jackson." He pumped Marina's hand, then turned to Reed. "Let me guess: Professor Reed. I've read all about your books. And you must be Sam."

He grabbed a chair from the neighboring table, pirouetted it round and squeezed himself in between Marina and Grant.

Grant shot Muir a quizzical look. "Did we make the papers?"

Jackson waved a waiter over and ordered a beer. "Never get it cold enough in this damn country," he groused good-naturedly. "Still, better than the wine. I hear they make it out of pine cones. You believe that?"

"Mr. Jackson is attached to the Allied Military Mission," said Muir. It seemed an utterly inadequate explanation. "He flew in this morning."

"Holding the line against the Commies. You hear what Truman said the other week? 'We must assist free peoples to work out their own destinies in their own way.' That's what I'm here to do."

"Are you army?"

"Not exactly." Just for a second the bonhomie vanished, and Grant glimpsed something sharp and hard behind the floppy grin. Then the smile was back. "But I guess we're all on the same team, huh?"

"Mr. Jackson . . ."

"Call me Marty."

Muir winced. ". . . has been liaising with us in the search for Element 61."

"I hear you've been doing some great things." He leaned forward earnestly, resting his elbows on the table. "That cave on Lemnos—just incredible. I wish I'd been there."

Reed murmured something that sounded like a mutual sentiment.

"But now we've got to shift this thing up a gear. Intelligence says the Reds are all over it like a kike in a coin shop. They put one of their biggest guns on it—Colonel Kurchosov." He took a photograph from his shirt pocket and laid it on the table. It must have been snatched surreptitiously: blurred and underexposed, there was little to see besides a pair of narrow cheekbones, a thin moustache and eyes that almost vanished in the shadow of his peaked cap. It took a moment for Grant to realize that one eye was actually missing, covered by a black eyepatch. "This is the only picture we got, but we've heard plenty. He made his name at Stalingrad—not fighting the Nazis, shooting deserters. Guess the Sovs saw something they liked: the folks at Langley reckon he's Uncle Joe's golden boy."

Grant eyed the picture. "I think we ran into some of his friends on Lemnos."

"Muir said. So we gotta get to this thing before they do."

"Well, we have the tablet. That seems to be the best lead. However, the professor was just explaining how much work there is still to do before we can read it."

"Anything I can do to help, just let me know."

Reed looked startled by the offer, though it seemed genuine.

"Meanwhile, we think we've traced the tablet to a site on Cephalonia."

"Great. We'll check that out first thing tomorrow. I got a plane." He said it as casually as if he was talking about a pair of shoes. "Sam, I hear you're a good man to have around. You come with me."

Grant prickled; he felt an instinctive urge to refuse, but swallowed his objection. There was no point making an enemy of Jackson yet.

Jackson turned to Reed. "Meanwhile, you get back in that library and keep on with that tablet." He glanced at Marina. "You too, honey. And Muir can stay to watch your backs."

He looked around the table, fixing each of them with a serious stare. "I can't tell you how important this is."

15

Cephalonia, Ionian Sea

The plane kissed the sea, settled and glided smoothly toward the beach. When the water beneath was barely two feet deep, Jackson cut the engines and let the waves wash them the last few yards. Grant leaped down from the cabin and splashed ashore, heaving on the plane's strut to pull it up the beach. When it was secure, he pulled out the map they had bought that morning in Athens and studied it. "According to the application Belzig filed at the Ministry, the site should be somewhere up there." He pointed north, to a rocky hill that crowned the flat coastal plain.

"Looks like a nice spot."

"For an ambush," said Grant sourly. Bright sunshine and sea air couldn't lift him from his mood. He'd distrusted Jackson from the start and two hours in the plane enduring the American's cheerful banalities hadn't mellowed his feelings

"We can handle it." Jackson swung the leather rucksack off his shoulder and pulled out a Colt pistol. Jackson didn't hear him. "What are we expecting to find here, anyway?"

Grant shrugged. " 'Mycenaean substructures,' according to Belzig's permit application. Reed thinks we're looking for the palace of Odysseus."

"Odysseus? His palace was on Ithaca." He saw Grant's surprise. "What? Didn't you ever read the *Odyssey* in college?"

"No."

"Great book. But I guess what the professor says goes. He's a real Einstein, huh?"

Grant gave a razor-thin smile. "I guess."

They found a causeway that led across the marshy ground behind the beach and followed it. The ground grew firmer, rising toward a valley that divided the hill from the ridge to the west. Where the path forked they turned left and gradually wound their way up an ever-steepening slope until it came out on a wooded summit. A steady breeze blew through the trees; looking back, Grant could see the floatplane on the beach, shining like a mirror in the sun, and the arms of the bay curving out around it.

They spread apart, picking their way between the trees. The air was warm, even in the shade, but Grant was on edge. Though he was supposed to be watching the ground for signs it had been disturbed, he kept on glancing around. Away to his right, Jackson was stamping and crashing through the undergrowth like a boar. It was impossible to hear anything else, and that only made him more nervous. He scanned his surroundings.

Hello. The trees almost hid it, but away to his left he could see flashes of what looked like a painted wall. He forgot his fears and struck off down the slope toward it.

The trees thinned and Grant came out in a tight clearing. It looked like a giant molefield: mounds of earth were heaped all around it, though they must have lain untouched for years. Weeds and wildflowers covered their slopes; one even had a sapling sprouting out at the top. A lopsided wooden shack stood at the edge of the clearing, its door hanging open.

"Over here." His voice sounded uncomfortably loud among the deadening trees. He wondered who else could hear it. *Hardly matters*, he thought: they'd certainly have heard Jackson.

The American blundered into the clearing, snapping off three low-hanging branches on his way. He must have been feeling jumpy too: as he emerged from the undergrowth, Grant saw him slip the Colt into his trouser pocket. It bulged suggestively.

He peered inside the empty shed. "Looks like someone got here before us."

"The villagers probably broke in to get at the tools."

"Geez." Jackson shook his head in disgust. "No wonder the Reds do so well here."

"They're starving," said Grant bluntly. "They haven't had food for six years. And now they've become an international football, kicked from one country to the next. They're just desperate to survive. *That's* why the Communists do so well. They're the only ones who offer them hope."

Jackson looked at him incredulously. "Are you out of your mind? You can't say that kind of thing. After what happened on Lemnos, you gotta think the Reds are already on to us."

"They certainly have a knack of turning up . . ."

Grant spun round, the Webley suddenly in his hand. But he was too late. Across the clearing, a single eye squinted at him down the sights of a gun.

Reed and Marina sat facing each other at the long table in the library, divided by a rampart of books. Rumpled sheets of paper littered Reed's side of the table: half-filled grids, lists, diagrams, crossings-out and what looked like penmanship exercises. Opposite, Marina contented herself with a solitary book, a jotting pad and a sharp pencil. In contrast to Reed, her paper was almost empty.

She gave a sigh—the sort that invites an enquiry. Across the table, the white thatch of hair stayed bowed over its work. A nib scratched furiously on paper. "It's such a mess," she said, choosing a more direct approach.

Reed's horn-rimmed spectacles appeared over the books. "I'm sorry?" He looked startled—though whether by some discovery he'd just made, or simply at being reminded she was still there she couldn't tell.

"I've been looking at the *Odyssey* again—to see if I can find any clues about what Odysseus might have done with the shield."

"Explorers and philologists have been trying to map Odysseus's wanderings for centuries," said Reed. "It can't be done."

Her face fell. "Why not?"

Reed capped his pen and moved aside a volume of *The Palace of Minos* that was obstructing the view between them. Absent-mindedly, he pushed his glasses up to the bridge of his nose. "Who do you think wrote the *Iliad* and the *Odyssey*?"

She laughed. "If you go to school in Greece, you know there's only one answer to that: Homer. Pemberton used to tease me for thinking so. He said it was a trick question, that nobody wrote the poems. He said they were the products of centuries of oral tradition, handed down and adapted from one generation of poets to the next." A sadness crept into her voice. "He said that looking for what was original in the final poems was as hopeless as peering at a baby's face and trying to see the features of his great-great-great-great-grandfather."

"Pemberton had his opinions. I disagreed. I don't think a committee of poets could have come up with those poems. I think it would have needed a single mind, a single vision, to create something with such cohesive brilliance. But there's no doubt that the poet—or poets: I'm not saying that the *Iliad* and the *Odyssey* were necessarily written by the same chap—had a lot to work with. A treasury of myths, genealogies, folk tales, memories and traditions. Some of the elements in the poems are almost uncannily accurate—rivers that Homer could never have seen because they'd silted up by his day; types of arms and armor that had been out of use for half a millennium when he wrote. You've seen the boar's tusk helmet that Schliemann excavated at Mycenae? Perfectly described by Homer."

He must have noticed her attention wandering; he shook his head and straightened his tie. "I'm sorry. The point is, with regard to the *Odyssey*, that the poet had a number of different traditions to draw on."

"Well, he seems to have used them all—and mixed them up completely. In some parts of the *Odyssey* Odysseus seems to be sailing around the Western Mediterranean; in other parts he's somewhere near Egypt; and books ten to twelve are filled with symbolic elements—clashing rocks, sirens, the islands of the sun—which are usually associated with the Black Sea region. Which is ridiculous! How can he expect us to believe that Odysseus—the cleverest of the Greeks, after all—would sail east into the Black Sea if he was trying to get home to Ithaca?" She sounded personally affronted by the idea.

"That's probably why Homer is so vague about it. After all, it's not as though he's got no sense of geography. He can be as precise as the Ordnance Survey when he wants to. He's stuck all these different stories together and he's trying to paper over the cracks."

Marina sighed. "As if we needed someone to make things more obscure . . ."

They both looked up as the door banged open. Muir strode in. "Any progress?"

Reed scratched a bushy eyebrow. "Marina and I were just discussing the many facets of Homer."

"Jesus Christ." Muir sank into a wooden chair. "Can't I leave you to get on with things? You're not going to find the answers in fucking poetry. Not unless Homer wrote a long-lost sequel explaining where this shield was buried. Preferably with a map."

He pushed back his chair and rested his injured leg on the table. "I cabled London about our friend Dr. Belzig—the German archaeologist—to see if he was known to us. Turned out they've got a file on him as fat as your cock. He was a paid-up member of the master race—one of Hitler's pet boffins, sent out to prove their crackpot theories. Did some work on the Cairo excavations in 1938, sniffed around Sparta the following year, then took himself to Cephalonia in the autumn of 1940. Spent the war on Crete. Numerous allegations of him using slave labor on his excavations there—locals compared him unfavorably to the Gestapo." He glanced at Marina. "As you know. Shame we didn't get our hands on him."

"What happened?"

"Saw the writing on the wall in 1944 and fled to Berlin. Perhaps he thought his beloved Führer would save him. Wrongly, it turned out—just meant that the Russians nabbed him instead of us. London says he was last heard of heading east on a very crowded train to Siberia."

"Do you think he told the Russians about the tablets?"

"If they thought to ask him. Based on recent events, I'd say they probably did. Which is why I'd be grateful if you stopped playing around with poetry and concentrated on translating that fucking tablet."

He glared at Reed—a wasted effort. All through the conversation Reed had been staring at the page in front of him as if hypnotized by it. Now he blinked twice and looked up, a puzzled smile on his face. "I'm sorry?" He paused, mistaking Muir's silence for a sign that a question had been asked. "I was just wondering if this library had a *Chrestomathy*."

Grant stared down the barrel of the gun. One eye squinted back, just about all he could see of a face almost completely buried in a thick black beard. In his flat cap, serge trousers and woollen waistcoat, he reminded Grant of the gamekeepers who had patrolled the woods on the local estate during his childhood. Now, once again, he'd been caught poaching.

"*Pios einai?*" the man growled. Then, in heavily accented German: "*Wer sind Sie?*"

"Grant." Moving very slowly and smiling all the way, he holstered the Webley. The rifle followed every movement. In Greek, he said, "We are looking for the . . ." He paused. What were they looking for? Watching the man with the gun, he could see that every second's delay only made him twitchier. ". . . the diggings."

Something rustled in the trees. Grant tensed—how many more were there? From the corner of his eye he saw Jackson's hand creeping toward his pocket. But the Greek had noticed it too. The gun swung round and the finger tightened on the trigger. Jackson let his hand drop back against his side.

The noise in the thicket grew louder. Something was moving behind the bushes. Grant tensed.

With a snuffle and a grunt, an enormous pig pushed through the branches, shuffled down the slope and began rootling around the base of one of the hillocks. Grant and Jackson stared in amazement.

"Eumaios," said the Greek, pointing to the pig. "I bring him to eat acorns."

"What's he saying?" Jackson demanded. His arm was tensed, as if an invisible piece of elastic was drawing his hand toward his gun.

"He's just feeding his pig. Pigs," Grant corrected himself, as four more trotted out of the forest and began combing the earth for treats. He smiled at the swineherd. "*Kali choiri*."

"What did you say?"

"I told him he had nice pigs."

The Greek lowered his gun. "*Kali*," he agreed. "The acorns make the meat very sweet."

"Someone else came to dig in this ground once. A German." Grant looked him in the eye. "Was it here?"

The swineherd gave him a crooked look. "You are German?"

"English."

"*Ela*." He leaned the gun against the tree and reached into the canvas bag slung across his shoulder. His hand emerged with a loaf and a slice of cheese wrapped in cloth. He tore off a hunk of bread and offered it to Grant.

"*Epharisto*. Thank you." Grant unclipped the canteen from his belt and offered the man a drink. Together, the three of them sat on the grassy bank and watched the pigs feeding among the heaped-up piles of earth.

"The German . . ."

"Belzig. His name was Belzig."

Grant's pulse quickened. He tried not to show it. "Did you know him?"

Again that suspicious look. "Did you?"

"No." Grant weighed his options for a second and decided to go for it. "But we have something that belonged to him. Something he found here."

The swineherd pried an acorn out of the ground and tossed it to the nearest pig, who snuffled it up enthusiastically. "Look at this," he said, sweeping his arm across the clearing. "So much history buried underneath. We spend our lives to try to dig it out, but always the present buries it again."

"What's he saying?" Jackson asked plaintively.

"Did you dig here?"

The Greek nodded. "Yes. I work for Belzig. Not a Nazi," he emphasized. He tapped the breech of his rifle. "I kill many. But before—before the war—I work for Belzig. I dig for him."

"What did you find?"

"Rocks." The swineherd pointed to the stone foundations poking out of the earth like teeth. "Old rocks."

"Pottery?"

"Pots, yes." He tore off another hunk of bread and chewed it noisily.

"And a tablet? A clay tablet, about . . ." Grant made the dimensions with his hands. "So big. With ancient writing on one side and painting on the other?"

The swineherd put down his bread and stared Grant hard in the face. "You have seen it?"

"A picture," Grant prevaricated.

"*Ela*." A faraway look came into his eyes. "We know it is special when we find it. Belzig's face, it was like a wolf. He says that nothing like it is ever found. He says it is the secret map to hidden treasure. Hah." He spat. "He should keep quiet. Socratis hear him."

"Who's Socratis?"

"My cousin. He works for Belzig also. One night he goes into Belzig's tent and steals it. Belzig is very angry—he wants to shoot everyone. But he never finds Socratis."

"What happened to Socratis?"

"I think he takes it to Athens to sell it. Is the war coming, we are very hungry. Stealing from Germans . . ." He shrugged. "They steal more from us."

"Did Socratis ever come back?"

"No. My uncle say he joins *andartes*. Germans kills him." He tossed an acorn in his hand and gave a sad smile. "So, Belzig has revenge."

"What about Belzig? Did he come back?"

"No. He takes away what he has found—maybe to Germany, I think. He never comes back to Cephalonia."

Grant thought for a second. "And this piece he found. You're sure there was only one? Not two?"

"Only one. And Socratis steals it."

"What's a fucking *Chrestomathy*? Sounds like a disease you don't want to tell your wife you've got."

Reed's face remained open and courteous. Only a small twitch at the corner of his mouth hinted at his disgust. "It's a book—or was. It only survives in fragments now."

"More fucking fragments. How are they going to help?"

Reed gave a thin, tested smile. "It may just give you what you want."

"A dictionary of Linear B?"

"The long-lost sequel to Homer."

Reed hauled himself out of his chair, rubbed his ink-stained hands on his trousers and pulled a long drawer out of the card catalogue. He flicked through the yellowed index cards, muttering to himself. "Here we are." He looked around at the stacked shelves, a man at a station trying to pick out a face in the crowd. His gaze gradually rose higher, until it came to rest on the topmost shelf of a bookcase that must have been twice his height.

"I'll get it." Marina wheeled over a ladder. It creaked and wobbled alarmingly as she climbed. Reed stood on the bottom rung to brace it, while Muir tried to look up her dress.

"If it's the long-lost sequel, why's it in the card catalogue? Don't tell me no one's thought to look there for the last two thousand years?"

Reed ignored him—so completely that Muir began to wonder if he'd actually spoken out loud. Stretching precariously on the top rung, Marina prised out a thick hard-bound book. A cloud of dust rose off the shelf; she sneezed, lost her balance and flailed around desperately. That didn't help. The ladder swayed like a pendulum, creaking so loudly Reed was sure it must collapse in splinters. With a small shriek, Marina let go of the book and grabbed on to the frame.

The book dropped like a stone and landed in Reed's arms with a thud. He winced, set it aside and held the ladder until Marina had got down safely. She tugged down her dress, which had risen up over her slip in the commotion.

Reed laid the book on the table and cracked open the cover. Two dead flies fell out of the title page.

"Maybe it hasn't been borrowed for two thousand years," quipped Muir.

"The *Chrestomathy* is a literary anthology: a sort of classical *Reader's Digest*. It was put together by a scholar named Proclus—about whom we know almost nothing—around the fifth century AD."

As Reed turned the pages, the others saw that it was no ordinary book. It was more like a scrapbook, made up entirely of small squares of typed paper cut out with scissors and pasted on to the blank pages. Often they had peeled away and been stuck back down with tape. It seemed to be a work in progress: many of the clippings had been scored out or amended in ink, or had new excerpts painted over them. Some were no longer than single sentences; others ran to complete paragraphs. All were in Greek.

"This is a collection of the fragments that survive." Reed ran his finger down the page.

"Fragments—you mean scraps of parchment or paper or whatever they were written on?"

Reed shook his head. "Very occasionally. Far more often they're small pieces of the text that come down to us through quotations in other works that have survived more or less intact. Think of Shakespeare. Even if we didn't have complete texts of any of his plays, we could still reconstruct them—partially—from all the subsequent scholars who've quoted them. Some of the quotations would overlap, in which case you could piece them together; for others you could guess their approximate position in the play by knowing something about its plot. Time and history try their best to erase our human endeavors, but they're hard to get rid of completely. They endure, like pottery shards embedded in the soil. Here we are."

His finger came to rest on a long excerpt that almost filled the page. "The *Aethiopis*, by Arctinus of Miletus."

"I thought you said it was by this fellow Proclus," said Muir.

"Proclus wrote the *Chrestomathy*," Reed explained patiently. "But he was only summarising other authors—in this case, Arctinus of Miletus. Later, some of the scribes who copied out the *Iliad* added excerpts from Proclus as supplementary material."

"It's so tenacious," Marina marvelled. "Almost like a virus, copying itself from one host to the next until it finds one that survives."

"Never mind that," barked Muir. "What does it say?"

"We should call the cops."

Grant stared at Jackson. They were walking back down the hill, their boots crunching on the twigs and acorns.

"His cousin stole this thing, right? So he probably knows more than he's saying. The way I figure it, we get the local boys in blue to bring him in for questioning. They're probably chumps, but who cares? Maybe they can soften him up a little. Either way, it puts him just where we want him." He caught Grant's incredulous gaze. "What? I read your file. I know what you did in the war. The girl, too. Is that shit true? She must've been some piece of work."

"We shouldn't get the police involved, not if we don't have to," Grant insisted. He shook his head angrily. Something didn't make sense, but he couldn't work out what it was. It was like trying to finish a jigsaw: there was only one piece missing—but the box was empty.

He realized Jackson had been saying something. "What?"

"I was saying we could bring in a team to dig up the hill. We're trying to find the other half of this tablet, right? If pig-man says they only found the one piece, then the other one's probably still up there. That's what the professor said."

"The second piece." Grant stopped in his tracks. "Belzig knew what that tablet was worth. If he only found half of it, why did he never come back to look for the other half?"

Jackson looked confused. "Why?"

But Grant had already forgotten him. He sprinted up the slope, pushing pell-mell through the branches. Haste made him careless. His foot turned over on a loose stone, pitching him forward; he stumbled, flailed out his arms and had almost regained his balance when an exposed tree-root caught him square on the shin. He toppled over, crashed through a bush and planted himself face first in the dirt.

Two piggy eyes stared at him down the barrel of a fat pink snout. The pig tossed its head; then, with a reproachful snort, went back to feeding itself.

On the far side of the clearing the swineherd was on his feet. "Do you forget something?"

Grant scrambled to his feet and dusted himself off. Half his face was caked with earth and his hand bled where he'd scratched it on a rock. "The tablet—with writing and painting. You only found one piece?"

"One piece, yes."

"And that was the piece that your cousin stole."

"Yes."

Grant took a deep breath, tasting the dry dirt on his tongue. "Tell me: was the tablet broken when you found it? Or was it complete? Whole?"

The Greek looked puzzled by the question. "One piece. We find only one piece."

"Yes. But . . ." Grant unbuttoned his shirt pocket and pulled out Pemberton's photograph. He thrust it into the Greek's startled hands. "Is this what you found?"

The swineherd stared at it. The double-exposure had left the image blurred and indistinct, but the outline of the tablet was clear enough.

"Well?"

The Greek shook his head. "We find one piece. This is only half."

Reed pushed up his glasses again. "As you know, the *Iliad* and the *Odyssey* drew on an established story cycle of the Trojan war. They dealt with specific episodes—the rage of Achilles, the homecoming of Odysseus. But once Homer had become so successful, other would-be poets also tried their hand at the Trojan war. Particularly, they wanted to fill in the gaps between Homer, so that eventually the whole tale of Troy—from the abduction of Helen to the final homecomings of the

Greek victors—would be set in epic poetry. It's hack work, of course, which is presumably why the texts haven't survived. No one believes that *Hamlet* would have been improved by five more plays on the subject of Danish medieval history."

He looked at Muir. "The *Aethiopis* is the long-lost sequel you wanted to the *Iliad*. It describes Achilles' final battle and death. And . . ." He ran his finger along the cramped lines of Greek, mouthing the words to himself. "What happens next. 'They lay out Achilles' corpse. His mother, the sea-nymph Thetis, arrives with the Muses and mourns her son. Then she snatches him up from the pyre and carries his body to the White Island.'"

His finger seemed to tremble as it hovered over the page, but his face glowed with amazement. "Of course. *The White Island*."

16

Paleo Faliro, Athens

THEY WERE back in the hotel, eating food that looked suspiciously like the previous night's leftovers. There were more guests there that evening, though few enough for their tables still to be spaced well apart, a far-flung archipelago in the empty sea of the dining room.

"The White Island was a sort of Greek Valhalla, a place where dead heroes went to enjoy the afterlife," Reed explained.

"I thought that was the Elysian Fields," said Grant. He was pleased to have some classical knowledge to offer, even if it was something he'd picked up from a girl on the Champs-Elysées in newly liberated Paris. He waited for Reed to acknowledge his contribution.

Instead, the professor just looked cross. "Well, yes." He jabbed his fork so hard at a piece of meat that the tines chimed on the plate. "To be honest, Greek conceptions of the afterlife were a little imprecise. The popular version that's come down to us—Hades for the torments of the damned, the Elysian Fields for eternal bliss—is a relatively late refinement of the scheme. It probably owes as much to our desire to project back our own ideas of heaven and hell. Certainly in Homer, the

Iliad in particular, there's no concept of the afterlife as an ongoing business. Immortality comes from the deeds you do in your lifetime and the glory you achieve. All that survives when you die is a shadow, a gray facsimile of the man you were."

"So where does the White Island fit in?" asked Muir.

Reed frowned. "Actually, cosmologically speaking it's a bit of an anomaly. There are a few analogous ideas: the Isles of the Blessed that Pindar describes, which are a sort of insular Elysian Fields. The Garden of the Hesperides, where the golden apples of life were kept, was also thought to be on an island at the edge of the world, though they're not quite the same thing. But geographically, the White Island was always thought to be somewhere in the Black Sea."

"Why there?"

"For the Greeks, the earth was a flat disc bounded by a great, cosmic river flowing round the circumference—the Oceanus. The Mediterranean was the axis across the middle. Passing through the straits of Gibraltar brought you into the Oceanus to the west; going out through the Bosphorus into the Black Sea took you out on the east side." He leaned forward. "The Black Sea was beyond the limits of the ancient Greeks' compass. It was the edge of the world, a no man's land where the realm of men and the realms of gods dissolved into each other. Naturally, anything you couldn't locate within the known world you assumed would be there. Especially if it had mythic or spiritual associations." His thick eyebrows tilted toward each other as he saw the look on Marina's face. "You disagree?"

"The Black Sea." She looked around the table, as if baffled that they didn't understand her meaning. "Don't you see the connection? Maybe it wasn't just geographical convenience that made the Greeks put the White Island there. So much of Odysseus's wanderings seem to take place in the Black Sea, but there's no reason for him to be there. It's not on his way home."

"It's probably a later story that's been interpolated into the myth."

"But what if it isn't? What if the White Island was a real place, a lost shrine or temple for dead heroes? Odysseus must have had a reason for sailing east when the home he was desperate to return to lay to the west. Perhaps he went there to deposit Achilles' armor at this temple on the White Island."

Jackson put down his beer and stared at her. "I'm sorry—are you saying that Odysseus was a real guy?"

"Of course he wasn't," said Muir. "We won't get anywhere chasing after myths and legends." He turned to Reed. "How did you get on with translating the tablet, before our Greek siren started leading you off on wild-goose chases?"

"I've got a rough idea of the characters." Reed unfolded a piece of paper. It was almost completely covered by a large grid of cabalistic symbols, about a hundred in total. Some were linked by arrows; others had question marks and notes scrawled in the margin beside them. "A few of them are a bit doubtful, but those tend to be less frequently occurring anyway." He looked at Grant. "Do you still have Pemberton's photograph?"

Grant fished it out and passed it across the table. "You can't make out the symbols on that. It's too blurred."

"Mmm," said Reed, not really listening.

Muir sparked a cigarette. "So—you've got the alphabet. What next?"

"Hmm?" Reed didn't look up. "It's not necessarily an alphabet, you know. Broadly speaking, there are three ways to represent language on paper. The most exact is alphabetic. Each letter represents one sound of the language. That makes it possible to spell out just about anything you can think of saying. Tremendously powerful and flexible—but, from a historical point of view, a relatively recent innovation."

"How recent?"

"A shade over two and a half thousand years ago, in its final form. Here in Greece. The ancient Greek alphabet was the first completely phonetic alphabet in the world. Arguably, it was the key that unlocked the extraordinary flowering of civilization that followed in the next four hundred years. Previous forms of writing were crude, ungainly systems. Words were passive receptacles, good for record keeping but not much else. The Greek alphabet was the first one to go beyond it, to make the written word an exact copy of the thoughts in your head.

Instead of being backward-looking and static, writing became this wonderful tool for expanding the mind's reach.

"But all that came afterward. Before that, there were two types of symbology: ideographic and syllabic. Ideograms are like the Egyptian hieroglyphs, or modern Chinese characters, where each symbol represents a word or a concept. It's purely graphic; there's no phonic link between what's written and the spoken word. A syllabic symbol-set, by contrast, breaks up the language into every possible combination of consonant and vowel and represents each one with a symbol. So in English you would have one character for 'ba,' one for 'be,' one for 'bi,' for 'bo,' for 'bu,' then for 'ca,' 'ce,' 'ci' and so on to 'zu.' The modern Japanese *hiragana* alphabet uses exactly this system." He didn't explain how he came to be so familiar with Japanese—there were only a few score people in the world who were cleared to know that piece of history and only one was seated at the table.

Grant did a quick mental calculation, five vowels times twenty-one consonants. "That would give you a hundred and five characters."

Reed beamed. "In English, yes. Which as chance would have it, is not far off the number of characters I've identified in Linear B. Ninety-three, to be exact. Not enough to be ideograms—though I suspect there may be a few for particularly common words; too many to be purely alphabetic."

"Terrific," said Muir heavily. "At this rate, in another three years we'll be getting somewhere."

"Not that it'll do us a hell of a lot of good without the rest of that goddamn tablet." Jackson sawed at his chicken with uncharacteristic gloom. "If this jerk-off Greek stole the thing, who knows what happened to the other piece?"

"Actually," said Reed, "I think I can guess."

He looked around the table, pleased with the incredulous reactions he'd drawn.

"What are you, Sherlock Holmes or something?" said Jackson.

"I always preferred to see myself as Mycroft, actually." Reed picked up the bag that lay by the feet of his chair and pulled out the tablet fragment. It was still inside the napkin he'd wrapped it in the previous evening.

"Let's begin with what we know. According to your swineherd, Belzig found the tablet intact. One of his workers then stole it and somehow it came to a dealer in Athens. By the time Pemberton found it in the shop, one tablet had become two fragments. Somewhere along the line the tablet broke in half. Or, more likely, somebody realized that the tablet would fetch more money in two pieces than in one."

"So what happened to the other one?"

Reed laid the photograph on the table next to the tablet. "Do you notice anything odd?"

Grant, Jackson, Marina and Muir craned forward to look. The photograph was so blurred it was hard to make out anything in detail.

"They're not the same." Reed let the significance of his words settle around the table. "The fragment in the photograph isn't the same as the piece we found in the shrine on Crete."

"Then how . . . ?"

"Both pieces must have been in the shop. This is pure conjecture, but I'd suggest that Pemberton only had enough money for one of them. He photographed the other."

"How come no one saw this before?" Jackson demanded.

Reed shrugged. "It's a terrible photograph. It's only from spending so long staring at the symbols that I noticed it."

"Bravo." Jackson and Marina were staring at Reed like some sort of magician; Muir looked as though he couldn't have cared less. "So both pieces of the tablet were in the shop, wonderful. But that's not much fucking use if the shopkeeper got a one-way ticket to Auschwitz. Who . . ."

He broke off. A waiter in a white jacket was gliding through the sea of tables toward them. He stooped down beside Grant and murmured something discreet in his ear.

Grant pushed back his chair. "Apparently someone wants me on the phone." He followed the waiter. Four gazes—suspicious, curious, surprised, hostile—followed him out.

At the reception desk the girl on duty deftly slotted a plug into the switchboard and handed him the receiver.

"Mr. Grant?" The voice was soft, precise, elongating the unfamiliar syllables.

"This is Grant."

"Listen to me. There is a car waiting outside your hotel. I advise you to get in it. You have two minutes."

"Who the hell is this?" Grant demanded.

"Someone you would like to meet. As a token of my good faith, you may bring one companion. You may also bring your gun, if it would reassure you, though you will not need it. Two minutes," the voice repeated. There was a click and the phone went dead.

Grant waved over one of the bellhops and handed him a drachma note. "In the dining room, a table with three men and a woman. Tell the woman to come here at once." He didn't have time to explain, let alone argue it out with Muir and Jackson.

Marina emerged from the dining room a minute later. Grant ran an appraising eye over her. She had made an effort for dinner—heels, nylons, lipstick, the whole show. It didn't quite fit her, he decided. Whereas some women could make themselves unattainable, on Marina it actually made her look more vulnerable, an earnest girl studying to please. Though she certainly looked good enough to draw long, lip-licking stares from the suits and uniforms in the lobby.

"What is this?"

Grant offered her a cigarette, lit it and hooked his arm through hers. "I'll explain in the car."

"What car?"

Grant escorted her to the door, feeling the stares they attracted. The doorman opened it with a flourish and they were out on the hotel steps. In the driveway, under an ornamental palm, a long-snouted limousine gleamed black in the sodium light. Its engine throbbed hungrily.

"In we get."

The car was a Mercedes. There was no one inside except the driver, who said nothing as he ushered them into the opulent interior and slammed the door. When Grant leaned back on the seat he felt a knot against his shoulders. He twisted round. A small hole, about the size of a .38 caliber bullet, had broken the leather and been inexpertly sewn up. Grant poked it with his finger. "Looks like somebody didn't enjoy the ride."

The car carried them on, up the empty road that ran along the seafront. Grant had supposed they'd be going to Athens, but the driver ignored all the turnings and continued straight on. Gradually, lights appeared in the night ahead, very high up. At first Grant thought they must be villages on a mountainside; then, feeling foolish, he realized the night had tricked him. They had arrived in Piraeus, the port of Athens, and the lights like strings of pearls in the sky traced the contours of cranes and looming hulls. Grant looked out of the window and stared through the barred gates and barbed-wire fences as they rushed past. It was like being whisked through a museum, each vessel an exhibit picked out in the floodlights. Some sat silent and ghostly; others hived with life as stevedores and longshoremen stripped them of their cargo like ants. A hand-painted banner, in Greek and English, hung limp against a freighter's hull: *USA feeds the patriotic people of Greece*.

They turned off the main road and darted through a succession of backstreets and alleys, each tighter than the last, until the car stopped. Grant thought perhaps the Mercedes had taken a wrong turn and couldn't get through, but in an instant the chauffeur had hopped out and was holding open the door. Grant just had time to glimpse boarded-up windows and political slogans daubed on the walls; then he was being ushered down a dank staircase. A metal gate protected the door—necessary, to judge from the dents and scratches in the wood. A battered sign above showed a figure draped in black standing in what looked like a canoe. Flickering neon letters beside it spelled out "Χαρον."

"Charon," Marina translated, though Grant could read it for himself. "The ferryman to the underworld."

A world of smoke and music collided with Grant as he opened the door. The smoke was thick enough to kill him, a solid cloud that seized his lungs as if he'd been punched in the stomach. It didn't drift or swirl; it just hung in the air under the cones of light cast by the low-hanging lamps. As well as the acrid bite of tobacco, Grant could taste a sweet undercurrent of hashish, and as he looked about him he saw bulbous water pipes on almost every table in the room. The patrons squeezed round them seemed to represent every conceivable stratum of Greek society: ladies in mink and pearls or in rouge and paste diamonds; men in evening dress, in overalls, in disarranged uniforms, in shirtsleeves and threadbare waistcoats all mingled around the *nargiles*, passing the coiled hose from one mouth to the next. No one gave Grant and Marina a second look.

On a low stage at the front of the room a five-piece band sat hunched over their instruments: a fiddler, a lute player, a man with a drum tucked under his arm and one with a flat dulcimer-like instrument resting on his knees like a cigarette tray. The only one who even seemed aware of the audience was the singer, a waif-like man in an open-necked black shirt, who stared at the microphone with deep, tubercular eyes. Grant couldn't understand the words, but the song was fast and impossibly sad.

A waiter appeared at his elbow and guided him to the back of the room, where a row of round booths lined the wall. Most of them were crammed with as many people as could jam on to the leather banquettes, but one, near the end, was almost empty. There were only two men inside it: one thickset, bulging in all the wrong places; the other small and light, his gray hair slicked back severely and his moustache carefully trimmed. Though dwarfed by his companion, you could tell from his face and his bearing who obeyed whom. He gestured Grant and Marina to take a seat opposite.

"Mr. Grant." He reached his right hand across the table; his left he kept out of sight, resting on his knee underneath. The skin was dry and waxy. "I am Elias Molho."

17

ELIAS MOLHO. Dealer in Rare Antiquities." Smoke curled on Grant's tongue as he said it. "I thought you were dead."

The gray-haired man smiled and spread his hands. "I am . . . as you see me."

"I heard the Nazis got you."

Molho's mouth twitched with displeasure. "Perhaps they did. Or perhaps it was convenient to me that people should think so. So many people vanished—even the Germans could not record them all. I chose to vanish on my own terms." He reached in his trouser pocket and pulled out a slip of paper. Grant recognized it from the tailor's shop, the one he'd written the hotel address on. "But now it seems you have been asking questions about me, Mr. Grant."

Before he could speak the waiter appeared again. He set two tumblers of whiskey on the table in front of Grant and Marina, and left without presenting a bill.

"From America," Molho said. "The first instalment of Truman's aid program."

Grant sipped his drink. He'd drunk enough cheap liquor, in underground bars from Cape Town to Moscow, to recognize the real thing when he tasted it. "Is this what you deal in? The black market?"

"Is there any other in Greece? All our markets are black now." Molho's face stayed still and courteous, but his eyes were hard. He nodded to the stage, where a full-breasted woman sheathed in a silver dress had taken over the microphone. "Do you know our *Rembetika* music, Mr. Grant? Before the war, it was a curiosity, music for addicts and thieves. The *rembetes* were a melancholy cult who thought that only their initiates understood the truth of misery. Now it is our national music."

He swirled his drink in his glass. The big man beside him said nothing, but watched the singer and drummed his fingers on the table in time to the music.

"I'm looking for an artifact. A Minoan tablet." Grant rushed out the words, almost stumbling over them. Everything since the phone had rung seemed like a dream and, as in a dream, he was frightened he would wake up before it finished. "Just before the war an English archaeologist came into your shop. He bought a clay tablet, or half of one, with writing on one side and a painting on the other. You remember the piece?"

Molho took a drag from his silver cigarette holder. "I sold many artifacts, before the Germans closed my shop."

"Not many like this. It's unique—or was, until you split it in two." Grant looked Molho in the eye.

The Greek nodded. "Mr. Grant, I am a businessman. Whatever I am selling—American whiskey, Russian cigarettes, pieces of clay—I need to get the best price. What people want most, they pay most for. If my customers want ten cigarettes at a time rather than twenty, or a half-liter of whiskey, or two pieces of stone instead of one, I sell it. Of course there is a risk. Sometimes instead of twice as much profit, I make twice as much problem for myself." Molho leaned back in the booth. "I must tell you, Mr. Grant, you are not the first man to come to me asking about a clay tablet. Soon after the occupation a German came to my shop. A Dr. Klaus Belzig." His eyes narrowed. "I see you know the name?"

"Never met him. But you told him Pemberton bought the tablet."

"Dr. Belzig was under the false impression that the tablet had been intact. I did not correct him; why should I? He asked me what happened to the tablet; I told him I sold it to a British archaeologist from Crete. I even showed him a copy of the receipt."

"So Belzig went off to Crete. But Pemberton was already dead."

"That was unfortunate for Dr. Belzig. And perhaps lucky for Mr. Pemberton. Dr. Belzig's methods were . . . notorious." Molho lifted his left arm from under the table. Marina gave a gasp of horror. A gold cufflink clasped the starched white shirt cuff—but there was no hand. Molho pulled up his sleeve a little to show off the grim stump, a rounded stub with scars like string round it.

Even Grant blanched. "Belzig did that?"

"I was only a Jew." He gave a grim laugh. "He told me I was luckier than the man who stole the tablet from him. He took one hand—and I gave him one name. I knew Pemberton was English. I did not know he was dead, but I thought he would be out of Greece. Safe. Belzig would never learn I had only given him half the tablet, because he would never find any of it."

"Christ."

Molho pulled his sleeve back down. "Perhaps Belzig did me a favor. Before, we heard rumors among the Jews. There was an uncle in Germany, or a cousin had a girlfriend in Warsaw. But no one really believed—how could you believe such a thing? After Belzig, I saw what the Nazis could do. So I disappeared."

Applause pattered round the smoky room as the singer finished her song. She left the stage and slid into one of the booths, sucking hungrily on the proffered pipe. Her place was taken by a man, slim and foppish. His black hair was slicked flat against his scalp and with his narrow moustache he looked almost like a Nazi. Grant wondered if it was supposed to be ironic.

The singer stood stiffly in front of the band. The bouzouki player began a fast lick, his fingers flying over the frets. Grant leaned forward. "And the second piece of the tablet? What happened to that?"

Molho held his gaze. "How much is that information worth to you? Will you take another hand?"

An electric howl cut through the room, silencing all chatter and gossip. Up on stage, the singer was clutching the microphone stand like a drowning man. His body contorted round it; you would hardly have believed such a slight man capable of such a sound. The howl trembled, then rose a pitch.

Grant's face stayed perfectly still. "I'm only asking. But there are other men who want it. Men like Belzig. If they find you . . ."

Molho drained his drink. "Are you trying to intimidate me, Mr. Grant?"

"Just giving you fair warning."

"I believe you. But—you understand—I am a businessman. If somebody comes into my shop and offers to buy something—maybe a clay tablet—for one hundred drachmas, I wonder if he will really pay two. Or if there is another man who will pay three. And what about you? I have not asked you why you want it—I am too polite. But I do not think you are an archaeologist, like Mr. Pemberton, or a collector. Are you a treasure hunter? I have heard from my sources that you are with two Englishmen and an American—as well as your lovely companion. I wonder, who are you working for?"

Grant gave a tight-lipped smile. "I sometimes wonder myself."

"You cannot be frank with me, I understand. So I cannot be frank with you. You understand." Molho smiled and stood. The heavy beside him stood too, just in case Grant had any ideas. "I will think about your request, Mr. Grant. Perhaps, when I have decided how much the information is worth, I will name my price. If so, I will contact you at your hotel."

Grant leaned across the table, only to collide with the bodyguard's fat palm shoving against his chest. "Don't take too long. There are too many people after this thing. Dangerous men."

Molho lifted his left arm and waved it at Grant and Marina, a chilling goodbye. "I know."

The Mercedes sped them back to the hotel through empty streets. Grant and Marina sat in the back and said nothing. In the corridor outside their rooms, they paused. To anyone passing, they would have looked like two lovers returned from a late evening dancing. Grant had his jacket slung over his shoulder and his shirtsleeves rolled up to the elbow; Marina had slipped off her shoes and clutched them in her hand, her feet more used to work boots than heels. Her face shone with sweat and a kohl tear smudged the corner of her eye. One of the straps of her dress had slid down over her shoulder.

"Goodnight," said Grant. In the silent corridor, deadened by the hotel carpet, it sounded more abrupt than he'd meant it. "Unless . . ." He moved a step closer. Marina's hair was thick with the spices of night and music: smoke and sweat, liquor and perfume. Perhaps all the hashish in the club had left him dazed. He lifted his hand and stroked the side of her face, pushing back the lock of hair that had fallen over her eye. She didn't pull away. He let his hand slide down: over her cheek, her neck and on to her shoulder. Tenderly, he pulled the strap back up.

"I've got a bottle of brandy in my room." He knew how false it sounded, but he needed the lie to cover him. It had been too long to take anything for granted.

"Just one drink," said Marina. She sounded almost dazed, automatic. She let him take her arm and guide her to his door, nestling against his elbow as he fumbled for the key. He slid it into the lock—and stopped. Molho's whiskey was warm inside him, Marina's perfume almost overwhelming, but there were some instincts you never forgot.

She sensed him stiffen and tilted her head to look up at him. "What is it?"

"Shh." Grant was staring at the door frame. A tiny corner of yellow paper peeked out from the crack between the locked door and the frame, almost invisible unless you knew to look for it. He always put it there when he left the room. But it wasn't quite where he'd left it. They hadn't just gone in; they—whoever *they* were—had also spotted the trap and tried to reset it. That meant they knew what they were doing. And the Webley was inside the room.

Grant pulled the key back out of the lock, keeping his hand on the door handle. Marina edged away, watching him in confusion. "Have you got your pistol?" he mouthed.

Without warning, the handle turned and the door flew inward. Still holding on to the handle, Grant was dragged forward into the room. He stumbled, caught his foot on something and sprawled forward on the floor. Someone came after him, but Grant was too quick. He rolled over and sprang up, took one step back and jabbed his opponent in the solar plexus. There was a groan and a muffled "*Geez*."

Grant stopped his fist mid-swing and stepped back. The man in front of him was doubled over in pain, but there was no mistaking the tight crew-cut, the broad shoulders and the navy blazer. Further back, Muir was sitting on the end of the bed with a cigarette in his hand.

"Where the fuck have you been?"

18

A STIFLING silence gripped the library. It was partially the weather, which after a week of April breezes had turned hot and sultry; partially the collective effect of more readers in the room. The Easter holiday was over, and the motley company of students, artists and academics who made up the British School's clientele had begun to drift back. They perched on desks around the room, earnestly poring over books that looked almost as ancient as the civilizations they told of. Sitting by the window with a newspaper, Grant felt as out of place as he ever had, oppressed by the worthy purpose around him. That and Muir's reaction the previous night.

"And that was all? He told you to go and you just went? Like a fucking puppy?"

Grant barely bothered to argue. "It was his home ground—and he had a gorilla next to him in case I tried something."

"If you'd told us where you were going—instead of sloping off with the girl like some salesman in Bognor—we could have followed you. We'd know a damn sight more if you had."

"There was no time. Molho arranged it that way. If you'd tried to follow us he'd probably just have dumped us." He remembered the hole in the car seat. "Or worse."

Muir jabbed his cigarette dangerously close to Grant's face. "Right now, this little Yid is our only link to the rest of the tablet. Next time he calls, don't you dare call your fucking girlfriend. You call me. Otherwise I'll have you off this caper and back in a cell in some shitty corner of the Empire faster than fuck. Understand?"

Grant put down his paper and went over to Marina. Her pile of books had grown, though she still had some way to go before it matched Reed's, opposite. He peered over her shoulder. "What are you working on?"

She leaned back so he could see—the curious book with its pasted-in patches of Greek. At the bottom, in a neat line of faded cursive script, someone had written what looked like a string of nonsense. "Paus.III:19:11; Strab.VII:3:19; Lyc.*Alex*:188; Arr.*Per*:21."

"Is that a crossword clue?"

Marina sighed. "They're references—places in the ancient texts where the White Island is mentioned. Pausanias wrote a guide to Greece, a sort of ancient Baedeker. Strabo was a first-century geographer. Lycophron wrote an almost indecipherable poem about the Trojan war and Arrian was a Roman functionary who wrote a description of the Black Sea to amuse the Emperor Hadrian."

"Do they say anything useful?"

"They all say it's somewhere in the Black Sea." She put down her pen. "Apart from that, they can't agree on anything. Pausanias and Lycophron say it's by the mouth of the Danube; Arrian only says it's somewhere in the open sea and Strabo puts it about five hundred stadia from the mouth of the Dniester."

"How far's that in real money?"

"About a hundred kilometers—but he doesn't say in which direction." She shuffled through her papers. "I also found a reference in Pliny—he claims the White Island is actually at the mouth of the Dnieper. You can't really rely on the ancient geographers for measurements, but both the Danube and the Dnieper estuaries are actually approximately one hundred kilometers from the Dniester."

Grant scratched his head. "So either it's by the Danube, or the Dnieper, or it's nowhere near either of them." He glanced across the table to Reed, lost in a whirl of symbols and photostats. "I thought he said this island was just a legend—some sort of mythic paradise for heroes."

"I think he was wrong. In all the references I've found, the only hero they ever mention is Achilles—or sometimes Patroclus, who was Achilles' companion. The White Island wasn't a *generic* paradise. It seems to have been specifically, uniquely, associated with Achilles."

"You think that makes it more likely to be true?"

"It must have come from somewhere. There's no comparable legend for any of the other heroes: there must be a reason why this particular story grows up around Achilles."

She pulled one of the books toward her. "According to Arrian, there's a temple to Achilles on this island. Pliny goes further and says that his actual tomb is there." Her eyes sparkled, bright as life in the dusty library. "What if it was—is—a real place? The lost temple of Achilles and his tomb inside. No one's ever found it."

"Because no one can agree where it is. Besides, even if it's all true, what's to say that this magic shield will be there?"

"I think it's where Odysseus brought it, as an offering to the dead hero on his way back to Ithaca. So much of his story takes place in the Black Sea, it makes no sense unless he was there for a reason."

"Maybe he was blown there by accident."

"There's no wind that could carry a ship all the way from Troy to the Black Sea. It was famously difficult even to sail up the Dardanelles. And once Odysseus gets to the Black Sea, he keeps on going east. Look." She grabbed another piece of paper, a list of points joined by flowing arrows. "These are the episodes whose imagery or associations suggest they take place in the Black Sea. They almost all happen in sequence, suggesting some sort of geographical coherence. And the centrepiece—the whole point of his journey there—is his visit to the underworld."

Across the Oceanus' stream,
A desolate shore where sirens scream
And heroes dream
Beach your ship at Persephone's bower,
Where poplars soar, where willows flower
And die that hour,
Then hasten down
To the mouldering House of Death.

"Odysseus goes there. In a chasm where two rivers meet he makes a sacrifice and he opens the door to Hades." She held the book so Grant could see. On the facing page, a woodcut illustrated the event with dark, heavy lines. A ship was drawn up on a beach fringed by poplars, so straight and high they looked more like the bars of a cage. In the middle of the page two white torrents cascaded down the flanks of a dark mountain and at the point where they met a tiny figure stood dwarfed beneath the stark crags. A haltered white ram waited on his left, a black ewe on his right, and the cliff in front of him yawned open.

Despite the warm room, Grant shivered. "You're saying Odysseus went down to hell?"

"He summoned spirits from the dead. To the ancient Greeks, Hades wasn't a place you physically went to. Travelling there was a spiritual process, a journey of the soul. They believed there were certain sacred places where the barriers between the worlds thinned—that if you went there and performed the correct rituals, you could commune with the dead. In the poem, when Odysseus comes to the far side of the Oceanus, he digs a shallow trench. He pours wine and milk and honey round it, then fills it with the blood of the sheep he's sacrificed. And the ghosts come. Tiresias the prophet; Agamemnon, killed by his wife Clytemnestra; Ariadne and King Minos." She paused significantly. "And Achilles."

Grant allowed himself to look impressed. "You think that Achilles' temple—his tomb—was the place where Odysseus went to the underworld?"

"Or perhaps that he went to the tomb, on the White Island, to offer the shield to the dead Achilles, and later the story was misremembered as a visit to the underworld."

"So all we have to do is find it." Grant looked at the two lambs in the picture, staring ahead at the monstrous cliff and awaiting their fate. "Do we have to sacrifice sheep to get there?"

"Let's hope we don't have to sacrifice anything else."

Grant left Marina and the professor to their books, and wandered out for a cigarette. Unsettling pictures filled his mind: lowering cliffs, pools of blood, ghosts like wraiths of cloud and carrion birds calling from the rocks. The images were so strong that he forgot to look where he was going. He walked through the library door and straight into a man coming the other way, almost knocking him down. A sheaf of papers flew into the air, blowing around the corridor like snow.

"Sorry." Grant reached down to help the man up. The gesture was ignored. With an irritated harrumph, he got to his feet and brushed himself off. He was a squat, ugly man, with a square head and thin fair hair cut very short. His skin was red and grainy, as if a nasty rash had consumed his face, and his close-set eyes burned with anger.

"*Pass auf!*" He took a step back. The piggy eyes widened—as much as they could—then narrowed quickly. "Next time, you must be more careful."

His English was almost impenetrably accented, but even so, Grant could sense something evasive in it. He looked closer at the man. Did he know him? Not that he could remember. But he couldn't shake the feeling that in that moment of anger there had been a flash of recognition.

The man picked up his papers and pushed past Grant into the library. Looking back through the glass pane in the door, Grant saw him sit down at the central table, two seats along from Reed.

"Probably nothing," he muttered, trying to convince himself. He'd been promising himself a cigarette for the last half-hour. And Marina was there to keep an eye on things.

He smiled at the girl on the front desk as he went out. The air around him felt almost as hot as the smoke in his lungs, but it was good to be free of the stuffiness inside the library. He wondered how men like Reed could spend their lives locked in those places. To him they were too much like mausoleums, necropolises of dead pages in dead languages.

The thrum of an idle engine disturbed the mid-morning air. Outside the gate, across the road, a green Citroën had drawn up on the pavement. One man sat in the front seat reading a newspaper; another lounged against the rear door and picked his teeth.

"Got a light?"

Grant spun around. Marina was standing in the shade of a plane tree, looking slightly surprised by how quickly he'd turned. She held out a cigarette expectantly.

"Who's watching Reed?"

"He's in the library." She gave a wary smile. "I wanted to talk to you. Last night . . ."

"Not now." Grant almost knocked her into the flower bed in his rush. He burst in through the front door, past the receptionist and raced down the corridor. A flock of bewildered, bespectacled faces turned up in surprise from their desks and carrels as he all but kicked down the library door.

Reed was still there, exactly where he had left him, peering up at Grant from behind a stack of books. At least he looked more surprised than irritated.

"Mr. Grant." The girl from reception must have run to catch up with him. Her face was flushed, her hair tumbling out of its bun. She looked at him with a mixture of astonishment and outrage. At last, her eye settled on the cigarette still jammed in his mouth. "You can't smoke in the library."

Grant spat out the cigarette and ground it into the wooden floor with his heel. Even he was struggling to hide his embarrassment. He let the door swing shut and walked, shamefaced, to Reed. One by one, the other students and academics turned back to their work.

"Was there a purpose to that little drama?" Reed inquired as Grant slid into the chair beside him. He looked around guiltily, as if worried to be associated with the blundering barbarian who had disturbed the library's sanctity.

"I thought . . ." The chair two places down, where the German had sat, was empty now. But what of it? This wasn't the war, where any foreign accent was automatically suspect and every German was an enemy. "I thought you might be in trouble," Grant concluded lamely.

"Only troubled by interruptions."

"What are you doing?" Marina had joined them. Behind Reed's back, she shot Grant an accusatory look.

"There was a man." Grant lowered his voice as he drew reproachful glares from the surrounding academics. "He looked suspicious." There was a touch of defiance in his voice. He realized how feeble it sounded, but his instinct had been right so often that he wouldn't apologize.

"Well, he didn't try to slit my throat." Reed's patience was evidently becoming strained, eager to get back to the maze of scribbles and squiggles on his desk. "And he didn't steal"—he looked down, the reflexive glance of a man checking his watch—"my bag . . ."

Grant followed his gaze down. Four wooden chair legs, two flannelled trouser legs, a pair of scuffed Oxfords—but no bag.

"My bag," Reed repeated. He sounded dazed. "It's gone."

"Was there anything important in it?"

"Important? The tablet was in there."

Grant barged through the doors and rushed down the corridor. He skidded to a halt by the receptionist's desk. "A German—fair hair, brown suit—did he come this way?"

His furious urgency squashed any thought of her scolding him. She simply nodded and pointed to the door. Her arm was still raised when Grant ran through it, down the steps and between the trees toward the gate. The green Citroën was still there: the back door slammed shut with a flash and the car leaped forward.

Grant ran into the street, just in time to suck up a mouthful of exhaust fumes and dust. He pulled out the Webley and emptied it after the fleeing Citroën. The rear windscreen shattered; pimples appeared in the green bodywork. The car slewed round; the driver struggled to control it but he had no chance. The car crested the pavement and slammed head-on into the side of a house. Shards of paint and plaster rained down over the smoking hood. The man in the passenger seat rattled his door frantically, but the impact had buckled it and it wouldn't open.

Smoke and steam from the wrecked engine had begun to cloud the picture; through the shreds, Grant saw the rear door open and the thief scramble out. Reed's leather satchel was hooked over his shoulder. He shouted something to the driver, then began running away down the street.

The man in the passenger seat was still struggling with the door as Grant reached the car. He'd pulled out a pistol and was hammering the grip against the side window. It shattered, leaving a jagged jaw of broken glass round the frame. In his desperation to get out, he hadn't noticed Grant coming and Grant didn't give him a chance. Before he could shoot, Grant reached in through the hole in the window, grabbed his arm and dragged it through. The man was still clutching the gun by its barrel; he tried to turn it round, but Grant banged his arm down on the windowsill, impaling it on the broken glass. The man screamed and dropped the pistol. Still keeping his arm immobilized, Grant bent down, picked up the gun and shot him twice in the chest. The bloody arm went limp.

Grant let go and ran round the back of the car, to see the driver stumbling toward him. He still looked dazed from the crash. One hand was half-raised, whether in surrender or defense Grant couldn't tell; the other was fumbling for something inside his jacket.

Grant didn't know how many bullets he had to waste, but he knew he had no time. He shot the driver—at that range, there was no question of accuracy—and then, as he tottered, kicked his feet from under him. Before he'd hit the ground, Grant was past him and running after the thief.

His quarry had already gone some distance down the street, but he was shorter and heavier than Grant, and cramped by Reed's bag. His brown linen suit flapped round him; his leather shoes slapped on the pavement; the people on the street stared as he ran past, but no one tried to stop him. With so many spectators, Grant didn't dare risk a shot. But he was making ground.

The thief reached a corner and looked round. He couldn't have missed Grant barrelling toward him, waving his gun like a lunatic. He shrugged Reed's bag off his shoulder and let it fall in the gutter, then sprinted across the street. Grant saw him and accelerated. The boulevard was wide and free of traffic—if Grant could catch him there he'd have a clean shot.

A bell was ringing off to his left, but Grant ignored it. He reached the corner, dropped into a crouch and raised the pistol. A line of concrete flower tubs barricaded the middle of the avenue, but the thief's head and shoulders were still clearly visible above, like a silhouette on a shooting range. It was a shot Grant had made a thousand times before.

And then the man vanished. With a whoosh and a rush and a tolling clang, a brown wall shut him off. A tram rolled down the avenue, impervious to Grant, to urgency, to anything but its own shunting progress. A couple of the passengers inside must have noticed the dishevelled Englishman at the edge of the road waving a gun: they pointed and pressed their faces against the glass, turning as the tram trundled inexorably on.

Grant ran forward, dodged round the tram's rear end and jumped up on the concrete tub. He searched the surrounding streets, scanning through the crowd of gray suits and black dresses. The German had disappeared.

A police car raced up the broad avenue and screeched to a halt. Grant laid the pistol in the flower bed and clambered down. Over on the pavement a familiar figure pushed through the gaping crowd. Marina had finally managed to catch him up. Reed's discarded bag dangled from her hands, but her face was grim.

Grant raised his arms in surrender as the police closed round him. "Did he leave the tablet?" he called.

She shook her head. "It's gone."

19

Hotel Grande Bretagne, Athens

"CHRIST, YOU know how to make a mess of things."

They were in a room at the Hotel Grande Bretagne. It wasn't as grand as it sounded. Taking the name at face value, the British army had moved in after the liberation in 1944 and never really gone away. Rooms had been commandeered, fittings stripped, furniture changed, walls and partitions knocked down and rebuilt, so that what had once been a de luxe suite was now a cramped office—albeit one with gold flock wallpaper and a crystal light fitting.

Grant sat in a hard wooden chair. It was uncomfortably like the one he'd sat in when he first met Muir in Palestine. Except this time Muir was angry. "I've got two dead Russians rotting on the street, and everyone from the British ambassador to the fucking librarian wants to know how they got there."

Grant leaned back against the chair and folded his arms across his chest. "They were Russian?"

"Well, they're not talking—obviously. But the car was registered to the Pontic Shipping Corporation, which is a local front outfit for Soviet State Security. Cigarettes, coins and the usual wallet fluff all point the same way." He saw the look of surprise on Grant's face. "Why? You were expecting the Salvation Army?"

"The thief—their accomplice—was German. I ran into him on the stairs—before he walked off with the bag."

"Shame you didn't shoot him too. Did you get a look at him?"

"Sandy hair, red face. Solid." Grant shrugged. "I'd recognize him again if I saw him."

Muir's eyes narrowed. "Would you?" He snapped open his briefcase and pulled out a thick dossier, flicking through the pages until he found the one he wanted. He passed it to Grant. "How about him?"

For once, it was a good clean photograph; posed, not snatched. That didn't make it more attractive. A man in bloused trousers and riding boots stood on top of a mound of earth and rubble. He held a spade which he had planted in the earth, a conqueror raising his standard on the ramparts of the city he had vanquished. He was younger, thinner and more handsome than the man Grant had met on the library stairs, but something in the proud face smirking down at the camera in triumph was irreducible.

"That's him. Who is he?"

"Klaus Belzig. Archaeologist, Nazi and all round nasty piece of work. File came through this morning in the diplomatic bag."

"You said he disappeared from Berlin in 1945." Grant's mind was working quickly. "If the men with him in the car were Russians . . ."

". . . They must have dug him up from Siberia, thawed him out and brought him in to help with the hunt. They know what they're looking for."

"Belzig was the one who found the tablet."

"And now he's got it back."

Something about the tablet triggered a flash of worry, a half-formed thought that Grant couldn't quite complete. Before he could think about it Muir had continued, "It could be worse. Reed says he'd already transcribed the writing that was on the tablet. If he can't decipher it, I don't suppose they can."

The other half. With a sickening lurch, Grant realized what had been worrying him. "Molho never told Belzig he broke it in half. Belzig thought it was intact, that Pemberton had the whole thing."

"So?"

"So now he knows—he's going to go after Molho."

Muir strode out into the anteroom and snatched the phone off its cradle. "Hotel Eurydice," he demanded. He drummed his fingers on the desk while he waited to be connected, then waved Grant over and thrust the receiver at him. "You talk to them. You speak the lingo."

Grant took it. "This is Mr. Grant—room thirty. Has anyone left a message for me?"

"One moment."

Grant covered the mouthpiece with his hand. "Did you and Jackson manage to find Molho's club this morning?"

Muir nodded. "Boards, bars, locks: no one home. Jackson left one of his men . . ."

Grant waved him to be quiet as the receptionist came back on the line. "No messages."

He rang off, then dialled the operator again and got the number for the Charon Club. He let it ring for ages, so long that the sound became mere echoes in his brain.

"*Neh?*" A woman's voice, sleepy and suspicious.

"Is Molho there?"

No answer.

"If he comes, tell him Mr. Grant rang. Tell him I need to speak to him. Very important. Yes?"

She rang off.

He couldn't go back to the library, so he went to the hotel. He lay on his bed and tried to sleep—he should have been tired, but the chase with Belzig had left him tense with adrenalin. Sunlight throbbed through the thin yellow curtains, diffuse and timeless. Someone—probably Reed—had left a book on his bedside table, a translation of the *Iliad*. Grant picked it up and leafed through it. At some point he must have fallen asleep, though he didn't realize it until a knock woke him. He sprang out of bed, grabbed the Webley and padded across the carpet to the door. "Who's there?"

"Me," said Muir. "Get your hat and your gun. Jackson's man just rang in. Molho's arrived at the club."

They almost ran out of the hotel. There was some sort of commotion at the reception desk as they strode past—Grant thought he heard the girl calling his name—but he was already halfway out of the door and ignored her. Muir drove, a pre-war Wolseley he had picked up from the embassy motor pool. His driving was as aggressive as the rest of him: he raced the car down the beach-front road with no regard for the holiday-makers, donkeys and pedestrians who made up most of the traffic.

They knew something was wrong the moment they got there. An army jeep had pulled up outside, blocking the mouth of the alley. An American soldier guarded it and another infantryman stood at the top of the steps that led down to the cellar.

The sentry by the jeep strolled toward the Wolseley. The driver's door almost flattened him as Muir leaped out. "Is Jackson here?"

Jackson was waiting for them inside, together with a man in a blue suit whom Grant didn't recognize. Smoke from the night before still clouded the air, but the music was gone. Stools and chairs stood stacked on tables, their legs in the air like sea urchins; half a dozen musicstands were tucked behind a curtain; a mop oozed water into its bucket. In a strange way it reminded Grant of the palace at Knossos. An archaeologist could find these artifacts in a thousand years and never understand what had happened there.

Molho lay in the middle of the room under a white sheet—a tablecloth that someone had thought to lay over him. He couldn't have been dead for long. Red smears stained the tablecloth, as if a careless diner had spilled a bottle of wine, and a dark pool seeped from under the hem.

"It's a hell of a thing," said Jackson. "They really did a job on him. Teeth, fingers, the works." He sounded brutally dispassionate, a tradesman delivering a bill of goods. "Whatever secrets he had, you can be damn sure he told them." With the toe of his shoe he tugged back the cloth to reveal the face. "That him?"

Molho's face was a horrific sight. Grant had seen worse in the war—not much worse, but enough to keep his composure. "That was him. Poor bastard." He'd liked the man, as much as he'd known him. It seemed impossibly cruel that he should have survived the war and all its horrors, only to meet this end. But then the world, as Grant well knew, could be an impossibly cruel place. "Cover him up, for God's sake."

Jackson kicked the sheet back over his face. "Mike here"—he gestured to the man in the blue suit—"was watching the place. When Molho showed, he scrammed to the nearest phone to call me. Missed the bad guys going in. Shame."

Mike grimaced. "I didn't realize they were in there until they came out. Jumped in a black Mercedes and drove off."

"Did you see the number plate?" said Muir.

"I did, but . . ." Mike shifted uneasily. "It's those goddamn Greek letters. You don't recognize them, you know?"

"Molho's car was a black Mercedes," said Grant. He gave them the number—another habit he'd learned at SOE.

"We'll get the local cops to put out a bulletin. Probably won't do jack, but you gotta try. We've got guys at the ports and airports too on Red watch. Maybe they'll show up there."

"They'd better turn up somewhere," said Muir tightly. "I think we have to assume that the Soviets came here to ask the same questions we wanted to put to him. I think we also have to assume that they didn't let him die until they had the answers. With Molho dead, Dr. Belzig's our only link to the second half of that tablet."

"You're assuming we have to find *him*." Three pairs of eyes turned to face Grant. "Even if Belzig does get the whole tablet, he's not going to be able to read it. Who's he going to come after then?"

Jackson and his colleague stayed to search the building for any records Molho might have kept. Muir and Grant drove back to the library to pick up Reed and Marina. No one spoke as they drove back along the beach-front road to the hotel. A low haze hung over the sea, blurring the island silhouettes on the horizon; it caught the light of the sinking sun and puffed it into a nebula of pink and gold on the water.

They trooped into the hotel in silence. All Grant could think of was a cold bath and a glass of beer, but as they passed reception one of the girls ran out from behind the desk and accosted him. "*O Kyrios* Grant." She thrust a slip of paper into his hands. "A message for you."

Grant looked at the paper. There was only one word, carefully written out in block Latin characters. Whoever wrote it had obviously struggled with the unfamiliar alphabet: the tentative strokes and wobbly lines looked more like a child's writing: *SOURCELLES*.

"Did you take this message?" Grant asked the girl.

She nodded. "On the telephone. He spelled it out very carefully."

"What time?"

She pointed to a small note in the corner: *13:47*. He must have rung just before the Russians arrived. Grant winced as he remembered the sight of the body.

"What is it?" Muir pulled the paper out of his fingers and examined it. "*Sourcelles*? What the hell is that?"

"Maybe the man who bought the tablet."

"And how the fucking hell are we supposed to find him? Get the Paris phone book? Ring the French embassy?" Muir turned away in disgust. But Marina was suddenly animated. She delved in her handbag and pulled out the slim notebook she had been using at the library. She flicked through the pages, then stopped. Wordlessly, she passed it to Grant, holding the page open with her thumb.

The paper was covered with her small, neat writing—all in Greek, except for one word that leaped out at Grant like a bullet between the eyes: *Sourcelles.*

20

North Aegean, near Thessalonica. Two days later

THE SEAPLANE soared high over the water like a messenger from the gods. In the dazzling sunlight the tips of its silver wings rippled like molten glass in a furnace. No wonder Zeus so often appeared as an eagle, Reed thought, for this was a god's eye view of a land that only gods could have made. The clouds below lapped round an archipelago of thrusting mountain peaks, while further west, where the clouds parted, the sun shone on the sea like a sheet of sapphire. He murmured to himself:

> *. . . the sandals of celestial mold,*
> *Fledged with ambrosial plumes, and rich with gold,*
> *Surround her feet: with these sublime she sails*
> *The aerial space, and mounts the winged gales;*
> *O'er earth and ocean wide prepared to soar,*
> *Her dreaded arm a beamy javelin bore.*

What would Homer have written, Reed wondered, if he could have seen his country from here?

It had taken them the best part of a day to track down Sourcelles, a day spent shouting into telephones and tapping out telegrams in the offices at the Hotel Grande Bretagne. From that little room, tentacles of enquiry had gone out all over Europe: first to consulates, libraries, universities, and—most often—the gray building off Victoria Street; then gradually closing in around tax offices, mayors and local police chiefs. By the end of the day Muir had been able to report back to Jackson at the hotel.

"Luc de Sourcelles. Naturalised Greek, but French originally, as you'd guess from the name. His family comes from Bordeaux—they were involved in shipbuilding, which is what brought him to Greece originally. He inherited a fortune, which he's mostly plowed into his collection of ancient Greek artifacts. He's a nut on the subject—obsessed with the age of heroes. Corresponded with Schliemann's widow—occasionally pops up to badger some obscure European archaeologist. They humor him because they hope he'll fund them. No one will say so, but everyone thinks he's a crackpot. Famously—if that's the right word—reclusive. Widowed, one daughter, lives in a mansion in Macedonia, outside Thessalonica. Ten years ago he wrote a monograph, published privately in Paris: *La Mort d'Achille et son Audelà*."

"What's that when it's at home?"

"*The Death of Achilles and his Afterlife*. His speciality. Marina found out about it researching the White Island. That's why she had the name in her notebook."

"Any good?"

"They didn't have it in the library," Marina explained. "I just found a reference to it in a footnote in another book."

"Huh. And you think he's the guy who bought the second piece of the tablet off the dead Yid?"

"It would make sense. The writing alone would have interested him—and then there's the painting on the back. Reed thinks there might have been something in the picture that hinted at Achilles, or the shield, or even the White Island."

"Did you manage to get in touch?"

"We tried to phone him but couldn't get through. There's been a lot of rebel activity up in the north of Greece—the lines may have been damaged."

Jackson had scowled. "Then we'd better go visit with him. And hope we get there before the Reds show up."

Thessalonica was a gloomy city spread round a bay. Ghostly mansions lined the waterfront; much of the port still showed the ravages of the recent war. Beyond, a few minarets raised their heads above the skyline, a reminder of more distant invasions. Even now, it felt like a city near the front lines of a war. As the seaplane chugged into the harbor, they passed between warships and transports waiting to discharge their cargo, their hulls as gray as the skies overhead.

A car met them at the docks, a black Packard driven by an American soldier. A serial number was stencilled along the hood of the car and another one along the right chest pocket of the driver. "Lieutenant Kirby," he introduced himself, reiterating what was written on his uniform. He couldn't hide his surprise as he looked over the rest of the group. Reed, in his donnish tweed and spectacles; Muir, who always looked to Grant like a black marketeer with his sharp suit and darting eyes; Marina, in a demure black dress belted at the waist; and Grant, whom he probably took for the mechanic. "HQ told me to take you wherever you want to go, sir."

"Did they say anything else?" said Jackson.

"Only that I shouldn't ask any questions."

Jackson clapped him on the shoulder. "Good man. Now, we need to get to a place called the Villa Pelion. Know it?"

"No, sir." Kirby pulled out a map and spread it over the Packard's hood. Grant leaned over to look; he was surprised to see that all the markings were in German.

"Greeks can't make maps for shit, sir," Kirby explained. "It's easiest to use the ones the Krauts left."

Jackson tapped the map with his pen. "That's the place."

Kirby looked worried. "The Reds are pretty busy up that way, sir. There's a radio in the vehicle—I could call in for some back-up if you like. Might take a little while, but . . ."

Jackson glanced at his watch. "No time. The bad guys want this guy too. Just get us there as quick as you can."

"Yes, sir."

Before they left, Kirby rummaged in the trunk and brought out a Sten gun with a folding stock. He handed it to Grant, who was squeezed in the front seat with Jackson. "You know how to use this?"

Grant nodded.

"Keep it handy. Just in case."

They drove out of the city, through the flat pasture and wheat fields that occupied the coastal plain. After so much famine, the crops were at last beginning to grow back, pushing their way between the concrete pillboxes and twisted steel tank traps that still littered the landscape. Not all the obstacles were in the past, either. Three times they had to stop to pass through checkpoints manned by Greek soldiers. Each time, Kirby's uniform got them through unmolested; each time, Jackson handed over a copy of Belzig's photograph with instructions to stop him if they saw him.

"What's the latest on the civil war?" Jackson asked, in between two of the roadblocks. "Are we winning?"

"You'd probably know better than me, sir." Kirby kept his eyes on the road. "I just got here. Officially, I don't arrive for another three months. But from what I hear it's not good. The DSE . . ."

"Who are the DSE?" Reed inquired from the back. The bumps and potholes had left him pale, and he pressed an arm against the ceiling to brace himself.

"*Deemo-kratikos Stratos Eladdas*." Marina winced to hear Kirby manhandling her language the same way he crunched through the Packard's gears. "Democratic Army of Greece. Commies, to you and me. From what I hear, they're doing pretty OK. They're not just taking pot-shots at convoys any more—they're trying to take the cities. Stalin's supplying them through Yugoslavia and Albania. And now the Brits have dropped out—no offense—if we don't hold the line here they'll roll us up all the way to Athens." He shook his head. "It's a helluva thing. But we're hitting back. Way I figure it, most of these guys are just peasants, sheep stealers. They won't have the stomach for a stand-up fight."

"Don't be so sure," Grant warned him. "Most of them learned their trade against the Nazis. Before that, they spent five years underground resisting the Metaxas dictatorship. They know all about fighting dirty little wars."

"Lucky for them they found someone to supply their guns," said Muir drily. His eyes met Grant's in the rearview mirror for a second, before Grant looked down at the Sten gun in his lap. If he had regrets, he didn't let them show.

After a few miles the road left the plain and began winding up into the hills. The higher they climbed, the lower the sky seemed to get. A hard ceiling of cloud pressed down on them, filling the spaces between the dark, scrawny pines that crowded the slopes. The road deteriorated to little more than a forest track. Kirby looked exhausted from the effort of wrestling with the wheel as he struggled to navigate the endless switchbacks, ruts, rocks and fallen trees that impeded their way. The rest of them held on to whatever they could and tried to gulp down breaths of air, while Grant gripped the Sten and scanned the impenetrable forest.

They passed a village—a mean place, half derelict. They would have assumed it had been abandoned if not for the shadows that moved inside the empty windows and splintered doorways, watching them pass. Jackson, squeezed between Grant and Kirby in the front seat, wriggled his hand inside his jacket to reach the Colt pistol tucked under his shoulder.

They came round a bend on the flank of the mountain and saw the house at last. They could hardly have missed it. A huge slice of the hillside had been carved off and levelled into two broad terraces across the face of the mountain. The lower level seemed to be gardens; above, buttressed by a huge retaining wall, perched a mansion that could have graced any estate in the Loire valley. Everything about it—from the lead tiles of its squat, steep-sided roof, to the white limestone walls, to the box hedges and gravel paths that surrounded it—could have been imported wholesale from France. Perhaps they had been.

The road ended at a wrought-iron gate. Two marble lions gazed down from the gateposts, aloof and disdainful. Grant jumped out of the car and tried the gate. It was locked, but there was a black brass button set into one of the pillars. He pushed it and waited.

Kirby craned his head out of the car window. "Nobody home?" His voice sounded small and feeble against the brooding immensity of the mountain; the cloud and pines seemed to swallow it up.

"You said he was a recluse. Maybe . . ."

Grant broke off and turned to look down the gravel driveway. He stared.

A stiff figure in a black raincoat and bowler hat was walking toward them, his crisp footsteps crunching on the path. He held a black umbrella erect in his left hand; a bunch of keys jangled in his right. There was something of the bank clerk or the railway station attendant about him. He came to a precise halt, three feet back from the gate, and stared at them through the iron bars. "*Oui?*"

A fat-bellied raindrop landed on the back of Grant's hand as Reed leaned out of the car window and said, "*Dites à Monsieur Sourcelles que le Professeur Arthur Reed est venu pour lui voir*."

The butler—he must be a butler, Grant thought—stepped behind the gatepost and pulled out a telephone receiver concealed within. He spoke a few words, listened, nodded. "Monsieur Sourcelles is honored that Professor Reed has come so far to visit. He would very much have liked to greet him. But—*malheureusement*—he is busy."

Grant resisted the urge to threaten him with the Sten gun. "Tell Monsieur Sourcelles it is very important. Tell him it concerns the clay tablet he bought in Athens in 1941. Tell him his life is in danger. Not from me," he added.

The butler stared at him, dark eyes in deep sockets. With obvious reluctance he picked up the telephone again and spoke a few more words. "*Oui. Oui. Bon.*

"Monsieur Sourcelles welcomes you."

The butler opened the gate and they rolled up the driveway, between flower beds and lawns, willows and laurel hedges. Further away, through the poplars that hemmed the estate, Grant could see the alabaster outline of a domed classical temple—presumably a folly, though beside the house it seemed almost rational.

The car ground to a halt at the foot of a stairway that led up to the main house. The rain was heavier now. Forgetting decorum, they piled out of the car, ran up the stairs with their jackets and bags held over their heads, and pushed through the open door. They waited there, trembling and dripping, until the butler reappeared to show them through.

The inside of the château—none of them could think of it as a villa—was stark and cold. Everything seemed to be carved from white marble: the floors, the stairs, the Corinthian half-columns set into the walls. Marble busts, all ancient, stared from marble pedestals and marble athletes flexed marble muscles in marble alcoves.

"Feels like a mausoleum," said Jackson, shivering. The only color came from the rich oil paintings that lined the walls between the columns. White-breasted nymphs tempted anxious heroes; alabaster goddesses turned feckless men to stone. A fair-haired woman wreathed in flowers admired herself in a golden mirror. In one, a twisted dwarf pressed an iron corselet against a woman's chest. Everything in the canvas was dark, except for the woman who shone with an almost ethereal whiteness. A blood-red scarf billowed behind her.

Reed stopped in front of it. "Van Dyck. The woman is Thetis; the dwarf, Hephaestus. And that"—he waved a finger at the iron breastplate, stopping it an inch short of the canvas—"is the armor of Achilles."

"Good to know what it looks like," muttered Jackson.

The butler showed them into a drawing room, where an assortment of second-empire furniture clustered round a marble hearth. The deep brocades and chintzes seemed all the richer for their stark setting, poised and elegant in the surrounding emptiness. Tall French windows lined the rear wall, leading on to a terrace. Raindrops spattered the glass, and the gardens below were almost invisible in the gloom.

A rumble of thunder rolled around the house, as if the whole mountain had turned on its foundation. A moment later came the lightning; for a split second everything in the room was cast in a sorcerous silver light. The fire spat sparks in the air and the dim electric lights flickered like candles. It took a moment for Grant's eyes to readjust—and to widen in surprise.

A man stood beside the fire, just in front of a chaise longue. He must have been lying in it before, though Grant hadn't seen him. His face was pale and lined, with a translucent quality that made the skin shimmer in the firelight. A mane of silver hair was slicked back almost to his shoulders. He wore a velvet smoking jacket and loose trousers. He was barefoot.

"*Mes amis*. Welcome."

21

THEY SEATED themselves on the stiff furniture. The butler arranged another log on the fire and withdrew. Sourcelles looked at Reed—as did everyone else. They all felt, instinctively, that it needed an uncommon power to contend with Sourcelles in his domain.

"Your visit is an honor, Professor Reed. You must know I admire very much your scholarship. But who are your friends?"

Reed cleared his throat. "Mr. Jackson and Mr. Muir, from the British and American governments respectively. Miss Papagiannopoulou, who was an assistant to John Pemberton, the English archaeologist, on Crete before he died. And . . ." A precise description failed him. "Mr. Grant."

Sourcelles flashed Grant an appraising look—not hostile, but careful. "Welcome. You would like some cognac? Some calvados?"

"No, thank you." Reed spoke for all of them—though Grant would have been glad of a gulp of something warm.

"*Bien.*" Sourcelles leaned back in his chaise longue, arranging himself like a cat. He took a long silver cigarette holder from a box on the side table, slotted in a cigarette and drew a deep draft. A nimbus of smoke gathered round his head. Everyone waited—but he seemed completely preoccupied, almost oblivious to them.

"Six years ago you bought a Minoan clay tablet from a dealer in Athens called Molho," said Reed. He spoke tentatively, like a student reading out an under-prepared essay in a tutorial.

Sourcelles twitched his shoulders, the merest shrug of indifference.

Reed continued, "The tablet was incomplete. It had been broken."

"By the man who sold it to you," added Grant. Sourcelles's eyes flickered like a snake's. "Did he tell you that? Molho sold the other piece to John Pemberton."

Sourcelles's gaze swept on to Marina. "You saw this? You have proof?"

"We had the tablet, until two days ago. A German stole it—though he'd probably say he was just reclaiming it, as he was the one who dug it up in the first place."

"What did it look like?"

"About this big." Reed framed the dimensions with his hands. "A dozen lines of Linear B script on the obverse. On the reverse, a faint painting showing the usual iconography associated with Minoan shrines. I imagine your piece looks very similar. Perhaps like this?"

He took out Pemberton's photograph, now dog-eared and creased, and passed it to Sourcelles. The Frenchman barely glanced at it. "This could be anything. I have many pieces in my collection. It is the best private collection of Mycenaean artifacts in the world, I think. *Private* collection," he repeated. Little puffs of smoke escaped his mouth as he said it. "It is not for public viewing."

"We're not the public," said Grant. "And we're not the only ones coming here to look for this tablet. Why don't you telephone the Athens police and find out what happened to Molho. He already lost a hand protecting you from Belzig. Did you know that?" He looked at Sourcelles's face, the skin like parchment that had been scraped clean, and decided he probably did. "Now he's lost his life—only this time he couldn't protect you. Belzig knows you have this thing. He'll come here; he's probably on his way already. Do you want to know what he did to Molho? It wasn't nice."

"And if I show it to you? What will you do with the knowledge you gain? I wonder, do you even know what you are really looking for?" Sourcelles gave Grant a piercing look, saw no answer and dismissed him with a sneer.

"The White Island," said Marina. She kept her eyes fixed on Sourcelles, ignoring the suspicious stares she drew from the others. Sourcelles gazed back. His mouth turned up at the corners in a smirk, though Grant couldn't tell if it was respect or satisfaction at some private victory.

"The White Island was the last resting place of Achilles, where his mother carried him after his death at Troy. It was also where his hero cult began. The tablet holds the key to finding it."

Sourcelles laughed, softly mocking. "Maybe. But how will you unlock it? Have you solved the code of the Minoan script?" He read the answer on their faces. "I think not. Many have tried to break it—I myself have tried, many times. The tablets are *comme une femme*. You possess her body, but her secrets she keeps to herself."

He blew a ring of smoke. "Do you know what the original *museum* was? It was not some exhibition hall, where the untutored masses could come and stare at relics they could never comprehend. It was a temple to the muses, *museion*, a sanctuary to the goddesses of memory. The men who worked there were a sacred order of priests and poets—not day trippers paying their two pennies to be entertained."

"Well, we're not tourists," blurted out Jackson. "Professor Reed is from Oxford University."

Sourcelles laughed. "I have been to Oxford. When I was a young man I went to all the capitals of scholarship. To Paris, to Berlin, to Oxford. I sat at the feet of the great men of learning and asked them about the Trojan war. They laughed at me. Even after Schliemann had proved Homer was correct, they could not accept it. They spun lies about him: that he salted his finds with trinkets he bought in the Athens markets; that his accounts of his digs were fiction; that he could not tell apart the different levels of his finds. Slanders. When he went to Troy, they said he would find nothing. When he found not one but half a dozen cities, they said that none of them could be right—they were too old, or too late, or there was no sign of a war. They mocked him, because their imaginations were too small to believe. Those same men, they thought I was another Schliemann, a little rich boy who would use his money to build fantasy castles. They had no time for heroes. They were small, mean-minded people who could not understand the true scope of the heroes. They were not worthy. So I resolved that as much as I could afford, I would collect the relics of the age of heroes and preserve their memory with honor.

"Besides, the White Island is not hidden, just as Troy and Mycenae were not hidden. If men have lost it, it is only because they do not believe. You know the story of Cassandra, the Trojan priestess whose fate was to speak the truth and never to be believed? She is the true heroine of the story: not Helen or Achilles or Odysseus. For three thousand years, the truth of the tale of Troy has been known to every generation—and every generation, in its feeble-mindedness, has refused to believe it."

"But all the sources contradict each other," said Marina. "According to whom you believe—Pliny, Pausanias, Lycophron, Strabo or Arrian—it could be at the mouth of the Danube, or the Dnieper, or somewhere in the open sea."

Sourcelles nodded. There was something almost paternal in his approval, a father admiring a precocious daughter—but also something voracious, hungry to lure her on. He rose and crossed to the cabinet on the wall. He pulled a slim brown volume from one of the shelves and laid it on the low table in the center of the room. Grant saw Sourcelles' name in gold on the cover. He opened it to a page that showed a double-spread map, flattening the spine as the others leaned in to look closer.

"The Black Sea." On the thick cream paper it looked like some sort of bodily organ, with the various rivers, straits and tributaries straggling from it like veins. "Here"—the northwest corner—"the Danube estuary, and here"—the northernmost point—"the Dnieper. In between, halfway, the Dniester. Between each is one hundred kilometers. *Alors* . . ."

He took a wooden compass from a tin and gave it to Marina. "*Mademoiselle*. You can show where is five hundred stadia from the estuary of the Dniester."

Marina calibrated the compasses against the map scale, then centered it on the narrow bay at the mouth of the Dniester and twisted. The faint circle she inscribed touched the mouths of both the Danube and the Dnieper.

"I don't see that that gets us any further," said Reed.

Sourcelles ignored him. "Pliny is a *fausse piste*—how do you say, a red herring. Here"—he tapped the mouth of the Dnieper with a silver pencil—"was the Greek colony of Olbia. It was founded in the sixth century before Christ by settlers from Miletus, who came to trade for furs and precious stones with the Scythians. Achilles was the local hero—the patron saint, you understand? They built a temple to him on a little island where the river joins the sea. But they did this because the story of the White Island was known, because already Achilles was associated with this place. Centuries later, writers and geographers remembered the story of the White Island; they remembered there was a temple of Achilles on an island near Olbia and they thought they must be the same thing."

"So if it's not there, it must be in the mouth of the Danube."

"*C'est possible*. That is what Pausanias and Lycophron believed, and there are many islands in the mouth of the Danube. But Pausanias never visited the Black Sea. He repeated what he had read in a much older source. And he mistranslated. The correct reading is not *in* the mouth of the Danube, but *opposite*."

With her finger, Marina traced the pencil arc she had drawn: out from the Danube estuary, through the open sea and back toward the north shore. Her finger glided across the map—then, at the circle's furthest point, hovered for a moment. At the tip of her nail almost crossed out by the pencil line running through it, a dark spot blotted the paper. It could have been an ink stain, or a squashed fly, but when Marina peered closely she could see . . . "It's an island." She blinked as her eyes adjusted back to the room. "What is it?"

"In Russian it is called *Zmeiny*, in Turkish they say *Yilanda*." Sourcelles smiled at their incomprehension. "They have all the same meaning. The Greek name is *Ophidonis*."

"Snake Island," said Marina and Reed almost simultaneously.

Sourcelles nodded. "You know the symbolism of the serpent. It crawls into dark holes in the earth, down into the darkest recesses where no man goes. It has the power of death—but also of life."

"Life?" said Grant skeptically.

Sourcelles drew a sinuous wave in the corner of the page, then bisected it with a straight line. "You know the pharmacists' symbol? The serpent curled round the staff. It is an ancient Greek symbol, the Rod of Asclepius. The snake is one of the earliest symbols of primitive life—sexless, timeless, able to regenerate itself by shaking off the old skin and leaving it behind. They were also associated with the gift of prophecy. The prophetess Cassandra had her eyes and ears licked by serpents when she was left alone by her parents, and this gave her her powers. And Apollo's priestess at Delphi was the Pythia, a pythoness in human form who entered a trance to deliver the oracle."

"Like the Minoan snake woman," said Grant. The image, the serpents writhing round her hips and breasts, had lodged unsettlingly in his mind.

Sourcelles raised an ironic eyebrow, the teacher surprised by the boy at the back of the classroom. "*Très bien*. According to Arrian, there was an oracle in the temple of Achilles on the White Island. So where is better to have it, this temple of the undying hero, this door to the underworld, than on Snake Island?"

"But that's in the fucking USSR!" Jackson exploded. He jabbed a finger on to the book. "Are you telling me that the Soviets have been sitting on this thing the whole time?"

Outside, lightning forked in the valley and rain drummed on the window like bullets. The sound of water flowed all around them, running off the roofs and gutters, and down the mountainside.

"Has anyone ever been there?" asked Muir more calmly.

Sourcelles waved the cigarette holder like a wand. "In 1823 a Russian officer in the Black Sea Fleet, Captain-Lieutenant Kritskii, put ashore. He passed his account to an academician at the Imperial Academy of Sciences and Belles Lettres in Saint Petersburg."

All five of them were tensed, leaning forward in their chairs. The fire crackled and spat out sparks that eddied and flurried up the chimney.

"Did he find anything?"

"He found the island lived up to its reputation." Sourcelles lit a fresh cigarette and tucked it in his holder. "It was crawling with snakes. Many birds, also. He could not move more than two paces without stepping on them. You have read the story in Arrian?" he said, suddenly turning back to Marina. She nodded slowly. "He said the White Island was filled with seabirds. Each morning they would dive down to the water and wet their wings in the waves, then fly up and sprinkle the water over the temple. Then they landed and mopped the temple courtyard clean with their wings."

Jackson shifted in his chair. "Can we skip the fairy tales? We haven't got time—not if Uncle Joe's got this thing in his goddamn backyard. Did this Krisski or Russki or whatever the hell his name was find anything important?"

Sourcelles eyed him with the sort of look that only a Frenchman could give an American. Then, turning deliberately to face the others: "He found an ancient temple."

Nobody knew what to say. They all gazed at Sourcelles, stupefied by hope, by greed, by the fear of what he might say next.

"Did he find anything else? Anything, uh . . . valuable?"

Sourcelles's eyes narrowed and he fixed Jackson with a raking stare. "A strange question. I wonder, Mr. Jackson—I have answered your tiresome questions as best as is possible; I have welcomed you into my house although you offered me only danger—but now I wonder, why is it you want to know so much about the White Island? Are you an archaeologist? What brings five such different and—excuse me—strange persons to my doorstep in these dangerous times? Have you been honest with me? I do not think so." He stared around the room: Muir defiant, Jackson plainly annoyed, Reed looking at his shoes. No one met his gaze.

"Legend says there was a great treasure on the island." Marina said it calmly, but her words electrified the room. Muir made a strangled, gurgling sound, as if he was suffering some sort of seizure. Jackson's hand edged inside the lapel of his jacket, toward the Colt under his arm; Grant reached for the Webley just in case. Only Reed and Sourcelles kept still, attentive. Sourcelles motioned for Marina to continue.

"According to Arrian, the temple on the White Island attracted lavish offerings from sailors who put in there. He describes mountains of silver bowls and golden rings, and hoards of precious stones. A treasure trove."

Muir's heart restarted; Jackson's hand eased back into view. Grant kept his fingers wrapped round the Webley.

"According to the text, they also offered many goats." A conspiratorial smile passed between Sourcelles and Marina. Grant didn't like it. "But no, as far as I am aware, Captain Kritskii found only stones. No treasure. Perhaps it was hidden in the bowels of the island. More probably it was looted long ago. The Black Sea has always been a haven for pirates and thieves." He inclined his head toward them with a chill smile. "If you go there, be careful of what you find. There was a reason the ancient Greeks feared the Black Sea as a place beyond the confines of the world, a liminal region peopled by savages. Wild Amazons, flesh-eating Laestrygonians, Sirens and serpents.

"You should not be fooled by the White Island's chaste name. Too much Christianity has made us think of the afterlife as a happy place of harps and choirs and soft clouds. The Greeks knew better. Even for heroes it was an angry, tortuous place. There is a story about the White Island in Philostratus that the ghost of Achilles instructs a passing merchant to bring him a certain slave girl from Asia Minor. When the merchant does so, Achilles feasts him royally in his temple, then sends him on. But as the merchant sails away he hears screams, horrible screams of impossible agony, coming from the island. It is Achilles, tearing off the girl's limbs one by one."

Jackson got to his feet. "Well, thank you very much Mr. Sourcelles. I guess we'd better be going. You've been, uh, very helpful to us."

The others stayed seated. "What about the tablet?" said Muir. "That's what we came for."

"What you came for?" Dark anger clouded Sourcelles's voice. He stood. The fire cast a long shadow back over the room. "You do not come to my house to demand something. My collection is my own. I do not share it with anyone. Unless you have some quid pro quo to offer me in return?"

"Let's go," Jackson urged. "We can find this island for ourselves. We don't need the tablet. Can't read the damn thing anyway."

"And what will we do when we get to the island?" Reed looked angrier than Grant had ever seen him. "We'd never even have got started on this hunt without the information on that tablet. What if there are more vital clues hidden on the second half? Whatever's on this island, it obviously isn't lying around in plain view."

"You keep your mouth shut," snapped Jackson. For a moment Sourcelles was forgotten in his own home as the three men stared each other down. He watched them from beside the fire, listening with detached fascination.

The mournful chime of a bell echoed through the empty house. Everyone looked at Sourcelles, who shrugged. "The doorbell. Jacques will see to it."

"Are you expecting anyone else?" Grant was already reaching for his gun.

"*Non*."

"It's probably Kirby," said Jackson. "Must be wondering what happened to us."

The bell chimed again. A flicker of annoyance crossed Sourcelles's face. "Where can Jacques be?" He crossed to the French windows and opened them. A blast of cold, damp air blew in and the din of the raindrops filled the room. Sourcelles peered out into the rain, though the garden was all but invisible in the gloom. "*Qui est là?*"

"No!" Grant realized what was happening a moment too late. Pulling Marina down, he dived toward the open door. He was still in mid air when the first bullet struck.

22

THE WINDOWS exploded in a storm of lead and glass. Sourcelles was knocked back by the impact; he collided in mid air with Grant and the two men fell to the floor. That probably shielded Grant from the worst of the blast. Jackson, who'd been standing nearest the window, wasn't so lucky; he reeled away clutching his face. Thin tendrils of blood covered it like maggots.

"Get back!" Grant shouted. Bullets were still flying over his head, but he couldn't see where they were coming from. "Get into the hallway." Shuffling back on his knees, he dragged Sourcelles into a corner. The Frenchman had actually been standing in front of the windows, so the flying glass had missed him, but that wouldn't help. Three wounds gaped in his chest where the bullets had struck, and he had left a thick smear of blood on the white marble floor. Grant looked for something to staunch the bleeding, but there was nothing within reach.

"The tablet. Where is it?"

Thunder roared over the mountain, temporarily drowning out the rattle of the machine-guns. It also drowned out Sourcelles's answer. Grant bent his ear close to the Frenchman's mouth, all the while trying to keep an eye on the shattered window frame. "*Where?*"

"The gallery." The guns had stopped, but now even the rain almost overpowered Sourcelles's voice. "It is in the east wing—on the top floor." He lifted a limp arm to his throat and tugged at his blood-soaked collar. Grant tore it open for him. He'd assumed the dying man just wanted to breath—but his fingers were still scrabbling for something. A leather cord hung round his neck. Grant lifted it and pulled out a small brass key from under the shirt.

"The Gorgon," Sourcelles whispered. "Behind the Gorgon."

He went limp. There was nothing more Grant could do. Keeping his back to the wall, he edged round the room to the exit. The others were there, sheltering in the hallway. Reed clutched Sourcelles's book to his chest; he must have snatched it off the table.

"Sourcelles bought it," Grant said. "The tablet's upstairs."

"That's not going to be much use if we can't get out," said Muir. "We don't even know what we're up against."

"Kirby said he had a radio in the car." Grant turned to Jackson. "Can you use it to raise the American HQ?"

Jackson nodded. "Gonna take a while for the cavalry to get here, though."

"We'll meet them halfway. There's an airstrip on the other side of the mountain. It won't be on their maps, but it's roughly between the villages of Enispe and Stratie, in the valley."

Jackson stared at him incredulously. "How do you know that?"

"I used it in the war."

Jackson might have argued, but at that moment an enormous explosion tore through the living room beyond. A cloud of dust and splinters swept into the corridor. Through the ringing in his ears Grant heard shouts from the terrace outside and more shots. They ran down the corridor, past the sightless row of marble heads. Ancient heroes watched them from above, frozen in their own battles. They stopped at the end of the passage, by the corner that led to the front hall and the main staircase.

"Give me your hat," Grant said to Jackson.

Jackson did. A bust of Socrates stood on a column about chest height just inside the corridor. Grant hung the trilby on its head, then crouched down and heaved against the pillar. It slid easily across the polished marble floor, past the corner, out into the hallway and . . .

Two cracks sounded almost at once: a pistol shot and the bullet chiselling into the marble. Half of Socrates' right cheek split off and crashed toward the floor. Before it hit, Grant had sprung out behind the column, trained the Webley through the narrow gap it made with the wall and squeezed off two shots. The trilby fluttered down. By the front door, something heavier thudded to the ground.

Grant glanced at Jackson. "Cover me."

He bounded into the hallway and dived behind the stairs. No one shot at him. He peeked out from behind the banister. A body in green fatigues, with a red star sewed on the sleeve, lay sprawled across the threshold. There was no one else there.

Grant waved Jackson forward. The American sprinted across the hall, flattened himself against the wall by the front door and risked a quick look out.

"Is the car still there?"

"Uh-huh. But I don't see Kirby."

"As long as the radio's there."

At a nod from Grant, Jackson dived out through the front door and rolled down the steps to the parked car. He crouched against its back tire. Grant waited for the bullets to come, ready to return fire at a moment's notice. No one seemed to have seen them.

Jackson edged his way round to the car's rear, popped open the trunk and pulled out a field radio. He struggled under the weight. Bracing it against his chest, he ducked his head round the Packard's taillight to check for danger. He shuddered. Kirby's corpse lay prone on the ground, bleeding into the gravel.

But there was no time to mourn. There was a movement behind one of the hedges. Grant saw it; he stepped out through the doorway and fired two quick shots, giving Jackson enough time to scuttle up the steps. He staggered under Grant's outstretched arm with the radio and collapsed onto his knees.

"Mind you don't break it," said Grant. He fired one more shot, then slammed the door shut. "Tell your headquarters to send a plane to the airstrip. We'll meet them there. Then find a back door and get out of here." He looked back to Marina. "You come with me."

"And where are you going?" Muir looked furious at being ordered about by Grant.

"We're going to find the tablet."

Grant and Marina left the others and ran up the curving stairs. The sounds faded behind them as they passed the first floor and carried on up. The stairs ended on the next floor in a square landing, with corridors leading away on both sides and a round window looking out over the gardens and driveway below. Grant peered through it. The rain was hard as ever, blotting the grounds into a drab canvas of greens and grays, but he thought he could make out a group of men huddled in the shelter of the retaining wall below the driveway. Something that wasn't lightning flashed and Grant heard a bang that wasn't thunder. He decided not to risk a shot. It was too far for the Webley and he didn't want to risk giving away his position.

"Where did Sourcelles say he kept the tablet?"

Marina's question drew him back to the task at hand. "The east wing." He thought for a moment, then pointed to his right. "That way." And . . . something else. "I think he said to look for the Gorgon. Does that make any sense to you?"

"The Gorgon was a monster, a woman with snakes for hair, tusks for teeth and brass claws instead of hands."

"Sounds like an ugly bitch."

"She's a manifestation of everything men fear about women's sexuality. One look from her could turn you to stone," said Marina, with a look that came close to achieving the same effect.

They moved down the corridor, opening every door they came to. This part of the house didn't seem to be much used—bedrooms with bare mattresses, bathrooms whose tubs were only filled with dust—but it still displayed a trove of artifacts. Most of it was pottery rather than sculpture: vases, amphorae, jugs and bowls with a dizzying variety of shapes. On the curved sides, black-glazed heroes shadow-boxed their miniature battles. More paintings hung on the walls: long portraits framed in heavy gold. Grant scanned them, looking for the Gorgon.

None of the women he could see fitted the bill. They reclined in swathes of gauzy cloth, careless of their nudity, looking on while earnest heroes did battle. One of the men was mounted on a winged horse, thrusting his lance into a creature that seemed to be some monstrous hybrid of a lion, a goat and a dragon.

Grant called Marina over. "Is that it?"

"That's the Chimaera. In the myths, the Gorgons were his aunts."

"I can see the family resemblance. Did you find anything?"

"No."

They'd reached the end of the corridor. A full-length portrait, larger than life, covered almost the entire wall, but the woman in it was far from a monster. Her skin was pale as ice, her eyes blue and piercing. She wore a high-peaked helmet and a silver breastplate of scaled armor, while her hands held a spear and an intricately decorated shield. Grant assumed she was Britannia, though he couldn't think why the Frenchman would want her in his house.

"Perhaps there's something on one of the pots," said Marina. "I didn't examine all of them. Maybe . . ."

Shouts in the stairwell cut her short. A moment later footsteps thudded on the stairs. Grant turned back.

"Look at the painting," said Marina.

"I hate to tell you this, but I don't think that's where our problems are coming from."

"Look at the painting," she repeated urgently. She reached for his shoulder and spun him round. "The shield."

The footsteps were getting louder—at least two pairs, Grant reckoned. They paused on the landing below and Grant heard muffled voices conferring. Reluctantly, he looked where Marina was pointing. The shield was almost head-high, so close that for a second all he could see were the individual flecks of gray and white paint. Then he saw it. In the center of the shield, embossed in the metal but seemingly with a life of its own, a suffocating face pressed out of the metal. Vipers sprouted from her head and curved tusks hung in her mouth like daggers. But it was her expression that was most terrible, drawn into a snarl of infinite, implacable hatred. Even in paint, Grant felt his bones stiffen just looking at it.

"The woman in the painting is Athena. When Perseus killed the Gorgon Medusa, he cut off her head and brought it to the goddess who set it in her shield. *That's* the Gorgon."

Grant grabbed the ornate frame and ripped the picture away. A hairline crack traced the outline of a door in the smooth wall behind, and a small hole invited the key.

"Hurry," said Marina. One of the men following seemed to have peeled off to clear the first floor; the other had kept on climbing. Grant could hear his footsteps turning as he reached the half-landing directly below their floor. "Give me your gun."

Grant handed Marina the Webley, then took Sourcelles's key from his pocket and slotted it into the hole. The mechanism moved smoothly. He heard a latch click and pushed against the door.

A low squeal echoed down the corridor as the hinges creaked. For a moment Grant froze, wondering if he'd been heard. Then he decided it was too late for that. He put his shoulder to the door and gave an almighty heave. It swung in with a shriek of protest. That ended any lingering hope that they hadn't been heard—but the door was open.

"Come on," shouted Grant. Pulling Marina after him, he dived through the doorway, just as a storm of bullets blasted apart the corridor. His enemy was sheltering behind the corner to the stairwell; he had reached his gun round and was firing blindly. Pots and vases exploded in clouds of red clay dust, and the painted heroes' armor was lacerated with holes. Together, Grant and Marina heaved the door shut, just in time to hear the first bullets hammering into it. It shuddered under the impact, but none came through. Grant locked it behind them. Only then did he turn to see where it had brought them.

Grant's first impression was that it felt like a chapel; Marina, more accurately, saw it was like the inside of a miniature temple. Corinthian columns ran along both sides of the high, narrow room, topped by low-relief friezes that she suspected weren't reproductions. At the far end, under the pitched roof, Sourcelles seemed to have installed the entire pediment of a classical temple, complete with a marble tableau of the gods. Tall glass-fronted cabinets were recessed in bays between the columns—the lower halves filled with drawers, the upper parts open shelves groaning under the weight of the sculpture, pottery and figurines they held. Some were so high that a wooden ladder had been left in the corner to reach them. There were no windows, but the entire pitched ceiling was made of glass, like a greenhouse or an orangery.

"This doesn't look like much." Grant peered at the artifacts on display. Compared with the finely decorated pottery in the hallway, or the lifelike marble heads downstairs, it looked more like child's work. The figures in the sculpted stone plaques showed no character or variation; the pots were painted with thick, unglazed bands of color.

Marina picked up a figurine—a familiar shape, a goddess with outflung arms, though without the detail of the one they had found in the cave on Crete. "This is the most valuable part of Sourcelles's collection. Everything in this room—apart from the friezes—dates from before the first Greek dark age."

She pulled out one of the wide, thin drawers. Laid out on a deep blue velvet cloth were six clay tablets, each about the size of a postcard and all etched with the tiny scratches of Linear B. She stroked a finger over one, feeling the inscribed figures like whorls of skin. The noise in the corridor outside had stopped; the only sound in the room was the patter of rain on the glass ceiling. Even that sounded softer, as though the rain was easing up—but perhaps it just seemed that way after the gunfire.

"They've probably gone to get reinforcements." Grant began rifling through the drawers, working his way down the bays on one side of the room. Marina did the same, though more slowly and methodically, on the other. Not all of them held tablets. Some were filled with figurines, or stone plaques or brooches; some pieces were intact, others only in fragments.

"Here." Marina lifted a piece out of the drawer in front of her and turned it over. Even though she had known what to expect, she still gasped. There was the painting, the same style as the drawing that had led them to the cave on Crete. The lines were faint with age, but she thought she could see the outlines of a boat, the zigzag patterning of waves, and bull horns.

Grant ran over, took the briefest glance, then looked up. "Let's get out of here."

The room suddenly seemed to pulsate as a volley of bullets struck the outside of the door, flat and muted like mallet blows. Whatever it was made of, the door seemed strong enough to absorb it—for the moment.

"They're back," said Grant.

"How do we get out now?"

Grant pulled out the Webley. "Cover your eyes."

"What?"

"*Look down.*" Without further warning Grant raised the Webley like a starter's pistol and fired three shots into the roof. He held Marina against his chest, protecting her with his body as a crystal rain of glass and water splashed over them. When the shattering of glass subsided, he looked up. Rain poured through a jagged hole in the greenhouse roof.

Grant took the wooden ladder from the corner and moved it under the hole. It swayed alarmingly as he climbed past the display shelves, higher and higher. But not high enough. Even as high as he could go, he was still left about three feet short.

The whole room seemed to shift a few inches as a massive explosion shook the house. Artifacts rattled on their shelves and a few more loose shards of glass came free of the roof and fell to the floor. Grant was pitched around like a rope end; Marina threw herself on to the ladder and hung on, desperately trying to weight it down. Behind her, the door had almost been punched off its hinges.

"They're trying to blow it open," she shouted up.

"I know." Grant looked around in desperation. On the shelf in the wall beside him he saw a withered metal blade that might once have been a sword. He took it, reached up and hammered it against the jagged edge of the hole he had made. "Watch your head," he shouted, as more glass cascaded down. Rain was still falling through the hole, running down into his eyes. The blade was slippery in his hands and his shirt was slicked against his skin. But he managed to hack away most of the glass from the lead window frame.

"*Hold on tight.*" He put down the sword, let go of the ladder with his hands and braced himself against the wall. With two quick steps he bounded up the last two rungs, swayed for a moment at the top like an acrobat on a tightrope, then lunged for the roof. His fingers closed round the frame—and almost let go at once. There was still glass embedded in the lead. It dug into his hands, drawing blood and a gasp of agony. Grant gritted his teeth. It was like dragging himself over a serrated knife edge. But there was no way down. And the banging behind the door was getting louder. He hauled himself up, over the edge, and collapsed in a wet mess of blood and water on the roof.

There was no time to recover. He looked back down into the room. Marina was standing at the foot of the ladder looking very small and worried.

"Get up here," he called through the rain. Behind her, a black snout had squeezed through the gap between the bowed-in door and its frame. The gun fired, but the angle was too narrow and the bullet struck one of the display cabinets instead. Something priceless and ancient shattered into dust and fragments.

Marina scampered up the swaying ladder, the tablet tucked into her belt. Grant pulled off his own belt and laid it over the broken window frame, letting the leather take the bite of the glass. He leaned out as far as he dared.

The house trembled again and this time Grant saw the yellow flames of the explosion licking round the battered door, then blasting it in. Marina jumped; the ladder tottered, swayed, then toppled over and crashed down on a stone sarcophagus in the middle of the room. Grant's hands closed round Marina's wrists. His hands were torn and bloody; for a moment he felt a stabbing pain and the horrible, heart-stopping sensation of her sliding through his fingers. Then she dug her nails into his forearm and he tightened his grip. She stopped falling and began to rise, flopping over the ridge of the roof just as the first of their enemies burst through the blown-out door below. He was still looking around, wondering where they'd gone, when Grant put two bullets into the top of his skull.

"Should improve the odds." Grant reloaded the Webley. Together, he and Marina ran to the back edge of the roof and looked down. The grounds behind the house were less mannered than the front garden: an open apron of lawn that ended abruptly in the front ranks of the surrounding pine forest. There, three sodden figures huddled in the trees.

"You first, this time." Grant found a drainpipe and almost pushed Marina over the edge in his hurry. As soon as she touched the ground he was after her, sliding down the slick metal pipe, trying to ignore the burning in his hands. Anyone watching from the windows would have had a clear shot at them, but that was a risk he had to take. They ran across the grass, their feet sinking into the soft turf and threw themselves into the cover of the trees.

"Glad you made it." Muir was crouched behind a tree trunk, his pistol poised to return any fire from the house. "Christ. You look bloody terrible."

"Did you find the tablet?" said Jackson from behind a rock.

Marina pulled out the damp tablet from her waistband and handed it to Reed. The professor's hands, white and bloated in the rain, trembled as he took it.

"Did you manage to raise your headquarters on the radio?"

Jackson nodded. "They have no fucking idea about this airstrip of yours, but they're sending a Dakota where you said. That's the good news. Bad news is they say the Reds are all over this mountain like a rash. They're not sure we'll get through. The other bad news is that they're running an aerial offensive against the Commies this afternoon. The guy at HQ said he'd try to call off the bombers . . ." He shrugged. "But I brought you this." Jackson passed Grant the Sten gun. "Only the one clip, so don't go crazy with it. Unless you have to."

Grant holstered the Webley and took the sub-machine gun. "I'll stay here while you get away."

"No," said Jackson firmly. "You're the only one who knows where this goddamn airfield is. We'll go together."

"Then let's go."

23

THEY SET off. It was slow going: the forest was thick and tangled, the ground soft. Marina, in particular, struggled with her high-heeled shoes. Eventually, she took them off, removed her stockings and walked barefoot on the carpet of pine needles. All of them were tensed, listening out for any sign they were being followed. The rain had stopped, though they hardly knew it with the steady drip of water from the trees.

"At least with Sourcelles dead, we don't have to worry about him telling the Russkis what he knows." Jackson pushed past a low-hanging branch. It snapped back, showering Reed with a spray of water drops. Grant, ahead of Jackson, looked back in disgust. "What? Don't look at me like some Boy Scout. You've played the game. It's not just what you know; it's what they *don't* know."

"I never thought killing civilians was the best way to achieve that."

"No? What about those Yid commandos you were busy selling guns to?" He raised an eyebrow. "Muir told me all about your dirty little past. You know what they did at the King David Hotel? Ninety-one dead. Do you think they give a damn about civilians?"

"They're fighting a war."

"So are we." Jackson looked as though he might have gone on at length. But Grant was no longer paying attention. He stopped and stared at the sky, his head tilted, listening for something. A moment later Jackson heard it too. The thrum of aircraft engines, high overhead.

"Is that ours? Could it've got here already?"

Grant shook his head grimly. "That's not a Dakota."

"You sure?"

Grant didn't bother to answer. He'd lost count of the times he'd spent crouched in foxholes or behind boulders, straining his ears for the sound that would spell relief. "I think we can assume your man didn't manage to call off the bombers."

"Shit."

A crack that had nothing to do with wood shattered the stillness of the forest. Grant spun round. The trees were as thick and dark as ever—he could barely tell the way they'd come. But someone was out there.

"Was there supposed to be a ground assault as well?"

Jackson looked as alarmed as the rest of them. "No."

"Then they're after us."

"What do we do?"

"We run. And hope the bombs don't get us."

Reed had never known the sheer physical terror of being a fugitive in hostile country. His war had been fought with paper and pencil in the huts at Bletchley Park. It hadn't been easy: some nights, when the U-boat packs were hunting, the pressure had been immense, too much for some men. But for Reed the stillness of the codes had always been a place of calm, the one corner of the war where battle was decided rationally. The torrent of numbers they battled every day could frustrate, baffle and deceive—but there was a fundamental order behind them, however well the Enigma machines tried to chew it up. And, like the ancient Greeks, Reed had never feared the rational.

But this—this was chaos. This was all the animal forces the Greeks had tried to consign to myth: the harpies, furies, gorgons and bacchantes that had haunted their imaginations let loose. Reed felt he was in a dream, clutching the tablet like a talisman. If he dropped it, he was sure, the chasing pack would be on him in an instant. And so he ran.

> *So two wild boars spring furious from their den,*
> *Roused with the cries of dogs and voice of men;*
> *On every side the crackling trees they tear,*
> *And root the shrubs, and lay the forest bare;*
> *They gnash their tusks, with fire their eyeballs roll,*
> *Till some wide wound lets out their mighty soul.*

The poetry thumped in his heart. He was aware of others around him—Grant, Muir, perhaps Jackson—breaking their stride to pause and return fire, but he carried on relentless. He had never run so far, so hard. His legs were like jelly. When the forest thinned into a bare clearing of rock and scrub he tried to run faster to get back into the safety of the trees, but couldn't.

Grant turned and squeezed off a few rounds from the Sten. It felt like some lethal fairy tale, being chased through dark woods by a shapeless malevolence. Perhaps they should have made a stand—at least that would have solved the risk of getting a bullet in his back. But the forest stretched away in every direction and their pursuers almost certainly had them outgunned. Probably outnumbered, too.

He reached the edge of some open ground, where a landslide seemed to have carried away the trees. Ahead, he could see Reed flailing frantically between the boulders. Grant fired a short burst into the trees. That might give them pause for thought, give him time to cross the clearing.

The blood was pumping in his ears—but for all that, it was a strangely silent battle. The shots were sporadic, quickly swallowed in the damp silence. So although the bomber was high overhead, he heard the buzz of its engines loud and clear. Despite the danger all around he looked up.

The storm had passed and a cool wind was pulling the clouds apart.

Grant could see pale-blue sky through the shreds of gray—and, passing in front of it, a dark shadow like a fly or a bird. As Grant watched, it split in two. Part of it seemed to break away, plummeting to the earth, while the other glided serenely on.

"*Run!*"

The others were already well across the clearing. There was no one to hear Grant's words but himself. He launched himself toward them, vaulting round the boulders and hurdling the roots and stumps that tried to grab him. Whoever was following them must have reached the edge of the forest: he heard shots, saw one of the rocks throw up a puff of white dust as a bullet struck it only a few feet away. His erratic course, zigzagging between the debris, made him a hard target to hit, but not impossible. The edge of the clearing was agonizingly close, twenty yards distant, but he couldn't chance it. He slid down into a pocket behind two boulders and peered through the crack between them.

For a second he saw them clearly: seven of them, all in green combat fatigues. They were spread out in a line along the edge of the forest, all with guns at their shoulders. Grant raised the Sten, wondering how many bullets he had left. Behind them, over the trees, a black comet crashed into the woods.

The world seemed to melt into flames. A pillar of fire rose up out of the forest, three times as high as the trees, which turned to tinder in the inferno. It was like no explosion Grant had ever seen. Instead of rolling away, the noise grew, swelling like a train rushing through a tunnel. A high wind blasted through the clearing; Grant was thrown against the boulder as the hungry fire sucked in all the air it could grasp. The wind swept his pursuers off their feet, picking them up like dolls and hurling them into the burning forest.

Black smoke crawled up the wall of flame and swallowed it. The wind subsided, drifting back over Grant like a wave running down a beach. He ran with it, scrambling over the broken ground to the line where the trees resumed. The others were waiting for him there.

"What the hell is that?" Grant's lungs felt as if they were struggling against a ten-ton boulder on his chest.

"Napalm." Jackson held a red spotted handkerchief against his mouth. "We use it for smoking out the Reds."

"Well, we're going to be served on toast if we don't get out fast." The far side of the clearing was completely ablaze and the fire had already started licking round its flanks.

"Did you see Belzig in there?"

"I didn't have time to look." Grant glanced back. A black figure ran screaming into the clearing. His head was bald, burned clean, and fiery shapes clung to his back like demons. Three bullets from Jackson's Colt ended his misery. Then they ran.

Black clouds hid the sky again, but this time they were clouds of fire, not water. Tendrils of smoke reached between the trees, chasing after them. Reed could only think of the Hydra, a slithery ball of sinuous necks and snapping heads. The fire seemed to have receded a bit, but every time he glanced over his shoulder it was still there, a dull orange glow behind the trees.

They reached an outcrop on the shoulder of the mountain, a rocky place, high and very exposed. From there, they could look down into the steep valleys that defined the mountain, and across to the slopes and summits on the far side. The valleys were dark and thickly wooded, with occasional flecks of white where a fast-flowing river showed through.

Muir pushed past Reed to the edge of the outcrop. "So where's the fucking airstrip, then?"

Grant pointed to the low saddle between the valleys, almost directly beneath them. The mountains on either side pressed close against it and the ridge itself looked barely wide enough for a goat track.

"We'll never land a plane there."

"I've done it before."

The metallic click of a bolt shuttling home cut through the open space like a gunshot. They turned. There was no point even trying to raise their guns. A dozen men were standing round them in a rough horseshoe, all armed. More could be seen in the trees and bushes beyond.

One of them stepped forward. He was a scrawny man, far too small for the gun he carried. He wore an expression of earnest concentration.

As he turned to share something with one of his subordinates, he showed a red star sewn on the sleeve of his shirt, like the one Grant had seen on the man at Sourcelles's house. When he looked back, a strange smile had spread across his face.

"Sam Grant," he said in heavily accented English. "We meet again."

Grant holstered the Webley and returned the smile with an uneasy grin. "Hello, Panos."

24

WHO THE hell is this?" Jackson demanded. "You know him?"

"Panos Roussakis—we met during the war. He was fighting the Germans on Crete."

Jackson pointed to the gun. "Who's he fighting now?"

"For Greece." Roussakis seemed to stand straighter as he said it and his grip on his gun tightened.

"You wouldn't like his politics," Grant warned. "Better not ask too many questions."

"And them?" The guerrilla jerked his gun at Grant's companions. His smile had vanished. "Who . . . ?"

He broke off, staring at Marina as if he'd seen a ghost. "You? Why are you here?"

He looked troubled, confusion written on his gaunt face. For the first time Grant began to feel worried. Roussakis looked at Jackson, then up at the sky, a mess of blue and black and gray. The bomber had vanished, but the smell of burning was all around them. "Why you bring them here?"

"The bomber's nothing to do with us. It's a long story—and we don't want to hang around. We've got a plane coming to pick us up from the airstrip. If you can just let us get there, we'll be out of your way."

Roussakis snapped something at one of his lieutenants. The guerrillas moved closer. "You come with us."

They surrendered their guns and marched in single file down the mountain. They had no choice. Roussakis's men surrounded them, keeping them under guard as they negotiated the precipitous stair of rocks and tree roots. The sun had come out, and the air was dense with the moisture steaming off the damp foliage. To Grant, it felt more like the Congo basin than northern Greece.

Jackson, walking behind Grant, asked, "How come you know this guy?"

"We worked together on Crete in the war. He led a group of partisans."

"So he knew Marina?"

"Not well. He and her brother had . . ." Grant hesitated, ". . . a difference of opinion."

"That would be one way of putting it," said Muir.

After what seemed like an interminable descent, the slope began to level off. Grant paused, sniffing the air. He could smell fire again, but not the sticky, oily fire that the plane had brought. This was tinged with the sweetness of pine resin—and the sizzling fat of roasting lamb. A pang of hunger shot through Grant's belly. He hadn't eaten since the morning. Now it was almost dusk.

Suddenly the trees thinned out. A hundred yards away sunlight shone through on to a thin scar carved out of the forest: the airstrip. It wasn't on top of the ridge, but on a natural terrace just below, so that the trees above hid it from almost every angle. The guerrillas had their camp in the forest around it: a handful of pup tents, a cooking fire and a few crates of ammunition. Two women in fatigues were roasting a lamb over the fire. To Reed, whose trip to the pictures was his weekly treat in Oxford, it looked like a scene from *The Adventures of Robin Hood*. He half expected to see Errol Flynn come through the twilit forest in his feathered cap. Instead, he saw something even more surprising. On the edge of the camp, branches had been lashed together to make the frame of a crude hut, open-sided and roofed with foliage. Roughly hewn log benches were lined up underneath it and all of them were filled with rows of children staring attentively at the front of the room, where a gray-haired teacher was writing on a blackboard. A few of them stared curiously at the new arrivals, wide-eyed under their mopped hair and pig-tails. Then the teacher rapped her pointer against the blackboard and they turned back dutifully.

"What are they doing?" asked Jackson.

"Their fathers are all wanted men. They can't go to the local schools, so their families bring them here."

Roussakis turned round. "*Quiet.*" He gestured to his men, who herded Grant and the others into a knot on the edge of the airstrip. The only sound was the unsettling chorus of the children chanting a nursery rhyme after their teacher.

"The last time we meet, I tell you never to see me again."

Grant took a step toward the edge of the circle. A rifle angrily jabbed him back. "Christ, Panos. You know I'm on your side."

"Yes? Once, maybe. Now I see you are with the Fascists."

Jackson couldn't contain himself. "Fascists? We're the good guys. In case you didn't notice, we spent four years helping fellas like you get rid of the Fascists. You want to know who the real heirs to Hitler are? Why don't you ask your buddies in Moscow?"

"There is a man from Moscow who comes here this morning. A colonel in the MGB. He has only one eye." Roussakis held a palm over the right side of his face to mimic an eyepatch.

"Kurchosov."

"So. You know him. And he knows you. He says: he is looking for an *Ameriki* and three English men. Enemies of socialism—very dangerous." Roussakis walked over to one of the ammunition crates and picked up a fat pistol with a barrel like a drainpipe. None of the others dared to speak. "He offers me money—gold—and many weapons if I go with him to find you."

"But you didn't go," said Grant.

Roussakis loaded a flare into the gun. "He has a man with him—a German. I know this man from Crete. A Fascist; they call him Belzig. He has killed many Greeks in the war. He makes them slaves; he makes them dig; he makes them die. A pig. So I say no."

Grant exhaled. "What happened to Kurchosov?"

Roussakis shrugged. "We have many men in this valley. Maybe he finds someone else who will do his work."

"I think we ran into them."

Roussakis said nothing. In the pause the distant hum of airplane engines drifted down through the forest canopy; not the harsh buzzing of the bombers, but the hollow chop of a Dakota.

"And what about her?" He pointed the flare gun at Marina. "It is not the first time I find the Papagiannopouli working with Fascists."

Roussakis aimed the pistol into the open sky and pulled the trigger. With a searing whoosh, a flare shot up and exploded high above the trees with a puff of red smoke. Half a dozen of Roussakis's men ran to positions along the sides of the airstrip.

"What happened to Alexei has nothing to do with this," said Grant. All the guns suddenly seemed to be pointing straight at him, deadly accusing fingers. He was also painfully aware of Marina's gaze.

"What do you mean?" There was an almost hysterical edge to Marina's voice now. A shadow passed over them: the Dakota, flying low to reconnoitre the runway. No one looked. "What about Alexei?"

Roussakis's eyes narrowed. "Grant doesn't tell you?"

"He was killed in an ambush," said Grant desperately. The moist air was thick around him; he felt ill.

"The British killed him," said Marina. "They were afraid that when the Germans were gone, the resistance would try to take over all Greece for Communism. They thought if they eliminated the Communist leaders they could keep Greece for themselves. So they had Alexei killed."

"No. Not because he was Communist. And not the British. They have tried—they send a man to do it, but he fails." Roussakis shot Grant a contemptuous look. "But I follow. I go there, to the gorge. I kill Alexei."

Marina stared at him. "You? Why?"

"You remember what happens three days before he died? All your men—massacred by Germans. There are surviving only three: you, Alexei and Grant."

"Alexei had sent us to Rethymno to spy out a German fuel dump."

"Because he knows. He knows what will happen. You know for why the Germans find your men? Alexei tells them."

Marina shuddered as if she'd been kicked in the stomach. Her face went pale. Grant reached out an arm to steady her, but she shook it away. "Why would he betray us? He spent his life fighting the Germans."

Roussakis shrugged. "Why do men betray their country? Maybe a girl, maybe gold? *Then ksero*—I do not know. But I look in his eyes, in the gorge of Imros, and I see it is truth."

Anything else he might have said was drowned out as the Dakota roared low overhead and thumped down on the landing strip. Its wheels barely bounced on the rain-softened earth. The pilot had done well to get it down, but he still needed all the space he had to bring it to a halt in time. Hidden alongside the runway, Roussakis's men readied their weapons and looked for his signal. He glanced at them uncertainly—and in that split second Marina pounced. She flew at him; in a single lithe movement she wrapped one arm round his neck and pulled him against her in a choking embrace, while the other twisted the pistol out of his hand. She pressed it against his right ear.

"Is he lying?"

The guerrillas surrounded her like a baying pack of hounds, jabbing with their guns and shouting at her to let Roussakis go. A hot breeze swept through the clearing as they felt the wash from the Dakota's propellers. But the answer on Grant's face was plain.

"I swore I would kill the man who killed Alexei," she hissed.

Roussakis gestured his men to be still. "If you kill me, you die. Your friends die, everyone dies."

At the far end of the runway the Dakota made a tight turn and readied itself for take-off. Grant could see the pilot through the windscreen, peering out as he looked for his passengers. The partisans, concealed in the trees, must have been invisible to him.

"Can I make a humble suggestion?" said Muir. All eyes—and several guns—turned toward him.

"You?" spat Marina. "What have you got to say? Did you give the order to kill Alexei?"

"Nothing to do with me. That was SOE's pitch—I was SIS." Muir flipped open his ivory cigarette case and lit a cigarette. "But as I see it, we could come over all *Hamlet* here and end up with a pile of corpses—or we could use some fucking common sense. Hands up everyone who wants to die here today."

He looked around the knot of men, the press of hard and angry faces. "Good. Now, your brother's dead and that's your tragedy, but if Mr. Roussakis hadn't got him then somebody else would. Maybe you'd have done the deed yourself, if you'd known the truth. So why don't we make a bargain? You let Roussakis go, he lets us get on that plane and we can all bugger off to more important things."

Marina tightened her finger on the trigger. The ring of men around her pressed closer. "If I let you go, will you let us get on that plane?"

"If I do, my hands are clean? There is nothing between us?" Roussakis could hardly speak with her arm strangling him.

"Yes."

"And the Yankee planes stop coming?"

Jackson frowned. "I can't promise . . ."

Muir whipped round. "For fuck's sake, Jackson. Think about what's important."

"OK, OK." Jackson raised his hands in surrender. "We'll stop the bombers." He shook his head in disgust and looked at Roussakis. "You're not going to win this war, you know."

Marina lowered the pistol and loosed her grip.

Roussakis rubbed his neck. "You cannot stop a better world forever."

They climbed into the Dakota, ducking in the propellers' slipstream. The sun had dipped below the clouds, and on the upper slopes of the mountain the forest was still burning. They saw the whole valley filled with a viscous golden haze. Reed hugged the tablet to his chest. Marina turned her head away and looked out of the window, trying to hide her tears.

"Think what Kurchosov's going to say when he finds out his own men helped us escape," said Jackson gleefully. "By the time he calms down, we'll have snatched the shield right from under his nose."

Grant glanced at him. "You will keep your promise to Panos? Send your bombers somewhere else?"

"Sure," said Jackson nonchalantly.

The plane banked and turned toward Thessalonica. Grant looked back, hoping for a last glimpse of the gilded sky. But the sun had gone, and the valley was lost in smoke and darkness.

25

IT WAS dark by the time they arrived back in Thessalonica. A staff car met them at the airport and took them to a small hotel. It had no restaurant; the only place they could find that would serve them food was a dingy *ouzeria* filled with old men playing backgammon and cards. The waiter brought them a tray of olives and stuffed vine leaves, which they ate hungrily.

When the plates had been cleared and the flask of ouzo topped up, Reed took out the tablet and laid it on the tablecloth. Molho hadn't broken it exactly in half—Sourcelles's fragment was larger than Pemberton's, about six inches square. They stared at the painting on the back. It was divided into three panels by two bands of zigzag lines, the stylized sea. In the top panel, just under the crumbling edge where Molho had snapped it, two figures, a man and a woman, stood on either side of a curiously shaped mound. Grant drew a sharp breath. Even three thousand years on he could still recognize the hollowed-out hill on Lemnos where they'd found the sanctuary of the Kabyri. And, in fact, when he looked closer he saw two tiny pot-bellied figures dancing under the mountain, waving hammers. A mottled disc stood between them.

"Those must be the Kabyri. I imagine the two characters in the margins are Hephaestus, the smith god, and Thetis, Achilles' mother." Reed's academic manner couldn't entirely hide his excitement.

"And that circle—that would be the shield?" said Jackson.

Reed put his hand against his head and tugged a lock of hair. "I suppose it must be."

"And there, that's the Trojan war, right." Jackson pointed to the next panel. The paint had faded here, but the image was still vivid enough. Grant was reminded of the carvings in the shrine on Lemnos. Chariots raced into battle, while under the walls of a hilltop city two files of armed men lined up opposite each other. Between them two men were engaged in combat. One had thrown his spear, which quivered in the other's round shield as he tried to draw his sword.

"Achilles and Hector." Marina made to touch the picture, then drew back her finger with a sigh of awe.

Fierce, at the word, his weighty sword he drew,
And, all collected, on Achilles flew.
So Jove's bold eagle, balanced in the air,
Stoops from the clouds to truss the quivering hare.
Nor less Achilles his fierce soul prepares:
Before his breast the flaming shield he bears.

Jackson looked at Reed sharply. "'Flaming shield'? What does that mean?"

Reed shrugged. "It's a common epithet applied to Achilles' armor. The shield was coated with gold. I imagine it just means it gleamed in the sun like fire."

"Huh."

"And I take it this is the White Island." Muir pointed to the bottom part of the tablet. The paint was badly chipped around the edges, but they could make out yet another mountain in the bottom right-hand corner, heavily painted in black. On its summit stood a white tower crowned with sacral horns.

"That must be the temple," said Reed quietly. "The underworld temple of Achilles."

He pulled a sheet of stiff paper out of his bag, a full-scale drawing he had made of Pemberton's piece. He slid it under the tablet. The edge of the drawing and the edge of the tablet fitted together almost perfectly. At last they could see the picture in full. The shrine in the Valley of the Dead stood in the top left-hand corner of what they could now see was the fourth panel, divided from the image below by the pointed waves. All five of them leaned in over the table and stared in wonder.

"Obviously it will require a considerable amount of study." Reed turned the tablet over, his intellectual mood as changeable as the Oxford weather. "However, at least we now have the rest of the text."

"Can you read it yet?" Muir asked.

"That's not the point. The immediate benefit is that we have a clean sample of Linear B. Everything I've deduced about the structure of the language so far has been inferred from our existing crop of Linear B inscriptions. Now that I have a new text, I can test my hypotheses, see if the rules I've inferred hold true. If my predictions are accurate, then I should be in an excellent position to start attempting a decipherment."

"To *start attempting* . . ." Jackson swallowed his ouzo. "Can't you ever just *do* something? How long will that take you?"

"I don't know." Reed's donnish affability had vanished, replaced with something curt and testy. Marina had seen a similar effect in Pemberton sometimes, when a new idea or challenge seized him. Courtesy, patience, tact—all went out of the window as the mind withdrew into itself.

"It took Champollion two years to crack the hieroglyphs—and he had the Rosetta Stone to work with."

"Two years?" All around the *ouzeria* locals looked up from their drinks and games to stare at the table of foreigners in the corner. Jackson lowered his voice. "Maybe you haven't noticed what's been going on the last few days, but we don't have two years. We likely don't have two weeks if the Reds are on to us. We need to get hold of this shield pronto, otherwise we're going to be on the wrong end of the last war in history."

Everyone at the table stared at him.

Jackson wiped his mouth with his napkin, aware he'd said too much.

"Let's just say you don't want to be around if the Russians get it. Sourcelles as good as told us where the White Island is. I say we go there straight away, before Belzig figures it out."

"But the island's in Soviet territory," Grant objected.

"All the more reason to get there as soon as we can. If the Commies figure out this thing's in their backyard, they'll have it in Moscow before we know anything about it."

Reed shook his head. "Even if you do reach the island, you won't just walk up to the temple of Achilles and knock on the door. Without the clues on the tablet you'll never find it. Grave robbers have been looting the Valley of the Dead on Crete for centuries: none of them ever found the baetyl shrine, until Pemberton turned up with his part of the tablet."

"That's not your problem. We've got instruments that can detect Element 61. If the shield's on that island we'll find it."

Back in his room, Grant stripped off his shirt and washed himself at the cracked sink in the corner. The whole day seemed to be caked on to his skin: Turkish tobacco from Sourcelles's silver cigarette holder; dried blood where the glass had cut him; soot from the fire and grease from the airplane. He scraped it off as best he could, and towelled his cut hands gingerly, then flopped down on the mattress. The bed was hard and narrow, but after the day he had endured it felt like heaven. He lay there for a few moments, barefoot and bare chested, enjoying the waft of air against his damp skin.

There was a knock at the door. He reached out for the bedside table and put one hand on the butt of the Webley. "It's open."

Marina came in. She was dressed simply in a white blouse and a high black skirt that emphasized her waist. Her hair was loose round her shoulders. She paused for a moment as she saw Grant's state of undress, then carried on into the room. Her bare feet barely made a sound on the floorboards. She sat down on the edge of the bed and Grant saw the silvered trails of fresh tears on her cheek.

"I can't stop thinking about Alexei," she said, perhaps by way of explanation. She turned to look Grant in the eye. "Is it true?"

"Which part?"

"All of it."

Grant raised his arm and stroked the hair that hung down behind her back. He could feel her skin through the thin cotton blouse. "You don't want to know."

She didn't move. "Tell me."

"You remember the ambush at Kastro? The entire band—Nikos, Sophoklis, Menelaos and the rest of them—all gunned down by the Germans. Two days later HQ called me in. Apparently Alexei had betrayed us. I was ordered to bring him to a rendezvous at a valley in the White Mountains, near Impros."

"You went to kill him."

Grant fell silent for a moment, remembering the taste of dust in his mouth. That awkward last embrace, neither of them meaning it. Thumbing back the hammer of the Webley and the look on Alexei's face when he realized.

"I couldn't do it. I looked at him and all I could see was you. I didn't know Panos had followed me."

Marina peeled away a splinter in the bedstead and snapped it in her fingers. "You never told me."

"It was better you didn't know. I wanted you to remember Alexei as a hero." Grant had stopped stroking Marina's hair. "Besides, I never had the chance. Roussakis almost killed me too—thought I must have been in cahoots with Alexei. He said if he ever saw me on Crete again he'd kill me. My career with SOE was over anyway: I'd disobeyed a direct order. They'd never have trusted me with a mission again. So I disappeared."

"I never knew."

"Alexei was an embarrassment to the British. They didn't want it to get out that one of their star allies had been turned by the Nazis. They buried it."

For what seemed an eternity neither of them moved. Grant lay back with his head on the pillows, while Marina sat on the edge of the bed, stiff-backed and still. Grant saw her wiping away more tears. Then she turned toward him, leaned forward and kissed him on the lips. "You should have told me," she whispered. "But thank you."

Grant reacted instinctively. He wrapped his arms round her and pulled her down on top of him. She came willingly. Her lips brushed his cheek, soft and dry against the stubble, her tongue flicking him with quick serpentine kisses. Putting his hand on her head, he steered her back toward his mouth. She forced her tongue inside him. He tasted aniseed, smelled tobacco and musk and perfume as her hair brushed his face.

Pressing her hands against his chest, she pushed herself up and swept her leg across to straddle him. Her skirt rode up over her thighs, revealing the cream silk slip underneath. Grant slid his hands underneath it and dug his fingers into her. She gasped. Swaying, she pulled back so that she sat up over him. She reached to her throat to unbutton her blouse, but Grant was faster. He put his hands on the hem of the blouse and tore it open, pulling it apart over her breasts. She lifted her arms over her head. The lamp on the side table lit her with a smoldering orange glow. Looking up, Grant saw her shadow swaying on the ceiling behind her. With her breasts cupped in the open blouse, her arms outstretched, the pursed skirt writhing over her hips, she seemed to have become an incarnation of the Minoan goddess: primitive, raw, quivering with creative power.

She pulled off her blouse. He reached up to touch her breasts, but she caught his hands in her own and pushed him back, holding him down. She leaned forward and let her nipples brush his chest. When she felt that Grant had stopped resisting her, she took a hand away and unbuckled his belt. She moved her hand lower, popping the buttons one by one, grinding her palm against his erection.

All of a sudden Grant thrust up. It unbalanced her; in that instant Grant twisted round so that they both rolled over. Now he was on top. She writhed and squirmed under him; she scraped deep welts down his back as she dug in her nails, but she couldn't dislodge him. He spread her thighs. She hooked her feet round the backs of his legs and squeezed her heels against his buttocks. Grant wrapped his arms under her slender shoulders, lifting her slightly so that her whole body was bent back against him.

He entered her and she swallowed him in darkness.

26

Black Sea, near Zmeiny Ostrov. Twenty-four hours later

THEY FLEW in low, at night. The only light inside the aircraft was a dim glow from the instruments, though occasionally they would see the navigation lights of ships plowing the sea below, tiny constellations like luminous plankton in the water. No one spoke. None of them had any illusions about the dangers that surrounded them.

Jackson, in the pilot's seat, looked out of the left-hand window at a smear of lights on the far horizon. "That's the border. We've just passed into Soviet airspace."

"If anyone's thinking of defecting, now's your opportunity," said Muir. He shot Marina a nasty look. Grant felt her stiffen against him.

"What's that?" Reed, squeezed into the co-pilot's seat, put his hand against the windscreen and pointed. Below and in front of them a white light pulsed in the darkness.

"According to the *Black Sea Pilot* there's a lighthouse on the highest point of the island," said Marina.

"That must be it, then. There's no other islands around here." Jackson banked the aircraft to his left, throttled back and put it into a slow descent. They'd timed it well: out of the right-hand window Grant could see the darkness softening to a purplish blue over the eastern horizon.

"Let's hope there's no angry gods waiting to tear us limb from limb."

They touched down on the water as the sun rose and taxied into a shallow bay. All of them stared, hardly able to believe where they were. In his mind's eye, without even being quite aware of it, Grant had expected something glittering and majestic: proud alabaster cliffs reflecting the sunlight like snow, or a wall of marble thrusting out of the sea. Even something like the white cliffs of Dover would have satisfied his imagination. But these cliffs were a russet brown. The only white Grant could see were the streaked bird droppings, of which there were plenty.

"Are you sure this is the right place?" said Muir. "Doesn't look very white to me."

"The name must be metaphorical." Reed sounded doubtful, as disappointed as the rest of them.

Muir hummed a few ironic bars of a Vera Lynn tune. Ahead, on the northwestern arm of the island, a flight of concrete steps ran down the red cliffs to a jetty. Jackson cut the engines and let the waves carry them the last few yards. The plane shuddered slightly as its pontoon knocked against the dock—then Grant had leaped down on to the dock and wrapped a rope round a rusting bollard. He looked over at the other side of the jetty, where a battered, paint-scarred rowing boat lay tied to an iron ring. "How many of the opposition are we expecting?"

"There'll be the lighthouse keeper. London thinks there might be a handful of Soviet engineers as well, putting in some sort of radio mast."

"Then it's just as well we came prepared."

Jackson passed round four M3 Grease Guns, and satchels with spare magazines and grenades. There was no sub-machine gun for Reed—instead, to his horror, he was presented with a small Smith and Wesson pistol. "I can't use that," he protested. "I've never fired a gun in my life."

"It's insurance," Jackson explained. "If you want peace, prepare for war. *Si vis pacem, para bellum*. Aristotle.' He beamed to see Reed's surprise. "Didn't think I knew that, did you?"

"I would never presume," Reed demurred.

Jackson pressed the gun into his hands. "This is the safety, this is the trigger and that's the end you point at the bad guys. Don't use it unless they're so close you can't miss." He clambered into the back of the plane and called to Grant, "Give me a hand with this."

They hoisted down a small wooden box, about the size of a crate of beer. It was surprisingly heavy. Grant had seen Jackson load it the night before and been curious. The only hint as to its contents was a serial number stencilled in black across the top.

Jackson checked his watch. "What time do you make it, Grant?"

"Five fifteen."

"Good. Let's hope they're still asleep."

They took the climb carefully, trying not to slip on the crust of bird droppings that slathered the stairs like spilled paint. Grant and Jackson carried the wooden crate between them, while Marina scouted ahead. She had swapped her skirt and blouse for baggy green combat trousers and a khaki shirt, but even they couldn't entirely mask the curves underneath. Something inside Grant clenched tighter as he remembered the previous night. For a moment an image flashed in front of his eyes: an undulating vision of silk, skin and perfume. Then his boot caught the lip of the step and skidded out from under him. He threw out a hand to brace himself against the cliff, but planted it in a thick dollop of guano. A flock of turtledoves squawked up out of a cleft.

Jackson glared at him. "Let's try not to do the Commies' work for them."

They came to the top of the stairs and peered over the edge. There was the lighthouse, barely two hundred and fifty yards away. It stood on a low summit, a squat octagonal tower about fifty feet high, with a single-story house beside it. A rocky track, scraped out of the island's thin earth, led up to it.

Jackson put down the wooden crate and took a blue cap with a red band out of his satchel. He pulled it on.

Grant gave him a sideways look. "You'll be shot for spying if they catch you."

"If they find out who we are, they'll shoot us anyway."

Leaving Reed and the crate at the top of the stairs, they fell in behind Jackson and started up the track. Grant scanned the surroundings, trying to look unobtrusive while still keeping the lighthouse complex in the corner of his eye. There was no cover on the island: no trees or bushes, not even any flowers. It was a dead place, little more than a landing for birds. Their nests were everywhere: Grant wondered where they found the twigs to make them.

A dark shape darted out from the edge of the road and slithered across their path. Jackson jumped; he swung his machine-gun off his shoulder and had whipped back the bolt before he saw what it was: a snake, thin and black, its jaws stretched wide apart round the speckled egg in its mouth. It disappeared into a hole on the far side of the road.

"Easy," said Grant. He gestured to the lighthouse. "Don't want them to think we're nervous."

"Right."

They reached the top of the ridge. The lighthouse loomed above, while the rest of the island spread out all around them. It wasn't large: less than half a mile long and perhaps quarter of a mile wide. The lack of trees made it seem smaller still. Grant couldn't see any sign of a temple, though there were a couple of unnaturally straight ridges on the western side, sharp creases in the blanket of couch grass. Otherwise, the only buildings were the lighthouse and its attendant cottage.

"Looks like you didn't need your fancy dress after all." No one stirred around the lighthouse. They were close enough now to hear the whir of its motor still spinning the lamp, like a clockwork toy slowly winding down. Gulls wheeled overhead.

Jackson gestured his gun at the cottage. The wooden shutters, stripped bare by the salt wind, were still closed. "I guess the engineers are in there."

Grant and Marina ran to the door and pressed themselves against the walls on either side of it. Jackson and Muir took up covering positions opposite.

Grant looked across at Marina and gave her a thumbs-up. "Ready?"

She nodded. The wind ruffled the ribbon that tied back her hair and her eyes were bright with excitement. Grant raised three fingers. *Two . . . one . . .*

The door swung in—a split second before Grant's boot would have made contact with it. An incongruous figure in longjohns and a woollen cap stood in the doorway, rubbing his eyes. "*Shto eta?*"

He never knew what hit him. Grant's boot smashed into his groin with all the force intended for the door. He doubled over with a howl of agony and staggered back under the impact. Grant, unbalanced, careered in, collided with him and went down in a tangle of arms and legs. He sprang up—and almost knocked into Marina coming in behind him.

"*Jesus Christ.*"

Grant looked around. They were in a small room with a table at one end, an iron stove in the middle and three bunks pushed up against the walls. Four of the beds were occupied by young conscripts, staring at him with varying degrees of confusion and terror as they emerged from under their blankets. Grant jerked the M3 at them. "Nobody move."

The man by his feet groaned and hauled himself across the concrete floor to the nearest empty bunk. Grant heard a movement behind him and flicked a quick glance over his shoulder. Jackson and Muir had come to the door and were peering in.

"You get them all?"

"Looks like it. I . . ."

A click sounded from the far end of the room. Grant looked up and for the first time noticed there was a door in the back wall. He cursed himself; he ran to it, punched three bullets through the flimsy plywood, then kicked it in. It was a bathroom, with a steel sink in one corner, a lidless toilet in the other and a fresh breeze blowing through the open window in between. Grant looked out, just in time to see a half-naked figure running toward the lighthouse. He lifted his gun to the window frame and fired, but the fugitive was already out of sight. All the bullets did was chip away the whitewashed concrete at the base of the tower.

"*Fuck.*"

Grant ran back through the bunk room, past Muir and Jackson, and out into the wan daylight. He was just in time to see the lighthouse door slam shut and hear a bolt shoot home inside. He raised the gun and dropped it almost at once. The door was a classic piece of Soviet workmanship, a solid steel plate built to resist everything the Black Sea's storms could throw at it.

Muir ran out of the cottage behind him. "What the hell's going on?"

"One of them just locked himself in the tower."

Muir swore, then shrugged. "I suppose he's harmless enough. He can't do anything there."

"Yes, he can." Jackson, who had emerged into the doorway, pointed up at the nest of wires strung round the top of the lighthouse. "That's a fucking radio antenna."

Grant ran round the octagonal tower. It had been built for navigation, not fortification: on its far side a row of iron staples in the wall formed a rough ladder up to the gallery round the light. Slinging the machine-gun over his shoulder, he started climbing. The lighthouse was in a pretty shabby condition: bare concrete patches showed where it had recently been repaired and little Xs of white masking tape still covered the windows, slowly peeling away.

The wind rose as he climbed higher. Now he could see the whole island spread out below him—and the sea beyond. Without breaking his ascent he checked the horizon: a few freighters and oil tankers, but nothing dangerous. Not yet.

He reached the top of the ladder and squeezed under the railing. Wherever the Russian had gone, he hadn't come up here: the glass dome was empty, except for the mirrored lantern still spinning on its turntable. Better still, there was a door. He tried the handle—and it gave. With a brief squeak of resistance from the rusted hinges it swung open, then slammed shut in the wind almost before he'd stepped through.

After the tumult outside, the lighthouse was eerily quiet. The lantern grumbled on its axis, and through the open hatch in the floor he could hear the muffled slapping of hurried footsteps. Grant dropped down the ladder, on to a narrow landing at the top of a staircase. He ran down the curving stair to the next floor. Through an open door he saw a plain, whitewashed room. A sandy-haired man wearing nothing but his trousers was crouched in front of a wireless set on a trestle table, twiddling frantically at the dial.

Grant slipped the gun off his shoulder and aimed it at the Russian's chest. With a panicked yelp, the man flung up his hands and edged away from the wireless set. Grant thought about shooting anyway, but decided against it. Whatever damage the Russian had achieved, it was already done.

Grant and Marina locked the prisoners in a storeroom in the base of the lighthouse—six engineers, plus the elderly lighthouse keeper Grant found cowering under his bed on the second floor. Jackson fetched Reed and the mysterious wooden crate. They gathered outside the lighthouse, looking apprehensively at the sky and the surrounding sea.

"How much time do you think we have?"

Grant looked reflexively at his watch, as if it might somehow show the answer. "I don't think he had time to get a message off. Even if he did, it'll take at least a couple of hours for them to get a boat here."

"Great," said Jackson. "Should be plenty of time."

Marina stared at him. "Are you familiar with the basic principles of archaeology?" she asked. "You cannot just pluck these things out of the ground. It would take weeks to survey this island."

Jackson knelt down beside the wooden crate and pried it open with the blade of his knife. Everyone peered in. Tucked in a bed of hay lay a black box about the size of a cinderblock. A chrome handle stuck out of the top, with some sort of gauge or meter at one end and a number of buttons and switches down the sides.

"What is it?" asked Reed.

"It's a Bismatron. It, uh, detects Element 61."

"They knocked that together pretty quickly, if they didn't even know it existed until three months ago," said Grant.

Jackson gave a patently false smile. "Don't ask me. I leave all that stuff to the smart guys. Anyway, if the shield's on this island this baby'll find it."

He flicked a switch. The needle on the gauge darted across to the far side of the dial, then settled back, twitching every now and again. A low hum rose out of the machine, overlaid with a steady chattering of squawks and clicks.

"Talkative creature," said Reed.

With Muir in tow, Jackson set off down the slope toward the west side of the island. Grant, Reed and Marina watched them go.

"Sourcelles said there was a temple on this island," said Grant, surveying the desolation. "If the shield's anywhere, it must be near that."

Marina reached in her pack and pulled out a slim book bound in brown cloth. "Sourcelles's monograph. It has a copy of the map Kritskii made when he came in 1823." She turned through the book. To Grant's unscholarly eye it looked as though someone had taken translations in half a dozen languages and thrown them together. Almost every page was a densely woven tapestry of French, Greek, Latin, German, Russian—even, in rare fragments, English.

Marina found the map and spread the book flat on her knee. It was a simple map. A few swirls sketched the main contours; dotted lines indicated the retaining walls Grant had seen from the top of the lighthouse. Plumb in the middle of the island, at its highest point, a subdivided square marked the temple. Grant looked around. From where they were, they could see the whole island: an almost too-perfect facsimile of the lines on the map.

"That's here," said Reed, voicing the conclusion they'd all reached. "We must be standing on top of it."

"But there can't be more than half a meter of topsoil." Marina pointed to the track they'd come up from the jetty. Its surface was bare rock, the same color as the cliffs. The earth embankments on either side were little more than a foot high.

"Then we shouldn't have far to dig."

They fetched the tools they had brought in the plane. Marina scratched a line in the ground that more or less bisected the ridge and they started digging. It didn't take long. On his third stroke Grant's spade rang on solid rock. In less than a quarter of an hour they'd cleared a trench about a foot wide and ten feet long, a ruddy stone scar in the grass.

"Even if the temple's foundations are here somewhere, there's not much space for buried treasure," said Grant, mopping his brow. Leaden clouds covered the sky and the breeze off the sea had died.

"There must be some sort of cave or tunnel in the rock. Like on Lemnos." Marina sat cross-legged by the rim of the trench and sifted the earth they'd excavated through her fingers.

"Jackson's magic box doesn't think so." A few hundred yards away, Jackson and Muir had reached the bottom of the slope and were standing at the cliff edge, little more than silhouettes against the heaving sea beyond.

"Do you think it can really detect this mysterious element?" said Reed.

Grant laughed. "It can certainly detect something. I've seen a similar sort of thing in the Congo. The prospectors use them."

Reed was intrigued. "Can it detect gold too?"

"The men who were using it weren't looking for gold." Grant got up and stuck his spade in the ground. "Do you know what a Geiger-Müller counter is?"

Reed shook his head.

"It detects radiation. The men who used them were prospecting for . . ."

"*Look at this.*"

Marina was sitting bolt upright. Her arms were filthy, smeared with dirt up to the elbows, but she had something in her hand. It just looked like a flat pebble to Grant. She spat on it and rubbed it on the knee of her trousers, then passed it wordlessly to Reed.

He squinted at it, scraping away some earth with his fingernail. His eyes widened. "Remarkable."

Grant snatched it out of his hand. It wasn't a pebble it was a black-glazed piece of clay that had been spun into a flat disc about the size of a coaster. A red serpent wound round the edge and in its center the letters "AX" had been scratched into the glaze.

Grant frowned, puzzled. “Who’s Ax?”

“Ach,” Reed corrected him with a throaty “ch” that sounded strangely Scottish. “Short for *Achilleus*.”

Marina took it back from Grant. “It’s a votive plaque. The ancient Greeks would have dedicated them with a prayer and left them at the temple. Like lighting a candle in church. It means the temple must have been . . .”

She trailed off as she realized Grant and Reed weren’t paying attention. They were staring over her shoulder, both of them listening to the low mechanical hum being blown in on the wind.

Grant grabbed his knapsack and pulled out his field glasses, scanning the leaden sky. “Yaks—two of them, coming in from the west.” He kicked a smattering of earth back into the trench to try to hide the scar. “Quick—into the house.”

“What about the others?”

Grant looked down toward the cliffs, then back to the west. Even with the naked eye the planes were now clearly visible, swooping in low beneath the clouds. “No time.”

They ducked into the cottage, still a mess of discarded blankets and abandoned clothes. They were barely inside when the whole building seemed to tremble: windows rattled and the tea urn fell off the stove as the two aircraft roared overhead. They seemed so close it was a surprise they didn’t hit the lighthouse.

“I thought you said the engineer didn’t have time to send an SOS,” said Reed.

“Well, someone did.” Grant looked out of the window. “They’re fighters. Must just have come to take a look.”

“They’ll see our plane,” said Marina. “What will they make of that?”

“Maybe we can reassure them.” Grant grabbed a green engineer’s uniform hanging over the end of one of the bunks. He pulled off his boots and trousers and tugged on the uniform. The trousers barely reached to his ankles, and when he pulled the tunic over his shirt the buttons stubbornly refused to meet.

“Is that how you plan to reassure them?” Reed asked doubtfully.

“Something’s better than nothing. If they don’t see anything, they’ll know something's wrong." Grant grabbed a forage cap to complete his ensemble, then laced his boots back on. "At least we can try."

He stepped out of the door and jogged over to the lighthouse. To his right he could see the planes banking sharply over the open sea to come back for another run. He took the stairs two at a time, ignoring the muffled shouts from the storeroom; he ran past the radio room, then backtracked and grabbed a pair of headphones from beside the wireless. He hooked them round his neck, hoping the Yak pilots would spot them.

Grant emerged on to the balcony, dizzied by the spiral stair. The planes were on to him almost before he could get his bearings. The blast from their engines was immense: the iron balcony shivered beneath his feet; the cap was snatched from his head and he had to brace himself against the railing to keep from being blown over the side. The planes banked again and roared back, so low he could see the pilots' faces behind the canopies, the flared intakes down the cowling and the stubby cannons behind the propellers. They seemed to be heading straight for him. He waved, tapped his ear to mimic a broken headset, then gave a cheery thumbs-up. Did Russians use the thumbs-up, he wondered?

At the last moment the two planes broke apart. They shot past on either side of the tower with an ear-splitting roar. Grant tried tugging the headset over his ears but it did nothing. He looked back to see the planes racing away behind him. Had it worked?

By the time he got to the bottom of the tower, Jackson and Muir had made their way back from the cliffs. They gathered in the bunk house, occasionally looking out of the windows to watch the planes still circling overhead like crows.

"Haven't they seen enough?" said Jackson. "Why the hell are they sticking around?"

Grant pulled on his trousers and buckled the Webley back on. "They've done their reconnaissance and they don't like what they've seen. My guess is they've been ordered to keep an eye on us until the Soviets can get a boat here."

"Shit." Jackson kicked the empty tea urn across the floor. "Can't we shake them off, make them think it's just a busted radio or something?"

"I tried that. Anyway, that excuse wouldn't have lasted long. There's supposed to be a team of radio engineers here, remember."

"We could wait until it's dark."

Muir looked at his watch. "That's hours away. They'll have half the Red Army landed here by then. And there's no way we can take off in the flying boat while they're around. They'd shoot us out of the water."

"And we still haven't got what we came for," said Jackson. "The Bismatron hasn't registered shit. It's deader than my grandpa's Johnson."

"Are you sure it's working?" said Muir.

"Kind of hard to tell if there's nothing to find."

Grant unbuckled his watch. Dangling it by its strap, he held it against the black machine. The needle twitched and the speaker emitted a series of pops like air being blown through a straw.

"It's working." He slipped the watch back on to his wrist. "Radium dial. Makes the numbers glow in the dark."

Muir's mouth tightened in a suspicious stare. "Very clever. Now have you got a parlor trick to get us off this fucking island?"

"We're not leaving without the shield," Jackson insisted. "There's . . ." He paused as the roar of engines overhead drowned him out once more. "There's got to be a way to find it."

Reed, standing by the door, cleared his throat. "Actually, I think I know where the temple is."

27

JACKSON LOOKED down at his feet, as if expecting to see a Corinthian column rising out of the concrete. "How exactly do you figure that, Professor?"

"Come and have a look. Quickly."

They trooped over to the doorway, glancing anxiously at the sky. The Yaks' orbit had taken them back out to the west and for the moment they were out of sight. Reed pointed to the lighthouse, to the patch on its wall where the concrete cladding had been chipped away. That was his own handiwork, Grant realized, from the bullets he'd fired at the Russian who'd escaped through the bathroom window. It had exposed the original wall underneath, square-cut lumps of stone mortared together.

"Look at that block. What do you see?"

Grant picked up his field glasses again. A soupy blur filled his vision as he twiddled the focus knob. Soft lines emerged from the haze, sharpened and resolved themselves into a circle, with thin lines in its center radiating to form a delicately veined rosette.

"That's not Russian workmanship," said Reed. "And look there."

Grant followed his gaze to the foot of the lighthouse. Now that he looked closer, he could see that the concrete coat didn't quite reach to the bottom. He ducked out of the house, ran over and knelt by the wall. He peeled back the grasses that grew around it to expose the foundation: layers of roughly finished limestone, huge blocks laid together with barely an ounce of cement.

Reed joined him. "There's your temple. The Russians must have dug up the remains and used them to build the lighthouse."

Grant looked back. The others were watching them from the bunkhouse door, while beyond the planes were circling round yet again. "We'd better get back under cover."

Jackson took the news badly. "When did the lighthouse go up?"

"Some time in the nineteenth century. It's mentioned in the Admiralty *Pilot* for 1894."

"The men who built it: do you think . . ."

Reed shook his head. "I doubt it. You couldn't have kept it a secret, not on this rock. It would have been the most sensational discovery of the age."

"So it's not here. *Fuck*." Muir kicked one of the bunk beds in frustration, then lit a cigarette. The nicotine seemed to calm him a little.

"It might be here," said Reed cautiously. "There could have been a tunnel complex under the temple, as on Lemnos. Perhaps your instrument wouldn't be able to detect it there."

"This piece of shit was built to detect . . . stuff . . . deep underground. I don't think a bunch of Stone Age wops could have dug deep enough to make a difference."

"They were Bronze Age, actually," Reed murmured.

"Anyway," said Marina, "the Russians must have excavated most of the site when they were digging the foundations for the lighthouse. If there was a cave, they would have found that too."

"Great. So the shield's not here and we are. What do we do now?"

"The best we can do is examine Sourcelles's tablet. The pictures on the back may hold some clues." Reed patted his pocket, where he had the tablet wrapped safely in a cigar box. "It worked on Crete."

Jackson stared at him incredulously. "I was actually thinking more short-term, Professor. Like, how the hell do we get off this island with those fighters overhead and probably the whole Black Sea fleet steaming over here?"

"We wait," said Grant. "Those fighters are going to run out of fuel sooner rather than later. When they go, we'll go." He cocked his head. "It sounds as if they're already on their way out."

He stuck his head outside the door. It took him a moment to find the fighters against the gray sky: they were higher than he'd expected, climbing steeply into the west.

"Looks like you're right," said Jackson. "They're giving up."

"Maybe." Grant shielded his eyes. There was something familiar in the way the planes were maneuvering for altitude: something ominous.

"*Get in the lighthouse!*" Grant shouted suddenly. "*Quick!*"

The fighters wheeled round and turned back, dipping their noses toward the island. Following Grant, the others ran across to the lighthouse, into the safety of its massive walls. The Russian pilots must have seen them—but they weren't interested in Grant. Their cannons opened fire. Lines of tracer streaked down like hard, phosphorous rain a couple of hundred yards away. Watching from the lighthouse doorway, Grant couldn't see them hit, but he knew where they'd struck. He imagined the shells stitching neat white lines of boiling foam in the waves, licking up toward the concrete jetty and . . .

The air shook with the explosion. From below the cliffs on the northeastern spit a cloud of flame and black smoke mushroomed up, hung in the air for a moment, then began to spread out in a canopy. A host of smaller explosions popped in the background like a string of squibs. Above, the pilots pulled out of their dives and banked sharply to avoid the smoke. Grant saw one of them dip his wings in an ironic salute; then the two planes climbed away and disappeared toward the western horizon.

"Now what do we do?" said Jackson.

They stared down at the jetty from the top of the cliff, trying to see through the smoke that still floated up from the floatplane's carcass. There wasn't much to see. The Yaks must have hit the fuel tanks—the plane had been blown to pieces. One of the pontoons floated like a basking shark; scorched pieces of metal bobbed in the water around it, or nestled in the rocks at the foot of the cliffs where they had already washed up.

"At least the rowing boat's still there," said Reed, trying to find something to be optimistic about. It was true: the concrete pier had protected the lighthouse keeper's little boat from the worst of the blast and the Russian shells, though it looked slightly lower in the water than it had before.

"We're not escaping in that. The nearest safe harbor must be two hundred and fifty miles away—if we even managed to find our way there without getting lost. I wouldn't trust that thing to get me across the Thames to Vauxhall." Muir coughed as the wind blew a puff of oily smoke in his face.

"The Russians won't leave us here for long," said Grant, glancing out to sea. "Remember, they still don't know who we are or what's happened here. They're just playing for time. Somebody must be coming to find out."

"And what do we do when they get here?"

They had plenty of time to think about it. Morning slipped into afternoon, but the fighters didn't return. Grant posted himself at the top of the lighthouse and scanned the horizon hour after hour, but there was no sign of any approach. "They're afraid of us," he announced. He'd come down from the lighthouse to get a cup of tea: Muir had managed to repair the urn in the bunk house. "The only way on to this island is through that jetty. A couple of men with machine-guns could pin them down for days.

"Just like Thermopylae," said Reed. The thought seemed to cheer him up. "Three hundred Spartans resisting the entire Persian army."

Marina arched her eyebrows. "And not one of them survived."

The afternoon crawled on. With nothing better to do, Muir and Jackson continued trawling the island with the Bismatron, in the ever-receding hope of finding a signal. Grant kept watch, spelled sometimes by Marina.

Only Reed looked totally unfazed by their situation. He sat in the bunk house with his notebook and a sheaf of papers, poring diligently over his work. No one disturbed him, except once when Muir looked in. He peered down at the large piece of notepaper, extended on every side by other scraps of paper sellotaped or pasted on, which formed the nexus of Reed's efforts, and grunted. "Any progress?"

"Hmm?" Reed was running through the pages of a notebook that seemed to contain nothing but long columns of the Linear B characters. "I'm working on the place names at the moment."

Muir's cigarette almost dropped out of his mouth on to the paper—which would have been unfortunate. "Have I missed something? I thought this was all still gibberish. How do you know they're place names?"

"It's a guess. But a good one. If you look at the original tablets that Evans found in the palace at Knossos, certain words appear at irregular intervals in the text but always in the same order."

"I don't follow."

"The Knossos tablets observe certain conventions." Reed searched for a metaphor. "Imagine you're trying to learn something about English by listening to the shipping forecast. The actual forecast varies each day, but the order of the stations never changes. If you looked at transcripts, you'd see the same words always appeared in the same sequence, although with differing intervals. Lundy, Fastnet, Irish Sea . . ."

"I see." Muir scowled. "So—what exactly? Are we looking at three-thousand-year-old weather forecasts?"

Reed sighed. "In the context of the Knossos tablets I imagine we're looking at tallies of taxes or tributes brought from the satellite towns of Crete. Presumably, each time the taxes were collected they were registered in the same order."

"And do any of them appear on our tablet?"

"That's not exactly the point. Place names are often preserved in languages when everything else is forgotten. Think of London. The name pre-dates the Romans, perhaps even the Celts, and it's survived Latin,

Anglo-Saxon, French, Middle English. It'll probably still be known in a thousand years. So if we can identify place names that survive—Knossos, for example—we've every likelihood of being able to put phonetic values on the symbols that spell them."

He pushed his spectacles back up his nose. "However, since you ask, there is one name from the Knossos lists that appears on our tablet." He rummaged on the table, looking for a piece of paper. "Here."

Muir peered at the three symbols—an ankh, a quartered circle and a simple cross.

☥ ⊕ †

"Where's that, then?"

Reed gave a shy smile, trying to hide his obvious self-satisfaction. "Well, if it appears on the Knossos tablets it's probably on Crete and it would make sense for it to be somewhere we've been. There's a modern settlement at the mouth of the Valley of the Dead called Kato Zakro—Old Zakro. The British School excavated there in 1901 and found evidence that there was a settlement there in Minoan times—probably a harbor on the main Aegean-Levantine trade route. So if one assumes that the name remains more or less the same, that would give values for these three symbols *Za-ka-ro*."

"Why '*ka*'?" Muir pointed at the middle symbol. "Why not just '*k*'?"

"Most of the symbols are syllabic—that is, a consonant sound and a vowel sound. If your word contains two consonants together, or a consonant on its own, you usually have to insert an extra vowel to spell it." His eyes flickered over Muir's shoulder for a second, then refocused. "So if you wanted to spell, say, 'biscuit' in a syllabic alphabet, you would have to write it '*bi-su-ki-ta*.'"

"Extraordinary," said Muir, shaking his head in disbelief. "Keep up the good work." He tossed a box of matches on to the broad sheet of paper. "You'd better have this."

"I don't smoke," said Reed politely.

"It's so you can burn it if we're caught."

Late that afternoon Grant saw a smudge on the horizon. He watched through the field glasses as it drew nearer: a Soviet patrol boat. On his way down to alert the others he unlocked the storeroom and pulled out the lighthouse keeper—a wiry man with wild gray hair, a straggly beard and a surly face. Through signs, Grant indicated that he should light the beacon.

"What the hell did you do that for?" Muir asked when Grant emerged. Dusk was coming early to the overcast sky and by tipping back his head he could already see the beam sweeping across the clouds above.

"We don't want the Soviets to lose their way in the dark."

"Don't we?"

"If they don't come, we're never going to find a way off this island." Grant strapped a knife round his shin and pulled down his trouser leg to cover it. "For now, we need to stay indoors. If they can't see us they'll start to wonder if we're here."

The sun sank behind the western horizon—agonizingly slowly for Grant, who watched it from the radio room in the lighthouse. He lost count of the times he looked out of the window, only to see that the sun had hardly moved. At least the patrol boat didn't seem in any hurry either.

At last, when it was dark enough, they set out. Grant was the last to leave: he bolted the steel door from within, then climbed to the top of the tower and shinned down the ladder on the outside. He rejoined the others behind the bunk house. Peering out, he could see the patrol boat's green and red navigation lights bobbing out at sea. Then, suddenly, they vanished.

"They're coming. Let's go."

They crawled on their hands and knees, trying to keep the hump of the slope between themselves and the Russian boat. To Reed, who had never liked the dark, it felt like an initiation rite into some cruel black cult. He couldn't see where he was going: his world became a dark and nasty place, alternately sharp with rocks or sticky with bird droppings. Unseen creatures flapped, croaked, slithered and hissed all around him. Once he put his hand in a nest and felt the eggs crack under him; his hand came away wet and he let out an involuntary whimper.

"Shh," came back Grant's stern whisper. "We're almost there."

"So are they," answered another voice—Muir's, probably. From over the hill to their left they could hear the throb of engines approaching the dock.

"Muir, you take the others on to the end of the peninsula." Grant had scouted it out that afternoon. Right at the very tip of the north-east corner a sliver of land extended its beckoning finger into the sea. "Wait there."

The darkness swallowed them quickly. As soon as they were gone, Grant and Marina turned left and began elbowing their way up the slope. Grant felt his way carefully, trying to weave a path between the nests that surrounded them like a minefield. Several times, Grant was almost smacked in the face by gulls rising up from their interrupted sleep. He could only hope that the boat's engines would drown the noise.

They came to the edge of the cliff and looked down into the little harbor. In the gray hues of darkness he could see the patrol boat just offshore. White foam bubbled at its stern where the engines held it against the tide, while on the foredeck he could see the machine-gun swivelling back and forth. On the concrete pier a small knot of men crouched in firing positions, rifles aimed at the clifftop.

"*Shit.*" Grant ducked back. He was too late: if he opened fire now he'd be a sitting duck. He thought about trying a grenade, but then the boat might take fright and leave altogether. And that was what he didn't want.

"Plenty of time," he told himself. He waited for his heartbeat to calm again—a technique that had served him well—then wriggled back to Marina. "We'll have to let them come up. I reckon they'll make for the lighthouse first."

"Shall we take them on the path?"

Grant shook his head. "Let them go. We'll wait until it's clear, then see if we can get down."

They edged away—not a second too soon. They heard heavy boots running up the stairs and a moment later a figure appeared at the top of the cliff. His silhouette seemed to fade in and out of darkness as the lighthouse beam swept round the sky. A second figure joined him, then a third. Others followed. With tense, jerky movements that betrayed their nerves, they fanned out from the head of the stair and formed a loose cordon round the harbor perimeter. Then they stopped.

"What are they doing?"

A shot broke the night air, followed by a ragged volley from along the Russian line. Marina raised her gun; instantly, Grant put his hand on her arm and pushed it back down. "They're just shooting at seagulls. Or else trying to scare us into returning fire."

The firing petered out, replaced by a babble of anxious shouts. Grant couldn't make out the words, probably wouldn't have understood them anyway, but the sense behind them seemed to be relief. That was good.

The unexpected flashes from the rifles had temporarily ruined Grant's night vision. While he waited for it to come back, he pressed himself into the ground and listened. The Russian soldiers still weren't moving—almost as if they were waiting for something. Then he heard it. A low hum to the west, growing steadily louder.

Grant eased his head up and looked out. Light from the lighthouse still blinked across the sky, a metronomic pulse flashing on the underside of the clouds like distant lightning or shellfire. He waited, watching. The hum got louder. Then, suddenly he saw it, picked out in the sky. It was a flying boat, with a smooth silvery skin and a strange, curved shape like a banana. It passed under the wand of light and disappeared again. A few seconds later Grant heard it splash down.

He grinned and edged himself over the top of the cliff. "That's our ticket off the island."

Lieutenant Maxim Sergeiovich Soloviev of the Soviet Naval Infantry watched the dinghy glide toward the jetty. The oars splashed in the water; in the back of the boat he could see a tall figure sitting stiffly, with a shorter and stouter figure slouched beside him. He glanced nervously up toward the encircling cliffs to make sure his men still had it secured. The instructions from Odessa had been vague, but the threat if he failed unmistakable.

The boat knocked against the pier, next to the floating wreckage of the American seaplane. The tall passenger clambered out. Soloviev clicked his heels together and saluted smartly. "Comrade Colonel."

The man returned it with a razor-sharp salute of his own. Soloviev tried to get a glimpse of him in the darkness. The face was gaunt and filled with violence: a white scar puckered his cheek from ear to jaw, and his right eye was covered by a triangular patch. It didn't make much difference, Soloviev thought: the remaining eye was sunk so deep in its hooded socket that it was as black and impenetrable as the other.

Soloviev took a deep breath. "Comrade Colonel, I am pleased to report we captured the harbor without incident. My men control the cliffs and are ready to advance on the lighthouse. If our enemies are still here, I believe that is where they will have barricaded themselves."

The colonel grunted. His companion had emerged from the boat now; over the colonel's shoulder, Soloviev caught a brief impression of a heavy, jowled face and short fair hair. He didn't seem to be wearing a uniform—though, as Soloviev had learned, those were often the men to fear most in Stalin's Russia.

"Do not underestimate them." Even on the warm night, there was something chilling and harsh in the colonel's voice. "Many of our men have already paid the price for such a mistake."

"And they have something that is very valuable to us." The other man spoke for the first time. His Russian was poor, the accent harsh. Soloviev wondered where he was from. Poland, perhaps? "It is imperative to take them alive."

Soloviev's heart sank. He looked to his colonel for reassurance, but got none—only a harsh twist of the mouth and a curt, "Be careful. Comrade Stalin will be most disappointed if you fail."

As if to echo his worst fears, at that moment a volley of machine-gun fire burst out from the cliffs away to his right. A second light appeared halfway up the tower of the lighthouse. Soloviev threw himself on to the dock, though the firing was wild and the bullets nowhere near him. To his shame, the colonel never moved, but simply swivelled his good eye round to see where the shots were coming from. Soloviev shamefacedly got to his feet and was further mortified to see he had bird droppings smeared all over his uniform. Up above, more shots rolled over the island as his men returned fire. Perhaps they had hit the gunman, for the shooting from the tower had stopped as abruptly as it began.

The colonel turned toward him. The promise of an eternity of Siberian winters seemed written in the harsh lines of his face. "Send the patrol boat round to the west to cover your advance. Then take your men and take that fucking tower."

Twenty yards away, crouched in the rocks at the bottom of the cliff, Grant watched the hapless officer run up the stairs. The patrol boat revved its engines and headed away from the pier. Its wake sent cold water sluicing round Grant's ankles, but he ignored it. Out on the dock the colonel gave the lighthouse one more look, as though something was puzzling him, then followed the lieutenant with his companion in tow. Grant tried to imagine the look on his face when he got inside the lighthouse.

But he wanted to be well off the island before that happened. The harbor was deserted now, except for a solitary guard posted on the jetty. A little further out the Russian flying boat bobbed in the water. It was too awkward a shape to try to bring to the pier; instead, the Russians had anchored it in the bay.

Grant pulled out the knife strapped to his leg and bit it between his teeth. Without a ripple he slid into the water and kicked his way toward the jetty.

Soloviev peered round the bunk-house wall and stared up at the tower. His men had cleared the cottage and found no one; all that was left now was the lighthouse. There had been no more shots fired from inside—perhaps his men had killed the gunman despite the Colonel's orders. A shiver went through him at the thought. But there must be others: the radio message had said there were four enemies on the island. Maybe the colonel could overlook one more or less.

He beckoned his sergeant over. "You have the explosive charges?" A nod. "Then open that door."

Grant moved noiselessly through the water, careful to avoid the razor-sharp fragments from Jackson's floatplane that littered the waves. He could still hear the rattle of gunfire drifting down from the plateau, see the flashes rippling on the tower like fireworks. The Soviets must still be shooting at shadows, but that was all to the good. It distracted the guard on the jetty: he had turned to watch the lighthouse, so he never saw Grant rising out of the water behind him. Grant grabbed an iron mooring ring, then took the knife from his teeth and stabbed it hard into the back of the guard's heel. He screamed and doubled over, twisting round to see who had attacked him. That unbalanced him. Grant reached up, grabbed his belt and dragged him into the water. He struggled for a moment, splashing and screaming, before Grant's knife slicing across his throat finished him.

Grant looked up at the cliffs. The shooting had stopped for the moment, but there was no sign he had been heard. He waved to where he thought Marina was and beckoned her down. Then he turned and swam over to the flying boat. It was an extraordinary aircraft, like nothing he'd ever seen: a long, upturned nose stretched out in front of the cockpit, while the single engine was mounted amidships directly above the cabin, overshadowing the windscreen like some monstrous cockatoo.

"As long as it flies," he muttered to himself.

He hauled himself up on the nose and slithered his way aft to the entry hatch.

Smoke billowed from the chaos of tangled metal that had once been the lighthouse door. Soloviev's ears were still ringing from the blast as his men stormed inside the tower. He waited; he was painfully aware of the colonel and his friend standing a few paces behind him, watching.

He heard sporadic shots from within the lighthouse, muffled by the massive walls, and he hoped his *kulak* sergeant had had the brains to remember his orders. Had they surrendered?

The sergeant appeared in the doorway. His face was streaked with soot, and grim. "Comrade Lieutenant, come and see."

Soloviev followed him through the twisted door. He took off his cap and flapped it in front of his face, trying to wave away the smoke that filled the lighthouse. He strode up the spiral stairs to the first floor. Through an open door he saw half a dozen men cowering in a small room. Most of them seemed to be in their underwear. "Are these the British?"

The sergeant shook his head. "Our men. We found them locked in a storeroom. It was lucky we did not use grenades."

"Then where are the British? Who was shooting at us from the tower?"

The sergeant didn't answer, but jerked his thumb up the next flight of stairs. As Soloviev climbed, he became aware of a strange rattling noise echoing down the stair shaft, like a tin can being kicked along a street.

He came out on the next floor—and stared in horror.

Grant guided the flying boat past the point, wrestling with the yoke against the brisk current that swirled round the island's tip. Even at low speed, the whole cabin seemed to shake with the vibration of the engine mounted over his head.

Behind him, Marina stood by the open hatch in the fuselage and scanned the dark shore. "There."

Grant saw them too, huddled together on a small finger of rock that dipped into the sea. He could only see two of them, but there was no time to look. A wave slapped against the hull and spilled into the cabin; it took all his concentration to hold the plane steady.

"I can't get any closer." He had to shout to make himself heard over the roar of the engine. "They'll have to swim for it."

Through the darkness he saw two men tottering on the edge of the rocks. One hesitated; then the other pushed him and he fell flailing into the water. The second followed more gracefully. The first one must have been Reed; the next looked like Jackson. But if that was so, where was Muir?

The plane rocked as the two men reached it and grabbed on. Marina hauled them in, dripping and spluttering.

Grant glanced back. "Where's Muir?"

Jackson picked himself up off the floor. Water streamed off him. "Didn't he find you?"

"I left him with you."

"He thought he saw another patrol boat coming in from the other side of the island. Said he was going to find you to warn you."

"Well, he didn't." Grant glanced out of the cockpit window. At the ridge at the top of the hill, he could see pinpoints of light waving in the darkness. "Shall I go and look for him?"

"No time." The lights on the hill seemed to be getting closer. "He'd do the same if it was us out there."

Without further argument Grant opened the throttle and turned the plane toward the open sea.

A metallic, metronomic beat filled the room, counting down the seconds of Soloviev's career. He was standing right underneath the lantern; above, he could see its beam reflected on the enclosing glass through an open trapdoor. In the middle of the room a slowly spinning axle descended through the ceiling and disappeared into the floor, no doubt to the engine room. It bulged in the middle where a long coil of rope had been wound tight round it. As the axle turned, it dragged the submachine gun tied to the rope end in slow circles on the floor. The trigger was still down and the gun ticked like a clock as the firing pin hammered against the empty chamber.

The sergeant pulled out his knife and cut the gun free. To Soloviev's relief, the clicking stopped. "A slip knot. They must have jammed it in the window. When the axle wound the rope tight, it closed round the trigger and started firing at us."

Soloviev staggered over to the open window and gulped in the night air. Outside, he could see the colonel and his companion standing by the bunk house, looking up. Their faces were in shadow, but he didn't need to imagine how they would look when he told them the awful news. But perhaps he could redeem the situation. The British must still be somewhere on the island.

Above him, the lighthouse lumbered on, revealing and hiding the world in passing phases like the moon. Soloviev stared out to sea, looking for solace in the still waves. Instead, to his utter and uncomprehending despair, he saw what looked like the colonel's flying boat gliding through the water—not in the harbor where it was supposed to be, but off the far north-eastern point of the island. His legs went weak; he sagged against the windowsill. A second revolution of the lantern revealed it struggling into the air, water streaming off its pontoons. On the third turn it was banking round to the west. By the fourth it had vanished.

The Soviet plane rose above the clouds. Grant eased back on the unfamiliar controls and relaxed into his seat. Jackson made his way forward and tapped him on the shoulder. With the engine mounted barely two feet over their heads, the noise inside the cabin was almost deafening. "Where are we going?" Jackson shouted in his ear.

Grant shrugged and tapped the fuel gauge. "We don't have enough fuel to make Athens."

"Gotta be Istanbul, then. That's the nearest safe harbor."

"Then what?" Grant glanced at the compass and nudged the yoke to correct his course.

"Then we find out what happened to the shield. And hope to hell the Commies didn't get Muir."

28

Istanbul. Next morning

GRANT WAS woken by a terrible cry. He sat up in bed, and had already thumbed off the Webley's safety catch before he realized what it was: the chant of the muezzin, dreamy and mysterious, drifting through the thin gauze curtains. The chorus echoed all over the city, from every minaret, like birdsong.

Curled beside him, Marina threw an arm across his chest and hugged herself against him. She was naked. Her tousled hair fanned out across the pillow; her eyes were closed; her bare leg wrapped round his. Grant reached across and stroked her shoulder, while she played with the hairs on his chest. He lay there for a few moments, soaking up the sounds, and the exotic smells of spice and dust that blew through the open window.

Marina's hand moved down. Her fingers drifted across the taut muscles of his abdomen, then lower. Grant tensed. Gently, he rolled her on to her back and slid on top of her. He pushed himself up on his arms so he could look down on her face, the sleepy eyes slowly opening with delight. He kissed her.

By the time Grant got out of the bathroom, Marina was already dressed. "I'm going to go to the library. Sourcelles mentioned something that I want to investigate and I think they have a *Suda* here."

Grant didn't bother to ask who or what a *Suda* might be. "I'll come with you."

"No. You stay with Reed—he needs protecting. I think he's on the verge of making a breakthrough."

Grant looked doubtful. "Really? All I've seen is scribbles. I thought he was getting nowhere."

"You don't understand how he works. Imagine the language like a nut he's trying to crack open. All this time he's been holding it in his palm: examining it, turning it round, knocking it to hear the noises it makes. You think he's learning nothing. Then, all of a sudden, he'll tap it in exactly the right place and the shell will just fall open for him."

"I still think you shouldn't go out on your own," said Grant stubbornly.

She blew him a kiss. "I'll be back by lunchtime."

Grant found Jackson eating a late breakfast in the hotel restaurant. The breakfast was meager—salty cheese, salty olives, salty bread and a hard-boiled egg—but the coffee was strong. Grant drank two cups.

"Sleep well?" inquired Jackson. He looked up from decapitating his egg and raised a suggestive eyebrow. He had raised it the same way when Grant and Marina checked into the same room the night before. Had he heard them through the thin walls that morning? Grant didn't care.

"Like the dead. Where's Reed?"

"In his room. He's been up since dawn. Seems to think he's on to something with the tablet. Which he'd better be. If they've got Muir, the Reds must have everything pretty much figured out. That tablet's our only ace and it's not much use if we can't read the damn thing." He looked around the empty restaurant.

"Where's Marina?"

"Library." Grant squeezed his olive so that the stone shot out of the end and bounced across the table. "She wanted to look up something Sourcelles said."

Jackson looked agitated. "You let her go on her own?"

"She can take care of herself."

"Jesus, Grant, that's not what I'm worried about. The Commies have been all over us since you stepped off the boat on Crete. And here in Istanbul . . ." He shook his head. "Christ, there's more Soviet spooks here than guys selling carpets. Hell, half the guys selling carpets probably are spooks."

"She can take care of herself," Grant repeated.

"You know what I mean."

"You're wrong." Grant's voice was hard; his eyes dared Jackson to go on.

"I hope so. Meanwhile, we've got business to be getting on with. With Muir gone, we need to get some back-up. I'll cable Washington and see if they've got any troops in the neighborhood we can borrow."

"Aren't we going back to Athens?"

Jackson shook his head. "No point—not until we know what the tablet says. The Black Sea still seems the most likely spot for finding the shield. Wherever it is, we're probably closer here than anywhere else."

"What about Muir?"

"We gotta assume the worst. He knew the risks. If he was a pro, he'll have put a bullet in his brain before the Reds got him." Jackson pushed back his chair and stood. "I'm going to the consulate. You stay here and watch Reed. If he finds something—or if anything happens—call me there."

Grant finished his breakfast, wandered out to buy an English-language newspaper from the kiosk across the street, then went back upstairs. Jackson and Reed were sharing the room opposite, and he rapped on the door to make sure the professor was all right. A muffled grunt suggested that he was and that any interruption would be unwelcome. With a sigh, Grant retreated to his room and flopped down on the bed. He could smell Marina's perfume on the sheets.

The taxi pulled away, leaving Marina alone on the quiet street. She walked up to a small wooden gate and rang the bell. Behind the whitewashed wall she could see the semidomes of a church, hardly remarkable in this city of domes and towers, and a tall, apricot-colored building like an inverted pyramid, each floor overhanging the one below. The paint on the door peeled away like skin, and crude political slogans were daubed on the wall, but inside the compound everything seemed peaceful.

A window in the door slid open. A suspicious eye surrounded by a wild sea of gray hair peered out. "Yes?"

"My name is Marina Papagiannopoulou," she said in Greek. "I've come to use the library."

The lines round the eye softened to hear the familiar language. The window closed, a lock turned, and a stooped priest in a black cassock and *kamilafki* hat admitted her.

Even Marina, who was used to scrabbling in the ruins of ancient civilizations, felt the age around her as she entered the courtyard. Not the age of Knossos, so remote that the gulf of history between them was unbridgeable, but the age of a grandparent or great-grandparent, a sense of faded glories, spent energy and endings, a life at peace with itself. She supposed it had been declining in this city for five hundred years.

To her surprise, the library turned out to be the church building she had seen from the street. She mentioned it to the priest, who gave a toothless smile.

"After the Ottoman invasion, the conquerors decreed it could no longer be used for religious purposes. His Holiness the Patriarch decided it would serve truth best to become a library."

There was something unsettling about stepping inside, past the golden gazes of mosaic saints, into the dim space. Wooden shelves sagging with books lined the walls and filled the spaces between supporting columns, while lacquered desks in a cruciform arrangement sat in the middle of the chamber under the dome. Marina seated herself at the near end, as close to the door as possible, and pulled the copy of Sourcelles's monograph out of her bag. She leafed through it, not entirely sure what she was looking for, but certain she would recognize it when she saw it.

Like the Hero himself, the White Island presents a troubling duality to those who attempt to explain it. On the one hand is its benevolent aspect as a haven, a "Sacred Harbor" in both the literal and metaphorical senses. In Arrian we find recorded the detail that Achilles would appear in dreams to passing sailors and guide them to the island, to the "most advantageous places to put in, the safest anchorages." On the island itself, Arrian and Philostratus both report the legend of the seabirds, of which there were very many, cleansing the temple through the brushing and flapping of their wings; though this is contradicted by the proverb quoted in Pliny (NH X.78) that "no bird flies over Achilles' temple on the island of the Black Sea where he is buried." In a similar vein, both authors repeat the idea that the livestock on the island offer themselves willingly to be sacrificed at the temple of Achilles, standing docilely before the temple and offering their necks to the knife (the idea of the "willing victim" is, of course, of fundamental importance to religious eschatology throughout history). The whole picture created is one of order and harmony, an Edenic (or, more accurately, Hesperidean) paradise where man and nature and gods live in complete sympathy to each other's needs.

And yet, as befits its status as a liminal place on the strange outer edge of the world, there is a serpent in this garden (literally so, if we consult the narrative of Captain-Lieutenant N. D. Kritskii concerning his 1823 visit to Zmeiny Ostrov); an aura of danger pervades the White Island. On this aspect the oft-neglected Philostratus of Lemnos is particularly loquacious. He relates the strange sounds sailors heard from the island: great voices that could "freeze the sailors with fright"; the sounds of battle, weapons and armor and horses. He states that no man was allowed to remain on the island past sunset. Most gruesomely, he tells the tale of the merchant whom Achilles commanded to bring him a slave girl. Thinking she was wanted merely for sexual gratification, imagine his horror when he

> heard her screams as the vengeful Hero tore her limb from limb and devoured her. Though the White Island may be a paradise of light for gods and heroes, for mortal men it is a place of savagery and darkness, not to be approached lightly.

Marina underlined a few words in pencil, then went to find the librarian—another priest. He took some convincing that her request was legitimate, but in the end gave in. He led her down a flight of stairs, along a dark corridor in the vaults of the old church to a locked room whose shelves were filled not with books but with boxes. These were locked too; he took one down and opened it on the small round table in the corner of the room. A single book lay couched on tissue paper inside. It looked ancient: a silver plate inlaid with jewels and colored stones formed the front cover, while its edges were black with age. Crumbs of the leather spine scattered the paper around it. Marina opened it reverentially.

The priest-librarian refused to leave her, but waited while she found what she wanted. The pages were brown and brittle, like spun sugar; each time she turned one she was terrified she would snap it. As soon as she had found what she wanted and copied it out, he took the book back and shut it safely away in its casket.

Back in the reading room, Marina pulled more books from the shelves and began reading. She worked diligently, glad of the solitude. She felt as though she could feel space and air around her after so many days in the stifling company of men. She knew what Muir and Jackson thought of her, what they suspected; she was tired of having to endure their sharp looks and sneers. There was something unpleasant, masculine, that inevitably went with them. Even Reed, of whom she was very fond, could be trying. And as for Grant . . . She crossed her legs under the table and turned back to her book. Grant was far too complicated to think about here.

She had almost finished when the priest from the gate entered and shuffled up to her seat. "There is a man at the gate to see you," he whispered. "*O Kyrios* Grant."

Marina looked startled: how had he found her? "Did he say why?"

The priest shook his head. "He said it was important."

Marina glanced at the books on the desk. She would be finished in another five minutes—perhaps she should just make him wait. But if Grant said it was urgent . . .

She stood, leaving her books where they were. "I'm coming back," she told the librarian as she left.

Grant didn't know what woke him—he hadn't realized he was asleep. His shirt was damp with sweat and his mouth was sour. He gulped down some water from the glass on the bedside table, though it was stale with dust.

He looked at his watch: four o'clock. A heavy afternoon stillness gripped the hotel; outside, even the muezzins seemed to have knocked off for a nap.

Still half asleep, he looked at his watch again. Where was Marina? She'd said she would be back by lunchtime. He sat up and looked around the room. None of her things had moved—and he'd have heard her if she'd come in.

Grant pulled on his shoes and went out into the corridor. He knocked on Reed's door and waited impatiently. His anxiety grew as the silence dragged on; what had happened to everyone? He tried the handle—not locked—and opened the door.

The room looked as if it had been ransacked. Books and papers lay strewn all over it, together with unfolded clothes, discarded shoes and half-drunk glasses of tea. Grant had no idea Reed could have brought so much with him. The curtains were still drawn, bathing the room in a dull amber light. And there in the middle of it all, sitting cross-legged on the bed in a silk dressing gown, was Reed.

He looked up, blinked and rubbed his glasses on the belt of the dressing gown. "Grant? Sorry—you should have knocked."

"I did." Grant picked his way through the mess and found a corner of the bed to perch on. "Have you seen Marina?"

Reed took one last look at the paper he'd been studying, then put it down, balancing it on his knee. "I thought she was with you. I haven't seen her all day."

"She went to the library first thing. Do you know where that is?"

"In Constantinople?" Reed had never reconciled himself to the change of name to Istanbul. "This city's been a center of learning for the last millennium and a half. It probably has more libraries than mosques. Did she say what she was looking for?"

"No. Yes, wait. She said they had something." Grant racked his brain. "A *Suda*?" He was about to ask if that meant anything to Reed, but he saw immediately from his face that it did.

"That must be the Ecumenical Patriarch's Library."

"Do you know where it is?"

"More or less. I'm sure you could take a taxi."

"Get dressed. You're coming with me."

Reed glanced about the room, as if surprised to see the mess around him. "I don't know that I'd be much help."

"You're not coming to be helpful. We've already lost Muir. If something's happened to Marina then chances are you're next."

They hailed a taxi and set off. Reed quickly decided that being chased by Soviet fighter planes and shot at by guerrillas held no terrors compared with taking a taxi through Istanbul. The driver seemed to think he was back in the imperial hippodrome, racing chariots wheel to wheel for the adulation of the masses; or perhaps one of his Ottoman ancestors, galloping his steed across the great Anatolian steppe. Neither, Reed thought, quite compared to the crowded streets and cramped alleys of modern Istanbul.

"Who's this *Suda* Marina was looking for?" Grant asked. The taxi swerved past a man with a donkey and veered right again to avoid an oncoming tram.

"It's a book, a sort of literary dictionary. It was compiled in the Middle Ages for the Byzantine court. It gives potted biographies of a lot of writers we'd otherwise never have heard of. Very few copies survive nowadays."

"What would Marina have wanted with it?"

"I've no idea. Perhaps she thought of another author who might have mentioned the shield, or the White Island."

Reed went silent for a moment as the driver executed a complicated maneuver, which seemed to involve lighting a cigarette, honking his horn, turning a hairpin corner and shaking his fist at the lorry he was overtaking all at the same time. Reed went white and mumbled something in Greek.

"What was that?" Grant asked, clinging on to the passenger strap.

"Homer":

> *Shot headlong from his seat, beside the wheel,*
> *Prone on the dust the unhappy master fell;*
> *His batter'd face and elbows strike the ground;*
> *Nose, mouth, and front, one undistinguish'd wound.*

Three near-death experiences later the taxi dropped them off outside the library gate. The window in the door swung open; the gray-haired eye examined them suspiciously. "Yes?" he said in Greek.

"We're looking for a friend. A woman. She came to use the library this morning. Have you seen her?"

The eye narrowed. "She was here this morning."

"*Was*? When did she leave?"

"Noon?" He sounded uncertain. "Three men came in a car."

Grant felt an invisible hand twisting a knife in his guts. "Did she say where she was going?"

"She said she would come back."

"Has she?"

"No." Another twist. "But she has left her work here."

Grant looked around desperately at the street, as if he might find Marina walking toward him, the most natural thing in the world. There was no one. "Can we see?"

The priest opened the gate with obvious reluctance and took them across the courtyard into the vaulted library. Marina's bag hung on the back of the chair where she had left it, with a single book on the table in front of it. A small slip of paper poked out between the pages.

Grant snatched it up. The title was in French, but the name on the front leaped out at him. "It's Sourcelles's book. She said she was interested in something he'd mentioned." Grant opened it to the page she'd marked. One sentence in particular caught his eye, one that had been partially underlined in pencil. He showed it to Reed, who translated the French:

> On this aspect the oft-neglected *Philostratus of Lemnos* is particularly loquacious.

"Who's Philostratus of Lemnos?"

Grant had grown so used to Reed's ready answers to his questions, to the smiles of indulgence or the twitches of impatience that came with them depending on his mood, that he barely thought about them any more. He had long since reached the conclusion that the professor was for all practical purposes infallible, a walking encyclopedia of the ancient world.

But instead of answering, Reed pursed his lips and looked blank. "Philostratus," he repeated. "A minor philosopher of the third century AD, I think. Not really my period—except that I seem to remember he wrote a biography of Apollonius of Rhodes, who wrote the principal poetic account of Jason and the Argonauts. That's probably why Marina wanted the *Suda*—to look him up."

Grant curled his hand into a fist to try to keep control of himself. "Well, *he* probably didn't kidnap her."

"If he's from Lemnos, he might have known something about the cult of Hephaestus."

They found the librarian. He looked suspicious at first, but a few sharp words from Reed persuaded him to unlock the cumbersome door and lead them down into the subterranean treasury. He opened the box and laid the crumbling book on the table.

Reed's hand trembled as he touched the silver-plated cover. "The young woman who was here this morning: did she look at this book?"

The librarian's wispy beard seemed to float in the darkness as he silently nodded. Reed turned the stiff pages; Grant marvelled at the tiny lettering, neat as type.

"Here we go."

> Philostratus. Son of Philostratus Verus, the sophist from Lemnos. He was a sophist in Athens, then in Rome when Severus was emperor until the reign of Philip. he wrote: Declamations; Descriptions (four books); Market-Place; Heroicus; Dialogues; Goats, or Concerning the Pipe; a life of Apollonius of Rhodes (eight books); epigrams; and other works.

"*Heroicus*," Reed repeated. "*On Heroes*. Do you know this work?"

The librarian nodded. Wordlessly, he gathered up the *Suda* and returned it to its box, then swept out of the vault. They followed him up to the reading room. He didn't head for the shelves; instead he went back to his desk. A wooden trolley sat beside it, piled with books waiting to go back to their shelves. The librarian plucked one from near the top, a slim volume in a black and red binding, and handed it to Reed.

When he opened it, Grant smelled a sudden blossom of almond and rose, a flower in the dusty desert of the library. "Marina must have been reading this," he said, imagining her perfumed wrist rubbing the page edges as she turned them. "What is it?"

Reed pulled out a chair and sat down at one of the tables, scanning the pages. Grant tried to swallow the desperate impatience seething inside him.

"It's an account of the Trojan war." Reed looked up. "It's a typical device in fiction of this period: the ghost of a minor character from the *Iliad* pops up and tells a weary traveller everything Homer got wrong. There's practically an entire literary sub-genre in late antiquity. What makes this one remarkable, for our purposes, is that it was written by someone who had intimate knowledge of the Lemnian cult of Hephaestus."

He gave a tired smile as he saw Grant's expression. "Your guess was right. According to the introduction, Philostratus was a priest of the cult of Hephaestus on Lemnos." Reed took off his glasses and rubbed his eyes. "He would have had an unrivaled knowledge of the cult's history, its innermost secrets. In fact, there appears to be a school of thought that the entire work is riddled with mystic double meanings that only initiates of the cult would appreciate: secret words that would appear wholly innocuous to the lay reader. But there is one thing particularly noteworthy in the text. He says[3]:

> The White Island lies in the Black Sea, toward the inhospitable side, which is on the left as you sail into the mouth of that sea. It reaches thirty stadia in length but not more than four in width. Both poplar and elm trees grow on it: some happen to grow wild, but others are planted by design around the temple. The temple is situated near the Sea of Maeotis (which flows into the Black Sea) and the statues in it are Achilles and Helen, crafted by the Fates.

"Where's the Maeotis Sea?"

"The Maeotis was the Greek name for what we now call the Sea of Azov." Reed got up and fetched an atlas from the shelves. But it was like no atlas Grant had ever used. The cartographers seemed to have been drunk: all the familiar outlines were distorted and even the places he recognized had been given unfamiliar names. Italy was no longer the tall, high-heeled thigh-boot he knew, but a stubby, clumsy workboot. It was not the world as it actually was, but the world as men had once seen it.

As Reed turned the pages, the contours slowly resolved. Vague lines became more precise; bays and inlets nibbled into the sweeping coasts and the amoebic continents evolved spines, appendages, limbs. Now the maps were printed, not hand drawn, their shapes recognizable as the modern world. Though the names were still strange and foreign.

"Here we are."

The map was of the eastern Black Sea, dated 1729. Reed pointed to where the Sea of Azov joined the Black Sea. "The Cimmerian Bosphorus." He shook his head, berating himself for some error or failing only he knew.

Now sunk the sun from his aerial height,
And o'er the shaded billows rush'd the night;
When lo! we reach'd old Ocean's utmost bounds,
Where rocks control his waves with ever-during mounds.
There in a lonely land, and gloomy cells,
The dusky nation of Cimmeria dwells,

"When Odysseus sails to find the portal to Hades, Cimmeria is the last country he passes before he crosses the Oceanus. Now, the ancient Greeks believed that the Cimmerians had been a real people who lived into historical times. According to Herodotus they lived around the north-east corner of the Black Sea. He says they'd all been slaughtered by subsequent invaders, but that their name lived on in . . ."

". . . place names," said Grant, remembering. "Always the last to go."

"Hence the Cimmerian Bosphorus. The Euxine Bosphorus—nowadays *the* Bosphorus—led into the Black Sea from the Sea of Marmara and the Aegean; at the opposite end the Cimmerian Bosphorus led out into the Sea of Azov. I believe nowadays it's called the Kerch Strait."

"And you think that's what Marina found: that the White Island is somewhere near there?"

"That's what Philostratus says—and the *Odyssey* agrees."

Grant peered at the map. "But there are no islands there."

A burst of frustration welled inside him; he slammed the book shut. "*Shit.*" Searching for whatever Marina had been working on had somehow staved off the feelings of helplessness. Now even that was a dead end. "We have to find her."

Reed looked at him with tired eyes. "And how will you do that in this city of almost a million inhabitants?"

"The police?"

"They'd be more likely to lock us up. We haven't even got our passports." He gave a sad shake of his head and touched Grant's arm. "I'm sorry. I suppose we'd better tell Jackson."

"Jesus Christ." Jackson threw a glass ashtray across the room. It punctured the flimsy wall, bounced off and landed on the carpet. Flakes of ash fluttered down around it. "This is your fault, Grant."

"Why are you looking at me? I didn't kidnap her."

"Get with the program. Nobody kidnapped her." Jackson paced the room angrily. "She's been spying on us for her Russian friends since day one. Why else do you think we keep running into them—because we use the same travel agent? How'd they find you on Lemnos? How come they found us in Athens—and ended up at Sourcelles's house half an hour behind us? How'd they get on to us on Snake Island so quick?"

"I don't know. The point is it wasn't Marina. She kept that tablet safe for six years without telling anyone."

"She probably didn't know what it was worth. Jesus! We should never have trusted her. Washington'll have my balls served up for breakfast in an omelette when they find out."

"And if she was a spy, why would she go now? There's nothing to go on except that tablet, and Reed's about to crack it."

A look of horror crossed Jackson's face. "Where is the tablet?"

"In my room." Reed had watched the whole argument from the safety of a corner. He looked embarrassed, a house guest forced to witness his hosts' marital bickering. "It's still there. I checked it ten minutes ago."

"She thought she was coming back—she left her things in the library."

"Well, gosh. That fucking proves it. You think it wouldn't have occurred to her to leave a false trail to slow us up, Einstein?"

Something snapped inside Grant. Before Jackson could think to protect himself, Grant had taken three strides across the room and lifted him up by his lapels. He slammed him into the wall, shaking him like a rat.

"Put me down."

"I'll put you down when you apologize."

"Apologize for what? Insulting your little Commie whore?"

There was no telling what Grant might have done next, but at that moment there was a knock at the door. All three men turned to look.

"Not now," snarled Jackson.

Either his words were too muffled to be clear, or they weren't understood. The door opened. An elderly porter in a white jacket stood in the corridor. His face went slack as he saw the scene in the room: "Telefon," he whispered, plainly terrified. He mimed a receiver with his little finger and thumb. "Telefon for Mister Grant."

Grant dropped Jackson and ran after the porter, almost pushing him down the stairs in his hurry. Jackson came after him. The receptionist stared at the look on Grant's face and mutely offered him the telephone. Grant was about to take it when Jackson pushed in his way. "The call's for me."

"Right. But I want to hear it too." Jackson turned to the receptionist. "Is there another extension?" He held up both hands and made the same bull's-horn gesture that the porter had made. "*Icki* telephone?"

The receptionist pointed to the opposite end of the counter. She rearranged the plugs in her switchboard, then nodded. Grant and Jackson took the handsets.

"This is Grant."

It was a bad line, full of hisses and electric crackling, but the voice was clear and cold. "My name is Kurchosov. I have your friend."

Grant's heart beat faster. He said nothing.

"I will offer her to you in exchange for the tablet."

At the other end of the counter Jackson covered the mouthpiece with his hand and mouthed, "Play for time."

"Your friend Belzig stole the tablet."

"There is a second piece." A dangerous edge crept into the voice. "The more important piece. You stole it from the Frenchman's house."

"We left it in Greece."

The line hissed. "For your friend's sake I hope you did not."

"It's no use to you anyway. You can't read it."

"We will decide that for ourselves—when you give it to us."

"I can't."

A dangerous edge entered Kurchosov's voice. "You will. We will meet you on the Üsküdar ferry at this time tomorrow. You will bring us the tablet."

The line went dead.

"Now do you accept Marina's not working for them?"

Jackson looked as if he was about to say something, then saw the dangerous look in Grant's eyes and swallowed it. Instead, he turned to Reed. "How are you getting on with the translation?"

Reed looked glum. "I thought I had it this morning. This afternoon I felt I'd as much chance drawing words out of a hat."

"Is there anything we can do to help?" said Grant.

Jackson took a drag on his cigarette. "Like what? If he can't read it, you sure as shit can't. And it's all goddamn Greek to me."

It wasn't a new joke, nor even very funny, but the effect on Reed was electric. He sat bolt upright, stared at Jackson, then leaped to his feet. "Excuse me," he mumbled and ran out of the door.

"What the . . ."

Jackson and Grant followed him into the room next door. They found him kneeling beside the bed, rifling through the reams of paper scattered on the floor.

"What is it?"

He turned to face them. His pale blue eyes were wide open, yet he barely seemed to see them. "I think I've got it."

29

NO ONE slept that night. Grant and Jackson took it in turns to stand guard in the corridor, fighting off sleep's advances with endless cigarettes and cups of coffee. Reed didn't need any stimulants. Every hour they knocked on his door to see if he needed anything; each time he waved them away. Hunched over his desk in a pool of lamplight, wearing his dressing gown over his clothes and scribbling furiously, he reminded Grant of something out of a fairy tale: Rumpelstiltskin, perhaps, laboring through the night to spin gold out of paper and clay.

Even when he wasn't on duty Grant couldn't sleep. He lay awake on his bed, shivering with caffeine and nicotine and fatigue. He tried not to think about Marina; when that failed, he tried to crowd out his fears with happier memories. That didn't work either. At three a.m., after his second spell on watch, he went up to the roof and stood on the terrace, drinking in the night around him. The hotel was in the Sultanahmet district, the heart of the ancient city. On his right he could see the tip of an obelisk in the old hippodrome; further over, the domes of the Blue Mosque tumbling over each other, and the spire on Ayia Sophia. For perhaps the first time in his life he felt the beauty of history.

When he went back downstairs, the corridor was deserted and Reed's door hung open. Grant broke into a run, then slowed again as he heard familiar voices inside the room. Reed was still there, slumped in his chair, while Jackson stared over his shoulder at something on the desk.

Jackson looked up. "He's cracked it."

Even allowing for his tiredness, Reed looked shaken—like a man who had peered behind the curtain of some sacred shrine and could not comprehend what he had witnessed.

"Jackson's joke turned out to be no more than the literal truth. The language—Linear B—is Greek. A very primitive, archaic form, but recognisably Greek."

"I thought you said Greek was suggested years ago."

"It was. But that was only guesswork: suggesting a key when we hadn't yet found the lock. It would have been like looking at an Enigma intercept, not knowing where it had come from, and saying it might be in German. It's all very well, but it's meaningless until you've dissected the code, learned its grammar and its syntax, and how it represents the language. You have to rebuild it from the bottom up—only then do comparisons with other languages do any good. In this particular instance we've been inconceivably lucky. It might have been a totally new language, or one only distantly related to one we knew. Instead, it's one of the most studied languages on the planet."

"You've done a great job," said Jackson warmly. "But what did you find out?"

Reed scratched the side of his head. "The implications are staggering. We all assumed the Mycenaeans were a pre-Greek culture, wiped out before the Greeks arrived. Now it seems they were there alongside. This is going utterly to rewrite the history books."

"Fuck the history books—what about the tablet?"

"Oh, yes." Reed handed him a piece of paper. "There's still work to be done—some of the constructions are hard to make out and there are several symbols I've only tentatively identified. But this should give you the gist."

Jackson and Grant leaned in to look.

"You know, we're probably the first people to read this language in almost three thousand years."

THE KING OF CRETE DEDICATED THE STONE TO THE MISTRESS OF THE LABYRINTH. BUT THE GODDESS DID NOT FAVOR THE MEN OF CRETE. THE BLACK SHIPS CAME TO ZAKROS AND TOOK THE STONE FROM THE LION'S MOUTH [CAVE?]. THE LEADER OF THE HOST BROUGHT THE STONE TO THE TEMPLE OF THE SMITH ON LEMNOS. IN FIRE AND IN WATER, THE INITIATES SWEATED METAL FROM THE STONE AND FORGED ARMOR: TWO GREAVES; A HELMET WITH CHEEK PIECES; A BRONZE CORSELET; AND A SHIELD OF BRONZE, SILVER, GOLD AND LEAD. BY THE WILL OF THE GODS, THEY GAVE THIS TO THE HERO WHOSE DEEDS ARE WELL KNOWN . . .

[next two lines illegible because of the break in the tablet. We may conjecture they relate the death of the Hero (Achilles?) and the inheritance of his armor.—A.R.]

. . . THEN OUR CAPTAIN, THE GOOD SAILOR, SWORE HE WOULD NOT KEEP THE TROPHIES BUT DEDICATE THEM TO THE HERO. BY THE WILL OF THE PRIESTESS, THE ROWERS TOOK THE CARGO BEYOND THE LIMITS OF THE WORLD. THEY SAILED ALONG THE COAST AND CROSSED THE RIVER. THEN SOON THEY CAME TO THE SACRED HARBOR WHERE WILLOWS AND POPLARS AND WILD CELERY GROW. THERE, IN THE MOUNTAIN BEYOND THE LAKE, THEY BUILT THE HOUSE OF DEATH. THEY PUT INSIDE IT GIFTS AND BURNED OFFERINGS, THE ARMOR AND THE SHIELD, AND ALSO MANY CUPS AND VESSELS OF GOLD AND SILVER. THEN THEY SAILED HOME WITH MANY ADVENTURES.

"So all we need to do is work out which river they crossed and then find the nearest mountain."

"Most of the sources talked about rivers in connection with the

White Island," Grant remembered. "But none of them could agree which. The Dnieper, the Dniester, the Danube . . ."

"And they're probably wrong anyway. Remember: it's more likely to be somewhere near the Kerch Strait and the Sea of Azov."

Jackson looked surprised. "Did I miss something?"

"I'll explain," said Reed. "In the meantime, I don't suppose we can find a map?"

"I've got the *Black Sea Pilot* we used to get to Snake Island. It's in my room."

Grant fetched the book, which came with a chart folded inside the back cover. He spread it out on the bed and stared at it. The lines swam and blurred in front of his exhausted eyes—but one stark fact was clear. "There aren't any islands. There isn't even a river."

"There must be," said Reed stubbornly. "The one thing all the texts agree on is that there's a river near the White Island. The whole point is that they have to cross the Oceanus to get to the world beyond."

"I thought they travelled by sea," Grant objected. "You can't cross a river at sea. You cross it on land, from one bank to the other. Unless it means they sailed past the mouth of a river. But there isn't one . . . what?"

He broke off as he realized Reed was staring at him—not with his usual impatience, but with genuine awe in his eyes. "That's it."

"What?"

"Try to see it through Odysseus's eyes." All Reed's age and weariness seemed to lift away as he spoke. "From the battlefields of Troy, you've brought your precious cargo up the Dardanelles and the Bosphorus into the Black Sea. You've sailed along the coast—you don't dare risk the open sea in those days—but even that is fraught with danger. Your ships have been attacked by cannibals, almost destroyed by storms. You're like Marlow in *Heart of Darkness*: you're off the edge of the world, into the white spaces at the edge of the map. You pass the land of the Cimmerians, and there—just where you're expecting to find it—you come into the mouth of a river. Not just any river: a great river nine miles wide and—if they looked upstream as they sailed across—no end in sight. The Oceanus."

At last Grant began to understand. "The straits."

"The current flowing out of the Sea of Azov into the Black Sea would have given the impression of a great flowing river. And they would have seen what they were expecting. They sailed across." Reed tapped the map on the eastern side of the straits. "And here, on the far shore of the world, they found the White Island. That has to be it."

"*Has to be*?" Jackson echoed. "Three days ago, it *had to be* Snake Island. We almost got ourselves a one-way ticket on the trans-Siberian railway finding out we made a mistake there."

"That was based on the wrong texts. Philostratus is different—he was a priest of Hephaestus on Lemnos, for heaven's sake. And his account is consistent with Homer."

"Of course it is," said Jackson. "He probably had Homer on his desk when he was writing his own book."

"The whole conceit of the *Heroicus* is that it's a self-conscious attempt to 'correct' Homer. Philostratus wouldn't agree with him unless he felt he had to—it undermines his literary purpose. Philostratus must have known something to put it where he did."

"Maybe he didn't know enough," said Grant. "It doesn't change the fact that there isn't a single island along the coast east of the Kerch Strait."

Reed went quiet.

"What about the strait itself?" Jackson waved his hand over the map where two arms of land came together to form the strait. The west side seemed solid enough, but the eastern arm looked like a moth-eaten scrap of cloth, so full of lakes and lagoons that there was more water than land. "That whole area looks like a chain of islands that got silted up."

"According to this, they're all low-lying and marshy," said Grant, consulting the *Pilot*. "The tablet talks about a mountain."

"And it says they sailed *past* the river. If that spit was ever broken into islands, they would have seemed to be islands *in* the Oceanus—the strait. We need to look further east."

"There aren't any islands there," Grant repeated.

"Perhaps it isn't an island."

They both stared at Reed as if he had gone mad. With his wild hair and haggard eyes, it wasn't hard to imagine.

Jackson spoke very slowly. "Are you trying to tell me that after all this the White *Island* isn't actually an island?"

Reed had the decency to look embarrassed—though Grant could see it was just a mask, thrown up automatically while his mind churned behind it. He flipped through his notebook. "Here we are. You remember the *Chrestomathy*, in Athens?"

"The lost poem. The sequel to Homer."

"Well, Proclus's summary of it, yes. After Achilles' death, 'They lay out Achilles' corpse. His mother, the sea nymph Thetis, arrives with the Muses and mourns her son. Then she snatches him up from the pyre and carries his body to the White Island'?"

"Not exactly tearing holes in the island theory, is it?"

Reed ignored him. "Now, the Greek words Proclus uses for the White Island are Λευκην νησον—*Leukin nison*."

"What does that mean?"

"'*Leukin*' is 'white' and '*nison*' is 'island.'"

Jackson rolled his eyes. "Is there a point to this?"

"In certain circumstances *nison* can also mean peninsula. Elsewhere in the epic cycle, for example, the Peloponnesian peninsula is referred to as *nison*."

"Why would they do that? Didn't they have a word for peninsula?"

"Greek poetry is metrical—that is, you have to fit the words into a certain syllabic rhythm. There are some words that will never fit the rhythm and *chersonesos*—the correct term for peninsula—is one of them. So while a prose writer would use *chersonesos*, a poet couldn't possibly. He'd have to find a synonym that fitted the meter."

"But is the *Chrestomathy* a poem? The bit you read out didn't sound very poetic."

"It's a prose summary, but of an epic poem. It's entirely possible Proclus just copied down phrasing from the original poem when he abbreviated it."

"So you're saying the White Island is actually the White Peninsula?" Despite everything, Jackson had to laugh. "Doesn't sound so poetic, I'll give you that."

"And nobody's ever thought of this before?"

"Not as far as I'm aware." Reed shrugged. "It's like water flowing down a hill. Once the first drop finds its way down, the rest follows its course. With every drop the stream flows faster, the channel gets gouged deeper, the way becomes more certain. Nobody even thinks to question the direction."

"Sure, whatever." Jackson wasn't interested in metaphors. He looked back to the chart, smoothing it out to keep it from curling up at the ends. "So we want a peninsula with cliffs, somewhere east of the strait." He traced the shoreline with his finger. "There's a bit of a promontory here."

"Doesn't look like much," said Grant doubtfully.

"It shouldn't. It's not supposed to be particularly large."

Reed consulted the *Pilot*. His eyes darted over the page—then, abruptly went very still. "What's the name of that point?"

"Cape Rusyaeva."

" 'Cape Rusyaeva,' " Reed repeated. " 'Bold, lofty cliffs at the foot of a range of weathered mountains, divided by numerous narrow valleys. Shingle beaches below; fish cannery on western shore, possibly deserted. The color of the cliffs is a remarkable white.' " He closed the book with a bang. " 'Appears from distance like an island.' "

A silence gripped the room as they digested it.

"It does fit," Grant said at last.

"The White Peninsula." Jackson shook his head in wonder. "I've got to hand it to you, Professor, you've come up with the goods this time."

"It doesn't mean anything," Grant warned. But he himself didn't completely believe that. "Even if it's the right part of the map, we're still looking at an area of miles, perhaps dozens of miles. An area that also happens to be part of the Soviet Union," he added drily.

"All the more reason we've got to get there fast."

"What about Marina? Now that we know where the temple is, we can trade the tablet."

Reed nodded, but Jackson was watching him with a strange, unsettling gaze. A cold look came over his face. "We're not giving the Commies anything—not until that shield's safe in Tennessee. Sure as hell not while it's lying in a cave somewhere in Soviet territory."

Grant could only stare at him. "You're not going to abandon Marina. Not after everything she's done for us." Grant took a step toward him.

Jackson held up his hands in mock surrender. "OK, OK. All I'm saying is we need to be smart about this. Not throw away our aces to pick up a queen."

"She's not a card, Jackson. Anything the Russians do to her, you'd better believe I'll do the same to you."

"Right." Jackson took a deep breath and sat down on a wooden chair. "Let's just remember we're all on the same side—and we all want the same thing."

"Do we?"

"Yes. I want to get Marina back, I honestly do. She's a good girl. But believe me, if the Russians get their hands on that shield you're going to know about it in the worst way you can imagine. So we'll get both. What time is it?"

Grant checked his watch again. "Just past four in the morning."

"And we're due to meet Kurchosov at six tonight, right?" He leaned over the map and measured the distance with his thumb and forefinger. "Four hundred and fifty miles. We've still got Kurchosov's plane here. If we leave now, we can be there by dawn. If the shield's there, the Bismatron should get us on to it. We'll whisk it out from under their noses and be gone before they know it. Then we'll hightail it back, and be here in time to trade Kurchosov the tablet for Marina."

"And if we don't make it back in time?"

Jackson shrugged. "Then meeting Kurchosov's going to be the least of anyone's problems."

30

Black Sea, east of Kerch Strait. 7:58 a.m.

THE PLANE touched down with a puff of spray, racing in under the slate-gray sky. The cliffs reared up out of the sea, stark white, with the higher walls of the mountains looming behind them. It all felt strangely familiar to Grant, rushing in to a hostile shore. But whereas in the war—or even a month ago when he had landed the guns at that fateful beach in Palestine—he would have felt a keen edge of excitement, this time he couldn't summon the energy. An unsettling lethargy had him in its grip; even the bucking boat felt dead beneath him. He hoped it wasn't an omen.

They came in under the cliffs and throttled back the engine, scanning the shore for a place to land. Seabirds circled above them, launching themselves off the cliffs with haunting cries and plunging down into the sea. Grant saw one swoop out with a fish wriggling in its beak; water showered off as it flapped its wings to gain height. He remembered the story Sourcelles had told them about birds cleaning the temple with the spray from their wings, and shivered.

Three hours earlier, still before dawn, they had assembled on a dock in front of an unmarked warehouse on the Asian shore of the Bosphorus. A light rain had been falling, coating the rusted metal and cracked concrete with a fresh sheen that gleamed orange in the sodium lamps. With ships' engines throbbing in the background, the air thick with coal smoke and engine oil, it had felt like a fitting beginning to a journey to the underworld. Just before they were due to depart a lorry had pulled up next to the gangway. Grant remembered the hiss of its tires on the wet dock. Three men in combat fatigues had jumped out. Two of them quickly transferred half a dozen duffel bags from the lorry to the Soviet flying boat, while the third came across to greet them.

"Lieutenant Kowalski, US Marines." He'd started to lift his hand in a salute, then remembered his orders and diverted it into an awkward handshake.

"Jackson. This is Grant."

He'd shaken Grant's hand and looked at Reed. "Who's he, Lincoln?"

"I borrowed them from the embassy," Jackson explained. "They were all they could give me, this time of night. Just because Kurchosov's holding out for the tablet, I figure he's not going to give up looking himself. If he shows up again I want some cavalry with us this time."

Grant had checked around the deserted dock, wondering what lurked in the shadows beyond the chain-link fence. "With luck, he won't know where to go."

"He's got Marina and she'd already figured out the whole Philostratus angle."

"She won't talk."

Jackson had looked as though he'd have liked to say something, but thought better of it. "Let's hope so."

"There."

Round the end of the promontory the cliffs split apart. Grant looked for willows or poplars, but saw nothing but a field of reeds waving gently behind a shingle beach. A small lagoon lay behind that, cradled inside the arm of the beach—but open at one end, where a shallow channel spilled into the sea. They taxied the plane toward it. The white cliffs towered over them; the pulse of the propeller echoed back off the high walls, drumming into their skulls. The channel was so narrow Grant feared they would surely snap a wing against the cliff, or be dashed into it by a rogue wave.

The flying boat nosed into the lagoon and came to a stop in the still water. They leaped out into the foam, slipping and struggling as the rocks slid away under their feet. Kowalski's men made the flying boat fast and unloaded the equipment. While they did that, Grant walked up the shingle slope to the back of the beach. Beyond, he could see a tight ravine filled with trees and bushes. A small river trickled out of it into the lagoon.

Reed joined him. Even there, on the shores of the Soviet Union, he was still neatly dressed in a suit, a waistcoat and a tie. His one concession to practicality was his boots, black army boots that poked incongruously from under his tweed trousers.

"Heroes' temples were always supposed to cause lush vegetation to grow up around them. It was thought to show the fecundity of the hero's presence."

"Doesn't make it any easier to find."

Reed didn't answer. He stared about him at the lonely bay: the sepulchral cliffs, the dark sky, the keening birds and the pebbles that rattled like bones.

Soon shalt thou reach old Ocean's utmost ends,
Where to the main the shelving shore descends;
The barren trees of Proserpine's black woods,
Poplars and willows trembling o'er the floods:
There fix thy vessel in the lonely bay,
And enter there the kingdoms void of day.

"At least it sounds like we've got the right place this time."

Grant heard footsteps crunching up the beach behind him. He turned and saw Jackson.

"Where to now, Professor?"

Reed shrugged. "The *Odyssey* talks about a river. I suppose we should follow it."

They made their way round the edge of the lagoon, splashing through the shallows and reeds, until they reached the place where the river entered it. Kowalski's men struggled under the weight of all the equipment they had to carry: as well as their rifles and packs, they had brought picks, shovels, the Bismatron and what looked to Grant like blasting charges.

Jackson reached a small islet of broken stones and looked back. "Does it have a name, this river?"

"Homer calls it Acheron—the River of Grief."

Jackson shook his head in mock despair. "You sure know how to pick 'em. Don't tell me where it leads; I don't want to spoil the surprise."

They followed the river inland. Grant led the way. There was no path, no way through the undergrowth at all. In the narrow valley the trees grew so close together they were all but impenetrable. They hid the sky, stretching their branches toward the light like the hands of the damned. Many of the smaller trees seemed to have been choked off completely by their taller rivals, but they had no space to fall. Even in death they stayed upright, their leafless corpses black and rotting. The only way through was to stick to the river, hopping from rock to rock, sometimes wading through. Mercifully it wasn't deep—little more than a stream—and the water never came much above their knees. Even so, they struggled to avoid the undergrowth. Creepers trailed from the overhanging trees like snakes, snatching at their hair, while half-submerged stumps and branches lurked in the stream to trip them.

There was almost nothing to see beyond the water and the woods, but gradually Grant had the impression that the valley was narrowing around them. The ground got steeper; the stream quickened. Ahead he could hear a rushing noise that seemed to float above the trees. He came to the bottom of a little cataract, where the fast-flowing water frothed and bubbled, and looked up. Not far ahead he could see cliffs and sky framed between the trees like a doorway.

The rushing noise had become a roar. Grant scrambled up the last few rocks, ignoring the water splashing all over him, soaking his shirt and trousers. He halted at the top, crouching on a flat boulder, dripping.

He had come to the top of the valley. The forest stretched away on either side, curving round to meet the cliffs that curved back to join them. The round hollow between was filled by a broad pool which emptied into the stream where he stood. The surface of the lake was black and fathomless, except at the foot of the cliffs where it bubbled and frothed under the impact of the waterfall cascading down from the heights above.

Jackson and Reed clambered up beside him, crowding on to the boulder like castaways on a raft. Kowalski and his men waited below.

"Now what?"

Reed gazed at the waterfall. "According to Homer, we should come to a place where two other streams join the river."

"What are they called? The river of hurt and the stream of pain?"

"The River of Fire and the River of Lament, actually."

"Sorry I asked."

Grant pulled the tablet out of his knapsack and unwrapped it, trying to shield it from the spray blowing across the pool. "It looks like two streams in the picture. Unless they're just contours in the mountain. What does the Bismatron say?"

Jackson scrambled back down to rejoin the marines. Grant saw him take the Bismatron out of its box and turn it on. The rush of water drowned out whatever noise it made; the needle barely flickered.

"Not much." He frowned at the dial. "Maybe something. I guess we have to go on." Jackson pointed to the cliffs beside the waterfall. "Can we get up there?"

Grant eyed it up. It wouldn't be easy. The cliffs weren't impossibly high, perhaps fifty feet, but the white stone was icy smooth, even without the fine coating of spray from the waterfall. "Sure," he said casually. "Have you got a rope?"

With one of Kowalski's men in tow, Grant splashed his way round toward the waterfall. The others watched from the far rim of the pool. It was hard even getting close to the foot of the cliff: it seemed to drop well below the surface of the lake, so there were few rocks to stand on.

Where the trees and the cliffs joined, Grant paused. There didn't seem to be anywhere to stand—except maybe a rocky shelf that protruded a few inches from the base of the cliff a few yards away. Grant peered into the pool but saw only his own reflection on the black mirror.

"I'm wet enough anyway," he muttered. He shrugged off his knapsack, slung the coiled rope over his shoulder and jumped in.

The water was warmer than he'd expected and in this corner of the pool the current actually pressed him back against the cliffs, rather than sucking him out toward the spout. He kicked through the water and hauled himself up on to the shelf, shivering to be in the breeze again. The cliff thrust out at him, chest to chest; he couldn't stand without the feeling he might fall backward at any moment.

He looked over to the marine watching from the shore. "Wish me luck."

Grant was no stranger to climbing. As a boy he'd spent hours crawling all over the chalk headlands at Flamborough as a man he'd hauled himself up more walls and cliffs than he cared to remember. But this was a different challenge. The surface of the rock was soft and undulating, like skin. The only way to get any purchase was to spread himself like a lizard, clinging on to the low swellings in the cliff. He could only move by sliding his hands up inch by inch. Even on the smooth rock his fingers were soon rubbed raw. His wet clothes weighed him down, though at least the shirt stuck to the cliff face as much as his own body. Sometimes, that seemed to be the only thing holding him up.

He glanced down. That was a mistake—not because he feared heights, but because he saw how little distance he had come. He turned his attention back to the cliff and struggled on. For a short while the slope angled in a little and the going got quicker. Then, suddenly, the cliffs bulged again, more than vertical, hanging out over him. There was no hope he could squirm up that. He pressed his cheek to the rock and glanced right: no way round. To his left the waterfall suddenly seemed thunderously loud.

There was no alternative. Bracing his legs as best he could in the shallow hollows in the cliff face, he lunged upward. His palm slammed against the overhang; his arm shuddered; his fingers closed—and felt a thin pucker in the rock. Not a moment too soon. Just as he touched it his foot lost its purchase. He kicked out, thrashing to find a foothold, but his boots just skidded off the rock. For a moment he dangled in space, his whole weight crushed into his fingertips.

He could have let go, fallen, trusted to luck and hoped for the pool to catch him. It hardly crossed his mind. Inch by inch, pound by pound, he hauled himself up. The tendons in his fingers felt thick as hawsers; the cramp in his hands was almost unbearable. Even the bones in his arms ached. He reached up again and this time his hand closed round something firmer. Hope gave him strength; his toe found a small dimple in the rock and he pushed himself up. With a gasp of release he hauled himself over the lip of a small ledge. It was tiny, less than a foot deep, but to Grant it felt like a football field.

When he had caught his breath he looked up. He was still well below the summit, but the way was easier now. A thin crevice split open the cliff—not much, but enough to worm the toes of his boots into. After what he'd already endured, it was almost as good as a ladder. He worked his way up and at last hauled himself over the top of the cliff. He lay there for a moment, breathing hard and rubbing his arms.

"What have you found?"

The faint shout from below drew him back to the present. He looked down. Reed and Jackson were still standing on the boulder at the head of the stream, staring up like frogs on a lily pad.

What had he found? He looked around. He had come into a high, steep-sided valley, almost like a sunken meadow. There were no trees, only the stream winding through the thick turf. It was surprisingly placid here; even the noise of the waterfall seemed distant and muted. In a strange way it reminded him of Scotland. At the far end of the valley, in front of another cliff, two stone columns stuck out of the ground like tusks.

He unhooked the rope from his shoulder and tied a bowline round an outcrop of rock. He tossed the rest of the rope over the cliff. Then he lit a cigarette. In a few minutes the first marine had pulled himself up, followed—at varying speeds—by Jackson and the others. Reed came last, with the equipment, harnessed into the rope and hauled up by the marines. He didn't seem to have suffered from the ordeal; in fact, his face shone with excitement. He looked around in wonder. "Remarkable," he breathed. "Like a lost world—stout Cortez and all his men. We might be the first men to tread here for three thousand years."

"Let's hope there aren't any more coming."

A breeze whispered down the valley. Soaking wet from scrambling through the stream, they shivered. Grant looked back at the way they'd come up. The forested slope hid the beach, while the sea had all but disappeared in a smear of fine haze.

They headed up toward the two pillars. The ground was soft, the grass thick and abundant. Wild celery grew in the crooks of the stream's meanders. A desolate quiet filled the valley.

It ended in another cliff, the walls curving round like the stern of a ship to close it off. As they drew near, they examined the rock pillars they had seen from the waterfall. They were colossal: they stood on either side of the stream, almost thirty feet from base to top. The white stone had been weathered smooth, but Grant, looking at them, had the sense that there was something indelibly *artificial* beneath, as if the columns had been cased in molten wax that still modelled the man-made contours under the surface. The more he looked at them the more he convinced himself he could see human shapes shrouded in the stone: bulges that could have been hips and shoulders, dips where the megalithic waists should have been. At the very top, hard to see from below, each pillar tapered to a conical cap that might once have been a head. And, on the right-hand column about three-quarters of the way up, two swellings that Grant felt sure had once been breasts. He pointed them out to Reed, who nodded.

"Philostratus describes two statues in the temple, 'crafted by the Fates.' He claims they were Achilles and Helen."

"Helen of Troy?"

"Precisely: the face that launched a thousand ships." He saw Grant's confusion and chuckled. "Yes, she's not usually associated with Achilles. But there's an obscure version of the legend that claims she actually came to live with Achilles on the White Island."

"Why would she do that? I thought the whole point of the Trojan war was to get her back to her husband. Doesn't it rather spoil the ending if she runs off with another man?"

"And a dead one at that." Reed sighed. "The Greek myths have been tidied up and reordered immeasurably in the last two and a half thousand years—not least by the Classical Greeks themselves, who were appalled by the mess their ancestors had left them. Other versions of the myth said that Hecate was the woman who came with him, or Medea, the witch more commonly associated with Jason and the Argonauts." He threw up his hands. "Take your pick. It's most likely that they were all aspects of the female goddess."

"The snake woman?"

"Indeed."

Grant looked at the right-hand pillar again. Even eroded by the ages, he thought he could see something of the goddess's high hourglass figure in the stone. He remembered the tiny figurine in the cave on Crete; and then, with his next breath, Marina, kneeling over him on the hotel bed, her blouse torn open and her arms outstretched. He checked his watch. Eight hours until Kurchosov's deadline.

He shook his head to clear it. "If these are the statues, this must be the place."

"And look." Reed was staring at the cliff. Behind the stone pillars, hidden until now by their bulk, they could see two spouts of water tumbling down the cliff. Both emerged from holes in the rock, cascaded down through deep-cut channels, then flowed across the earthy ground to meet at the head of the stream a few yards in front of the cliff. The surface of the water bubbled where they joined and eerie wisps of steam rose off it.

There the dark rock o'erhangs the infernal lake,
And mingling streams eternal murmurs make.

Jackson looked at Reed. "Which one's the River of Fire?"

Reed walked forward. He passed between the two pillars—for a second Grant saw them as the posts of a giant door—and knelt by the left stream. He dipped his finger in. "It's warm," he exclaimed. He stepped across to the far bank and tried the other channel. "This one's icy cold."

Standing back a little, as if reluctant to step between the pillars, Jackson gazed at the cliff behind. At its foot the two becks enclosed a small triangle of land that came to its point where the waters met. The wall behind was smooth and unbroken.

"What do we do now?"

First draw thy falchion, and on every side
Trench the black earth a cubit long and wide.

Kowalksi grunted. "What does that mean, Shakespeare?"

Reed fixed him with the polite, vacant smile he reserved for only the most irredeemably obtuse pupils. "It means you have to dig a hole."

They took their spades on to the triangular strip between the streams. While Reed watched, the others cut away squares of sod and piled them in a turf wall round the stream bank, then began excavating the black earth beneath. The soil wasn't deep, and it wasn't long before their spades rang on stone.

Jackson paced impatiently. "What exactly are we looking for?"

"Homer says Odysseus spoke to the dead by squatting in a pit. If we're correct in our surmise that there was actually a temple here, I imagine we'll find it somewhere beneath our feet."

"Is there anything else we can do?"

"You could pour offerings to the dead. Homer specifies milk, honey and wine, followed by a scattering of barley grains."

"Sir, take a look at this."

They looked round. They had cleared the sod and earth from a rough pit about three yards across now, down to the bedrock two feet below. At the back, just in front of the cliff, a square of black earth filled the rock. The marine stuck his spade in, thrusting it down as far as he could. The blade sank in without a sound.

"Seems to be some kind of hole that's been filled in with dirt."

"Clear it. I'll get . . ." He broke off. A low drone, like a bumblebee echoed above the valley. "What the hell is that?"

Grant squinted up, but the raft of clouds pressed too low to see anything. "Could be nothing." But again his instinct warned otherwise. "Maybe a routine patrol. The Soviets have plenty of bases around the Black Sea."

"Tell me about it." Jackson glanced uneasily down the valley. "Kowalski, take your men and make sure there's nothing coming up behind us. Grant, you dig."

Kowalski led his men at a run back toward the top of the waterfall. Grant began hacking away at the hole. It seemed to be a sort of shaft sunk into the rock, barely two feet square. It wasn't easy to excavate: for each shovelful of soil he prised up, half of it had slipped off the spade before he could lift it out of the hole.

A few feet away Jackson had got out the Bismatron and was kneeling beside it. He flicked a switch. Grant heard it crackle into life. There was a blast of static, then a rapid series of pops like the distant sound of a car backfiring.

"Shit," Jackson breathed. "This thing's going off like the fourth of July. We have to be close. How're you doing?"

The hole at Grant's feet was now almost two feet deep. The spade was all but useless there: he couldn't get any sort of angle on it at all. He pulled it out, stood on the tip and bent back the handle until it was at a right angle to the blade. That was a bit better; now he could use the spade to scoop the soil out like an oversized ladle.

Inch by inch the hole got deeper, but still there was no sign of an end. Grant was down on his knees now, plunging the spade up and down like a piledriver. Even then he could barely touch the bottom.

He thrust the twisted spade into the soft earth once more, pulled it toward him to scoop soil on to the blade and lifted. It didn't come; instead, he almost pitched himself forward into the hole. He peered in. The flattened tip of the spade seemed to have caught on a lip inside the rock; he could see a dark crack between the earth and the stone. He pushed the spade back and jiggled it around. The crack widened; loose soil tumbled into it and vanished into unseen space beneath. There must be a tunnel or a chamber underneath the shaft.

"Have you got a torch?"

Jackson grabbed one from the pile of equipment and tossed it to him. He and Reed gathered round, peering over Grant's shoulder as he shone the beam into the chasm at the bottom of the shaft. All he saw was earth and darkness.

"Down we go," he muttered. He sat on the edge of the shaft, dangling his feet down inside. He tapped his hip to make sure the Webley was there and gripped the flashlight tightly. Then he jumped.

31

GRANT'S FEET sank into the soil at the bottom of the hole and kept on going. He threw up his arms to cover his head as he slid under the lip of the shaft. He hadn't stopped; in fact, he seemed to be gathering speed. Rolling and tumbling in the dark, he felt himself sliding helplessly down a slope. Loose earth and tiny pebbles cascaded down all around him: under his collar, down the neck of his shirt, into his ears and mouth. For a moment he felt a flash of weightless terror at the thought that he might fall forever. Then he landed with a hard bump and lay still. Earth slithered down over him; it piled up round his shoulders as if threatening to bury him.

He spat the dirt out of his mouth and sat there for a moment, rubbing the bruises on his arms and shoulder. A thin, watery light filtered through the shaft above him: as his eyes adjusted he could see rough rock walls on either side of him and stone steps that seemed to lead still further down. He slowly got to his feet.

The light went out. Grant heard a scream, then a thud and a flailing above him. Before he could move, something heavy slid down the mound of earth and slammed into him. His legs were knocked out from under him; he fell forward and rolled down the stairs.

"Grant? Is that you?"

"Reed?" Grant came to rest and risked opening his eyes. One of his ribs felt as if it had cracked, and there was a pain in his ankle that he had no time to think about. "Christ, next time shout before you jump down a dark hole."

Clearly shaken, Reed stood and stumbled down the passage toward Grant. He was barely out of the way when another shadow dropped through the shaft and came tumbling to the bottom of the slope.

"My God," said Jackson's voice in the darkness. "It's really real."

Grant flicked the switch on his flashlight. Nothing happened: he must have broken it when he fell. He threw it aside and pulled out his lighter. The damp walls shone in the light of the naked flame; the shadows rippled over them as he moved slowly forward. He edged his way carefully down the shallow stairs. Ancient as they were, they had none of the round edges or glassy surfaces usually worn into old steps.

"Looks like they haven't had many visitors," said Jackson behind him.

The tunnel ended in a thick, slanted doorway of dressed stone. A black mouth seemed to yawn open between its pillars, but as Grant reached his lighter into the shadow between the pillars dim shapes swam out of the darkness. He stepped back, holding up the lighter so that its glow reflected off the frame. Heavy bronze doors blocked his way. The metal had faded to a greenish-brown, crusted with age, but the patterns embossed in it were still visible. A pair of giant serpents writhed up the main panels, while four birds sat in the corners and stared out. There were no handles.

Grant put his shoulder to the crack between the two doors and pushed. The metal cracked and flaked away; the doors bowed in but didn't budge.

"Careful," said Reed. "If those are as old as we think they are, they're absolutely unique."

Grant took a step back and eyed the door with an appraising look. Then, before Reed could stop him, he swiveled round and slammed the flat of his boot into it. With the crack of tearing metal and a horrified cry from Reed, the door broke off its ancient hinges and fell in. A cloud of dust coughed up around it, and the whole corridor resounded to the clang of bronze striking stone.

"Geez. You sure know how to make an entrance." Jackson pushed past Reed and shone his flashlight through the doorway. "So this is it." He turned back and looked at Reed. "Congratulations, Professor. You've done it."

Grant stepped through the open door and stared in amazement. For weeks it had been a place glimpsed only in his dreams, a mysterious chamber veiled in shadows. Of all the things he'd imagined, the last thing he'd expected was that it would seem familiar. And yet, following Jackson's flashlight beam as it circled the room, he had the unreal feeling of having been there before. It was an almost perfect replica of the shrine on Lemnos, a single round room whose masonry walls soared up to form a beehive dome high above their heads. Grant wondered if the ancient builders could possibly have carved the whole sanctuary out of the rock, or if they'd adapted an existing cave. Either way, it was an extraordinary feat of engineering, by men so far beyond the borders of their civilization.

"Of course," said Reed. "I should have expected it for the grave of a hero. This is a classic Mycenaean *tholos* tomb. Those stairs we came down would have been the *dromos*—the sacred approach road."

The flashlight beam played over the walls. There were no carvings in the stone; instead, the lower reaches had been plastered and painted. Some of the plaster had peeled away; in places black mold bloomed across the frescoes, but the rest of it remained, faded and wan. In a daze, Grant walked across and held his lighter up to the wall. Even close up the pictures were so faint that they seemed immeasurably distant, as if he was peering at them through cobwebs. Some of the scenes looked identical to Lemnos: men harvesting corn, sheep on the hills, a bull trussed up beside a poplar grove. There were images of war: elongated chariots rushing into battle; a walled city; a line of ships drawn up on a beach; men with shields as tall as themselves impaling enemies on their spears.

As Grant stepped closer to examine the figures, his foot kicked something. He crouched down and held the lighter flame closer. At the base of the wall, a thick heap of debris littered the floor. It must be fallen plaster or stone—but even as he thought it, Grant felt it couldn't be right. He reached out and picked up a piece. Through the crust of dust and grime he felt the hard chill of metal.

He snapped the lighter shut and put it between his teeth. The pool of light around him vanished. He felt for his shirt-tail, still damp after wading through the lake, took it, and rubbed it vigorously against the object in his hand. *Who do you think you are?* he asked himself. *Aladdin?* He took the lighter out of his mouth and sparked it with his thumb. No genie had appeared—but from the black lump in his hand, a golden eye stared unblinking out at him.

Grant almost dropped it in his amazement. "Over here," he called. He polished it some more while the others ran over, working back the boundaries of the exposed patch of gold so that it spread across the face of the object. It was a cup, he saw, a beaker with a high rounded handle like a teacup, and pictures of deer and lions worked into the metal. He handed it to Reed. "How much is that worth?"

Reed took the cup with trembling hands, like a father holding his child for the first time. "I can't imagine."

Grant took Reed's flashlight and moved the beam along the wall. The ridge of piled-up treasure ran unbroken all round the room. Now that he knew what he was looking at, he could make out individual shapes among the debris: plates and bowls, cups, crowns, statues and swords. He tried to imagine how it would look all polished up, a hoard of heathen gold. "There must be half a ton of this."

"Forget that." Jackson took the flashlight back from Reed and aimed it at the walls, moving it in tense, erratic jerks. "We don't have the time. Where's the goddamn shield?"

They scanned the chamber. Unlike the shrine on Lemnos, there was no altar, no ring of gas flames, no hole in the floor for an initiate to crawl through. The circular walls continued smooth and unbroken. Except . . .

"There." On the far side of the room a recessed door interrupted the curve of the wall. They hurried over. Corroded metal pins stuck out of the sides of the frame, but the door they had once hinged had crumbled away long ago. Jackson beamed the flashlight through the aperture.

Grant glimpsed a small chamber with elaborately carved walls; then the view was blocked out as Jackson stepped through the doorway.

"*Careful.*" Reed grabbed Jackson's sleeve and pulled him back. He pointed to the ground. Just inside the door, right at Jackson's feet, a shallow pit about three feet deep yawned in the floor. Jackson shone the flashlight in—and recoiled with a sharp hiss of breath. At the bottom of the pit, skeletal prongs of white bone protruded from the patina of dust and dirt that caked the floor.

"Those aren't—human?" Even Jackson's normally bullet-proof confidence sounded shaken.

Reed took the torch and shone it around the pit. "I think it's a bull." The beam picked out a dull brown horn sticking up in the corner. "It must have been sacrificed when they dedicated the temple. In Greek hero cult a pit usually fulfilled the function of an altar."

"How did they get the bull down the entrance shaft?" Grant wondered.

The three men skirted the pit and edged into the chamber. It was a small room, but almost every inch of its walls was covered with carvings: hunts, sacrifices, battles—even after three thousand years the life in the stone had lost none of its savage intensity. In the far wall two niches flanked a huge sculpted roundel that seemed to bulge out of the stone. Inside them . . .

"The armor!" With a cry of delight Reed ran to the alcove and lifted out the object inside. He held it above his head as if he was about to crown himself. In that position it was easy to see that it was, or had been, a helmet. The dome tapered to a strange, key-shaped spike, while rounded cheek pieces projected down like rabbit ears. Grant, no historian, thought it looked more like Kaiser Bill's Prussian cavalry helmet than the angular, slit-faced headpieces he had always imagined in ancient Greece.

"And the greaves." Reed crossed to the other alcove and pulled out two lumps of metal that looked like hollowed-out split logs. "These would have protected his legs. *Achilles'* legs," he added in absolute wonder.

"Maybe if he'd worn them backward he could have protected his heel."

"But where's the goddamn shield?" With the flame from Grant's lighter, and Jackson's flashlight, there was plenty of light to see by in the small room. Apart from the two pieces of armor, and the bones in the pit, it was empty.

"Maybe in the pit?"

Jackson jumped down and began scraping away the grime that caked the floor with an ox bone. Grant scanned the walls, looking for a chink or crevice that might betray a hidden door or secret chamber. Nothing. Inevitably, his eyes returned to the massive round carving between the two alcoves. The workmanship on it was much finer than the rest of the room. The figures were smaller and the designs seemed more intricate—though it was hard to tell with all the black age that covered them. In fact, the closer he looked, the more he realized it had a different texture to the surrounding walls.

"That's not a carving."

He stood in front of it. That close to, he could see each individual figure: men and women, shepherds and plowmen, lawyers and merchants, soldiers and gods—a microcosm of the world. He rubbed it with his arm and felt cold metal through the sleeve of his shirt. It came away black—but on the surface in front of him a golden smear illuminated the dirty metal.

No one spoke. Jackson scrambled out of the pit, opened his pocket knife and worked the blade into the thin crack between the shield and the surrounding stone. It fitted its carved socket almost perfectly, but gradually—carefully—he and Grant managed to prise it free. They lowered it to the floor and leaned it up against the wall—even with two of them its weight was immense. Then they stepped away, almost pushed back by its power, and stared at the shield of Achilles.

32

"Is that it?"

After so much effort, so much struggle, there was something inadequate about finally seeing the shield. It was perfectly round, though chewed at the edges, about three feet across and curved like a lens. Under the coat of grime the embossed designs gave its surface a mottled, almost organic look, like tree bark. Grant wondered if it had ever been used in battle.

"How are we going to get it out of here? We won't fit it through that shaft we came down."

Jackson stared at him, then back at the shield. "We have to. It must have come down there once upon a time, right?"

"Perhaps we shouldn't move it."

"*What*?" Jackson swung round toward Reed. "Have you been asleep in class for the last three weeks? We didn't come here just to prove a theory, snap some pictures for the folks back home and go. The whole reason we're here is to take this thing back to get the metal out of it."

"And Marina," Grant reminded him.

Jackson looked confused for a second. "Right—Marina." He grasped the shield in both hands and strained to lift it. Half carrying, half dragging, he moved toward the door.

"*In modern ages not the strongest swain, could heave the unwieldy burden from the plain*," Reed murmured. He looked at Grant. "Do you have your pistol with you?"

Grant pulled out the Webley and showed it to Reed. "Why?"

"If Mr. Jackson takes another step, please shoot him."

Grant couldn't believe he'd heard him right. "Excuse me."

"Ask him what he intends to do with the metal from the shield—if we manage to get it out of here."

Jackson glared at them with a look of pure fury. "Are you crazy? Put that gun down."

The Webley wavered in Grant's hand. "What the hell are you on about, Professor?"

"He's wasting time," hissed Jackson. "He's in league with the Russians."

Reed looked calmly between the two of them. "This mysterious Element 61 has a name now, I believe. They called it *Prometheum*."

"How do you know that?" Jackson demanded. "It's classified."

"You shouldn't leave your ciphered messages lying around your hotel room. Have you come across Prometheus, Grant? He was a Titan; he stole fire from heaven and put it in the hands of men."

Grant stared at Reed, then at Jackson. His legs were hidden behind the shield and his face was in shadow. "Are you saying . . ."

A noise outside the door interrupted him. Forgetting Jackson, Grant turned and ran back into the main chamber. It was much brighter than before—a mustard-yellow light filled the dome, illuminating the painted warriors and the treasure at their feet. Grant barely noticed them.

She was standing a few feet in front of the entrance, holding up the lantern so he could see her face. It was scratched and stained with mud; a purple bruise ringed her right eye where they must have hit her and her hair was tangled. She still wore the same clothes he had last seen her in: a white blouse and a black skirt that hugged her hips, now torn and filthy.

"Marina!" He ran toward her. She lifted her head and gave a tired smile—but there was no joy in it.

"Halt there."

The voice, harsh and cold, rang out of the passage behind her. Halfway across the room Grant stopped as if he'd been kicked in the guts.

"Drop your guns. Drop them or I will terminate her now."

A tall, lean figure stepped through the doorway. His boots rang on the stone floor. He wore a green uniform with the gold bars of a full colonel on the epaulettes. His cheeks were hollow, his thin gray hair slicked back to his skull, his one eye sunk in darkness. A triangular black patch covered the other. In his arms he cradled a tommy-gun, which he aimed at Marina. "Put them down," he said, jerking the gun. "You and the American."

"Forget it," said Jackson. "She's one of them."

Grant ignored him. He looked at Marina and saw the defiance in her eyes.

"You know what we said in the war," she said in Greek. "No compromises; no sentiments."

"That was our war. This . . ." Grant was numb. His muscles refused to move. More men ran down behind Kurchosov and fanned out around the room—too many, now. All of them carried guns.

"OK," Grant said flatly. "You win." He bent down and laid the Webley on the floor.

Behind him Jackson was still hesitating. Kurchosov swung the gun round and pointed it straight at him. "I will count to three, Mr. Jackson. Then I will kill you. *Odeen . . . dva . . .*"

Grant heard the Colt clatter on to the ground.

He looked back—and paused. At the back of the chamber he could see someone moving in the darkness to the right of the door. He stared in disbelief. "Muir?"

Muir stepped out of the shadows. An unpleasant leer played across his face. He took out a cigarette and lit it. "If you're waiting for me to rescue you, you're in for a nasty fucking disappointment."

Kurchosov turned to Muir and shook his hand. "Well done, Comrade. Comrade Stalin will be a happy man."

"We'll break out the Beluga when we've got the shield in Moscow."

"Christ, Muir." Jackson ground his heel against the floor. "There's a word for men like you."

Muir gave a wicked grin. "I always was a hopeless romantic."

"Do you have any idea what they're going to do with that shield?"

"Do with it? Why the hell do you think we went to all this fucking trouble?"

Muir turned as another man came striding out of the passage. As he stepped into the lamplight, Grant recognized Belzig's stocky frame and straw-blond hair. He seemed to be wearing the same brown suit he had worn that day at the library in Athens. But then, he was a prisoner too, Grant supposed.

"Is it here?" Even his ugly voice was touched with a childlike awe as he stared around the great domed chamber. "*Mein Gott, ist das schön.* Have you found the shield?"

"It's in there." Muir pointed to the side chamber. Between them the Russian, the German and the Scot seemed to have settled on English as their common language. "Mind your step when you go in."

Belzig hurried across, snatching the lamp from Marina's hand as he ran past. He ducked under the doorway. The gasp of astonishment from inside the little chamber echoed around the dome.

"That's not all." Muir took a lamp from one of the Russian soldiers and beamed it at the black hoard on the floor. He picked up a cup and tossed it in his hands. "It may look like junk, but there's more gold in this room than in the Bank of England. A nice bonus for the party."

"Indeed. It will take much time to remove it. The Americans made us pay heavily to take the valley."

"Did any of them survive?"

Kurchosov gave a dismissive twitch of his head. "Not even those who surrendered." He looked back to the center of the room where Grant, Marina, Jackson and Reed stood huddled together. "What about our prisoners?"

Muir shrugged. "They've all worked for British Intelligence—even the professor. Let the interrogators at the Lubyanka sink their teeth into them when we get to Moscow, and out what they know."

Kurchosov pursed his lips, then nodded. "*Da*. But first the shield." He snapped something in Russian; two of his men put down their guns and ran across to the side chamber. Grant eyed up the guns. Too far away.

The men returned, carrying the shield between them. Belzig trailed behind. They held it up like a sporting trophy for Kurchosov to inspect.

"So this was the shield of the god Achilles. The first hero of the great war of East and West. Only now it is the East who have won." He stroked his fingertips over the metal, then pulled them away as if he'd been burned. He glanced at Muir. "Is it safe?"

"God knows." He exhaled, watching the smoke curl up off the shield. "You'll need to test it in the laboratory."

"Then we must get it out of here."

The soldiers fetched two lead-lined blankets. They sandwiched the shield between them and trussed it up with ropes, then carried it out of the door into the passage beyond. Grant watched it go with indifference; beside him Jackson trembled with anger.

"Put the prisoners away until we are ready."

The remaining guards herded their four prisoners toward the side chamber, making sure to keep well back. They were almost there when a commotion by the main door paused them. They all looked round. Belzig and the two soldiers had returned. They still had the shield.

"It does not fit through the hole," Belzig explained.

Anger flashed on Kurchosov's face. "It must. How else could it come in otherwise?"

Belzig took out a handkerchief and wiped the sweat from his forehead. "Perhaps there was another entrance. Perhaps they have built the temple round the shield, so that no one can take it away. But it does not go out now."

"Can we drill? Make it wider?"

"It's three feet of solid rock," said Muir. "You won't drill through that in a hurry—not without specialist equipment."

"Then we cut the shield apart."

That prompted a squeal from Belzig. "You cannot! This is the most priceless treasure in the world—proof of the greatest myth in human history. It must be preserved, studied by scholars."

"Why? As soon as Comrade Stalin has inspected it, it will be melted down for its materials. They are what is valuable." Kurchosov gave a cruel laugh as he saw Belzig's horror. "You wish to argue, Comrade? Better to pray we do not also liquidate you."

Muir chuckled. "More to the point, can you cut it up? Under all that shit you can see there's a core of solid iron. Did you bring a cutting torch?"

Kurchosov's mouth curled up in frustration. "*Nyet.*" He thought for a moment. "So, if we do not make the shield smaller, we make the hole bigger."

"I told you: we can't drill . . ."

"With explosives."

The soldiers cut off lengths of rope and tied the prisoners' hands behind their backs. They pushed them into the chamber and left them there. Through the open doorway Grant saw them working their way round the main chamber, scooping the treasure into canvas sacks. He couldn't bear to watch. Instead, he looked across the chamber to Jackson, who lay against the wall on the far side of the pit.

"Now that we're all on a one-way trip to Moscow, why don't you tell us what this was about."

Jackson sighed. "OK, you want a story? Arms and the man and all that shit? How much do you know about the atom bomb?"

"I know I don't want to be near one when it goes off."

"Right. Well, just right now you're as safe as you were ten years ago. There aren't any."

"I thought the Americans were building dozens of them."

"We are—we did. Only thing is they're all sitting in a vault in New Mexico and the worst thing they can do is make your dick fall off." He leaned forward to take the pressure off his bound hands. "I don't know the science. All I know is there are problems. There's this thing called reactor poisoning: you run the factories that make the bomb fuel too long and eventually they go bad. At the same time, we find out that the bombs we have made aren't like fine wine: they don't age too good. So the bombs we thought we had, no one knows if they work any more, and we can't build more because the factory's closed for repairs. Truman's trying to face down the Soviets, and the only thing stopping Uncle Joe from rolling his tanks all the way to Paris is that he's convinced we've got a pile of bombs to drop on Moscow if he makes a move. And, at this moment in time, we don't."

Grant took a deep breath, trying to absorb the information. He had seen Hiroshima and Nagasaki on the newsreels, and not really understood it. "So this Element 61—Prometheum—it can make an atom bomb?"

"Well, nobody knows for sure because nobody's ever laid their hands on it. But they've done the math. That's how things work now." He shook his head, trying to dislodge a drop of sweat that had run down into his eye. "A bunch of geniuses sit in a room with their slide rules for three years and at the end of it they make a weapon. Hell, the Hiroshima bomb they didn't even bother to test before they dropped it. Just so long as the sums add up."

"And did Muir know this?"

"Muir knew what it could do. He didn't know why we needed it so bad. I hope. *Shit*." Jackson kicked his heel against the floor. "Jack-off bastard. He's played us all for dupes."

Against the far wall Reed stirred. "Does it matter?"

"*Does it matter*? Have you been listening to a word I said?"

"Very carefully. You said Stalin was held in check because he *believed* in the power of your country's atomic arsenal."

"Which we don't have."

"But he doesn't know that. If anything, your escapades here will only have made him wonder why you should be so desperate to lay your hands on this rather unlikely source of material."

A shadow fell through the doorway. "Just thought I'd pop my head in to say hello." It was Muir. With his damp shirt pressed against his skin he looked leaner than ever, almost feral. The look on Jackson's face was just as primal: he seemed as though he might lunge at Muir and tear him to pieces. The steel snout of a tommy-gun poking round Muir's shoulder made him think better of it.

"Come to spy on us some more?"

"I've retired now, actually. Looking forward to a sunny cottage in the workers' paradise."

"How long's it been going on?" Jackson's anger subsided as quickly as it had risen. All that remained was bitter defeat.

"Some time. I made some friends at university. Even then, a few of us could see that the Soviets were the only ones with the guts to stand up to the Fascists. Some young idiots went off to throw their lives away with hopelessly romantic deaths in Spain. We wanted to do something that would actually make a difference. We wanted to help them."

"Help them with what? The gulags? The show trials? The executions?"

"They saved the world," snapped Muir. "Us, the Yanks—we were just a sideshow. They won the war on the Eastern Front, grinding out victory one life at a time. Do you know how many of them died? Millions. And now look what you're trying to do to them. Do you know why the Americans are so desperate for Element 61?"

Muir fixed Jackson with a cool, inquisitive stare. Jackson gazed at the floor and fiddled with the bonds behind his back.

"The men in Washington want to make an example of their erstwhile allies. Give the Soviets something to think about. Not Moscow or Berlin—but maybe Stalingrad. Prove they can do what the Nazis never could."

"That would be an edifying spectacle," murmured Reed. "And what are you going to do with it?"

Muir shrugged. "Isn't it obvious?"

A numbness seized Grant—the same feeling he'd had in the White Mountains when he'd aimed his gun at Alexei and tried to pull the trigger. He looked at Jackson, who returned the look with cold defiance, then at Muir. "I don't know who's worse—you or him."

Jackson's face was hard and lifeless. "I guess you'll find out now they've got their hands on it."

"Nothing changes," said Reed. He nodded at the carvings on the wall, the long tableaux of miniature men, horses, chariots and arms. In one of the panels two warriors stood between a mound of heaped-up armor and a pile of naked corpses. In another a man dragged a coffle of women toward the open door of a tent.

"Maybe," said Muir. "But I doubt there'll be many heroes in the next war for poets to sing about."

The guard behind him muttered something. Muir nodded and turned to leave. "I'll see you later, perhaps. Just wanted to clear things up for you, for old times' sake. I hope it wasn't too much of a surprise."

"Not really," said Reed, unexpectedly. "You always were a shit."

Silence settled over the little room like dust. In the main chamber outside they could hear the clank and clatter of the temple's treasure being swept up, occasional shouts from the soldiers. Jackson shuffled himself into a corner apart from the rest of them and pretended to sleep. Reed stared contemplatively at the carvings on the wall.

Grant wriggled his way closer to Marina. "Did they hurt you?"

"A little. Not much—they didn't need to. Muir had told them everything."

"If we ever get out of here I'll kill him."

He couldn't see her face, but he knew she was smiling. "The look on Jackson's face when he found out Muir was one of them . . . It was almost worth it."

"He's going to have the last laugh." Grant twisted round so he could see her. "This isn't anything to do with you. Maybe you could persuade them—your brother, after all—make them think . . ."

"No." She tipped her head back against the wall. "Even if I could, I would not leave you."

"We'll get out of here somehow."

"That does not improve your situation, necessarily," said a voice from the door.

All four of them looked up. Belzig was standing in the doorway. He was no longer the proud Aryan archaeological conqueror, he had been in the photograph. His back was stooped and the clumsy tailoring of his suit only emphasized the ragged body underneath. Heavy lines circled his eyes.

"Have you come to gloat?"

Belzig muttered something to the sentry and stepped into the square chamber. He walked across to the far wall and lifted the tarnished helmet from its alcove. He held it in front of him, staring into the bowl as if he could see the ghost of the ancient face inside, and mumbled something.

Grant stiffened. "What?"

"I have come to offer help."

"Why?"

He jerked his head toward the door. "Do you think I am one of them? They are philistines, monsters. They do not know what they have. They will destroy this shield, this priceless artifact, and only to make a bomb. It was made by gods; now they take its power and make themselves gods." He stared into the shadows inside the helmet. "Also, now they possess it they send me back to Siberia. Or worse." He twitched with a shiver that seemed to come from the marrow of his bones. "I cannot go back there."

Jackson sat up straight. "What are you suggesting?"

"They are few. Your soldiers fought well, killed many. Now there are only four guards, and Colonel Kurchosov and the English spy." He reached into his suit pockets and pulled out two pistols, the Webley and Jackson's Colt. "If I free you, you can kill them."

"Are you doing this out of the kindness of your heart?"

Belzig looked puzzled by the idiom. "If you escape, you take me to America. You give me pardon. You know how they call it in Germany? A *Persilschein*."

"Washes whiter," Grant muttered. He stared at Belzig. He remembered Molho's missing hand and the horrific corpse they had found in the Piraeus nightclub. He remembered Marina's stories of Belzig's activities on Crete. Most of all, he thought of the smirk in the photograph. The monsters which the ancient Greeks had tried to banish to the underworld—the hydras, gorgons, basilisks and Cyclops—still walked the earth. The man in front of him, with the rash on his face and the ill-fitting suit, was one of them.

"Sure," said Jackson. "Who needs to rake up the past. You get us out of here, I promise you a first-class ticket to the USA. Maybe we'll even find you a job at the Smithsonian."

"And the shield—you protect it?"

"On my mother's grave."

That seemed to satisfy him. He pulled out a clasp-knife and squatted behind Jackson. In a moment Jackson's hands were free. He rubbed his wrists, then grabbed the Colt while Belzig cut the others loose. Grant picked up the Webley. It was good to feel its weight back in his hand.

"Here's what we do."

Corporal Ivan Serotov gripped his sub-machine gun and leaned against the wall. He was desperate for a cigarette, but he resisted the temptation. He knew what the Colonel would do to him if he saw him smoking on duty. He could hold out. They had almost finished clearing the temple: by the door, his comrades were hauling out the last sack of treasure. Then it would be a short flight to Odessa, the cargo delivered and two weeks on the sandy beach at Yevpatoria. He wondered if all that black junk they had carted out was really gold. Surely it had to be, if the Colonel would spend precious time removing it. There had been so much of it. Surely no one would miss a single cup if it went missing in transit. That would fetch a few roubles in Odessa—which he could convert in turn into vodka or women. The prospect made him smile.

He heard footsteps and half turned to see Belzig walking out of the prisoners' room. He was carrying what looked like a rusty helmet. Serotov scowled. He hadn't marched all the way to Berlin just to end up taking orders from this Fascist. At least he wouldn't be weighing down the plane on the way home. Kurchosov had made it clear what was to happen to him.

Belzig paused and jerked his head back toward the door. "More treasure there," he said in broken Russian. "You should tell Kurchosov."

A very un-Marxist notion started to form in Serotov's mind. He turned round and peered through the open door. Three of the prisoners—the American, the old man and the woman—sat against the back wall with their hands behind their backs. The fourth . . .

Without warning a heavy shove against his back sent him stumbling into the room. He tripped on something and sprawled forward. He dropped his gun and threw out his arms—but the ground wasn't there. He fell face first into the pit, screaming as he landed on the exposed bones jutting up like spikes from the floor. The last thing he saw was a pair of horns looming in front of his eyes. Then something heavy landed on him, an arm reached round his throat and he knew no more.

Grant stepped out of the pit and wiped the knife on his trousers. His hands were covered in blood. He glanced through the doorway to Belzig. "Is it clear?"

To his consternation, the small, heavy eyes were wide with confusion. "*Ja—nein.*" He shook his head. "They have gone."

"What?" Grant picked up the tommy-gun and thrust it into Marina's hands. "Cover me." Crouched low, he dived through the door, rolled to his left and swept the Webley around the main chamber.

It was empty. A kerosene lantern sat on a wooden crate in the middle of the room, and the bundled-up shield leaned against the wall beside the entrance, but otherwise there was nobody. He lay there for a second in the dust, checking again, but there were no corners in the room, no shadows. It was empty.

He got to his feet and brushed himself off. Jackson and Marina had followed him out; further back, Reed was peering round the door.

"They've gone."

"But the shield's still here." Keeping the tommy-gun trained on the main entrance, Marina edged across the room to where the package lay. "They can't have abandoned it."

"Maybe they're having a cigarette break."

Nobody knew what to do. There was nowhere to hide—but no one to hide from. They drifted into the middle of the room, under the towering dome, guns half raised against a non-existent threat.

A nasty thought crossed Grant's mind. "You don't think they're about to set off . . ."

"*Ivan? Bistro poidyon!*"

A pale figure had appeared at the main entrance, standing over the door Grant had kicked in. He had a tommy-gun in his hands but it wasn't raised. He stood there for a moment, staring at them stupidly—and, stupidly, they stared back. Then he turned and ran.

"*Nein!*" Belzig, who was nearest, dropped the helmet and ran through the door into the passage beyond. Grant heard feet clatter up the stone stairs, then angry shouts and a shot.

"No—wait."

Grant threw himself to the side of the room a split second before the explosion. From outside, a deep, booming roar shook the dome of the temple; it rolled down the passage and burst into the room like an ocean wave. The bronze door was torn off its hinges and flung across the chamber; the lamp fell over and went out. Darkness swallowed the room. A great cloud of dust and debris blew in through the door, billowing out to fill the high vault. Jackson, who had been standing in front of the door, was snatched up by the blast and hurled against the back wall in a blizzard of stone. Rocks rained down; Grant covered his head with his hands, while Marina hid herself under the shield. Only Reed, safe in the side chamber, was spared.

Grant didn't hear the noise subside—his ears were still ringing—but he knew the worst was over when the floor stopped shaking. He peered through his fingers, then looked up. Dust and smoke still choked the room, but at least the rocks had stopped falling.

He got to his feet and staggered over to Marina, trying not to twist his ankle on the debris strewn across the floor. By the entrance, a pool of water was spreading across the floor. "Are you OK?"

She couldn't hear him—he couldn't hear himself—but she understood. She nodded, then felt her leg and winced. "Maybe not so good."

"We need to get out of here." Grant found the tommy gun on the floor where Marina had dropped it. Its barrel was bent like a paperclip. He kicked it aside and ran to the entrance, splashing through the shallow puddle that had formed round it. It was a testament to the ancient builders' skill that the vast door frame remained intact. The lintel alone must have weighed a hundred tons.

Grant peered round the corner and blinked. The top of the staircase had been blown open: it was no longer a tunnel but a deep trench open to the sky. The roof had fallen in, and huge slabs of rock now formed a steep ramp up to the world above. Water slopped over the edge and trickled down the slope, a new stream flowing between the cracked boulders and rubble into the temple. Somewhere underneath it all, he supposed, was Belzig.

He waited a moment, watching for movement. He saw none—but then, he couldn't see much. Billowing clouds of dust still filled the air, diffusing the sun into a muddy half-light. He would have to risk it. But not without protection.

He ran back to where Marina lay and ripped the coverings off the shield. Leaned up against the wall, to the side of the door, it had been well protected from the blast. He spun it round. The leather strap, if it had ever had one, had rotted away long ago, but there were two brass rings sticking out of the back. He slid his arm through them and lifted.

The weight was immense. Grant wondered how any man could ever have carried it into battle and still managed to wield a sword or a spear. Perhaps, he admitted, Achilles had been worth his reputation. But it was better than being shot. He walked back to the doorway, resting the shield against his thigh, and checked the passage again. Still nothing but smoke and dust. He edged through the door and began to climb, picking his way over the rubble. It was slow, awkward work: keeping the shield in front of his body as he dragged himself up the broken slope. The rocks grew larger; the cracks between them widened. But the dust was thinning, the light getting brighter. He scrambled up the final incline, his feet slipping and sliding on the wet stone, and staggered into the light.

The first thing he saw was the bodies. Whether it had been a stray bullet or whether the Russians had panicked when they saw Belzig trying to escape, the charges must have gone off too soon. Two Russian soldiers lay sprawled on the ground like abandoned toys, bloodied and battered. Dust gathered in the creases of their uniforms.

He heard a sound behind him and spun round, bringing up the shield to cover his chest. That saved his life. The shield shuddered with the impact, and Grant's body with it: dirt and corrosion flaked away to reveal gold and bronze underneath. But it didn't break.

Grant looked over the shield's rim. Kurchosov was standing a few yards away, beside one of the monolithic statues. The explosion must have surprised him too: his uniform was torn, his face smeared with dirt and blood. His eyepatch had been ripped away to reveal the scar beneath: a puckered contortion of skin that twisted together into a knot where the eye should have been. He looked dazed.

Grant lifted the Webley and shot him through the eye. The .455 caliber bullet went straight in. Afterward, Grant could have sworn he heard the hiss of hot lead sizzling on the eyeball for a fraction of a second. A geyser of blood erupted from the socket, and the rock walls around them echoed with a hideous roar. Grant shot him twice more and the noise stopped.

Beyond the corpse, at the base of the statue, something moved. Grant looked up, just in time to see a shadow disappearing behind it. *Muir*. He crouched down behind the shield, glad to rest its weight on the ground, and aimed the Webley at the pillar. The barrel fanned from side to side as he wondered whether Muir would come right or left.

"Give up," he called. After so much noise, his voice sounded stark in the misty silence. "Kurchosov's dead."

No answer. Grant slipped his left arm out of the shield's loops. Balancing it against his knee, he picked up a small rock and threw it toward the pillar. It skittered across the rubble and came to rest at the foot of the statue. Still there was no response.

"Muir?"

Something grated on the stone behind him. He turned; the shield overbalanced and fell on the ground with a resounding clang. He lifted the Webley—and stopped himself just in time. It was Jackson—but not the Jackson who had breezed into the hotel in Athens in his white tennis shoes, all sunshine and pomade. His hair was wild, his clothes torn. His face, under the blood and bruises, was pale as a ghost. He clambered out of the hole and stared numbly at the gun pointing at him.

"Shit." The voice was dead, past caring. "Not you too."

"I thought you were Muir. He's . . ."

Grant's head whipped round as he heard rapid footsteps beyond the pillar. He sprang to his feet. Through the haze of dust he saw a dim figure sprinting away. He loosed a shot—then, when the figure kept going, he started to run.

The air cleared as he descended the valley. Now he could see Muir plainly, his coat-tails flapping behind him and his wiry arms jerking spasmodically as he scuttled toward the top of the cliff and the waterfall. He still had a gun. Grant saw him start to turn and immediately fired the Webley. It was a wild shot: he had little chance of hitting him while running at full tilt, but it changed Muir's mind. He put his head back down and carried on.

But he could not go far. He came to the top of the cliff and stopped. Grant slowed to a walk. Muir turned. If he'd raised his pistol even an inch, Grant would have shot him right there. Instead, Muir held it away from his body and let it drop over the edge of the cliff. The two men stood there for a moment, face to face, breathing hard.

"Mind if I smoke?"

Grant nodded.

Muir reached into his jacket and carefully took out the ivory cigarette case. He snapped it open. When he'd lit the cigarette, he threw the match into the stream. The current caught it and propelled it over the waterfall. Muir watched it go. "You've chosen the wrong side," he said without bitterness. "You'll see. The Yanks'll ruin everything."

"I didn't choose any side. You chose me."

Muir took a long drag on his cigarette. The smoke seemed to inflate him somehow: he stood up taller, lifted his chin. "I suppose they'll hang me when we get back."

Grant shrugged. "We're not at war—not officially."

"Better if we were. Then they might shoot me. At least I'd die with a fucking cigarette . . ."

"*You Red traitor asshole son-of-a-bitch.*"

A blur of movement rushed past Grant and flew at Muir. Muir lifted his fists to defend himself but it was only a gesture, without strength. Jackson's momentum carried him straight into Muir's body. They wrestled for a moment on the edge of the cliff; then, locked together, they fell.

Grant rushed to the edge and looked down. He was just in time to see the splash—then nothing. The black water closed over them. A few minutes later he saw their corpses bob to the surface by the spout where the pool poured into the stream. The bodies teetered for a moment on the lip of the weir, then vanished.

Grant turned back. As he did, he felt his foot kick something. It slithered across the damp rock and came to rest on a patch of moss. Muir's cigarette case. The dull ivory stared at him like an eyeball on the black moss, white as death.

33

Oxford. Trinity Term 1947

HOMER NEVER intended that the shield of Achilles should be considered as an actual, literal object. The shield, as described in the *Iliad*, is meant as a metaphor for the world—a flat disc, made by a god, surrounded by the Ocean river, in whose compass lie all the stars, sun and moon; war and peace, commerce and agriculture; work and leisure; gods, men and animals."

The undergraduate looked up nervously. He'd padded this paragraph out a bit in a slightly desperate attempt to eat up tutorial time. So far, his tutor didn't seem to have noticed. It didn't occur to him that his tutor might be quite as eager as he was to let the tutorial slip by painlessly.

"But, in reality, this glittering artifact is forged from words, not metal. Clearly, the poet expects his readers to suspend their disbelief during the *ecphrasis*. Such a cumbersome weapon would have been wholly impractical on the field of battle. For all its poetic depth and power to dazzle, we must—with regret—dismiss the shield as fiction, a triumph of Homer's imagination, written at a time when the technical practice of Bronze Age warfare was merely legend."

Reed stared out of the window. Outside in Turl Street, women in summer dresses flirted with men in blazers and flannel trousers. Behind the college walls, croquet balls knocked each other on the immaculate lawns. Reed was oblivious to it. In his mind's eye he was at the top of a cliff, straining on a rope with Grant as they tried to lower the shield without dropping it in the pool. He was tripping his way back down the overgrown stream, splashing through the shallows as he tried to support Marina with her broken leg. He was back in the lagoon, scrambling into the seaplane, praying no more Russians would come.

He realized his student was waiting to continue, deferring his essay to whatever great thoughts Reed's distant stare portended. Sometimes, he decided, there were distinct advantages to having a reputation for abstract brilliance. He smiled. "Go on."

"What is significant is the fact that Homer gives the shield to Achilles. He seems to be saying that Achilles grasps the entire world in his hand. When he fights, it is the world itself which shivers under the blows.

"In this age of atom bombs and a National Health Service, the unbridled violence and haughty elitism that Achilles embodies may fail to rouse our sympathies." The undergraduate glanced up, wondering whether this was too daringly relevant, if his ethereal professor had ever heard of either atom bombs or a National Health Service. "Odysseus, the man who prizes wit over strength, who suffers for ten years to return home and save his family, seems a more realistic hero in this country, in this century.

"But, I suggest, if we are to build a better world, it is Achilles who offers the parable of salvation. True, he spends much of the *Iliad* governed by rage, heedless of the destruction it wreaks on those around him: his fellow warriors, his friends, even his most intimate companion Patroclus. But the poem is the story of his *humanizing*, his journey away from unthinking anger into an understanding of his responsibilities to the world.

"In metaphorical terms, we all exist on the shield of Achilles. When the warriors gird themselves for battle we tremble. If we are to survive the new perils of the modern age, we must hope that the destructive rages which drive men can be tempered by reason, by engagement and most of all by compassion."

He shuffled his essay back together and put the papers down.

From his wing-back chair, the professor looked as if he might be asleep. "Tell me," he said at last, "do you believe in Homer?"

The undergraduate looked alarmed. He hadn't prepared for that question. "Well, erm, Mr. Schliemann's finds in Turkey obviously pose some questions. And Mycenae." He thought desperately—and, to his surprise, found an answer. "I don't believe it actually matters."

A white eyebrow rose in surprise. "No?"

"The poetry is what matters. That's real. It's survived intact for two and a half thousand years, much longer than anything made of metal or wood. And . . ." He tried to think of something to expand his point. He was saved by a knock at the door.

"Beg your pardon, Professor. There's a gentleman in the lodge to see you. Says he's come from London."

Reed didn't appear surprised; he'd expected this ever since he got back to Oxford. There was no point delaying the inevitable.

"Would you mind coming back in an hour?" he said apologetically. "I shan't be long."

Hardly able to believe his luck, the undergraduate picked up his essay and darted out of the room. A few moments later the porter showed in his visitor, a young man in a blue suit who sat forward on the sofa and held his hat.

"Wright," he introduced himself. His face was kind rather than handsome, but there was a lively intelligence in his eyes and a suggestion of humor gently kept in check. "Thank you for seeing me, Professor."

Reed waved graciously.

"It's about a colleague of mine, a man named Muir. I understand you had some dealings with him."

"I worked with him in the war. He came to me a few weeks ago. He wanted help tracing an ancient Greek artifact. I believe he was working with the Americans."

"So we've gathered." Wright twisted the hat in his hands. "And not much else, unfortunately. He was a bit of an odd fish, Muir. Frankly, there's a suspicion he may have been involved in some rather queer business."

Reed tried to convey a distinct lack of surprise. "He always seemed a little . . . unorthodox. What's he done now?"

"Well, that's what we're trying to find out. You see, he's gone missing. We were rather hoping you would shed some light on it."

Wright stayed for an hour. Reed answered his questions as best he could—which was to say as little as possible that was flatly untrue, or easily disproved. Wright took copious notes, frowning as he tried to keep up.

"We're also trying to trace this Mr. Grant."

"Yes," said Reed. "I can see that you would. I don't suppose you'll find him."

"Do you have any idea where he might . . ."

"Not really. He may have mentioned Canada."

Wright looked surprised. "Oh. That's certainly news to us. Thank you."

He stood and shook Reed's hand. At the door he paused for a moment. "This . . . Homeric artifact. You don't think there was anything in it, do you? No chance of it turning up?"

Reed smiled. "I shouldn't think so."

The plane flew south-west through the night, high above the sea that had seen so many gods and heroes pass. Grant manned the controls; behind him, Marina lay on the floor under a blanket, her leg stretched out in a splint.

Reed made his way forward and squeezed into the copilot's seat. "Where are we?"

Grant checked his watch. "Just past the Dardanelles. We should make Athens in another couple of hours."

Reed squirmed round and looked back down the cabin. At the rear of the plane, lashed to a steel bulkhead, the battered shield stared back at him. A canvas sack, bulging with all manner of strange shapes and nubbles, sat beside it.

Grant saw his gaze. "Imagining how it'll look in the British Museum?"

Reed sighed. "You know we can't keep it. The Americans would have it in a flash."

Grant banked the plane left a little. "Do you really think it could be used to make a bomb?"

"Are you willing to take the risk?"

Grant didn't answer. They flew on in silence for a few minutes. Reed pointed to a small island of lights in the darkness below. "That must be Lemnos."

"Maybe we should land there. Hide it in the temple we found until it all blows over."

"No. Even there, someone will find it eventually."

"Someone'll find it anyway. You can't unfind things."

"It's already been missing for three thousand years. If it were lost for another three thousand, I shouldn't complain."

Grant stared at him in surprise. "But the shield changes everything. It proves it was all true: Homer, Achilles, Troy—everything. It's . . . it's history."

Reed stared out of the window. "That's exactly it. The world has enough history—more of it every day. But no one's making any more myths. And we need them. When I heard Schliemann talk in Kensington, it wasn't the fact that all this was true—it was being allowed to believe that it *might* be true. It's *wonder* that inspires us—the wondering, the delicious not-knowing. A sense of something just out of reach. History brings that back within our grasp."

He unbuckled his seat belt and moved to the back of the plane. Grant didn't try to stop him. A howling gale blasted into the cabin as the cabin door slid open. Under her blankets, Marina stirred and opened her eyes. Holding on to the struts in the roof, Reed tottered to the shield and untied it, pulling away the lead blankets that had wrapped it. He knelt in front of it for a moment, staring at the images of life teeming in the metal. Then he got up, rolled it to the door and heaved it into the whirling darkness.

The plane flew on into the night. Down on the water, nobody saw the small splash the shield made—or, if they did, they assumed it was just a dolphin broaching the waves. The water was deep; the shield sank quickly. And if a siren's haunting song ever echoed down to the deep place where it came to rest, or a kraken slithered past, or the shadow of a sea nymph flitted overhead, history never knew.

HISTORICAL NOTE

Linear B was actually deciphered in 1952 by Michael Ventris and John Chadwick. The story of their achievement, one of the great intellectual feats of the twentieth century, is told with elegant clarity in Chadwick's *The Decipherment of Linear B*; and in full scholarly detail in their joint work *Documents in Mycenaean Greek*.

All the classical authors referred to in this novel are genuine and all the quotations from them are accurate. Reed's quotations from Homer are from the translations of Alexander Pope.

ACKNOWLEDGMENTS

Researching this book required travelling almost as much as the characters in it. Though my journeys usually involved less danger, they certainly provided as great a sense of wonder and discovery. For that I owe thanks to Colin Macdonald, who graciously showed me around the Villa Ariadne at Knossos when I turned up on his doorstep; Lucy and Nik Ftochogiannis at the Apollo Pavilion on Lemnos, whose homemade wine I promised to mention; James Harrop, with whom I discovered lost cities and fried pancakes on the natural gas flames at Cirali; and my Greek family—Helen, George and Panos Hayios—for their help and hospitality during my trips there.

Back at home, Yulia Kovas and Isabella Paul provided Russian and German translations, while my sister Iona helped with the classical references. Dr. Jonathan Burgess was kind enough to share an early draft of his monograph on *The Death and Afterlife of Achilles*, possibly unaware of how I would misuse his research. My agent Jane Conway-Gordon provided constant support and regular sustenance. At Random House, my editor Oliver Johnson encouraged my vision of the book and gave it his usual masterful commentary, while Charlotte Haycock kept everything running smoothly. Both were hugely supportive in the face of a daunting schedule, which made a great difference. I'm also grateful to Richard Ogle, Rodney Paul, Claire Round, Louise Campbell, John Kelly and Richard Foreman for all their efforts on my behalf.

My wife Marianna was, as ever, an indispensable partner in all my creative endeavors.